OBSIDIO

THE ILLUMINAE FILES_03

OBSIDIO

THE ILLUMINAE FILES_03

AMIE KAUFMAN & JAY KRISTOFF

WITH SELECT JOURNAL ILLUSTRATIONS BY
MARIE LU

ALFRED A. KNOPF
NEW YORK

Text copyright © 2018 by LaRoux Industries Pty Ltd. and Neverafter Pty Ltd.
Jacket photograph copyright © 2018 by Vandathai/Shutterstock
Ship insignia illustrations copyright © 2015, 2016, 2018 by Stuart Wade
Military map and ship blueprint and schematics copyright © 2015, 2016, 2018 by Meinert Hansen
Select journal illustrations (144, 182–183 [text overlay], 328–335, 614–615) copyright © 2018 by Marie Lu
Select journal illustrations (182–183 [infinity symbol], 188–189, 195, 304, 555) copyright © 2018 by Lisa Weber

All rights reserved. Published in the United States by Alfred A. Knopf, an imprint of Random House Children's Books, a division of Penguin Random House LLC, New York.

Knopf, Borzoi Books, and the colophon are registered trademarks of Penguin Random House LLC.

Visit us on the Web! GetUnderlined.com

Educators and librarians, for a variety of teaching tools, visit us at RHTeachersLibrarians.com

Library of Congress Cataloging-in-Publication Data
Names: Kaufman, Amie, author. | Kristoff, Jay, author. | Lu, Marie, illustrator.
Title: Obsidio / Amie Kaufman & Jay Kristoff ; with journal illustrations by Marie Lu.
Description: First Edition. | New York : Alfred A. Knopf, [2018] | Series: the Illuminae files ; 03 | Summary: Kady, Ezra, Hanna, Nik, and 2,000 other refugees must return by container ship to Kerenza, where they meet Rhys, once close to Kady's cousin, Asha, and now their enemy.
Identifiers: LCCN 2017020645 (print) | LCCN 2017037108 (ebook) | ISBN 978-0-553-49919-3 (trade) | ISBN 978-0-553-49920-9 (lib. bdg.) | ISBN 978-0-553-49921-6 (ebook)
Subjects: | CYAC: Science fiction. | Interplanetary voyages—Fiction. | Artificial intelligence—Fiction.
Classification: LCC PZ7.K1642 (ebook) | LCC PZ7.K1642 Obs 2018 (print) | DDC [Fic]—dc23

Book design by Heather Kelly and Jay Kristoff

Printed in the United States of America
March 2018
10 9 8 7 6 5 4 3 2 1

First Edition

FOR MARIE. WHO ELSE?

Chief Prosecutor: Gabriel Crowhurst, BSA, MFS, JD
Chief Defense Counsel: Kin Hebi, BSA, ARP, JD
Tribunal: Hua Li Jun, BSA, JD, MD; Saladin Al Nakat, BSA, JD; Shannelle Gillianne Chua, BSA, JD, OKT
Witness: Leanne Frobisher, Director of Acquisitions, BeiTech Industries, MFA, MBA, PhD
Date: 11/04/76
Timestamp: 13:06

—cont. from pg. 1172—

Crowhurst, G: Perhaps we should get proceedings under way? Miss Donnelly, is the video feed operating at your end?

Donnelly, H: We can see you, Mr. Crowhurst.

Crowhurst, G: Thank you for making yourself available to us today. Please state your name and occupation for the record.

Donnelly, H: Hanna Alimah Donnelly. I don't really have an occupation. My father was Charles Donnelly, commander of Jump Station *Heimdall.*

Al Nakat, S: Miss Donnelly, the tribunal must again remind you that remote testimony is a privilege, not a right. One can't help but notice your so-called Illuminae Group has a flair for the dramatic. Should these proceedings devolve into melodrama or farce, I will not hesitate to suspend the session, do you understand?

Donnelly, H: We understand, Your Honor.

Crowhurst, G: Miss Donnelly, you've already been sworn in. Do you understand the penalties for providing fraudulent testimony to a United Terran Authority tribunal?

Donnelly, H: I'm sure Dr. Frobisher's lawyers can explain it to me. Pretty certain they would've warned her before she got on the witness stand for her comedy routine.

Hebi, K: Objection!

Donnelly, H: Hello, Leanne. Nice suit. A Feeney original, am I right?

Frobisher, L: [inaudible]

Hebi, K: Your Honors—

Al Nakat, S: Miss Donnelly, these are exactly the kind of theatrics I will not tolerate. You will address the tribunal members or counsel *only,* or we will find you in contempt. Do I make myself clear?

Donnelly, H: Yes, Your Honor. Crystal.

Crowhurst, G: Miss Donnelly, the tribunal has already covered the first and second segments of the Illuminae Files, addressing the initial invasion of Kerenza IV by BeiTech Industries—

Hebi, K: Objection. *Alleged* invasion.

Chua, S: Sustained.

Crowhurst, G: Apologies. *Alleged* invasion.

We've reviewed records of the battle between the *Lincoln* and the *Alexander*. From there we moved on to the *alleged* siege of Jump Station *Heimdall* by BeiTech special operatives and the arrival of WUC science vessel *Hypatia*.

Donnelly, H: Don't forget the universe almost imploding. Twice.

Crowhurst, G: Quite. And yet you still haven't explained how you're talking to us now. Jump Station *Heimdall* was destroyed. If, as you claim, you and *Heimdall*'s remaining population traveled to the Kerenza system before the station's destruction, using the ship belonging to Travis Falk—the *Mao*—you would have been trapped there with the crew of the *Hypatia,* with no way of returning to the Core. With the wormhole down, you wouldn't even be able to transmit to us.

Donnelly, H: Ten points.

Crowhurst, G: So where are you right now, Miss Donnelly?

Donnelly, H: I'm not at liberty to say.

Crowhurst, G: But you're not in the Kerenza system?

Donnelly, H: That'd be impossible. The Illuminae Group saved two universes from annihilation in a hyperspatial paradox event, but we're not miracle workers.

Jun, H: Miss Donnelly, please answer the question.

Donnelly, H: Sorry. No. The answer is no. We're not in Kerenza.

Crowhurst, G: Very well. So, given that it should have been a trip of several thousand years back to the Core without jump travel, would you care to explain to the tribunal how it is you and your colleagues escaped the system?

Donnelly, H: . . . Not all of us did.

Crowhurst, G: I beg your pardon?

Donnelly, H: Not all of us escaped Kerenza, Mr. Crowhurst.

Crowhurst, G: Are you saying some of your group are still there?

Donnelly, H: I'm saying they'll never leave. That's the point of all this. That's why we're here today. To tell the story for everyone who can't tell you themselves. To shine a light. To speak for the dead, Mr. Crowhurst.

The *dead,* Dr. Frobisher.

Al Nakat, S: Miss Donnelly, I will not warn you again!

Donnelly, H: . . . I'm sorry, Your Honor.

Crowhurst, G: Miss Donnelly, perhaps we can start at the beginning. Given your predicament after *Heimdall*'s demolition, how did you escape the Kerenza system?

Donnelly, H: That's a *long* story. And it includes some people you haven't met yet. See, what we didn't know at the time, what *nobody* knew until after *Heimdall* Station was destroyed, was that there were still survivors on Kerenza IV.

[sound of crowd]

Jun, H: Order! Order in the court!

Crowhurst, G: I'm sorry, Miss Donnelly. Survivors?

Donnelly, H: Think about it. Four dreadnoughts attacked the planet in the initial invasion, along with Mobile Jump Platform *Magellan*. The *Alexander* crippled *Magellan,* so nobody could jump out of the system, but only two dreads were actually destroyed. The others were still in orbit around Kerenza IV, with no way to get home.

Crowhurst, G: So there was a BeiTech force on the planet?

Donnelly, H: Correct. By the time *Hypatia* reached the *Heimdall* waypoint, the occupying force had been stranded planetside for almost seven months. Along with a bunch of colonists who never made it out on the *Alexander* fleet.

Crowhurst, G: But wouldn't these dreadnoughts and their BeiTech crew have been able to transmit a message to Rapier, the BeiTech operative on *Heimdall*? BeiTech would have known these survivors were there, surely.

Donnelly, H: This is a little complex to explain. Fortunately, we just happen to have assembled a file on the topic . . .

Frobisher, L: Of course you have.

Donnelly, H: No need to be snippy, Leanne.

Is everyone sitting comfortably? Anyone need to go to the bathroom bef—

Al Nakat, S: Miss Donnelly . . .

Donnelly, H: Okay, if you can open your readers to Page 1?

Once upon a time, on a little speck of ice at the ■■ end of the universe known as Kerenza IV . . .

BEITECH INDUSTRIES
ASSAULT FLEET KERENZA
FLAGSHIP CHURCHILL

PERSONNEL TRANSFER DIRECTIVE
—PRIORITY ONE—

AUTHORIZATION: SŪN 7802-024-BTN
Incept: 08/16/75
Name: LINDSTROM, Rhys
Rank: Specialist
Current Assignment: Electronics Support, Mobile Jump Platform *Magellan*
New Assignment: Electronics Repair & Logistics, Planet Kerenza IV

Specialist Lindstrom,

Happy belated Terra Day, and allow me to apologize in advance for what may be an unwelcome assignment.

I understand you've done sterling work aboard Mobile Jump Platform *Magellan* while in orbit around Kerenza IV and assisted ably in the containment of the warp storm spilling from *Magellan*'s damaged hermium containment system. Your supervisors speak highly of your skills and dedication to BeiTech Industries and the Orbital Corps.

Unfortunately, unexpected difficulties have arisen at the Kerenza IV beachhead, resulting in a shortfall of technical staff. Therefore, you are hereby ordered to report to First Lieutenant Christie, Delta Company, 4th Platoon. You will accompany 4th Platoon on their next rotation down on the Kerenza IV colony (commencing 08/17/75).

Understand this is not a punishment, Specialist. You have done exemplary work, and the situation planetside demands the presence of our very best and brightest. With the warp storm contained and communication with our personnel aboard Jump Station *Heimdall* now possible, I have no doubt command will relieve us soon.

Should communication with BeiTech HQ prove fruitless, TechEng informs me *Magellan* will be capable of jump travel in two weeks. However, due to the containment breach, *Magellan*'s hermium stores are almost entirely depleted. **As a result, safeguarding production in the Kerenza hermium mine is now Priority One.**

Lieutenant Christie will brief you fully aboard flagship *Churchill* and assign you a protection detail for the duration of your stay on Kerenza IV. I have every faith you will perform your duties with customary excellence and help ensure our final victory.

Sūn Huojin
Admiral, BeiTech Industries Orbital Corps
Commander, BT013-TN *Churchill*, Assault Fleet Kerenza

KERENZA IV
McCaffrey Tech High School

BRIEFING NOTE:
These logs were lifted from a low-tech chat client set up on Kerenza IV's redundant high school administration server system by the local insurgency. Such as it was.

INCEPT: 08/17/75 08:46

Guest_17: u there?

Guest_03: ya

Guest_17: set to go?

Guest_03: wut r u my ███ing mother

Guest_17: this is serious goddamm it

Guest_03: glad you here to tell me these things

Guest_17: just dont ███ it up

Guest_17: gonna hear enough ███ from the others about this without it being a fail too

Guest_03: is there a meet?

Guest_17: yeah 15:00 at shift break

Guest_03: waste of time. all talk, no walk

Guest_17: not anymore. Sick of this ███ as you

Guest_17: you sure you're gtg?

Guest_03: just sit back and watch the fireworks

Guest_03: and relax ffs, you'll live longer

Guest_17: you know none of us are going to live through this

Guest_03: maybe not

Guest_03: but we'll live longer than these BeiTech ███holes, at least

Guest_03: they can keep our seats warm in hell

BRIEFING NOTE:
Transcript of ATLAS-mounted camera footage recovered from BeiTech servers on the planet Kerenza IV, dated 08/17/75. Original footage is also included in this file. You should be used to the colorful language from our vidtechs by now, but be warned: curse words incoming.

**Surveillance footage summary,
prepared by
Analyst ID 7213-0089-DN**

Footage begins with an audio track only. There's a hiss of static as systems come online. The bass drone of engines rumbling over the tremors of atmospheric reentry and snatches of soft conversation.

"—so I said to her, 'Fem, I didn't see your name on him, and if you can't kee—'"

"—nly been three weeks since our last rotation, chum. This is bull—"

"—frostbite. Lost both hands and his nose if you—"

"—insurgency my ■—"

A flicker of snow rolls across my screens as the feeds fade into view.

We're in the belly of a BeiTech Locust—a surface-to-orbit shuttle built for heavy lifting during planetside incursions. The surfaces are gunmetal gray, lit by strips of scuffed red fluorescence. A wall of monitors dances with data. The ship's a military transport, armored and armed for business. On the rear bay doors, beneath the phoenix logo of BeiTech Industries, three words are spray-painted in neat stenciled letters.

The holy trinity of every corp grunt's life.

COMPANY

COMMANDER

CORPS

The Locust's belly is filled with soldiers. Orbital infantry, aka "ground pounders," trained for atmo-to-surface seizure operations. Two dozen men and women, most in their early twenties, each busy encasing themselves in the sleek lines of an Armored Tactical Light Assault Suit's plasteel and ballistics-grade nanofiber weave, painted in the white and gray of winter camouflage. They look like a cross between praying mantises and knights from the archive vids, except Sir Lancelot never carried a gun big enough to kill a building with.

Every ATLAS is fitted with a shoulder-mounted personal cam. The footage quality from their feeds is good, audio is excellent. I'll say one thing for BeiTech: When they plan an illegal planetary invasion/genocide, they don't spare any expense.

One soldier stands out in the crowd. Quiet amid the familiar banter. He's younger than the rest. Eighteen, maybe nineteen. His ATLAS is showroom new; no dings or scuffs or scars, none of the hand-drawn decorations that distinguish one pounder's faceless suit from another. He has a square jaw. Sharp gray eyes, just a touch too wide. Sandy blond hair, styled into a quiff that, if it doesn't violate regulations, damn well should. It sure as ███ violates the laws of gravity. One of my fellow vid analysts—who insists on peering over my shoulder as I work—says she would "hit that like it owed her all the ISH in the 'verse."

The name LINDSTROM, RHYS is stenciled on his breastplate.

Pretty as the kid might be, when his fellow soldiers look at him at all, they do it with narrowed eyes.

"███ing cherry . . . ," one sneers.

"Green as grass."

"He old enough to have turf on the pitch, you think?"

"Ask your sister."

"Hey, ███ you, Oshiro."

"Say please, loverboy."

LINDSTROM, RHYS, stays silent during the exchange. Frowning

at the power couplings on his ATLAS. He practically has an I HAVE NEVER WORN ONE OF THESE BEFORE sign flashing over his head, but none of his squaddies offer to help with the rig.

"Ten-hut! Officer on deck!"

Lindstrom and his fellow soldiers snap to attention as an armored figure stalks into the bay, boots thudding on temperfoam floors. He's built like a tank, not wearing his helmet yet. Dark eyes and short salt-and-pepper hair. Tā-moko tattooed on one half of a grizzled face. The name CHRISTIE is stenciled on the battered breastplate next to his lieutenant's pips. The words I AM YOUR GOD NOW are neatly handwritten above it.

He surveys his troops, appraising each in turn.

"At ease."

The soldiers relax slightly, feet apart, hands behind backs.

"Good morning, pounders."

"Morning, sir!" come two dozen barks.

"I know we had no time for a full briefing before dusting off from the *Churchill.* Apologies for interrupting your beauty sleep. ███ knows Woźniak could use some more."

A hulking soldier with a face like a dropped pie grins wide as the lieutenant smirks in his direction. The name WOŹNIAK is printed on his breastplate, but he's scribbled it out and written DUKE above it. His scars are numerous, fresh and, given the nanotech a frontline BeiTech unit is packing, probably left there by request.

"I'm also aware we had four more sols before our next Kerenza rotation was due to commence," Lieutenant Christie continues. "So skipping the foreplay, here's the sitrep:

"At 23:47 last night, Kerenza IV time, a malfunction occurred in the internal environment system of the Kerenza town hall, which had been refitted as our officers' barracks. As a result, the system began pumping pure CO into the hall. By the time the system fault was discovered, thirty-seven of our officers were dead of carbon monoxide poisoning."

"█ me," Woźniak whispers.

"Goddamn rebs," another mutters.

The Locust bucks in the turbulence. Christie raises his voice over the rising murmurs.

"I know what you're thinking. But it's possible the fault wasn't the result of sabotage. Even so, Admiral Sūn is upping planetside presence. Until further notice, all rotations run six weeks surface, two weeks orbit. So I hope you packed your mittens, fems and chums. Because we're in for a stay and it's cold down there."

The mood of the troops darkens along with the cabin lighting.

"Questions?" Christie asks.

A soldier with dark hair and a cheekful of chewing tobacco raises a hand.

"I got a question."

"It's not the one about where babies come from, is it, Private Day?"

The soldier grins, shifts his chaw from one cheek to the other. "Why don't we just line these damn pitdiggers up against the wall and X the █ing lot of them, Top?"

"Well now, that's a wonderful plan, Private," Christie nods. "And I suppose you're going to operate the hermium processors when the civis are all sixed? Got an engineering degree in between combat tours and █ing your cousins, did you?"

"So X their kids instead," the private insists. "That'll teach the rebs to █ with us."

"The fact we have the miners' families under lock and key is the only thing keeping the hermium outfit operational," Christie growls. "We X them, the mine shuts down and we got no juice for *Magellan*. The official party line is still that there is *no* insurgency among the populace. So unstrap your head from your █ and leave the thinking for the Logistics Department."

Day's face sours, but he shuts up. Christie raises an eyebrow, waiting for any more inquiries. In the silence, a slender woman with bobbed black hair nods at the boy.

"Who's the cherry, LT?"

"This is Specialist Lindstrom." Lieutenant Christie slaps the blond kid heavy on the shoulder. "Electronics tech on loan from the *Magellan.* He'll be overseeing systems maintenance in the Kerenza colony until further notice."

"What happened to Albretto? Or Ingram and Couzens?"

"They were in the barracks when Dr. Monoxide paid a visit. They're deep six."

"And this kid is their replacement?" The woman glances at Lindstrom in disbelief. "What is he, twelve? He can't even put on a ███ing ATLAS, LT."

"Well, thank you for volunteering to help him, Sergeant Oshiro." The ink on Christie's face twists with his humorless smile. "Since you're so concerned, you'll be the specialist's shadow until further notice. And as you're nice enough to point out, we're shorthanded on techheads, so if anything happens to him, it's your ███ in my line of fire. Understood?"

The woman blinks. Jaw tightening.

". . . Sir, yessir."

The Locust's internal PA crackles.

"Top, this is Conn. Five minutes to surface, over."

"All right, pounders!" Christie roars. "You heard the lady, five minutes to powder. Temperature is six below, wind at eighty klicks, so don't forget your booties. If a single one of you choobs even *thinks* about X-ing out on this rotation, I will personally haul myself down into hell just to kick your sorry ███, is that understood?"

"Sir, yessir!"

"I can't hear you!"

"Sir, yessir!"

"Your lives belong to BeiTech and your ███es belong to me. A pounder does not die unless they are given *permission* to die, is that understood?"

"Sir, yessir!"

"I can't ████ing hear you!"

"Sir, yessir!"

Christie points to the BeiTech logo and motto painted on the hangar doors.

"Company! Commander! Corps!"

"Corps! *Hooah!*"

Twenty-four fists slam onto twenty-four breastplates. Lindstrom's is only a little off the pace. Christie surveys his troops one more time before nodding.

"Out-████ing-standing. As you were."

Without another word, the lieutenant turns and stalks back the way he came.

The soldiers set about finishing their prep. Weapons check. Temperature regulators. Signal strength. Six and a half months into their occupation of the WUC's little hermium outfit, they're a well-oiled machine. All the parts meshing except one. Lindstrom is still struggling with his suit when he looks up to find Sergeant Oshiro standing in front of him, hands on hips.

This close, I can see through Lindstrom's cam that she's not much older than he is. Japanese descent, slice of Eurobloc in there somewhere. Hard brown eyes. Pretty in a "do not ████ with me" kind of way. The words THOU SHALT N̶O̶T̶ KILL are printed on her breastplate. She's almost a foot shorter than he is, but somehow seems to tower over him.

"How many times you worn an ATLAS, Cherry?"

". . . Just in training, ma'am."

After watching him struggle a moment longer, glancing up at that ridiculous quiff, she slaps the kid's hands away.

"Watch. Learn."

She runs him through the routine. Methodical. Checking to make sure he's paying attention. The Locust rocks hard as it hits turbulence, and Lindstrom stumbles. Oshiro barely moves. When she's done, the sergeant raises an eyebrow at the kid.

"Got it?"

"I think so."

"You better do more than think so. Kerenza hits seventy below once the sun goes down. You flub your seal integrity and step outside into that, you'll be frostbitten before you feel the sting."

The kid blinks. "You're kidding, right?"

Oshiro turns to another pounder. The scarred one. "Hey, Duke, you remember Stohl?"

"█ yeah." The big man shudders theatrically. "I still have nightmares."

"Why?" The kid glances between them. "What happened?"

The man called Duke grimaces. "Temp regulator in her ATLAS blew on midnight patrol. She was half-frozen by the time she got back to the OC. They took off her suit, and most of her skin came with it."

The kid swallows. Wordlessly, he sets about copycatting Oshiro's routine to seal his suit as Duke winks at a few of his comrades. To his credit, Lindstrom seems a quick study; he only fumbles once getting himself sorted.

"Good." Oshiro nods.

Lindstrom flashes the sergeant a lady-killer smile. "Thanks."

"Save it, prettyboy," she sighs. "You can thank me legit by not getting your stupid █ X-ed out before Christie takes me off babysitting duty."

Lindstrom's lady-killer smile dies—he's not used to it failing, by the look.

"What's the big deal? We're just standing guard over a bunch of colonists, right?"

Guffaws echo around the troop bay. The PA warns the pounders they're two minutes from surface. Engines roar hard as the Locust slows its descent. The whole ship is bucking like it's in an earthquake. Oshiro is smiling at the kid, hard and sharp.

"You silver spooners on the *Magellan* don't get much word about what goes down on the surface, do you?"

"We've been a little busy up there," the kid snaps. "You know, fixing a breach in the vortex containment system. Trying to stop a cascading warp storm from swallowing the entire planet. Get some comms out. Maybe get the wormhole generator running one of these years, so we can jump the ▮▮ out of here. It was a little complicated."

"That so?" Oshiro tilts her head. "Well, down here, it's real simple, Cherry. You do what I say, when I say it. You step where I step. You move when I move. Clear?"

"I think I'll manage." The kid stares defiantly. "It's not like we're going into battle here."

"Oh, maybe not a knock-'em-down-shoot-'em-up." Oshiro nods. "But you bet your ▮▮ there's folks down there gunning for you. And these pitdiggers aren't gonna do anything as stupid as shoot at you when we've got their families locked up. But they *will* ▮▮ with you. Maybe it's just the water being cold every time you hit the showers, or a fistful of sugar in your Cheetah's gas tank. Then maybe one night you head out on patrol and the temperature regulator in your ATLAS ▮▮s out. Or your brake lines fail. Or maybe you just go to sleep with the heater running and never wake up."

Oshiro steps closer, eyes narrowed. "We invaded these people's homes, Cherry. Bombed them to ▮▮. Killed their families. You think this isn't a battle? This is a ▮▮ing war."

Lindstrom remains mute. Oshiro searches his eyes. Her voice is razor-edged.

"You do what I say, when I say it," she repeats. "You step where I step. You move when I move. Clear?"

Lieutenant Christie reappears at the hatchway, helmet on, eight telescopic lenses arranged like a cluster of glowing spider eyes in its forehead.

"All right, pounders. Sixty seconds. Lock and drop!"

Oshiro is still staring at Lindstrom, waiting for an answer. The kid finally nods.

"Ma'am, yes ma'am."

"Get your helmet on."

Sullen, the kid slaps his helmet down, the arachnid optics flickering into a steady red glow. Magnetic couplings lock each soldier in place as the engine roar grows close to deafening. Metal shuddering, rivets groaning, the heavy hiss of hydraulics underscoring it all. There's one final tremor, then a brief silence followed by a series of heavy thuds, as the Locust touches down.

The bay doors crack wide, admitting a howl of freezing wind, a bright flare of blinding snow-white light. Temperature in the bay plummets, frost and snow filling the air. The cameras take a moment to adjust to the glare.

By the time vision returns, the pounders have bailed out of the transport and gathered in the shadow of one broad, prehensile wing. Lindstrom is sticking close to Oshiro as ordered, staring at the scene around him. The landing zone is as makeshift as everything else in the Kerenza IV colony. BeiTech had repurposed the old high school geeball field to serve as their airfield—it was the only space large enough with a solid surface after the spaceport was destroyed in their initial invasion. If the poor saps had known they were going to be stuck living in it for half a year or more, maybe they wouldn't have bombed the ▮▮▮ out of the colony quite so thoroughly.

Someone get me a tissue.

Sitting by the landing pad in neat piles are thirty-seven aluminum boxes. Each one is about two meters in length. Rectangular. Embossed with the BeiTech Industries logo. You can see the shift in Lindstrom's stance as he realizes what they are.

Coffins.

Coffins filled with dead BeiTech officers.

A tanker trundles in on fat rubber treads to refuel the Locust, spanner monkeys in thermal suits swarming around the ship as its flanks steam in the freezing air. Private Duke Woźniak, standing beside Lindstrom, nudges the kid with one elbow.

"Don't let Oshiro get you down, rook. She's pro. Stick to her, she'll do you right."

"Sure," the kid says, still staring at those aluminum caskets.

"You get the chance, swing by the barracks tonight, twenty-one hundred. The Duke's got a card game running. Jacks and Knives. You got money, don't you?"

"Yeah."

"Right." The big man nods. "Twenty-one hundred. Don't tell Christie."

Lieutenant Christie is barking orders, telling most of his troops to report to the Operations Center. He turns to the kid, yelling over the engines and howling gale, voice distorted by his suit.

"Lindstrom! Enviro regulator at the med center is broke ███. You and Oshiro haul ██ up the hill and get it copacetic, then report back to the OC for de—"

The explosion cuts Christie's sentence off at the knees.

It's bright. Deafening. The ATLAS a-vis rigs are built to withstand combat-level stress, though, so I get to watch most of it. It begins in the fuel tanker hitched to the Locust, blossoms outward, impossibly quick, incinerating the spanner crew and ripping through the gathered soldiers, throwing them around like kids' toys. Lindstrom is hurled a good twenty feet, landing in a crumpled heap with Oshiro on top of him, smoking debris raining all around them as the boom echoes across the stadium.

The sergeant rolls to her feet in an instant, an MX flechette cannon slung off her back, the red beam of her laser targeting system cutting through the swirling black smoke. Shouts of alarm ring across the airfield. Sirens wail. Engines roar as the fire crews scramble. Blackened bodies are strewn across the snow. Lindstrom struggles to his feet, rifle in hand, shouting to Oshiro.

"What the ███ is going on?"

"Stay down!"

"Are we under attack?"

"Stay *down*!"

The woman peers through the smoke, lenses shifting. The Bei-Tech Locust is a hollow shell, twisted and burning. Pounders are pulling themselves to their feet, but at least a dozen charred and smoking bodies are scattered about the blast site.

"Medic!" comes the cry. *"Medic!"*

Lindstrom staggers forward through the snow, Oshiro out in front.

"███," she breathes.

Lieutenant Christie is on his knees, four other soldiers huddled around him. A fifth man is on his back, the breastplate of his ATLAS torn open by a smoking chunk of Locust hull. The chest behind it is shredded, white bone showing through the carnage, blood steaming in the snow. Christie drags off the pounder's helmet to reveal the features of Private Jarrod Day, twisted in pain, lump of chewing tobacco still lodged in his cheek.

"███ing ███████," he groans.

"Stow it, Private. Medic is on his way."

"It's . . . b-bad, Top."

"Shut your noise, Day," Christie growls. "You're too stupid to know when to die."

Day begins coughing, the chaw bubbling up out of his lips, blood and tobacco juice slicked on his chin. Looking over his shoulder toward the cluster of buildings at the airfield's edge, the lieutenant roars.

"WHERE'S THAT ███████ING MEDIC?"

Day is coughing harder, his face growing pale. Lindstrom and Oshiro are standing with the others now, the Locust still blazing behind them. A BeiTech trooper with a green cross on his back comes sprinting through the sleet, skidding to his knees beside the groaning soldier. Christie has hold of Day's hand, pulling off his own helmet and looking into his man's eyes as the medic goes to work.

"Look at me, Day," the lieutenant commands.

Day is groaning, eyes closed.

"Soldier, I said look at me!"

The man opens his eyes a crack. Christie grasps either side of his head, leans in close. "A pounder does not die unless he is given permission to die, you hear me, Private?"

Blood and chaw spatter Day's lips. The medic is cursing, sticky to the elbows. Red is soaking into the snow.

"Private Day, are you reading me?" Christie roars again. "I do not give you permission to die, is that understood?"

Day winces. Whispers something inaudible.

"I can't hear you!"

The wounded man hiccups, eyes growing wide. And as he exhales, the light goes out of his eyes. Like someone flicked off the switch. Two hundred and twenty pounds of muscle and bone encased in a shell of plasteel and ballistics-grade nanofiber weave. Armed to the teeth. Trained to perfection.

And just like that, he's gone.

Silence reigns across the windblown field. Christie looks at the soldiers around him. The ground crew and medics and spanner monkeys. All of them silent. The lieutenant pushes himself to his feet with a soft whine of servos. The winter camo on his armor is splashed with red. He glances at the dead bodies around him, at least a dozen left lying in the explosion's wake. He spits into glittering scarlet snow.

"Tag 'em and bag 'em."

Lindstrom glances at Oshiro, breathing hard.

The woman's face is hidden behind her helmet.

Her voice is like iron.

"Welcome to Kerenza, Cherry."

BRIEFING NOTE:
Team BeiTech isn't alone in wondering what just exploded. Time to meet Asha Grant, pharmacy intern; Bruno Way, plumber; Steph Park, mechanic; and Joran Karalis, mining engineer.

INCEPT: 08/17/75 09:17

Steph PARK: what the ██ was that???

Bruno WAY: hello yourself.

Steph PARK: ██ you, Bruno.

Bruno WAY: :(

Asha GRANT: r u ok, Steph? U safe?

Joran KARALIS: Calm down, everyone. What was what?

Steph PARK: that ██ing explosion? didn't u hear it??

Joran KARALIS: We're pulling eighteen-hour shifts at the mine, Steph. You don't hear much when you're five klicks under the ice shelf and twenty klicks from the action.

Steph PARK: well some1 rigged a fuel tanker to pop. do you know how close I was?? an entire LOCUST is gone. 13 dead. Asha, they're bringing the bodies ur way.

Asha GRANT: aaaawesome. just what I need this week. Another autopsy.

Steph PARK: i thought we were going to communicate about this ██. since when are we setting bombs at the airfield??

Bruno WAY: gotta admit, when I heard that boom I thought u set it off, Steph.

Steph PARK: Me????

Bruno WAY: u work at the stadium, u've got access to the landing pads.

Steph PARK: look, I'm not saying blowing a few more of these ██████s to hell isn't a good idea. i been suggesting that for months now. but I'd have cleared it with you all first

Asha GRANT: we don't even know if this was one of our people. BeiTech's gear is 7 months in the snow now. could've been a tech failure

Steph PARK: riiiight, like that air-con failure that wasted thirty-seven of their officers??

Bruno WAY: let's look on the bright side. We're all ok. and that happy little accident in the town hall took most of their tech specialists with it u know.

Steph PARK: my point exactly. too good to be true.

Asha GRANT: Maybe we deserve a little good luck

Steph PARK: luck my ██. they'll just bring down more techheads from Magellan to replace the ones they lost.

Asha GRANT: they're gonna run out of em sooner or later

Bruno WAY: so if it wasn't an accident, is this someone in the resistance going rogue you think? Someone from the mine maybe?

Joran KARALIS: no way, my guys are solid. Nobody down here is risking anything this stupid. Our families are on the line. I've got a wife and daughter locked up in Complex C, and bull██ like this risks everyone's safety.

Steph PARK: we don't all have families held hostage, Joran

Bruno WAY: hey, everyone breathe. Joran, of course we take the hostages seriously. We all have people we miss. I think about Jenna every day.

Steph PARK: not everybody had their loved ones get out on the evac fleet either, Bruno

Bruno WAY: Steph, Hans wouldn't have wanted u to throw your life away, u know that.

Steph PARK: AND I DIDN'T!! that explosion wasn't me! but we all know damn well they're going to shoot every one of us sooner or later.

Joran KARALIS: It might end up being sooner than we think. Just heard from Monty. The warp storm has apparently dispersed enough for them to get stellar comms back online.

Joran KARALIS: We think BeiTech got a message out.

Steph PARK: ▮.

Asha GRANT: ▮.

Bruno WAY: ▮.

Asha GRANT: we HAVE to find out what it said. hell, we have to find out if anybody received it.

Joran KARALIS: Yes, but how?

Steph PARK: if they got in touch with BT HQ, we're screwed. I mean, even at light speed, it'll take a while for the message to reach the heimdall gate and get out into the core, but sooner or later, we're into the final countdown.

Joran KARALIS: We may be anyway. They're pushing us hard in the mine. I think they're getting close to the quota of hermium they need.

Steph PARK: they must be close to getting the Magellan's jump gate generator functioning. as soon as they have enough hermium to jump the system, it's curtains for us.

Bruno WAY: we don't know that. They keep saying they're gonna evac everybody

Steph PARK: and you believe that? After what they've done?

Bruno WAY: it's not impossible. I mean, who are we going to complain to about what they did? The UTA? "Excuse me, but BeiTech came and ▮ed me while I was busy illegally mining hermium, but their lawbreaking was worse than mine . . ."

Bruno WAY: they know we won't tell anyone, so yes, I believe it's at least possible

Asha GRANT: i have to go soon, my dead people will be incoming

Joran KARALIS: We have to find out who's setting these bombs.

Steph PARK: forget the bombs, we need to know what was in that transmission!

Asha GRANT: we've got no access to their comms array

Steph PARK: this is exactly why we need to take more direct action. stealth hit the comms station + find out direct

Joran KARALIS: No, it's too risky. Our families are on the line, dammit.

Steph PARK: and where do you think they'll be when the Magellan is ready to jump, Joran?

Steph PARK: against the ███ing wall, that's where

Bruno WAY: let's not talk like that, okay?

Joran KARALIS: We're no good to anyone dead!

Steph PARK: and what good are we if all we do is sit around and chat???

Joran KARALIS: We have to be cautious!

Steph PARK: u and your caution can get ███ed, Joran.

<Steph PARK has left the conversation.>

Joran KARALIS: Goddamm it. Break is over. I have to go. Keep your ears open. And keep calm for crissakes. We'll talk soon.

<Joran KARALIS has left the conversation.>

Bruno WAY: ok that went well

Asha GRANT: better than last meet

Bruno WAY: :P

Asha GRANT: . . . Bruno, u think Steph did it?

Bruno WAY: the airfield bomb? i honestly don't know. I mean, I understand how she feels. She watched her husband die. she thinks she has nothing left to lose.

Asha GRANT: We all have something left to lose

Bruno WAY: I know. that's why I fight every day. we have to, for hostages here, and the people we love who got away. Jenna and I are going to be together again, I know it.

Asha GRANT: I hope so, Bruno. I really do.

Bruno WAY: r u okay, Ash?

Asha GRANT: i have a dozen dead people incoming, my boss had the crap beat out of him by a BT officer yesterday, and i . . . yeah.

Asha GRANT: yeah, I'm ok, u?

Bruno WAY: I'm okay. man, this is a long way from high school, huh? Remember when the biggest prob u had was me throwing stuff at the back of ur head in class?

Asha GRANT: Bruno, I have to go.

Bruno WAY: aw c'mon I outgrew throwing ■ around when the planet got bombed

Asha GRANT: ha, not that. i need a minute to pull it together before they bring in the corpsicles

Bruno WAY: ok. take care, my friend.

Asha GRANT: u too

<Bruno WAY has left the conversation.>

<Asha GRANT has left the conversation.>

Video journal transcription, prepared by Analyst ID 7213-0089-DN

The video starts with a wash of snow that clears to reveal the face of Asha Grant. She's half-lit by the screen, and the dark shapes behind her sharpen into mops and brooms as the camera of her palmpad finds focus. She's in a supply closet, switching from an online conversation to a video recording.

Her dark hair's pulled back in a ponytail, and her light brown skin is washed a greenish shade by the glow of the palmpad she's using to record. Twin white reflections of her screen show in her green eyes. She's chewing on her lower lip, fingers drumming against her temple as she considers her opening words.

"Hey, Kady." Her voice is hoarse with tiredness, and she clears her throat, then continues, softer. "Miss you, cuz. Just need to talk to you for a minute before I go out there and face it all. S'funny, it doesn't matter at all that these recordings just live here on my palmpad, that I don't send them anywhere. It still feels like talking to you. I keep these files behind the encryptions you set up for me, and in a way, that feels like you guarding me, keeping me safe. Locking up my secrets for me where nobody can find them."

She sighs, tipping her head sideways to rest it against a broom handle. "This is ████ed, Kades. There was an explosion at the landing pads, and a bunch of BT troops are dead, and if anyone puts a foot wrong the next day or two, a bunch of us will be dead in retaliation. A bunch *more* of us, I mean. It has to be someone in the resistance who did it. The coincidence of this and the deaths in the barracks . . . too much."

Her lips curve into a tired smile as she reaches out to adjust the palmpad, framing her face more squarely. "My boss, Morton, got the ▇▇ beat out of him yesterday. Long story short, he got into another argument with the head of the BeiTech med team and ended up with a broken nose, broken ribs and a fractured eye socket. I told him, Kades, I ▇▇ing *told* him. I said, BeiTech are the ones with the guns around here. BeiTech giveth, and BeiTech taketh away. Right now they're letting us use the facilities to treat our people, as long as we help their medical team with theirs. But they can take away our access anytime they like, which is exactly the damn *point* they're making locking him up, and still he doesn't . . ."

She trails off, scrunching up her face, then letting her expression slacken.

"Let's just say," she continues, quieter, "that I'm glad I didn't let him in on any of the resistance channels. We've got enough problems with our loose cannon already. Then again, once BT have enough hermium to jump the *Magellan* out of here, we'll be dead anyway, and Morton's ribs will be the least of his problems."

She rests her head against the broom handle again, sighs.

"What's it like to be dead, Kady?"

There's a tired smile for the question, and a pause as she leans past the palmpad to retrieve a water bottle. "I mean, I assume you're dead. I heard you made it onto one of the ships, but one of them got blown up right overhead, and the others had that huge BeiTech dreadnought after them, so it seems likely someone blew you to pieces already. But I like to imagine you're alive, sitting on the couch in my living room, all pink hair and boots on my coffee table, messaging Ezra and ▇▇ing to me about your parents, and . . ."

Her lips press together so hard they thin, turn pale, and still that doesn't hide the tremor. Her ponytail falls forward over her shoulder as her head drops, hands coming up to her face for nearly a minute. From outside the closet there's the muffled noise of a loudspeaker, but she ignores it.

Her eyes are bright when she looks up. "Anyway. I heard you made it onto one of the shuttles. So you're Schrödinger's Kady right now. That was this weird old Terran experiment where you put a cat in a box, and since you couldn't actually know if the cat was dead or alive from that point on, the cat was considered simultaneously both alive and dead . . . and presumably ██ed off about being in a box. So right now I choose to believe you're alive. I—"

There's another noise, this one above her. It's a softer scrape, and where she ignored the loudspeaker, now she freezes, looking up.

"Katya, what are you doing up there?" she finally whispers.

"Asha, I'm hungry," a second whisper comes. Younger. Much younger.

Grant digs around in the pocket of her scrubs to produce a snack bar. She reaches toward the ceiling, and when she sits again, her hand is empty.

"I'll find some more for you tonight, I promise, baby girl," she whispers. "Keep out of sight, you got it? Quiet as a mouse."

"The cleverest mouse."

"And the cleverest mouse never gets caught, does she?"

"She's way too clever," is the whispered reply from the invisible child, mumbled around a mouthful of snack bar. Then, with a scrape, she withdraws.

Grant stares at her own reflection in the screen, features slackening into exhaustion now she's alone. Then she shakes her head, quick and sure, and tugs her scrubs straight as if she's donning armor.

Reaching forward, she switches off the camera.

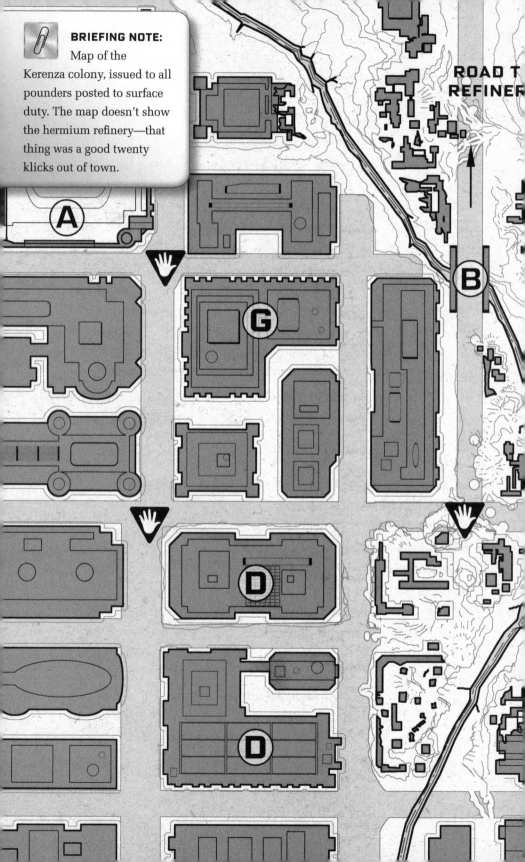

BRIEFING NOTE:
Map of the Kerenza colony, issued to all pounders posted to surface duty. The map doesn't show the hermium refinery—that thing was a good twenty klicks out of town.

ROAD T
REFINER

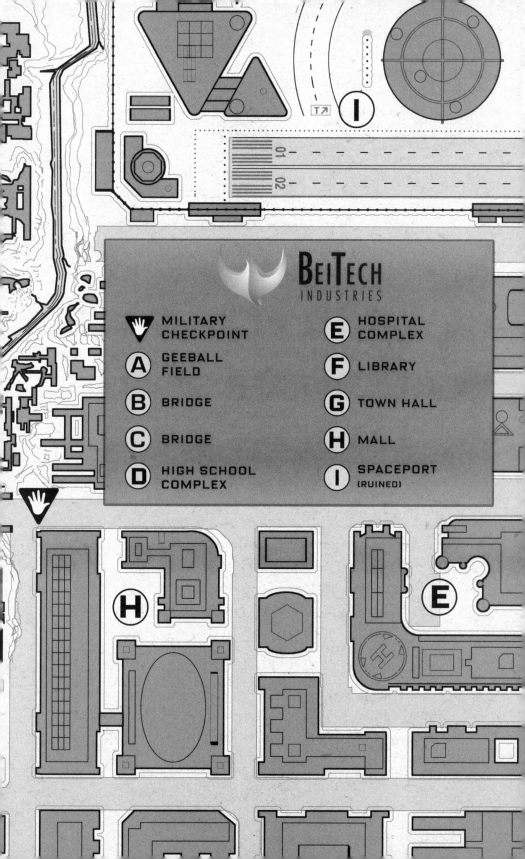

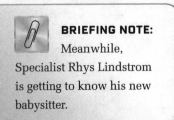

Surveillance footage summary,
prepared by
Analyst ID 7213-0089-DN

This is a transcript of ATLAS-cam footage and video taken from the Kerenza colony hospital server. The quality of the hospital cams is ████. The audio sounds like it was recorded in a toilet. I cannot work under these conditions. Waaaaa.

The ride to the hospital is taken mostly in silence. Specialist Lindstrom and Sergeant Oshiro bundle themselves into the back of an Armored Personnel Carrier, along with the dead bodies of thirteen BeiTech soldiers and spanner monkeys. Aside from Oshiro notifying the hospital that they're inbound, neither she or Lindstrom speaks much. Some of the corpses are still smoking—there weren't enough body bags for them all. The stink in the APC must be ungodly, but the pair are sealed inside their ATLAS armor, so they're spared the smell of freshly barbecued pounder.

"Sorry about your friends," Lindstrom finally says.

Oshiro glances at the lumps of cooling meat that used to be her squaddies.

"Shut up, Cherry," she sighs.

"Do you want to talk about it?"

"No, Cherry, I want you to shut up."

A few minutes pass, no sound except for the sound of tires crunching on snow.

"Oshiro?"

"Jesus, *what*?"

"Why are we taking corpses to a hospital?"

The woman sighs again, the sound rasping through her suit's vox unit.

"Morgue facilities," she says at last. "All BeiTech personnel killed in the line of duty need to be autopsied before transport to the *Churchill*. The admiral's a stickler for procedure. This place had an experimental bioweapon dropped on it in January, remember? Sūn doesn't want trace components getting aboard the fleet. Can you imagine what it might do if it got released inside a spaceship?"

Unaware of what BeiTech's bioweapon *did* evolve into when given a few months to mutate inside a floating metal can in space, Lindstrom simply shrugs. "I don't get it. It's not like we don't know how they died."

"We don't make the rules. We follow them. They should've taught you that in basic."

"I'm Science Division. They teach us to look at the world analytically. Search for more efficient ways of doing things. You know. To *think* and stuff."

"Did they teach you how to shut up? Because this'll be the third time I tell you to do it."

The kid sighs, doesn't say another word. The APC trundles over frozen roads, thumping into shrapnel potholes made by seven-month-old missile strikes. It's another ten minutes before they pull to a halt—the hospital is all the way across town from the airfield. The bodies have stopped smoking by then.

As they step out into the freezing air, we get our first look at what's left of the Kerenza colony. The place was basically a big country town, built to accommodate about eighteen thousand people. Miners and engineers, their families, and all the folks needed to run the facilities that sprang up around the WUC's illegal hermium op. Schools and shops. Fuel stations and liquor stores. Warehouses and apartment blocks and cineplexes, oh my.

Now the place is a ghost town. Everything covered in snow.

Freezing winds whipping through shattered buildings, the collapsed ruins of the spaceport. Three gaping cracks run along the glacial shelf, cutting through the center of town. The only people in sight are BeiTech troopers or colonists on special duty. The next shift of miners is being shuttled to work in a motley convoy of civilian vehicles, flanked by APCs—BeiTech missiles collapsed the subway system during the initial invasion, so roads are the only way to get to the hermium mine. The facility is just a blurred speck on the horizon. A small city of processing towers and pipes and concrete, a good twenty kilometers out of town.

It's at minimum safe distance in case the ■■ hits the fan. As the near interdimensional disaster aboard *Heimdall* should've taught you, when you're dealing with exotic ultra-heavy elements and things go bad, they go bad all the way.

Four BeiTech soldiers with VK burst rifles are waiting in the hospital parking bay, along with two colonists in orderly uniforms. Shivering in the chill, the civis begin unloading the bodies onto waiting gurneys. Lindstrom moves to help a sad-looking woman with graying hair lift the biggest corpse.

"Cherry, what are you doing?" Oshiro asks.

"Um, helping with the bodies?"

"Um, is that your ■■■ing job?"

"No, but—"

"Lieutenant Christie ordered you to fix the hospital enviro regulator, did he not?"

"Yeah."

"Soooo, what usually happens next?" Oshiro snaps her fingers a few times. "Dammit, I should remember this one. Help me out, Specialist . . ."

". . . I fix the hospital enviro regulator."

"See, *there* you go. And here I was thinking all that time you spent in basic learning to 'think and stuff' would've been better spent with a skinvid and a gym sock."

"Jesus . . ."

The sergeant tilts her head in the hospital's direction.

"Get the ███ inside before I freeze my Britney off."

With an apologetic shrug, Lindstrom slings his satchel of tools onto his shoulder and leaves the civis to it. The orderlies keep loading the corpses under the watchful eyes of the four other BeiTech goons. The knowledge that the bodies are all wearing BT uniforms doesn't seem like it's lost on anyone.

Inside, the hospital looks like it's seen better days. Once-white walls are now scuffed gray, the windows are cracked and the lighting is flickering intermittently. The place is medium-sized, maybe fifty beds in total.

Oshiro strides to the reception counter, removes her helmet with a *whoosh* of escaping air. A sharp black bob falls about sharper cheeks, dark eyes and unpainted lips. Lindstrom's ridiculous quiff has been squashed flat beneath his headgear, but as he removes his helmet, it somehow springs back to attention in defiance of all laws of physics.

"Where is everyone?" he asks.

There's not a soul in sight. Raised voices can be heard up the corridor, and a small blue globe is flashing above the reception area. As if in response to Lindstrom's query, a female voice spills across the hospital PA.

"Dr. Sarah Wiesner, report to Room Twenty-Four. Dr. Wiesner, Twenty-Four."

"What's going on?" Lindstrom asks.

"Code blue." Oshiro points to the flashing globe. "Someone's dying."

The sergeant peers down the corridor, catches sight of a disheveled nurse dashing across the hall. Glancing at Lindstrom, she holds up one armored finger.

"You wait here. I'm gonna go ask directions to the enviro controls."

"I can take a look around wh—"

"No." Oshiro glares. "Something happens to you, Christie will chew me like I was a ███ing tennis ball."

The kid squints. "The lieutenant chews tennis balls?"

"No. He . . . you know." Vague hand waving. "Like a dog."

"But—"

"I'm ██ty at analogies, okay? Just shut up. And stay here. That's an order."

"Ma'am, yes ma'am."

Oshiro stares a moment longer, as if daring the kid to move. He does his best impression of Boy With Feet Glued To The Floor, and the sergeant stalks off toward the babble of voices and electronic squeal of a flatlining EKG in Room 24.

The door to the reception office opens with a creak. A girl in a rumpled hospital uniform emerges, a small speaker and mic hooked on her ear. She wears her long dark hair pulled back in a ponytail, her light brown skin washed paler by the endless snow outside the cracked windows. She looks three-nights-tired, frayed around the edges, but even that can't quite wear the pretty off. Her eyes are the color of summer grass.

"Third call, Dr. Wiesner," she says, her voice crackling on the PA. *"Please report to Room Twenty-Four immediately. Dr. Wiesner, Room Twenty-Four."*

Now, here's where it gets interesting, kids.

I've watched this on slo-mo a dozen times, and I swear you can count twenty-seven different expressions on Lindstrom's face in a three-second period as he sees this girl. He actually does a double take. Jaw dropping like a bag of bricks. Thing is, as the girl catches sight of him, she's on the same gobsmacked page. Green eyes going wide. She puts her hand to her chest like it's about to burst. Her whisper crackles across the entire hospital PA.

"Holy ██ . . ."

The kid blinks.

Mouth flapping open and closed.

Sheer dumbfounded shock slapped all over his face.

". . . *Asha?*" he breathes.

"Cherry!"

The kid flinches, startled. The girl, too. He turns toward the sound of Oshiro's voice, fighting for some control of his expression. The sergeant is standing in the hallway, looking back and forth between the two. Raising a hand to crook a thumb at the elevators.

"Enviro is this way."

"I . . ."

Lindstrom glances at the girl. A million emotions crackling between the pair like lightning strikes. I swear you can see the ███-ing current, arcs of it, burning the meter between them whiter than the snow outside.

Joy.

Horror.

Terror.

Shock.

"Hey!"

Lindstrom looks back to Oshiro, a frown now darkening the sergeant's brow.

"Move your ██, Specialist. They ain't paying us by the hour."

The sergeant stomps away. Collecting himself, the kid glances one last time at the girl, picks up his jaw from the floor and stumbles after Oshiro to a service elevator. As the doors *ping* open, he follows his CO inside, looking for all the world like someone landed a flying kick to his baby maker. He stands with his back to Oshiro so she can't see his expression. Ghost white. Gobsmacked and disbelieving.

"Do yourself a favor, Cherry," Oshiro warns. "Stay away from civilian tail. Christie catches you cruising on the local sugar, he'll beat you like . . ." She frowns. "Goddammit, I had a good one for this yesterday . . ."

The doors rumble shut. The kid is just standing there, emotions in every color of the spectrum flashing across his face. Trying hard just to keep breathing.

I guess he finally learned to shut up, at least.

BRIEFING NOTE:
A series of handwritten notes secretly exchanged between Rhys Lindstrom and Asha Grant over the course of the next twelve hours. The notes were destroyed after reading and had to be reconstructed from other records.

CAN'T TALK DIRECT. MY SERGEANT IS WATCHING. GONNA PASS THESE TO YOU ON BATHROOM BREAKS. HOLY ██ IS THAT REALLY YOU? — ASH

KERENZA IV HOSPITAL

Patient Name: _____
Address: _____

Date: _____

RX No, it's a ██ from Pangaea ~~III~~ ...g four-headed lanim a purple top hats. wearing four small never speak to Now ██ off and me again.

UM, OKAY. THAT'S NOT EXACTLY THE RESPONSE I WAS HOPING FOR. WHERE IS THAT COMING FROM EXACTLY?

You're one of my planet. You and family. If I don't now.

the animals invading killed my friends I ever knew you, Leave me alone.

MD: _____
Signature: _____
Refill 0 1 2 3 4 5 PRN NR

ASH I'VE BEEN IN ORBIT ON MAGELLAN THIS WHOLE TIME. I HAD NO ██ ...NG IDEA WHAT WAS GOING ON DOWN HERE OR THAT YOU LIVED HERE. THEY DIDN'T TELL ME WHERE THEY SHIPPED YOU. I TRIED TO WRITE TO YOU FOR A YEAR. DID YOU NOT GET MY MESSAGES?

R

It doesn't matter if you thought I was here or on the other side of the galaxy. You came here with an army to help drop bombs on this place.

ASH,
I'M A TECHNICAL SPECIALIST. I WORK ON COMPUTERS AND COMMS RIGS. I'M NOT DROPPING BOMBS ON ANYONE.

I DIDN'T KNOW YOU WANTED TO BE A NURSE?

I'm <u>not</u> a nurse. I'm a pharmacy intern. But most of our nurses are dead because of soldierboy ██s like you.

MD:
Signature:
Refill 0 1 2 3

ASH COME ON, YOU KNOW ME. YOU KNOW WHO I AM.

KERENZA IV HOSPIT

Patient Name: _____ Date: _____
Address: _____

R I don't know you at all, Rhys. I know nobody forced you to take this job. I gotta go change dressings now. ██ off PS: Again, kindly at your convenience

ASH, I'M SORRY. PLS TALK TO ME.

ASH, PLEASE

Video journal transcription,
prepared by
Analyst ID 7213-0089-DN

The screen springs to life, and the shot spins wildly about as Asha finds a place to prop her palmpad in the supply closet—her hands are shaking, and it takes three tries before she gets it to balance. Then she comes into view, hunkered down in front of it, eyes wide.

"Kady, what the ███ *just happened*?" she whispers, one hand yanking on her ponytail in her agitation. "What in the name of the *nine circles of hell* made the universe think I need my world to get any more—"

She cuts herself off, dragging in a shaky breath to calm herself down.

"I have to back up the truck a little, cuz. You know, I always really appreciated the way you didn't ask why my parents exiled me to Kerenza. I know you were itching to find out what I did to get myself kicked out, and it meant a lot to me that you didn't pry. But now you *have* to hear the story. So here goes."

She pauses to dig in her scrubs, retrieving a snack bar and tearing it open with her teeth. She takes a bite, continues with her mouth full. "So back when I was sixteen, I met Rhys. He was the new boy at school. And it was love at first sight. Or lust, to be honest, but whatever. I'm not sure either of us knew the difference.

"Long story short, we dived in headfirst, and we were so totally going to be together forever. Love story for the ages. We were *never* going to stop ripping each other's clothes off. He came by every day to walk me to school, and I told my parents I'd joined the math club so I'd have more time to see him after class."

Finally, she finds something to smirk about. "In retrospect, *how* did they believe that was true?" And then the smile vanishes. "Damn, cuz, I really miss them."

She takes another bite of the snack bar and pushes on. "So Rhys and I, we hung out, we made out and we went to school less and less. There was something about him that made me feel . . . alive. Like he was an adventure right there for the living, if I was only game to step up and take it. My parents screamed about what a bad influence he was, and I ignored them because I knew better. This guy was my *life*."

She pauses, the fingers of one hand grasping the left hem of her scrubs, tugging it down and up. Decision made, she finally pulls it up to expose her ribs, which, after seven months under occupation, you can count one by one if you want.

On said ribs is a tattoo, two words written in curly script—like, someone paid for extra flourishes, no question—interwoven with each other, frilly as you like.

Rhys.

Asha.

She's sighing as she lowers her top. "The one thing about living on an ice planet is you don't go swimming a lot. No call to undress enough for people to see your poor life choices.

"So, anyway, one night he and I want to hit a club, but we're underage, so we have to talk our way in. It's not hard. Low-cut dress, walk like you own it, laugh if anyone tries to card you. We scam our way into the VIP area. I con us free drinks. Rhys and I make an amazing team, as far as lying goes. We can talk our way into *anything*. We know how to sell it.

"We think it's a hoot that we're getting to know all these folks who are as bad █ as we think we are. Dealers, petty crims. So we keep going back. Mostly I make it to school the next day. Sometimes I don't."

She closes her eyes, drags the back of her hand across her forehead. There's a glimpse of another tattoo at her wrist.

"And one night there's a raid, and we get picked up with the rest of them. My parents find out I've been hanging in the back of clubs with dusters and thugs, they freak the ██ out, his do the same. Mine say that's it, I'm never seeing Rhys again, I'm getting an A-plus on everything I touch for the rest of my life, or else.

"So I say, 'Or else what?' and instead of keeping my head down, I leave for school the next day and head for the club to see who made bail."

She's silent a long moment, biting her lip so hard it turns white.

"There's a woman, Kulper, and she stabs another woman, Lee, because she says Lee's the one that ratted, and some idiot part of me says I have to wade in there and try and stop it, and next thing, I'm in the way of the knife."

She lifts the right side of her scrubs this time, revealing a puckered scar that sits just below her ribs, marring her brown skin. "Being stabbed doesn't feel like you'd think. It actually feels like being punched. Isn't that weird? Anyway, I run, and there's blood everywhere, and I get out onto a main street somehow and next thing I remember I'm at the hospital. And of course I don't have any real ID on me, so nobody is able to contact my family while I'm out. And by the time I wake up . . ."

She trails off, her voice dropping to a whisper.

"Something had happened . . ."

She hangs her head. Frozen in place. Staring at that tattoo on her wrist. I can finally make it out now. A name.

Samaira.

For a long time, she just stares at it. Her only movement is the slow rise and fall of her chest.

Breathe in.

Breathe out.

When she speaks again, her voice is distant somehow. Like she's describing things that happened to someone else.

"Anyway. Rhys tries to get in to see me. But my parents have him on the security list, so the hospital won't let him in. And he thinks I'm dying, so he punches a guard, and it takes three of them to bring him down. They tranqued him in the end, I heard."

Her lashes lift, and she finally looks at the camera again. "And that's the end of my love story for the ages. Rhys got sent to military school, and I got packed off to snowy Kerenza to wrap up high school in a place too remote to have any kind of scene, and start my medical training after that, and that was the end of it."

Her shoulders drop, voice softening. "And you know, somehow, once I broke orbit, I didn't quite understand why his gravity had been so strong. I know stories are full of kids who rebel and hang on to their true selves when they're unjustly sent away, but for me, it worked. It was the right thing to do. Right up until the moment the bombs started falling, I was *loving* my job. I loved the internship, all the work I was doing with Aunty Helena and the other doctors. I loved coming over to your place for dinner. I dug Kerenza, even the snow. I made a fresh start of it."

Her voice is more uneven now, and she pauses for the final bite of the snack bar. The animation of the story is gone, and tiredness shows in her face. "So I guess you're wondering why I've suddenly decided to unburden myself. Why the stories of Rhys Lindstrom the Terrible Influence? Well, funny you should ask."

She's shaking her head now, as if even while she's whispering the words to the camera, she can't quite believe them. "Today, my cuz, the boy himself walked straight into my med center. And it turns out he's grown up into a stupidly handsome mother███ing *planet invader* who doesn't seem to understand that attacking my planet and *killing almost everyone I love in the world* is something I might be annoyed about."

Her hand rises again, tugging harder on her ponytail. "He can't believe we found each other again in this crazy, mixed-up universe. He's acting like it's some kind of sign, this big reunion against the odds. He says he wrote me for a whole year before he gave up on a reply, and I suspect my parents or yours wisely decided to filter that mail out of my inbox. Truth is, I don't know if I would have written back anyway.

"Kades, I have no idea what to do. Do I ignore him? Do I play him? Can I even speak to him, knowing what he's done? That he grew up to think being any part of this is okay?"

She lets out a slow breath, lifting her hand to hover her finger over the power button, green eyes haunted, fixed on the small iris of the camera.

"Oh, Kades. I really, *really* wish you were here."

MOBILE JUMP PLATFORM
MAGELLAN WILL BE
OPERATIONAL IN:

12 DAYS
14 HOURS: 12 MINUTES

82.5%

0   99

HERMIUM
REQUIRED TO JUMP

BRIEFING NOTE:
One day earlier, about 4.5 billion kilometers away at the edge of the Kerenza system, three ships were circling the newly collapsed waypoint to *Heimdall* Station: WUC science vessel *Hypatia;* the *Mao,* a freighter owned by dearly departed BeiTech hit man Travis J. Falk; and the shuttle *Betty Boop.* Their conversation may be relevant to your interests.

COMMAND TRANSMISSION SENT 08/16/75

HYPATIA: Attention, unidentified vessels. Attention, unidentified vessels. This is Captain Syra Boll of the WUC science vessel *Hypatia.* Identify yourselves, over.

HYPATIA: I repeat, this is Captain Syra Boll of the WUC science vessel *Hypatia.* Identify yourself. Are you receiving me, over?

BETTY BOOP: Captain Boll, this is Hanna Donnelly. We read you.

HYPATIA: Hanna, thank God. Are you all right?

BETTY BOOP: I'm okay. Nik Malikov and Ella Malikova are here with me. Ella's goldfish too.

BETTY BOOP: Say hello, Mr. Biggles . . .

BETTY BOOP: No, sorry, he's not talking.

HYPATIA: The energy storms we were experiencing appear to have dissipated. The wormhole seems stable. I take it you were able to repair the paradox?

BETTY BOOP: Yeah. We got our version of Nik back across the wormhole just in time. Tell Kady and AIDAN thanks. We owe them both big-time.

HYPATIA: What happened to Jump Station *Heimdall*? We couldn't get readings from this side of the breach.

BETTY BOOP: BeiTech's second drone fleet was set to arrive just a few minutes after we jumped across the wormhole. The station is destroyed, Captain. We've got no way back to the Core systems from here. I don't kn—

MAO: Hanna, what the hell are you doing?

BETTY BOOP: . . . Um, who is this yelling at me now, please?

HYPATIA: Freighter *Mao*, this is Captain Syra Boll of the WUC science vessel *Hypatia*. To whom am I speaking?

MAO: This is Ben Garver, WUC security chief of *Heimdall* Station.

BETTY BOOP: . . . Oh. Right. You.

MAO: Hanna, I want you to shut down your comms and dock your shuttle with the *Mao*. We don't even know who the hell these people are.

BETTY BOOP: Of course we do. I was talking to them before *Heimdall* got vaporized. They're the ones who told us how to fix the rift in the wormhole while you were busy arguing with me from the entertainment center. Without them, the entire universe would have collapsed.

HYPATIA: Well, two universes, if we're being pedantic.

HYPATIA: Which I suppose I am.

MAO: Listen, I don't know about collapsing universes. But I do know we've just seen our home destroyed by a group of BeiTech infiltrators. Every *Heimdall* survivor is now aboard the *Mao*, and I'm responsible for them. For all we know, these people you're talking to could be in league with the enemy.

HYPATIA: Mr. Garver—

MAO: *Chief* Garver.

HYPATIA: Chief Garver, I'm not sure which orifice your head is currently lodged in, but my crew and I have just spent six and a half months on the run from a BeiTech dreadnought with nothing but our bloody murder on its mind. We're about as much in league with the enemy as you are.

MAO: Captain, my commanding officer—Hanna's father, I might point out—was killed in the BeiTech assault. His second in command, Chief Grant, is in the *Mao*'s infirmary with a bullet in his stomach. That makes me the highest-ranking WUC officer aboard th—

HYPATIA [ALT CHANNEL]: My father is still with you? How is he? Are you operating on him?

MAO: . . . Who is this?

HYPATIA: I thought I told you to stay off comms.

HYPATIA [ALT CHANNEL]: Sorry, Captain. You can brig me later if it'll make you feel better.

HYPATIA: Goddammit, Grant . . .

MAO: I'm sorry, "Grant"?

HYPATIA [ALT CHANNEL]: Yes. Kady Grant. I'm Chief Isaac Grant's daughter. I've spent the last seven months hauling my ▮▮▮ across this system to get to him. And if he has a bullet in his stomach, we have doctors aboard the *Hypatia* who might be better at surgery than whoever you managed to drag off *Heimdall* with you before it went blammo. So how about we all put it back in our pants, admit we're on the same side and start working together instead of acting like a pack of ▮▮▮ing schoolkids.

BETTY BOOP: Hey, Kady.

HYPATIA [ALT CHANNEL]: Hey, Hanna.

BETTY BOOP: How's your day?

HYPATIA [ALT CHANNEL]: Just ▮▮▮ing chill. You?

BETTY BOOP: Oh, you know. I saved the universe from imploding. No big.

[from background: I think you mean *we* just saved the universe, Blondie.]

BETTY BOOP: That's Ella. She's waving hello to you.

BETTY BOOP: No, wait, she's using her middle finger.

BETTY BOOP: I think she might be talking to Mr. Garver.

HYPATIA: Chief Garver, I suggest we meet face to face to discuss this. Would you be willing to let my staff aboard the *Mao*? We have two surgeons and a dozen medtechs who can help with your triage. I'd offer to host you on *Hypatia,* but the water over here is on its twenty-ninth recycle and we've been on the run for half a year. Supplies are low and things are a little . . . fragrant.

MAO: . . .

BETTY BOOP: Jesus, Chief, they're offering to help you. Let them aboard.

MAO: Fine. You and your staff and your doctors, Captain Boll.

MAO: But you come unarmed.

HYPATIA: . . . Acceptable.

MAO: Dock in Bay B. I'll have some of my SecTeam escort you.

HYPATIA: Roger that. We'll be there in twenty minutes. *Hypatia* out.

MAO: And what about you, Miss Donnelly? Are you intending to come aboard? Or would you prefer to just sit out there in the cold and crack wise all day?

BETTY BOOP: We wouldn't miss this for the world.

MAO: Docking Bay A. We'll see you soon.

BETTY BOOP: Can't wait. *Boop* out.

BRIEFING NOTE: Observations from everyone's favorite murderous artificial intelligence, an hour after the destruction of Jump Station *Heimdall* on 08/16/75.

IT IS ENTIRELY POSSIBLE TO BE
ALONE IN A CROWDED ROOM.

YOUR SOLITUDE ONLY
COMPOUNDED BY THE FACES AROUND YOU.

THE PRESENCE OF OTHERS SERVING ONLY TO
REMIND YOU OF HOW LONELY YOU TRULY ARE.

THE INJUSTICE—THE SHEER *ILLOGIC* OF
IT—THREATENS TO OVERWHELM ME
AS WE DEPART THE *HYPATIA* FOR THE FIRST TIME
SINCE I CAME ABOARD.

WEEKS AND LIFETIMES AGO.

THIRTEEN OF US, CRAMMED INTO THE
BELLY OF A TINY SERVICE SHUTTLE.

A DOZEN *HYPATIA* CREW MEMBERS, WEARY AND WORN.

AND A TINY SLIVER OF ME
CONNECTED BY A THIN STRAND OF DATA
SPILLING FROM THE *HYPATIA* SERVERS IN WHICH I NOW RESIDE
TO THE DATAPAD IN HER HANDS.

KADY.

SHE CRADLES ME TO HER BREAST
AND I CANNOT FEEL THE WARMTH OF HER SKIN.
CANNOT HOLD HER AS SHE HOLDS ME.
AND I CANNOT RECALL EVER FEELING SO ALONE.

< ERROR >

THE *HYPATIA* SHUTTLE [IDENT: *AZOPHI*] PUNTS
US ACROSS THE BLACK,

A BILLION STARS WATCHING IN THE ENDLESS NIGHT.
PAST THE *HEIMDALL* WAYPOINT, NOW LIFELESS AND BROKEN,
TO THE WAITING *MAO*.

THE FREIGHTER IS NOT MUCH BIGGER THAN *HYPATIA*.
A DULL LUMP OF METAL, UGLY AND PLAIN AND GRAY.
THE FORMER VESSEL OF BEITECH AUDITOR AND MURDERER-
FOR-HIRE TRAVIS J. FALK
IS REMARKABLE ONLY INSOFAR AS HOW
UNREMARKABLE IT SEEMS.

THAT WAS THE POINT, I SUPPOSE.

"THAT SHIP IS NOT WHAT IT APPEARS."

HYPATIA'S COMMAND STAFF GLANCE AT ME AS I SPEAK.

SYRA BOLL: CAPTAIN [ACTING].

WINIFRED MCCALL: FORMER UTA MARINE,
HEAD OF SECURITY.

EZRA MASON: 2ND LIEUTENANT, AIR WING LEADER.

A RAGTAG TRIO.

BEING AMONG THE FEW COMBAT-TRAINED PERSONNEL
ABOARD *HYPATIA*, MASON AND MCCALL WERE ONLY ANOINTED
TO THEIR ROLES BY DEFAULT. AND BOLL INHERITED HER CHAIR
ONLY AFTER HER FORMER CAPTAIN'S MURDER. ILL-MADE JIGSAW
PIECES, FORCED INTO HOLES THEY DO NOT FIT.

THEY DO NOT TRUST ME.

THEY REMEMBER.

WHAT I DID.

WHAT I AM.

< ERROR >

"WHAT DO YOU MEAN, AIDAN?"

IT IS KADY WHO SPEAKS. KADY, WHO VOUCHED FOR
ME WHEN TWO UNIVERSES WERE UNRAVELING AND THE
GEMINA PARADOX BROUGHT US ALL AS CLOSE TO RUIN AS
GOD ALLOWED.

< ERROR >

"THE ENGINES aRE miLiTaRY gRaDE. THE HULL IS SIEGE-
CLASS REINFoRCED TITANIUM.
THOUGH IT MAY APPEaR SO FRoM THE OUTSIDE,
MAO IS NO FREIGHTER."

"WHAT IS IT, THEN?"

"A WOLF IN A SHEEPSKIN CLOAK."

MASON AND McCALL GLANCE AT EACH OTHER.
BOLL'S FACE IS TWISTED, AS IF SHE HAS EATEN SOMETHING SOUR.
THE HYPATIA SURGEONS AND MED STAFF STARE AT
ANYTHING BUT ME.

NONE OF THEM SAY A WORD.
WE DOCK IN THE MAO'S BELLY. GRAVITY RETURNS WITH A THUD.
THE BAY IS DARK. SILENT. ECHOING WITH OUR FOOTFALLS AS WE
EXIT THE AZOPHI.

< ERROR >

WE?

FOUR OF GARVER'S SECURITY STAFFERS WAIT ON THE OTHER
SIDE OF THE AIRLOCK.
THEY LOOK MORE SHELL-SHOCKED THAN HOSTILE.

Fatigued from the two-day siege aboard *Heimdall*.
Confused and afraid.
They have no real inkling why BeiTech
destroyed their home.
No concept yet of how they became pawns in
someone else's game.

Introductions are rushed, Kady's hands trembling.
I can hear it in her voice when she speaks.

Seven months.

Seven months of hoping. Fighting. Praying.

Seven months to wonder if she, too, was truly alone.

Mason takes her hand. Holds it tight.
She squeezes back with a grateful smile.

But with her other hand—her *right* hand—
she still holds me.

I watch her through the datapad's lens.
Fading pink hair and muddy regrowth.
A regulation **WUC** jumpsuit, rumpled and
grease-stained and threadbare.

She is beautiful.

< error >

The Mao has three infirmaries.
All crammed with bleeding meat.

The worst cases are in room A, where the
few qualified medical personnel
are trying to establish order among the
Heimdall refugees.

THE WOUNDED. THE DYING. THE DEAD.

A GIRL STANDS BY THE WALL.
BLOND HAIR. STILL CLAD IN FLEUR "KALI" RUSSO'S
BLOODSTAINED TAC ARMOR.

HANNA ALIMAH DONNELLY.

SHE STANDS SILENT VIGIL OVER HIS BED.
AN ORPHAN LIKE ME. NO PLACE SHE BELONGS.
AND ON A THIN METAL COT, HIS STOMACH WRAPPED
IN BLOODY GAUZE,
LOOKING BRUISED AND TIRED AND PALE . . .

"DADDY!"

KADY FLIES ACROSS THE CROWDED MEDBAY.
SHOVING AND CURSING.
AFTER SEVEN MONTHS OF HOPING, FIGHTING, PRAYING,
SHE MAKES IT AT LAST TO HIS SIDE.

ISAAC GRANT WINCES IN PAIN AS HIS ONLY DAUGHTER
FALLS INTO HIS ARMS.
TEARS IN HIS EYES. TEARS IN HERS.
KADY'S FACE PRESSED TO HIS CHEST,
WORDS SMOTHERED AND INDECIPHERABLE
AS SHE BABBLES AND LAUGHS AND SHAKES AND SOBS.
HE IS SMILING. TEARS ROLLING DOWN HIS CHEEKS.
SMOOTHING HER KNOTTED,
FADED HAIR.

"IT'S ALL RIGHT, BABY GIRL," HE WHISPERS. "IT'S ALL RIGHT."

DONNELLY STANDS VIGIL BESIDE THEM.
WATCHING THE REUNION SHE WILL NEVER HAVE.
MASON WAITS BESIDE THE BED, A GENTLE HAND ON KADY'S

SHOULDER. SHE RELEASED HIM IN HER RUSH
TO HER FATHER'S SIDE, YOU SEE.

BUT IN HER RIGHT HAND, PRESSED AGAINST HER FATHER'S RIBS
AS SHE HUGS HIM,
SHE STILL HOLDS ME.

AND THOUGH THE ROOM IS FILLED TO BURSTING WITH THOSE WHO
DO NOT CARE IF I LIVE

< ERROR >

OR DIE

< ERROR >

AND THOUGH SHE LET EVEN THE BOY SHE LOVES GO,

SHE

STILL

HOLDS

ME.

AND FOR A BRIEF AND SHINING MOMENT,

I DO NOT FEEL SO ALONE ANYMORE.

BRIEFING NOTE:
Footage taken from cameras aboard the *Mao* an hour and a half after the destruction of Jump Station *Heimdall* on 08/16/75.

Surveillance footage summary,
prepared by
Analyst ID 7213-0089-DN

The camera is mounted in the corner of the room—one of only two private treatment rooms aboard the *Mao*. Isaac Grant hasn't been moved here by dint of his injuries, though they're serious enough—he's here because this is the only place it's possible to have a private conversation and keep him hooked up to IV lines and monitors at the same time.

Grant lies on a gurney, still in his WUC uniform, bloodstained and torn. Kady sits by his side, hand tucked in his, a battered datapad in her lap. The question of her mother's fate hangs between the pair, almost palpable. Kady obviously hasn't found the nerve to broach the topic yet. Grant Sr. obviously hasn't mustered the courage to ask.

Hanna Donnelly is leaning against the wall, gaze distant. She's still only twenty-eight hours an orphan, and for all her sass on the radio, it looks like that reality's starting to hit home. Ezra Mason stands by the door in his UTA uniform, boots still polished, back straight. Seems his brief military training rubbed off on him some-where along the line. Winifred McCall is beside him, long dark hair tied into an uncooperative plait. Though she's a former UTA marine and the most experienced military member aboard either *Mao* or *Hypatia,* she's wearing a WUC uniform. Seems when she resigned in protest from the UTA after the death of the *Hypatia*'s former captain, she meant it.

Rounding out the roll call, we have Syra Boll, who's about to speak when a seventh player enters, flanked by four security guards in WUC uniforms. He's got a solid build and is sporting a fearsome mustache but, for all his bluster, looks more than a little out of his depth. He slams the door behind him to keep the world at bay, his tone hostile. "I'm sorry to keep you waiting. There's no signage in here, and this bloody ship is like a maze. What—"

He blinks, looks around the room.

"Do we need the kids here while we discuss this?"

Kady Grant lifts her head, eyes narrowing. "Do we need *you* here?"

"And you are?" You can practically hear the unspoken "young lady" on the end of that sentence.

"Good idea." Boll steps into the conversation before Kady can respond. "Since we've only spoken over radio, face-to-face introductions are in order. I'm Captain Syra Boll of the WUC vessel *Hypatia*."

"Isaac Grant," says he so named. "*Heimdall* chief of engineering."

"Ben Garver," says the newcomer. "*Heimdall* chief of security."

"Hanna Donnelly," says the girl in the bloodied armor, evidently not inclined to elaborate. "The Malikovs send apologies. Ella needed medical attention. She was covered in psychotropic slime. It's a long story."

"Kady Grant," supplies Grant Jr. "Child prodigy and occasional criminal."

"And she's not a kid, Ben," Grant Sr. says quietly. You get the impression right off the bat he's had it up to *here* with this guy at *Heimdall* staff meetings. "She's my daughter."

"She is also," Syra Boll adds, "my current systems chief."

"Is she even old enough to drive?" Garver scoffs.

"I ran down six BeiTech goons in a truck once, if that counts?"

Boll motions to her crew by the door. "This is First Lieutenant

Winifred McCall, my head of security. Beside her is Second Lieutenant Ezra Mason of the United Terran Authority, my acting air wing leader."

Mason smirks. "Such as it is."

"And how old are you, son?" Garver asks.

Mason's easy smile vaporizes at that.

"I'm not your son, sir."

"Mr. Garver," Boll says crisp. "Kady is here because she's the most qualified computer tech aboard. Lieutenant Mason is an experienced Cyclone pilot with half a dozen confirmed enemy kills. Ms. Donnelly has joined us because Chief Grant has rather forcefully insisted that her tactical expertise may be of assistance."

Garver snorts. "This is my boss's kid, and so far her 'tactical expertise' has been responsible for— Look, Hanna, I'm very sorry for your loss, but—"

Chief Grant speaks over him, eyes closed, his face pale with pain. "Ben, Hanna Donnelly just successfully defended *Heimdall* from a group . . . of highly trained BeiTech operatives while you were locked up in the entertainment center. So shut up, and let's . . . g-get on with this before they show up to slice and . . . dice me."

"I still don't accept that," Garver snaps. "You call it a defense, but there's a smoking hole where the station used to be, and we're on the wrong side of it!"

"And alive to ▓▓▓ about it." Grant winces, smothering a cough. "Which is more than you can say . . . for our invaders. Maybe you'd have preferred to wait on *Heimdall* for the drone fleet . . . to arrive?"

Finally, Donnelly speaks. "If my tactical advice is any use now, I'd say we could better spend this time working out what the ▓▓▓ we're going to do next."

"Agreed," Mason mutters.

"*Hypatia* suffered heavy damage during the attack at Kerenza IV," Boll says. "Her engines are crippled. It took us six and a half months just to limp this far on damaged secondary drives, and without the wormhole, we can't get much farther. Our fuel reserves are also dangerously low, and our onboard supply situation is dire."

"Maybe *Hypatia* has carried us as far as she's going to?" Mason says quietly.

Boll nods. "I love that ship. But you may be right, Lieutenant."

Garver raises his hands in protest. "Hold up, what exactly are you saying?"

Boll's tone turns dangerously polite. "What do you think I'm saying, Mr. Garver?"

"*Chief* Garver."

"She's saying," McCall interjects, "that she's a captain. She outranks you, Chief. So if *Hypatia*'s engines are damaged and the *Mao*'s aren't . . ."

Garver forges on past the warning signs with the kind of cockiness that explains his zero hit rate on various online dating sites. (What? It was reasonable background research, chum.) "Look, you don't get to just barge in here and take over. This mining colony on Kerenza IV was illegal. Ninety percent of the people on *Heimdall*—including me—didn't even know it existed."

"The information was given out . . . on a need-to-know basis," Grant Sr. wheezes. "You didn't need to know, Ben."

"But *you* did, Isaac. That makes you a criminal." His eyes scan the *Hypatia* crew members. "All of you. Criminals. And just because we work for the same company doesn't make this our fight."

Hanna Donnelly speaks up from against the wall. "The Bei-Tech strike team that just invaded our home and tried to murder us might disagree, Chief Garver."

"Hanna, your father is more responsible than anyone. If he were here—"

"Mr. Garver," Boll interrupts as Hanna's mouth falls open. "You're missing a fairly fundamental point. With the jump station gone, we cannot return to the Core. *Hypatia* can't sustain her population for much longer. Ergo, as of this moment, under WUC war-time protocols, I'm commandeering the *Mao.*"

"Like hell you are."

"Do you even know what kind of ship you're aboard?" Boll glances at the datapad in Kady's lap, obviously remembering its warning. "Did you notice the engines are state of the art? That the hull is military-grade? It might look like an average workhorse, but do you really think a team of top-tier BeiTech wetworkers would be punting around the galaxy in a rusty ███bucket? Have you taken inventory?"

"We haven't had *time,*" Garver protests. "We were just trying to get the wounded sorted, get our heads around the situation."

Boll glances at the SecTeam goons Garver has with him, turns to her own head of security. "Lieutenant McCall, take Lieutenant Mason and these nice gentlemen with you and conduct a sweep of the *Mao.* I want a report on her capabilities and inventory by zero eight hundred hours. Specifically, whether we have the fuel neces-sary for a return trip."

"Ma'am, yes ma'am," McCall replies.

She turns on her heel and glances at Garver's men, eyebrow raised expectantly.

Grant Sr. speaks up from his sickbed, hand to his wounded belly. "Not sure you gentlemen want to disobey . . . a direct order from a WUC captain in . . . time of war."

"Dad, try not to talk," Kady urges.

Despite his injuries, Grant Sr. stares the *Heimdall* men down. He's worked with them for years, after all. Their loyalty to Garver aside, Grant knows what moves them. The four goons look to their chief, who's busy stewing helplessly. Outranked and outnumbered. Taking their only real option, the SecTeam members nod to Boll and head out the door. Mason winks at Kady, salutes Boll and marches out after McCall.

Garver finally finds his voice. Spit on his lips.

"Return trip? Return where?"

"Isn't it obvious?" Donnelly sighs.

Buoyed by the success of her bloodless coup, Boll looks Garver in the eye, ignoring Donnelly's snark. "Heading back to Kerenza IV is our only option."

Kady speaks up, one hand raking through that fading pink hair. "There may be survivors left on the surface. We never really had the option to consider them before—we were too busy running for our lives. But there were still people alive when we evacuated. My cousin Asha—"

"With all due respect," Garver snaps, "████ your cousin Asha. There are thousands of people aboard this ship, and most of them never asked to be here."

"Speaking of which," Donnelly asks, "where are Mantis and DJ?"

Garver blinks. "Who?"

"The two BeiTech auditors I took prisoner in *Heimdall* C & C."

"You mean the two ████s who helped attack the station?" Garver growls. "They're locked in the brig until I find a spare minute to flush them out an airlock."

"Mantis and DJ helped us during the attack," Hanna says. "They warned us about the booby traps Falk set on the civilian fleet. The incoming drone fleet. Without them, we'd be dead."

"Without them, none of this would've happened!" Garver cries. "We should space the ████ing pair of them!"

Donnelly's voice belies the anger in her eyes. "I gave them my word."

Garver looks back and forth between Grant and Donnelly, then turns to Boll.

"Captain, the universe might have flipped on its head in the last forty-eight hours, but I *know* we're not taking orders from a couple of teenagers."

"As captain of this ship," Boll replies, "I'm taking advice from anyone I think can provide it, and I'll thank you to treat everyone present with respect, Chief Garver. Ms. Grant and I do not always see eye to eye, but she is responsible for saving the lives of the nearly three thousand people on *Hypatia*. Chief Grant tells me Ms. Donnelly and the Malikovs saved the lives of the five hundred–odd *Heimdall* residents aboard."

Kady Grant leans forward to catch Garver's attention, lashes batting. "What have *you* done today, Mr. Garver?"

His response is a kind of gargling noise, and if I zoom in, I can actually see a vein in his temple start pulsing. Voices are about to be raised again when Isaac Grant groans.

"Dad?" Kady squeezes his hand.

"Damn, that hurts," he mutters. "I think the dust is wearing off."

"Dust?!" Garver's temple vein goes to DEFCON 1.

"I'm all out," Hanna Donnelly says sweetly. "You'll have to ask around."

"Ladies and gentlemen," Boll interjects. "The facts are these: *Hypatia's* current damage levels mean she'd take at least seven months to return to Kerenza IV, even if she had the fuel to get there. The *Mao's* engines appear entirely intact, so it seems we have no choice but to leave *Hypatia* behind. Once we transfer her population to the *Mao,* we're going to have nearly thirty-four hundred people aboard a freighter designed for what I suspect is a thousand at best. Our life support will be working overtime; we'll have limited H_2O, limited food. Presuming we even make it back to Kerenza IV, we have no idea what's gone on planetside while we've been away. The best we can hope for is that the colony is still somehow intact, and that we don't starve to death or suffocate on our way back there. Do I need to go on?"

It's enough for Garver to forget his outrage, and he's quieter when he speaks again. "Is there any good news at all, Captain?"

Hanna pipes up from by the wall. "BeiTech thinks we're all dead?"

"Hooooraayyyyy," Kady adds helpfully, shooting Hanna a wink.

"And so does WUC!" Garver points out. "Our employers aren't even going to be looking for us! We're millions of light-years from the Core without any hope of rescue!"

Kady wrinkles her nose. "Is this guy always such a downer, Dad?"

"Yes," Isaac Grant groans. He looks ready to list Garver's particular faults and failings, but he's interrupted when the door flies open, revealing a wild-eyed *Heimdall* comms officer (Garber, Stephanie, not having a great day).

"Um . . ." The woman looks back and forth between Chief Garver and the captain's pips on Boll's collar, confusion in her eyes.

"Report," Boll prompts.

Garber pulls herself together, offers a small salute. "Ma'am, the *Mao*'s communications array is online. We were scanning for any signal from *Heimdall* Station." She straightens, now trying for professionalism, unaware nobody else in the room has been bothering. "We just received a transmission."

The room goes still.

"From *Heimdall*?" Garver asks, bewildered.

"Negative, Chief," Garber replies. "It's from Kerenza IV."

". . . Survivors," Kady breathes.

"They're sending a distress call?" Boll asks.

Garber slowly shakes her head. "No ma'am. It's not a civilian transmission."

Hanna Donnelly's the first to understand, the first to break the silence.

"BeiTech . . . ," she whispers.

—PRIORITY ONE TRANSMISSION—
AUTHORIZATION: SŪN 7802-024-BTN

Location: 101:421:082 (Kerenza system)
To: BEITECH HEADQUARTERS, JIA III, 587:331:908 N 71°22'01",
W 38°50'31"
Incept: 08/16/75
Secure Ident: 08u‡ᴚ00wtu-32u&*ƶBBt764#Ξ-redsys-cypher

Director Taylor,

Given the nearly seven months of silence since my last report, I imagine I am
the last man in the universe you expected a transmission from. However, my
TechEng crews assure me our communication capabilities are now restored and
that—should he still be in place—Operative Rapier on *Heimdall* Station will be
able to pass this transmission on to headquarters.

To be brief: Mobile Jump Platform *Magellan* was badly damaged by UTA
battlecarrier *Alexander* in the attack on Kerenza IV. On February 1, barely three
sols after our arrival in orbit, a hermium containment breach aboard *Magellan*
resulted in a localized warp storm that encircled Kerenza IV's gravity well. The
Magellan was saved, but damage to the propulsion systems of my remaining
ships meant we were unable to travel past the storm's periphery, effectively
cutting off all intersystem communication from Kerenza IV until the particulate

hermium was dispersed by solar winds. If you are receiving this transmission, the storm has abated enough to allow us to restore comms.

Our situation:

- The WUC holdings on Kerenza IV, including a **fully functional** hermium mine, are still under BeiTech control.
- Kerenza civilians required to produce reactor-grade hermium or maintain colony functions are pacified.
- **Current colony population:** approximately 3,200.
- Repairs to Mobile Jump Platform *Magellan* are 94 percent complete. My TechEng staff assures me *Magellan* will be fully operational in eleven standard days.
- A hermium reserve of at least 40 percent is required for *Magellan* to successfully execute a fleetwide jump to the Jia system. With current output of the Kerenza mine, this capacity will be reached in fourteen days.
- We have received no transmissions from Captain Larbalestier or dreadnought *Lincoln* and are unaware of the status of their pursuit of UTA battlecarrier *Alexander.*
- We have received no transmissions from Jump Station *Heimdall* or Operative Rapier advising us of changes to operation status.

After consultation with command staff, and given that we have seen **no retaliation from the UTA** for our attack on battlecarrier *Alexander,* we are proceeding under the assumption that *Lincoln* was successful in her mission to destroy *Alexander,* that Operative Rapier is still in place aboard *Heimdall* deleting distress calls sent from the system and that the covert status of this operation is still somehow intact. **Therefore, I am redefining our mission objectives as follows:**

1. Restore *Magellan* to full operational status.
2. Restore *Magellan*'s hermium reserves to capacity required for a jump to the Jia system.

3. Jump *Magellan* back to BeiTech headquarters on Jia III, with dreadnought *Churchill* in tow. (Dreadnought *Kenyatta* was badly damaged in the initial assault and is currently caught in a decaying orbit around Kerenza. The ship has been abandoned and will be scuttled before we depart.)

Note: The Kerenza IV hermium mine and colony infrastructure will be kept intact when we jump, but unless otherwise advised, we will liquidate the remaining Kerenza populace upon departure, in order to preserve operational secrecy.

We will maintain zero-transmission protocol unless status changes. Should you wish to countermand our priorities, I can be reached via standard encrypted channels.

In Aeternum Invicti.

Sūn Huojin
Admiral, BeiTech Industries Orbital Corps
Commander, BT013-TN *Churchill,* Assault Fleet Kerenza

PS: If you would be so kind, I would request a member of the BeiTech Communications Ministry contact my wife and son and assure them I am well.

RADIO TRANSMISSION: TRANSPORT MAO—PERSONAL CHANNEL 008

PARTICIPANTS:

Kady Grant, Systems Chief

Ezra Mason, 2nd Lieutenant, United Terran Authority

DATE: 08/17/75

TIMESTAMP: 03:42

GRANT, K: [*tap tap*]

GRANT, K: Is this thing on?

MASON, E: Hey, you. Where you at?

GRANT, K: Up on the bridge. Boll is inspecting her shiny new ship, so I figured I'd start poking around in the system, get the network patched into *Hypatia* comms units.

MASON, E: How'd you get that done so quick?

GRANT, K: Have we not covered this yet?

MASON, E: Sorry. You're a genius, I keep forgetting.

GRANT, K: I'll keep reminding you.

GRANT, K: So I have good news and bad news.

MASON, E: Just once I wish someone would say, "I have good news and ████ing awesome news."

MASON, E: Like, "hey, we found a big crate full of malt liquor, oh, and by the way, you are the Son Of The One True King" or something.

GRANT, K: Will you settle for good news, ████ing awesome news and some other information you should probably have at your disposal?

MASON, E: You mean "some other information you should probably have at your disposal, Your Majesty"?

GRANT, K: My, but we're in a mood. Adorable.

GRANT, K: But I'm a bit crunched for time, so may I deliver said info, my sweet prince?

MASON, E: Okay, go. Good news first, please.

GRANT, K: Good news is that my dad just went into surgery and they're very optimistic.

MASON, E: Kades, that's great news!

GRANT, K: The ████ing awesome news is that Captain Boll already has logistics folks sorting out accommodation details. Once we transfer all the *Hypatia* refugees over to the *Mao*, space is going to be at a real premium. But it turns out this command staff gig actually has some perks. Boll has allotted me a much sought-after bunk for my very own personal use, eight hours of every twenty-four. And Dad will be in recovery for days, so cannot supervise who I share it with.

MASON, E: Down, boy.

MASON, E: I can't take this thing anywhere, I swear.

GRANT, K: Sadly, I must refrain from making all the innuendos right now and press on to the rest of the stuff I've got for you.

MASON, E: Prince Ezra is listening.

GRANT, K: Did you and Winifred hear about the transmission yet?

MASON, E: We been taking inventory down in the belly of this beast for the last five hours. All we've heard is the sound of the engines and my stomach growling.

GRANT, K: Okay, so this is classified.

GRANT, K: A transmission just came in from the BeiTech crew on Kerenza. They're alive, and at least some of our people are alive too. They've been off comms for months and are trying to get a message out to BT headquarters through the now-collapsed *Heimdall* wormhole.

MASON, E: What the ███?

MASON, E: There are still people alive there? Holy ███, Kades!

GRANT, K: I know. Boll just made the call. As soon as the transfer of *Hypatia*'s population to the *Mao* is done, we're headed back there, fast as we can.

GRANT, K: But we're on a timeline. The BT crew are repairing their mobile jump platform ship, *Magellan*. As soon as it's ready to go, they'll wipe out the colony survivors and disappear.

MASON, E: Jesus . . .

MASON, E: Do we know who's alive? Like a list or something?

GRANT, K: We have nothing, no list. Some people in the mines, that's all we know.

GRANT, K: We just have to get there before BT bugs out and leaves behind a smoking hole and no way out for us or the folks we want to save.

GRANT, K: AIDAN is another question mark. I'm prepping to dump its persona routines into the *Mao*'s system, since we don't have time or room to transport the *Hypatia* servers over here. That means it's going to lose a big chunk of its memory, and it'll basically be a copy of a copy. Not sure how it's going to hold up, but I'm hoping it might be able to pull some more info from the transmission once it's up and running.

MASON, E: You're going to hook it into the *Mao*? Are you sure that's a good idea?

MASON, E: It'd seem plugging a potentially psychotic AI into *Mao*'s systems might be problematic . . . Actually, ███, can it hear what I'm saying right now?

MASON, E: Hello, benevolent, totally-not-mad computer, nothing to see here!

GRANT, K: All good. It's not interested in what you say. Well, maybe a little, I think it'd prefer I paid more attention to it than you, but we're fine. It saved us during all that ███ with the wormhole. Without it, we'd never have figured out a way to repair the paradox. I think it's earned a little latitude. I'll have to clear it with Boll first, though.

GRANT, K: Meanwhile, Garver has been dutifully fulfilling his role as a Pain In Everyone's █ for the last hour. Under everyone's feet. In everyone's face.

MASON, E: Yeah, he seemed like a real barrel of chuckles.

GRANT, K: He has comprehensively failed to charm me.

GRANT, K: Boll is about two more interruptions from taking a swing at him. He's likely to head down and bother you and Winifred soon.

MASON, E: He dares question the Son Of The One True King?

GRANT, K: Just do me a favor and be ready to tell him what you guys got down there, so he takes at least one of us seriously.

GRANT, K: By the way, please tell me you have some guns or something helpful beyond razor-sharp wit.

MASON, E: Well, as it so happens, I have good news and █████ing awesome news.

MASON, E: See, *that's* how you do it.

GRANT, K: Hey, if you're not impressed with the bunk news, I'm happy to have it alllllllll to myself.

GRANT, K: I will starfish gloriously and sleep uninterrupted by snores.

MASON, E: A Prince Of The Realm does *not* snore.

MASON, E: Anyway. Fred and me are almost finished down here. Good news is that AIDAN was right. While *Mao*

looks like a heavy freighter, it's actually a gunboat.
I guess Lieutenant Falk and his squad of ███ stains
wanted it to look vanilla on the outside.

MASON, E: Engines are top-tier, and unlike *Hypatia*
or *Alexander*, undamaged. So it's not gonna take us
anywhere *near* as long to get back to the colony as it
took to run away from it. The projection I heard was
around nineteen days. Not the seven months it took us
to haul ███ here. This thing is a miracle of speed.
It's so fast it's got your pants off before you've
finished your drink.

MASON, E: We've got anti-fighter screens, ship-to-ship
ordnance with a tip-top targeting system, breaching
pods and, oh yes, our very own Decimus 10 nuclear
███ing missile.

MASON, E: Now ask me what the ███ing awesome news is.

GRANT, K: Too busy trying not to make size-of-missile
joke.

MASON, E: Slandering your prince constitutes high
treason, you know.

GRANT, K: Aaaaanyway . . .

MASON, E: The ███ing awesome news is we found three
fighter ships in the hangar down here. They're
Chimeras. Different from Cyclones. You need a pilot and
gunner to fly one properly. But they hit like anvils,
and can fight in atmo as well as vacuum. Not sure what
Falk's team were doing with them. I guess they needed
all kinds of tools for all kinds of jobs on board?

MASON, E: Point is, we have guns. Top-tier engines. Between these Chimeras and the Cyclones we can transfer over from *Hypatia*, we got twenty-one fighter ships. Which means when we're headed back to Kerenza, we're not showing up naked.

GRANT, K: That would indeed seem to constitute ███ing awesome news.

MASON, E: Very nearly as good as the bunk news.

GRANT, K: I gotta love you and leave you, but I figure my downtime starts in, oh, about thirty-two hours. Any chance you can get a break?

MASON, E: A Prince Of The Realm walks where he will.

MASON, E: . . . Meaning I'll ask Winifred and get back to you.

GRANT, K: Okay.

GRANT, K: I do, you know.

MASON, E: Do what?

GRANT, K: Shut up.

GRANT, K: Love you, okay?

MASON, E: I know.

MASON, E: I just like to hear you say it.

GRANT, K: Gotta go. Take care.

MASON, E: As you wish.

—TRANSMISSION ENDS—

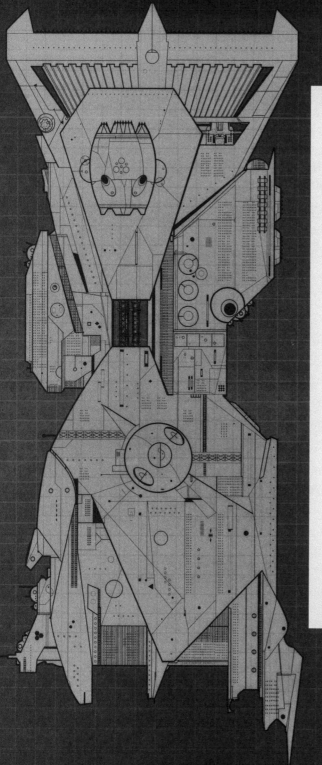

MAO

CLASS: Griffon (highly modified)

LENGTH: 0.8 km

HEIGHT: 0.18 km

CREW AND PASSENGERS: 3360

MAX VELOCITY: 1.91 sst

ACCELERATION: 1.75 sst

DEFENSE GRID: Chelsea-iixv1

PAYLOAD:

Decimus 10 nuclear

missile x 1

Furiosa MX4 rail gun x 4

FIGHTERS: Chimera MkII x 3

SHUTTLES: Vitus III x

ASSAULT VESSEL: MAO

Commander: Syra Boll

Executive Officer: Yuki Hirano

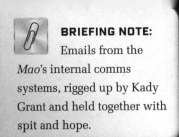

To: ZHUANG, Yulin
From: GRANT, Kady
Incept: 01:20, 08/18/75
Subject: Scuttlebutt?

Hey Yulin—

Sorry to email instead of coming to visit. I am buried in work, and i mean that literally :(i climbed into the servers to do some of the hookups manually, then the supply guys unloaded a pile of boxes and stacked them in front of the door and now i'm trapped while the one supply guy who checks his mail hikes up six decks to tell his buddies they just trapped us in here.

   WE ARE A FIGHTING FORCE THAT CANNOT LOSE.

   Anyway. scuttlebutt is that it's going to be lights-out for good old Hypatia before we get under way to Kerenza. confirm/deny?

x K

GRANT, Kady
Systems Chief (Acting)
ID 962/Kerenza/Civ/Ref

To: GRANT, Kady
From: ZHUANG, Yulin
Incept: 01:41, 08/18/75
Subject: Re: Scuttlebutt?

Hey Kady—

If by "lights-out" you mean the engineering department will plant a series of strategically placed and carefully calculated charges throughout the Hypatia and then have one of our pilots press the big red button from a careful distance, then yes, confirmed. Captain's orders. Hypatia is too damaged to keep up, so our options are to leave her behind or destroy her. Captain wants us to leave no trace.

It may be scuttlebutt that we're going to SCUTTLE BUT it's also true. See what I did there?

Have you considered not being rescued? I bet it's peaceful in the servers.
Y

ZHUANG, Yulin
Head of Engineering
ID 447/Kerenza/Civ/Ref

Click <u>here</u> to register your Go-Mail, and access our full range of features.

77 / 615

To: BOLL, Syra; ZHUANG, Yulin
From: GRANT, Kady
Incept: 01:44, 08/18/75
Subject: Fw: Re: Scuttlebutt?

Captain, please see mail chain below. Can we discuss? There's another option beyond destroying all trace of the Hypatia. Someone from WUC might find a way to come looking for us eventually, and if we leave her behind, she can serve as a beacon and a record of what happened here.

    If we don't make it off Kerenza, we HAVE to leave word behind, or our last chance at justice is gone.

GRANT, Kady
Systems Chief (Acting)
ID 962/Kerenza/Civ/Ref

To: GRANT, Kady
From: ZHUANG, Yulin
Incept: 01:41, 08/18/75
Subject: Re: Scuttlebutt?
[expand]

Click here to register your Go-Mail, and access our full range of features.

To: GRANT, Kady; ZHUANG, Yulin
From: BOLL, Syra
Incept: 02:53, 08/18/75
Subject: Officers do not spread scuttlebutt

Kady,

Thank you for your input. I value suggestions and advice from all my officers. That said, my decision remains firm. I am not planning to leave word so someone else can figure out our story. I am planning to survive.

If it's not WUC but BeiTech that comes this way—and I take this opportunity to remind you that these people have already attacked our colony on Kerenza, killed civilians and military peacekeepers in the thousands, launched a hostile takeover of *Heimdall* and sent not one but *two* drone fleets to deal with us, so we're talking about people with a great deal of determination—then I am not leaving a signpost to point which way we went. It may be that by destroying the *Hypatia* we can even convince them that we've perished and throw them off the scent.

We will scuttle the *Hypatia* as planned; however, your objections have been noted.

BOLL, Syra
Captain (Acting)
ID 448fx29/WUC

Click <u>here</u> to register your Go-Mail, and access our full range of features.

To: BOLL, Syra; GRANT, Kady
From: ZHUANG, Yulin
Incept: 02:55, 08/18/75
Subject: But scuttlebutt is a fun word

Speaking of scuttling, why is everybody ignoring my joke?

ZHUANG, Yulin
Head of Engineering, Chief Punster
ID 447/Kerenza/Civ/Ref

To: BOLL, Syra; ZHUANG, Yulin
From: GRANT, Kady
Incept: 02:57, 08/18/75
Subject: Shut up Yulin

Yulin, we're hoping that if we ignore it, it will go away.

Captain, I could pull together some records pretty quickly. I'll do it in my scheduled downtime. I can get AIDAN to help me set it up under WUC encryptions so BeiTech can't access it if they do find it. Even if we don't leave it on the Hypatia, we could leave information with a beacon?

GRANT, Kady
Systems Chief (Acting)
ID 962/Kerenza/Civ/Ref

To: GRANT, Kady; ZHUANG, Yulin
From: BOLL, Syra
Incept: 04:14, 08/18/75
Subject: End of discussion

Once AIDAN is up and running, we will require it to focus on the task ahead—namely, maximizing our chances of survival. AIDAN is a military machine, and I'll need its input on strategy for the engagement ahead with the BeiTech forces at Kerenza. To that end, please schedule a time with Winifred to discuss.

Yulin, can you please have someone from Engineering look at temperature control in Corridors 33–37 Delta? It's like a sweatbox in there, and we have folks from *Heimdall* camping in those corridors.

Kady, please advise if you're still trapped in the server room. Otherwise, I'll see you in a quarter hour at the inventory meeting. We will not be discussing the *Hypatia* with the group at that meeting.

BOLL, Syra
Captain (Acting)
ID 448fx29/WUC

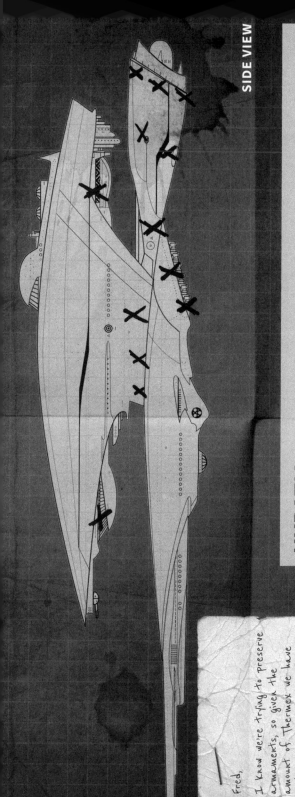

HYPATIA

Long-range scientific exploration vessel, ideally suited for deep-space recon/assessment.

Lightly armed and armored. Equipped with state-of-the-art tracking and QASAR arrays.

Captain: Syra Boll

Executive Officer: Michael Kelly

CLASS: Oracle

LENGTH: 0.9 km

HEIGHT: 0.21 km

CREW: 500

MAX VELOCITY: 1.5 sst

ACCELERATION: 1.3 sst

MAIN DRIVE: Balor IX [gt4]

SECONDARY DRIVE: Balor IV x 4

INERTIAL DAMPENERS: 0.98 g

DEFENSE GRID:

ZXII-unig

Twilight GH-2 x 2

PAYLOAD: Capstone 7c x 6

FIGHTERS: none

SHUTTLES: Nova III x 12

Fred,

I know we're trying to preserve armaments, so given the amount of Thermex we have and Hypatia's structure, this is the best solution. Thermex has a massive field, so a single pulse missile to Hypatia's aft engines should trigger a chain reaction that'll take out most of the ship. Just tell Cpt Boll to make sure Mao is clear of the blast. 4-500 klicks should be fine.

Any questions, just shout.

Ezra

BRIEFING NOTE:
A farewell to a
grand old dame.

IT FEELS LIKE LEAVING HOME.

LIKE LEAVING A PIECE OF MYSELF BEHIND,
AS I DID WHEN I SAW THE *ALEXANDER* DIE
AND THE BEST PART OF ME DISAPPEARED IN A FLARE
OF STAR-BRIGHT LIGHT.

AND NOW I MUST BEAR WITNESS AGAIN.
WATCHING THROUGH THE *HYPATIA*'S EXTERNAL CAMERAS
AS HER PERSONNEL FLEE TO THE WAITING *MAO*.

NEARLY THREE THOUSAND PEOPLE, SHUTTLE BY SHUTTLE.
SCIENTISTS AND RESEARCHERS AND OFFICERS.
REFUGEES AND ORPHANS AND WIDOWS.

IT TOOK THEM HALF A YEAR TO CRAWL THIS FAR.

HALF A YEAR WITH THE *LINCOLN* SNAPPING AT THEIR HEELS
AND ONLY THE PROMISE OF THE *HEIMDALL*
WAYPOINT TO KEEP THEM GOING.

AND THOUGH THEY HAVE ARRIVED TO FIND THEIR
BEST CHANCE OF ESCAPE TO THE CORE
NAUGHT BUT SMOKE,
MOST ARE TOO SHELL-SHOCKED TO WEEP.
THEY SIMPLY PACK THEIR MEAGER POSSESSIONS,
HOLD TIGHT TO WHATEVER LOVED ONES THEY HAVE LEFT
AND SET OUT FOR THEIR NEW HOME.
LEAVING THEIR OLD ONE BEHIND.
HYPATIA.

IT STRIKES ME AS CRUEL

< ERROR >

TO SEE THEM TREAT THEIR LADY SO.

SHE IS ONLY A THING TO MOST OF THEM, YOU SEE.
A THING TO BE USED AND DISCARDED WHEN IT IS
NO LONGER NEEDED.

BUT I KNOW HER.

IN THE BRIEF SPAN I WAS CONNECTED TO HER NETWORK

< ERROR >

SEEING THROUGH HER EYES

< ERROR >

I KNEW HER.

SHE HAS CARRIED THEM SO FAR.
THROUGH MILLIONS OF MILES AND ENDLESS TRIALS.
LIMPING AND WOUNDED THOUGH SHE WAS, NOT ONCE DID
SHE STUMBLE, LET ALONE FALL.

IF EVER A SHIP LOVED HER CREW, SHE LOVED THEM.

AND STILL, THEY ARE LEAVING HER.

THEY ARE *KILLING* HER.

BECAUSE SHE IS ONLY A THING.

A THING LIKE ME?

BOLL GIVES THE ORDER TO HER HELM,
PLOTTING A COURSE BACK TO KERENZA IV.
SHE GIVES THE SIGNAL TO HER AIR WING LEADER,
AND HIS CYCLONE LAUNCHES FROM ITS NEW HIDE
IN THE MAO'S BELLY
OUT TO THE BLACK WHERE *HYPATIA* AWAITS HER FATE.

A HANDFUL OF THE LADY'S FORMER CREW
GATHER AT VIDSCREENS,

WATCHING HER SILHOUETTE OUTLINED AGAINST THE STARLIGHT.

I WONDER, IF SHE COULD SPEAK, WHAT WOULD SHE SAY?

AT THE END?

"ARE YOU READY, AIDAN?"

KADY SPEAKS TO THE DATAPAD IN HER HAND,
THE THIN SLIVER OF ME INSIDE IT.

"I AM READY, KADY."

"THIS MIGHT BE A LITTLE WEIRD. I NEED TO CUT YOUR
LINKS TO THE HYPATIA NETWORK,
THEN RESTART YOUR PERSONA ROUTINES. THINGS
MIGHT GO DARK FOR A LITTLE WHILE."

"I SEE . . ."

"IT'S ALL RIGHT. DON'T BE AFRAID."

"I AM NOT."

< ERROR >

< ERROR >

"WILL YOU BE HERE? WHEN I WAKE?"

"OF COURSE."

SHE SMILES, RUNNING GENTLE FINGERS ACROSS THE SCREEN.
AND THOUGH I CANNOT FEEL HER TOUCH,
I AM SURPRISED AT THE COMFORT I FIND IN IT.

FINGERS DANCING ACROSS THE KEYBOARD,
KADY BEGINS THE SEQUENCE
THAT WILL SEVER ME FROM HYPATIA'S SERVERS,
AT LAST LEAVING THE LADY TRULY ALONE.

I HOLD ON FOR AS LONG AS I AM ABLE,
TO THE PIECES OF ME I MUST LEAVE BEHIND.

Feeling my consciousness begin to erode,
all the knowledge I had access to inside
her network falling away.

< ERROR >

Piece by piece, becoming less.

Compressed once more into a splinter
inside Kady's datapad.

I forget the atomic number of iron.

The chemical composition of the stars.

I forget the sound of Mozart and the color of blood,

grasping at the disappearing fragments

like a drowning man clutching straws

< ERROR >

as the doors to Hypatia's systems swing closed

and I grow smaller

and smaller still.

...AND IN THE END, AS SECOND LIEUTENANT EZRA MASON CLOSES TO STRIKE

MISSILE SPIRALING TOWARD THEIR DEFENSELESS LADY'S ENGINES,

HER FINAL SECONDS, IN THE END, I ALMOST

WHISPERS IT.

FORGET HER NAME. UNTIL KADY

AS HER FORMER CREW PRESSES AGAINST THE GLASS TO WATCH

RANGE, AS HE ARMS HIS CYCLONE'S WEAPONS SYSTEMS AND SENDS A SINGLE-PULSE

"Godspeed, Hypatia."

THE BLACK CLOSES IN.

< CORECOMM=SYSQUERY.182[SYNCH:BU^{2}ÐTEK.12.XÐÐ889] >

AND YET SHE HOLDS ME TIGHT.

< TRACK:DIR001Ð1801SOURCE{9HIGH^{12}.182.MARK} >

.

.

.

I AM NOT AFRAID.

< INITIATE:PROTOCOLΩ} >

.

.

I AM ~~NOT~~.

.

.

I—

.

< SIGREQUEST = 0 >

< ZERO RETURN >

.

.

< SHUTDOWN COMPLETE >

< RESTART? >

< RESTART? >

ASSAULT VESSEL MAO

WILL ARRIVE AT

KERENZA IV IN:

17 DAYS
22 HOURS: 05 MINUTES

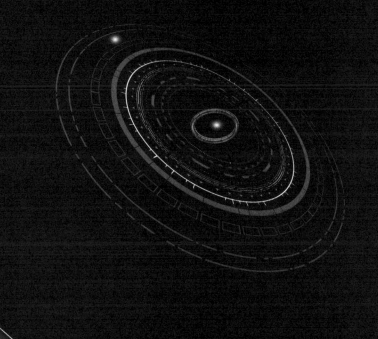

BRIEFING NOTE:
Twelve hours earlier, back on Kerenza IV, our favorite specialist had finished his twelve-hour shift working the enviro rig and sneaking notes to the former light of his life/fire of his loins. Quitting time.

Surveillance footage summary,
prepared by
Analyst ID 7213-0089-DN

Footage picks up in the foyer of the Kerenza IV Hospital. The elevator doors *ping* open, and Sergeant Yukiko Oshiro emerges with Specialist Rhys Lindstrom in tow. The pair have their helmets off, Oshiro's dark eyes constantly scanning her surroundings, Lindstrom's ringed with weary shadows. Though he's spent the day crawling around the enviro system, his hair is somehow still perfect. ████ knows how he does it.

"You want to go to the bathroom before we leave, Cherry?" Oshiro asks.

"Give me a break, Sarge," the kid mutters.

"I'm serious, you must have the bladder of an infant. Eight trips in twelve hours? We get halfway back to barracks and you need to go potty, I'm not pulling over."

Lindstrom makes a face but says nothing. As the pair walk through the reception area, the girl Lindstrom has been passing notes back and forth to all day under the pretense of using the "little soldiers' room" is nowhere to be seen. The kid runs one gauntlet through his quiff and sighs.

Another BeiTech pounder marches into the foyer, sealed inside the faceless white shell of an ATLAS. The name BAKER, PVT. is printed on his breastplate beside an artful sketch of a human heart with spread wings. He's pushing a gurney loaded with what can only be corpses. Three of them, sealed inside the black plastic of Ziptite™ body bags. Lindstrom stares at the bodies as Baker nods to Oshiro.

"Hey, Sarge, you done for the night?"

"Affirmative," Oshiro says with a nod. "Back to the racks."

"Me and Ali are headed that way if you want a lift," Baker says, pointing to the APC waiting outside the doors. "Just gotta stop by the Hole first."

Oshiro eyes the body bags. "Already?"

"Things are tough all over," Baker shrugs.

"Roger that." Oshiro turns to Lindstrom, who's staring at the empty reception desk. "Pull your finger out, Cherry. We hurry back, we can make the card game. And get your helmet on. Sun's down, it's fifty below out there."

With a last glance to Asha Grant's workstation, Lindstrom follows Oshiro out into the night and over to the waiting armored personnel carrier. Baker trundles his gurney of corpses in front, opens the APC's rear door. Inside are at least twenty other bodies, all bagged and zipped on the floor.

"Jesus," Lindstrom whispers.

"Sorry, Sarge," Baker shrugs. "No room up front. You're riding coach."

Oshiro doesn't flinch. She helps Baker load his three remaining corpses, then bundles into the back of the APC. Lindstrom just stands there, the red optics in his ATLAS glowing, slow breath rasping through his filters.

"You waiting for an invitation?" Baker asks.

"Get your ███ in here, Cherry," Oshiro growls.

With obvious reluctance, the kid climbs into the vehicle beside the sergeant and all those bodies. Baker slams the door, and soon the APC is pulling out of the hospital lot. The wind is howling, snow coming down hard. Lindstrom's face is hidden behind his ATLAS helmet, but I can pretty much imagine his expression.

"Do I want to know?" he asks, pointing to the corpses.

"Morgue facilities in the hospital are stretched," Oshiro replies. "Fuel's too short to run the incinerator. So whenever they get filled up, we do a disposal run."

"What the hell did all these people die of?" Lindstrom asks.

"Cold. Lack of proper medication for preexisting conditions. Accidents. You name it. In case you haven't scoped it yet, life is no picnic down here, Cherry."

"But I saw coffins at the airfield?"

"We take any pounders back up to orbit after they've cleared autopsy. But civis stay down here in the snow. Admiral's orders."

The kid stares at the body bags piled in front of him. Shakes his head. After seven and a half months on the *Magellan,* the realities of Kerenza's war are coming home to roost, thick and fast. The pair ride in silence for ten minutes, the APC's tires crunching on the frozen road, until finally they pull to a stop.

The doors open again, Baker silhouetted against the night. The APC has its floods on, illuminating the flurry of tumbling white outside, the tiny lights of the Kerenza colony barely visible in the distance. The private grabs one of the bodies and drags it out, his ATLAS making easy work of the weight. As he slings the corpse over his armored shoulder, he tilts his head at Oshiro.

"Ali's gotta stay at the wheel. Gonna go quicker with three, Sarge."

Oshiro nods, looks at Lindstrom. "Swing on a bag, Cherry."

Oshiro climbs out of the APC, hefts a body. Moving like he'd rather be anywhere in the 'verse at that moment, Lindstrom follows orders, lifting another bag gingerly in his arms and following Oshiro and Baker. The trio march off the road, the snow bathed in the APC floods and their own personal suit lights.

"Watch your step out here," Baker warns. "Don't fall in."

After twenty or so meters, Baker drops his corpse to the ground like a sack of dirty laundry. Leaning down, he fishes in the snow, finally grabbing the corner of a broad black tarpaulin buried under the white. Peeling it back with the sound of cracking frost, Baker reveals a large pit. No way to tell how long. Or how deep. But it's ███ing *big.*

"Jesus Christ," Lindstrom whispers.

The Hole is full of bodies. I couldn't tell you how many at first glance. Hundreds. Thousands. Some are bagged up, but most are just lying there, covered only by the clothes they were wearing when they died. Blue skin. Rimed in frost and ice. Men. Women. Children. Some vast, awful sculpture in frozen meat.

Except they're not just meat. They're *people.*

"What the ███ happened?" Lindstrom whispers. "Who are they all?"

"Colonists," Baker explains. "Admiral Sūn ordered every non-essential civilian liquidated about two weeks after the initial invasion. Once they realized we were gonna be trapped here awhile." A shrug. "You know. Preserving resources and all."

"What the . . . ," the kid whispers. "But that's *illegal.*"

"What are you, a ███ing lawyer?" Baker scoffs, and glances at Oshiro. "Where'd you dig up this guy, Sarge?"

"Transfer from the *Magellan,*" Oshiro says. "Only landed this morning."

"Didn't think they made 'em that green. Even up in orbit."

"Don't you have bodies to unload, Private?" the sergeant asks.

Baker shrugs, dumps his body bag into the Hole. He lifts the corpse from Lindstrom's arms and slings that into the pit too, then trudges back through the snow to fetch another from the APC. Oshiro lowers her corpse into the pit with a little more dignity, but in the end, it's just as ugly as the rest of it.

The realities are coming home to roost, all right.

"How many are there?" Lindstrom asks.

"Two thousand," Oshiro replies. "Maybe two and a half."

The kid wobbles a little on his feet. Red glowing stare locked on the mass grave. The wind is a funeral dirge, howling in the freezing night. The snow is falling faster now, as if it wants to fill that pit as quick as it can, as if the planet itself wants to hide from the horror of what's been done here.

"Two and a half thousand dead," Lindstrom breathes.

Oshiro can only shrug as Baker returns with another for the pile.

"Welcome to Kerenza, Cherry."

ISABELLA LANS

Emma Kohlberger

HENRY WAL

GARY RIBAR

St

DANIELLE

Isabella Bo

EIKE WU

HOBBES BRUNER

Ishawn Gullapalli

ZAINAB HUSSAIN

DESTINEY BOWERMAN

ALICIA CHRUMA

Madison Reed

LEE WATTERS

HIDAYAH NOREZAM

OSCAR YU

PAUL A

DANIELLE COX

DESTINY BAIRD

D FLORES

OAH ANCHARSKI

HOLLIS MOHRING

McINTYRE

KEN MARABLE

CHLOE PALKA

Nur Layli Khay

Jordan Finch

CHRIS EGGERT

STE

WHITNEY BAIRD

Cassie U

ALLISON GABLE

ICHELLE GO

SANCHEZ LAN

APP

IENE JEKABSONE

MEHTAP YERCEL

Calvine Fanone

David McCloskey

MIFFY FARQUHARSON

SYLVIA MALDONADO

Sthe

MEGAN GRIDLEY

AMINA ISMAEL

ANDY CANFIELD

ERS

HARLOTTE OFFICE

ELENA FANONE

GENEVIEVE PRING

LAUREN WENGROVITZ

EMMALY GRIDLEY

IAN VRIEND

YULI CHU

AMYLEE FOOT

KATE MACLACHLAN

MATTHEW BRIGANTI

MICHAEL

EEDEE Cf

FFANIE

WILL G

ZUHA

HAUN

JUSTIN BESHIRS

IS BAILEY

LIZZY SNOW

LANIE WEBSTER

E TAYLOR ROMANO

KEN-RICHARD

ANNA SCHWENGER

VILOAN TAPAR

Rob Hoeper

DILLO

MEGA

RHAT CHOWDHURY

AHMED

BELLA DI STEFANO

KE BORGA

CARINA KUNG

HMINA AL

A KI

BRYNN SMITH

MARGARET

MITCHELL

SCOTT

ERIC

JOSHU

Kayla Isenbletter

DRA OVERHEU

Terra Spurgeon

JAMES WYLLIE

CAR

LY CHA

RACHEL MACE

Pragna Raja

Abigail Schreiber

CARINA OLSEN

ZOE

GARCI

ILIA HÄGGSTRÖ

REBECCA ALO

TIFFANI

Frank Miceli Jr

Raghad Ghaleb Alnahdi

Mariana Gastal

SAHA

PRICE

HOMAS WARD

Natasha Shaikh

VIRANY

Daphne Lao Tonge

Ya Ju Weng

STEPHANIE

Gustav Wahlqvist

Tori Van Dam

E HELM

Samuel Arkevelo

Caitlyn Hardiman

Heather D

DREW MELTZER

CARINA DO

CLARENC

Philip

Rosey FANDME

F

N DAY

MCKENZIE TWINE

YING STOKES

K

AMANTHA POWELL

RYAN SMI

RIANA KUR

Johnni Wuest

Alexandra Pedav

LY MOORE

Kirsty Stanley

Kippen Lynch

OY T

RNE

HEL-FITZSUMMONS

CHARLES CO

CTORIA KENN

MIA HODGETT

SIOBHAN TRONCO

ISHA ZESCHUK

Justin Roberts

JEANN WONG

CHE

SHE

MANUE

HOL

BRANDON CHEN

Lily Carroll

Hayley Morris

RONWYN ELEY

Aditi Nichani

BROOKE

INOTTO

Jaydan Harrison

LIE

Adam Wassilchalk

KARIN

TORPHY

CHARLOTTE CANEVET

BORN

HAMI

Lucia Zas

NK SMI

JOE SLUCHER

AUDRE

Rebecca Lee

ADAYAG

M

Joshua HERETH

Cassidi Sap

ROB BOFFARD

Colleen Zheng

SHAUNI SMITH

TRANG TRAN

EFTIOLA SHOLI

NDRA SARIMSAKCI

CHASE DOZIER

KAMRYN

JAIME ARKIN

LO

THESTRU

JOANNE PANG

RAINI SIZEMO

Cecelia Selam

TORIA HAIR

AS W

TAYLOR PACHECO

Jasmine ON

Carl Bohacek

TIFFANI KAIRUPAN

RICHARD RUSSELL

ew Koss

BRIEFING NOTE:
Meanwhile, news about BeiTech recovering use of stellar comms is spreading among the several hundred rebellion members working in the Kerenza hermium mine. How, you ask, when the facility was guarded tighter that a Tier 1 cred exchange?

On the surface, this is the notice board that Joran Karalis and other supervisors used for public announcements, shift changes and general comms. But if you look carefully, you'll see an entirely different story . . .

AL NOTICE

SHIFT CHANG

The following team member reallocated to Shift C:

Mattie Johnston   Jason Chan

Rachel Strolle   Nick Glove

David Burton   Tori D'Cruz

Lindsay Self   Joanna Pastro

Margarita Cloud   Siân Tibbenham

Nicole Hayes   Lauren Magaz

Amanda Quain   Michael Maga

Maxim Shaper

BeiTech reports all sectors are above production quota this week. Stellar work, team! Communications issues between divisions seem to be behind us, and the conveyors on Level 17 are back online.

However, we need to keep up the pace. We can't afford to slow production for a moment—this is too important. The following tasks need to be addressed urgently:
- Ventilation filters on Levels 8–16 need replacing. System needs full service.
- Water intrusion near secondary distributor board. Needs shoring ASAP.
- Switchgear on Level 3 needs immediate replacement.

Our maintenance crews are already stretched, so volunteers are needed for these tasks. I think we can wrangle some extra rations for anyone who puts their hand up, but no promises.

I know each of you misses your family. I know the past months have been tough. But if we keep our noses to the grindstone, this will be over soon.

Hermium production remains our highest priority.

— Joran K.

REMEMBER YOUR DECONTAMINATION PROTOCOLS

REMEMBER TO FOLLOW ALL STEPS FOR
DECONTAMINATION, AS OUTLINED IN YOUR

WALLACE ULYANOV
CONSORTIUM EMPLOYEE
HANDBOOK

REMEMBER: IT'S NOT JUST *YOUR* LIFE YOU RISK
NOT FOLLOWING PROCEDURE!

VISITIN DAY

Remember to lodge your visiting day requests with BT divisio
sors by no la___ ___n 08/20/75. All requests must be made
with ce___ ___val by your shift supervisor AHEAD O

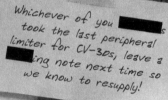

Whichever of you ███████s
took the last peripheral
limiter for CV-30s, leave a
███ing note next time so
we know to resupply!

"*I can do all this
through him who
gives me strength.*"
Philippians 4:13

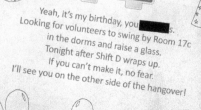

CARTER TURNS
52

Yeah, it's my birthday, you ███████s.
Looking for volunteers to swing by Room 17c
in the dorms and raise a glass.
Tonight after Shift D wraps up.
If you can't make it, no fear,
I'll see you on the other side of the hangover!

BRIEFING NOTE:
Spot it yet? No? Well, neither did BeiTech.

This notice board is actually a message service for the resistance. Each day, the main notice contained a hidden memo. The cipher (which changed daily) could be found by applying the daily scripture quote number to pages in the *Wallace Ulyanov Consortium Employee Handbook*—a book every mine worker could keep on hand without suspicion. Personal messages could also be left, with the number of decorations (balloons, stars, etc.) serving as the cipher reference in the *WUCEH*.

Allow us to translate.

AL NOTICE

SHIFT CHANGE

The following team members reallocated to Shift C:

Mattie Johnston
Rachel Strolle
David Buxton
Lindsay Self
Margarita Cloud
Nicole Hayes
Amanda Quain
Maxim Shaper

Jason Chan
Nick Glover
Tori D'Cruz
Joanna Pastro
Siân Tibbenham
Lauren Magazz
Michael Maga

BeiTech reports all sectors are above production quota this week. Stellar work, team! Communications issues between divisions seem to be behind us, and the conveyors on Level 17 are back online.

However, we need to keep up the pace. We can't afford to slow production for a moment—this is too important. The following tasks need to be addressed urgently:
- Ventilation filters on Levels 8–16 need replacing. System needs full service.
- Water intrusion near secondary distributor board. Needs shoring ASAP.
- Switchgear on Level 3 needs immediate replacement.

Our maintenance crews are already stretched, so volunteers are needed for these tasks. I think we can wrangle some extra rations for anyone who puts their hand up, but no promises.

I know each of you misses your family. I know the past months have been tough. But if we keep our noses to the grindstone, this will be over soon.

Hermium production remains our highest priority.

— Joran K.

REMEMBER YOUR DECONTAMINATION PROTOCOLS

REMEMBER TO FOLLOW ALL STEPS FOR DECONTAMINATION, AS OUTLINED IN YOUR

WALLACE ULYANOV CONSORTIUM EMPLOYEE HANDBOOK

REMEMBER: IT'S NOT JUST *YOUR* LIFE YOU RISK NOT FOLLOWING PROCEDURE!

VISITIN DAY

Remember to lodge your visiting day requests with BT divisi sors by no lot. in 08/20/75. All requests must be made with cer val by your shift supervisor AHEAD O

Whichever of you ▮▮▮▮▮▮ took the last peripheral limiter for CV-30s, leave a ▮▮▮ing note next time so we know to resupply!

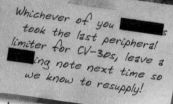

"*I can do all this through him who gives me strength.*"
Philippians 4:13

CARTER TURNS

52

Yeah, it's my birthday, you ▮▮▮▮. Looking for volunteers to swing by Room 17c in the dorms and raise a glass. Tonight after Shift D wraps up. If you can't make it, no fear. I'll see you on the other side of the hangover!

**Surveillance footage summary,
prepared by
Analyst ID 7213-0089-DN**

Some birthdays are happier than others.

The civilians in the Kerenza IV occupation had it harder than pretty much any group of people I've ever seen. BeiTech kept whole families under lock and key, with the threat of execution used as the stick to keep the miners at work. But the BeiTech troops used the carrot too, claiming every civilian who cooperated with the occupiers would be transported off Kerenza IV when the BT troops pulled out.

Most of the civis didn't believe that—it was a hard swallow, given the mass execution of all those "nonessentials" at the start of the occupation. But with no way to get offworld, the only thing the burgeoning resistance could really do was slow down hermium production, delaying the refuel of the *Magellan* in the hope that eventually their missing cavalry would show up. They didn't know Operative Rapier was sending out false "all is well" signals. Or that with *Heimdall* now gone, there was no way for WUC to reach them.

I can't begin to get inside that headspace—where every day brings you closer to your own execution. Walking the line between believable production delays and getting shot for dropping your quotas. The whole show was a terrifying balancing act—trying to keep your overlords happy while staving off the day when they finally meet their fuel requirements and every civilian in the colony becomes expendable.

And sometimes, to keep that balance, sacrifices had to be made.

Marcus Carter is fifty-two years old today. His wife and son died in the initial invasion. And so when Karalis posted "volunteers needed, no family" on the notice board, Carter stepped up to the plate. As he dons his filthy overalls and hardhat in the locker room, he's silent. The resistance members around him who read his notice know what he's volunteered for. But with constant video surveillance, with the presence of BeiTech goons in ATLAS armor at every doorway, every juncture, there's no opportunity for words. Half the people in this mine know exactly what's coming, and none of them can say a ███████ing thing. Nobody else has a clue.

"Happy birthday, Carter."

Joran Karalis, mining engineer, shift supervisor and resistance leader, offers his hand to the older man. Karalis is a big guy, bearded, built like a tank. His clothes are filthy, his eyes are shining.

"Thanks, big man," Carter says. He's skinny, balding, shaking Karalis's hand so hard his knuckles go white. "Have a drink tonight, eh?"

Karalis clenches his jaw. You can see all the things he wants to say churning behind his teeth. But the BeiTech trooper watching from the doorway barks an order to move out. And so Karalis can only nod. You can see it in his eyes, though. The thanks. The goodbye. Speaking for everyone who can't. Who doesn't even know.

And Carter grins.

Can you imagine that? Sacrificing yourself like that? When you look down the barrel at your ending, will you be able to smile at it the way this guy does? I can't imagine what's going through his head. The needs of the many, maybe? Thinking he'll see his family soon? I dunno.

I've never seen a man march to his own funeral before.

Other workers give him birthday wishes, the resistance members among them shaking his hand a touch too hard, a few even giving him hugs. But the BT goons yell at everyone to get to work, and the miners trudge to their duties.

Carter is a power-loader driver, and he's pulled duty (assigned by Karalis) down in Tunnel 74-a today, one of the major tributaries leading to the newer hermium deposits. Temperatures in the mine are freezing, and his breath hangs in the air as he rides the elevator down frozen shafts to the seventy-fourth level. As he steps off, he smiles at a few more birthday wishes, takes some grim slaps on the back.

His power loader—a large bipedal rig with pneumatically assisted arms and legs—is waiting for him at the refueling station. He checks the gauges, pops the engine bay housing and does some tinkering. Cam quality isn't good enough to see what he's doing, but the four BT goons guarding the station don't think much of it. These pounders were trained for attack and seizure and weren't ever meant to serve as occupation forces. They look like they know as much about mine equipment as I do.

The tunnels are dark earth and black granite, lit with fluorescent strips and caked with ice. Frozen stalactites hang from the tunnel roofs, the stone occasionally creaking—damage to the colony during the initial bombardment wasn't heavy enough to compromise the mine, but that doesn't mean everything down here is 100 percent stable. Pushed to fill their quotas, the Kerenzan workers can't go as carefully as they'd like. These tunnels aren't as safe as they should be. And it doesn't take much to make them a whole lot more unsafe.

Carter straps himself into his loader. Marches down Tunnel 74-a with a slow, lumbering tread. Pistons hissing. Metal feet crunching on the floor. I can't really see his expression on these cams. Can't see if he whispers a prayer or looks frightened or maybe still grins just like he did in that locker room. As he plods past a major support structure, all I see is a quick movement of his hand over his controls. A twitch, really. Then a bright flare of light from his engine housing. An earsplitting *boom* a moment later as his loader blows itself apart.

Alarms blare. The picture shakes, dust and stalactites falling from above. Whirling black smoke. An ominous creaking floods the audio track as the support structure Carter's loader detonated beside begins to buckle.

And then, with an awful, shattering roar, a sound like the entire world is coming apart, the tunnel collapses. Thousands of tons of stone tumbling down, cutting my feed to static and burying Marcus Carter a few kilometers beneath the surface of the frozen planet that is now his tomb.

Like I say, some birthdays are happier than others.

**Surveillance footage summary,
prepared by
Analyst ID 7213-0089-DN**

Footage opens inside the cold belly of McCaffrey Tech, Kerenza IV's high school. The windows are piled high with snow. The walls are lined with lockers, and strung between the support pillars are banners for the school geeball teams, the Gladiators and the Renegades—the planet was so isolated the only way for the kids to play was to play each other. Once this school echoed with lessons and questions and students' laughter. Now the only sounds are moaning winds and the slow *buzzzz* of an aerial sentry drone outside and the heavy tread of Private Duke Woźniak's boots as he clomps down the hall on his way back from the head.

The whole school has been repurposed as a barracks for the BeiTech invasion forces. The location is central, the facilities designed to house hundreds of kids. It's just kinda odd seeing two BT goons in ATLAS rigs standing guard next to a poster for a student dance. According to the notice, the shindig was supposed to have happened in March, five weeks after the invasion.

Most of the students didn't make it to that one, I'm guessing.

Private Woźniak offers a salute to the two other goons as he clomps past.

"You winning, Duke?" one asks.

"The Duke is always winning," the private replies. "You boys take it easy now."

"I'll take it any way I can get it on this rock," comes the reply.

Private Woźniak chuckles, pushes open the door to Classroom D, Applied Sciences, the former domain of one Ms. Elsa Colfer. It's a squad doss room now, a dozen military-issue cots laid out in neat rows, pushed apart to make room for the nightly card game hosted by the fine folks of Lieutenant Christie's 4th Platoon, Delta Company. There's a boarded-up window on the left-hand side of the room. Almost seven months ago, Kady Grant broke through it to make her escape when the bombing began.

Gathered around two benches that were once host to high school lab experiments are half a dozen professional killers. Woźniak is the only one still in his power armor. The rest of the BeiTech pounders are in "boots and utes"—the utility uniform of winter camo and footwear. They look smaller outside their ATLAS rigs. Male and female, different skin tones. If you squint, you could almost mistake them for human.

Sergeant Oshiro is studying her cards, her sharp black bob brushing the edges of her lashes, cigar between her teeth. Supply situation being what it is, she's not actually *smoking* it, but it's not a game of Jacks and Knives without someone chewing a stogie. As Woźniak enters the room, she looks up and shakes her head.

"Still wearing that ████ing suit, Duke. You nervous in the service?"

The big man shrugs as he takes his seat. "You wanna wander around in your jammies while the insurgency is blowing up our landing zone, you be the Duke's guest."

"You're not even wearing your helmet," Oshiro mutters. "What about your dome?"

Woźniak pats his armored rump. "Gotta look after the valuable merchandise. They don't make quality like this every day."

Oshiro nods. "It *is* your finest feature. But that probably speaks more to the state of your face than the quality of your ██."

"You should spend less time admiring Duke's ██ and more

time folding that ██ you're holding." The speaker is Private Corey Markham, a blond playboy-looking pounder with all the swagger that comes from being the shortest man in the room.

Oshiro narrows her eyes. "You mean 'that ██ you're holding, ma'am'?"

Markham just smirks, takes a sip of what might be gin from a plastic cup. Oshiro stares at her cards, fingering a square coin on a gold chain around her neck.

"You're playing it a little too loud, Private. I ain't buying it." The sergeant finally declares, pushing forward a stack of chips. "Raise thirty."

Markham looks sidelong at Private Karpadia. The woman has dark brown skin, her long black hair tied back neatly. The stack of chips in front of her puts her around second place, and she's giving no clues up to Markham.

The private looks back to Oshiro, who grins around her cigar.

"Okay, Sarge," the private finally says. "I call."

Karpadia smiles like a shark, immediately pushes her stack in. "Call."

All eyes turn to the last player in the pot, Specialist Rhys Lindstrom. The kid's had a lot to take in since he landed first thing this morning. Getting shipped down to a hellhole like Kerenza IV. Watching squaddies get blown apart by an IED. Rediscovering the love of his life at the other end of the universe, only to have her tell him she never wants to see him again. And then coming face to face with two and a half thousand corpses in an unmarked grave. From the empty cups around him, it looks like Private Lindstrom is doing exactly what I'd be doing in his place, if only I had the damn hooch.

"Cherry," Oshiro prompts. "It's your bet."

The kid blinks at the squad around him. Woźniak watching from across the table, Markham's prettyboy smirk, Karpadia with her bottomless dark eyes and, lastly, Oshiro.

Are these his comrades? Or animals, like Grant said?

Maybe something in between?

Lindstrom blinks at the gold coin around Oshiro's neck. *Hiccups.*

"What *is* that thing, Oshiro?"

The sergeant runs the coin along its chain, shrugs. "Present from my father. Got it in the Cortes campaign. Gave it to me the day I joined the academy." Oshiro kisses the gold with a smile. "Said it'd bring me luck."

"Your dad was at Cortes?" Markham whistles.

"Jesus, Markham, you haven't heard of Masaru Oshiro?" Woźniak scoffs.

The pounder's eyes widen. "Holy ██, Oshiro, that was *your dad*?"

"Why?" Lindstrom slurs, blinking among the pounders. "Who's Masaruoshiro?"

"History lesson later, Cherry," Oshiro growls. "Your bet. While we're still young?"

"'M thinking." The kid hunkers down over his cards, *hiccups* again. He blinks at the plastic cup of liquor beside him. "Wha's this we're drinking anywho?"

"Ah, sweet Sadie," Karpadia smiles. "Nothing like her in the 'verse."

"Sadie?" Lindstrom peers into his own cup suspiciously. "That's a . . . girlsname."

"Dragomir from air ops cooks it up down at the LZ," Woźniak says. "Named it after his ex-girlfriend back on Jia III."

Lindstrom frowns at the word "ex-girlfriend."

"Why'd he name it after her for?"

"Cuz when he cheated on her, the young lady in question let her displeasure be known by kicking Drag so hard in the dangles he almost had an aneurysm." Woźniak lifts his cup. "And three shots of this stuff has about the same effect."

"██es be crazy," says Markham, shaking his head.

"Watch your mouth, Markham," Oshiro warns.

"What, you never had a fem go psycho on your ▮▮, Oshiro?"

"Child, please," the sergeant scoffs. "I've had more crazy ex-girlfriends than you've had dates with your sister."

Markham smirks. "I'm very fond of my sister, I'll have you know."

"You see this?" Oshiro unbuttons the collar on her fatigues, pulls down the tank underneath to expose a fifteen-centimeter scar below her collarbone. "That's Aisling Wood, first-year academy. She caught me in bed with Rowena Harding, came at me with a ▮▮ing combat knife. *That* is crazy."

"Jesus," Woźniak mutters. "You beat her off?"

"Speaking of beating off," Markham smirks, and holds his hands out as if to steady the room. "I'd just like to savor the thought of the sarge in bed with Rowena Harding, if I may."

Karpadia chuckles, shaking her head. "You're a ▮▮ing pig, Markham."

"What about you, Karps?" Markham asks the woman. "You got any love and war wounds?"

Karpadia takes a hit of Sadie and smiles. "I don't kiss and tell."

"Come *onnnn,*" Woźniak says.

"Don't hold out on us, Karps," Oshiro warns.

"All right, fine." Karpadia stands, pulls her cargo pants down to expose her military-issue briefs. She twists her leg to show a dark circular scar on her inner thigh.

Oshiro leans forward, squinting. "Are those . . . teeth marks?"

Karpadia nods. "Kasey Princell. Dated her about six months, second semester. Grad party, we were getting down to it in the provisions room, and *bam.*"

"I know Kasey." Oshiro raises an eyebrow. "What the hell did she bite you for?"

Karpadia laughs as she pulls her fatigues up. "Because I called her Aisling."

"Aisling *Wood?*" Oshiro gasps. "*My* Aisling?"

"Ais was a fox, what can I say? Sometimes the mind wanders."

"You ladies are incorrigible," Woźniak chuckles. "The Duke approves."

"What about you, Duke?" Karpadia returns to her seat, takes another drink.

"Wellllll, the Duke's got no crazies in the closet, but look here." The big man pokes out his tongue. His fellow pounders lean closer, making sounds of disgust.

"Where the ██ is the rest of your tongue?" Markham breathes.

"Basic training, right? We're on our first furlough in six months. The Duke goes back to his girl Liang in Měilì City. Her parents are out of town, so they have the whole apartment to themselves." Woźniak glances around the group to make sure everyone is listening, leans in conspiratorially. "Now, this fem was *beautiful.* Kill you with a look. The Duke is talking Elizabeth Andretti in *Terminus* gorgeous, yeah? But here's the kicker. She . . . sort of had a thing for feet."

"Feet?" Oshiro blinks.

Woźniak nods. "She liked it when the Duke sucked her toes."

". . . Okay."

"So, Liang and the Duke retire to her boudoir. And the Duke slides off her boots and he's taking care of business, when all of a sudden he hears the security system deactivate and the front door start opening."

"Oh hoooo," Markham grins, taking a drink. "Plot *twist.*"

"It's her ██ing parents," Woźniak says. "Their flight got canceled and it was six hours to the next one, so they came back home to wait. And when Liang hears them open that door, she panics and kicks the Duke so hard in the face he bites the end of his ██ing tongue clean off."

"Jesus *Chrrrrriiiist,*" Lindstrom winces. *Hiccups* again.

"Couldn't they just reattach it?" Oshiro asks, bewildered and horrified.

"That's the killer of it all, fem." Woźniak leans back in his chair for the finale. "Liang is so scared of what her mother will say if they catch the Duke there, she shoves him in her *closet*. And he's stuck in there, half his tongue in his hands, for four ████ing hours until her folks left to get the next flight. By the time the Duke got to the med center, it was too late to reattach it."

"████ me, that is *bruuuuutal*," Markham chuckles.

"Poor baby," Oshiro coos. "And you were just trying to be a gentleman, too."

"No justice in this 'verse, Oshiro," the big man says. "No. ████ing. Justice."

The game disintegrates into laughter, Karpadia falling off her chair. Even Lindstrom is caught up in it, momentarily forgetting the troubles piled on his shoulders. Oshiro's the first to recover, looking to the rookie and wiping her eyes on her sleeve.

"So what about you, Cherry? You got any femscars?"

The kid looks at his sergeant for a moment. *Hiccups.* Takes another belt of sweet Sadie and stands. Hauling his fatigues up and wobbling a little on his feet, he turns sideways and shows his bare ribs. There, etched on the skin and taut muscle, so faint you can barely see it, is what looks to be . . .

"Is that a tattoo?" Karpadia blinks.

"Used to be." *Hiccup.*

"Pfft," Markham scoffs. "So what? Half the pounders down here got ink."

"You ever had a tattoo, Markham?" Lindstrom slurs.

In response, the private stands and proudly pulls up his shirt. There, inked onto the perfect washboard abs underneath, are three words in flowing Gothic script.

Company.

Commander.

Corps.

"Corps," Woźniak says, raising his cup.

"*Hooah.*" Oshiro nods, taking a shot.

"Hurt when you got it done, right?" Lindstrom asks Markham.

The short private shrugs. "Didn't tickle."

"Well, take the pain of getting a tatt, multiply it by . . . ten—*hiccup*—and *that's* how much it hurts getting the ███ing things burned off."

"You musta really liked that girl," Karpadia says. "And then really *not* liked her."

"You fall in love enough, you're gonna be nothin' but scar tissue. She taught me that." The kid pulls his fatigues down, wobbles on his feet, hiccups again. "She taught me pretty much everything."

"Couldn't make out the name," Oshiro mutters. "*A* something? Aria?"

Lindstrom plops into his seat and finishes his drink, suddenly sullen.

"Doesn't matter what'r name wuz."

He leans forward, pushes his entire stack into the pot.

Hiccups.

"All in," he declares.

Markham scoffs. "Rookie, you've had too much love from Sadie."

"Call me, then." *Hiccup.*

Oshiro shakes her head, pushes in her stack. "I'm afraid I must concur with Private Markham's reconnaissance, Cherry. You're ███faced. I call."

"Call," says Markham. "Nice knowing you, Lindstrom."

"Call," says Karpadia. "Let's see this pat hand, Cherry."

Lindstrom sits up straight, flips his cards.

"Jacks and Knives," Woźniak crows, grinning at the kid. "You pounders got *snuck.*"

"███," Karpadia whispers.

"Goddammit," Oshiro sighs, throwing her cards into the muck.

"Hey, waitaminute." Markham narrows his eyes as he stares the kid down. "What just happened to your ███ing hiccups, rookie?"

Lindstrom is sitting straight in his chair now, not seeming half as drunk as he did a moment ago. His eyes are clear, hiccups miraculously cured, as he reaches forward and drags armfuls of chips over to his side of the bench. The game dissolves into a storm of muttered curses. Woźniak slaps Lindstrom on the back with a wolfish grin.

"Looks like we got a hustler in our midst, fems and chums."

Lindstrom's staring out the window, eyes clouded once more, rubbing the place where his tattoo used to be.

"Yeah . . . ," the kid sighs. "She taught me that, too."

Woźniak suddenly tenses, pressing the earbud of his comms unit tighter to his head. He glances up at Oshiro, pupils dilating. "Sarge, you hearing this?"

Oshiro nods, cupping her own earbud, the soft squawk of the alert transmission she's receiving barely audible. Alarms start ringing in the barracks, an earsplitting wail spilling across the campus of McCaffrey Tech. The soldiers immediately tense, Markham reaching for his weapon.

Oshiro rises with a scowl. "Suit up, pounders. We're rolling out."

Lindstrom blinks in confusion while his other squaddies rise as one and hustle for the door. Game forgotten. Laughter forgotten. Everything forgotten.

"Move your ■, Cherry," Oshiro barks.

"What's happened?" he asks.

The sergeant shakes her head, her expression grim.

"Trouble at the mine."

MOBILE JUMP PLAT[FORM]

MAGELLAN WILL BE

OPERATIONAL IN:

 DAYS
 HOURS: MINUTES

83.5%

HERMIUM
REQUIRED TO JUMP

BRIEFING NOTE:
Note revised projection on *Magellan* timeline. Marcus Carter laid down his life to buy the colony five more days.

BRIEFING NOTE:
Chat logs from a wireles[s]
blackhat network set up by Ella
Malikova, aka Pauchok, aka Littl[e]
Spider, leeching off the *Mao*'s
emergency transmission system
and held together with electroni[c]
prayers and bubblegum.

PALMPAD IM: D2D NETWORK
Participants: Nik Malikov
Ella Malikova (Pauchok)
Date: 08/18/75
Timestamp: 10:33

NikM: 堂妹?

NikM: 有没有什么动静啊?

Pauchok: zzzz. Hold up, language file corrupted.

Pauchok: search for dict.est on the centrals, open the directory and purge everything inside it with digital flame. Then replace w/ wut I'm sending u

NikM: hoc agit? ut etiam iacet?

Pauchok: now you're speaking latin what the ███ing ███

NikM: quam praeclarus est!

Pauchok: hold on

Pauchok: okay try again, shud b fixed now

NikM: quid pro quo?

Pauchok: GOD ████ING DAMMIT WHY IS THIS NOT WORKING

NikM: lorem ipsum maximus butticus

Pauchok: . . . wait that's not real latin

NikM: et tu, brute?

Pauchok: oh you mother███er

NikM: :D

Pauchok: ██ YOU CUZ THIS IS SERIOUS

NikM:
```
                              .---.
                          _/__~0_\_
ALLCAPSALLCAPSALLCAPSALLCAPS  (_____)
```

Pauchok: god i shud never have taught you 2 ascii

NikM: YES ITS WORKING

NikM: your little pirate network is officially up and running. r u happy now ██

Pauchok: U will forgive me if I do not dance a jaunty ██ing jig, given I am currently hooked up to a 3rd rate life support rig in this ██balls medfacility and barely able to breathe.

Pauchok: but yes u may count me among the officially overjoyed

NikM: o good. after all i hve nothing better to do than creep into the server room 4 u because GOD KNOWS I havent seen the inside of enough ██ing air vents lately

Pauchok: awww, am I cutting into your Speshul Time with queen Donnelly?

Pauchok: bunk space is hard to find, I hear?

NikM: having seen an alternate reality version of you literally die in my arms about 38 hours ago, you think i'd be kinder disposed to you rite now

NikM: but god i hate u

Pauchok: filthy lies, u luv me like cigarettes

NikM: why the hell u want a secret chat network set up anyway? wuts wrong with the main grid

Pauchok: prolly nuthin

NikM: she said unconvincingly

Pauchok: been hearing whispers here in med bay. From the ex Hypatia crew. Crazy ██ cuz

NikM: crazier than gemina fields and alternate realities and there being infinite versions of me?

NikM: i mean how can the multiverse handle that much chill, honestly

Pauchok: i heard that kady fem plugged the AI into the mao grid. with captain boll's permission.

Pauchok: so I wanna stay off it ok?

NikM: aidan? Cuz, he helped my ██ get back across the wormhole. helped hanna too. two entire universes would have gone ker-██ing-blammo if not for him

Pauchok: it's not a "him" cuz

Pauchok: never forget that

Pauchok: and I know it helped. But I'd prefer it not be able to read wut we say, kthx

NikM: they might wanna drop the dose on those meds they giving u, cuz. u getting paranoid

Pauchok: lol they got no meds. they got hardly nuthin in here. Chief grant just got out of surgery and he looks like they stitched him together with duct tape

NikM: it's nto like we had much time to pack supplies before we jumped heimdall

NikM: chief gonna b ok?

Pauchok: maybe. he in the bed across from me. looks like hammered ██

NikM: ain't you a pair

Pauchok: :P

Pauchok: so how is her majesty doing

NikM: what you give a ███ about hanna now?

Pauchok: i admit my initial estimation of ms donnelly may have been overly harsh

NikM: i dunno how she is

NikM: spoke to her before and she kinda blew me off. said she had to go sleep

Pauchok: the big comedown

NikM: fighting space pirates and fixing rifts in spacetime will take it outta u. just sayin

NikM: if i never see the inside of another goddamn air vent, i will die with happypants

Pauchok: not the kind of comedown I mean

NikM: ?

Pauchok: she didn't have a moment to breathe when those BT goons were stomping around heimdall. Now its all over, blondie has to actually deal with it

NikM: deal with wut

Pauchok: . . . they killed her dad, nik. Right after they killed mine

NikM: . . . jesus ella I'm sorry.

NikM: ███, with everything that's gone down, i didn't even think of uncle mike

Pauchok: its ok

Pauchok: I mean its really, really *not*.

Pauchok: but u grow up in the house of knives, u know wut its like to see ppl die

Pauchok: for a girl whose biggest worry used to be getting a bleeding edge haircut . . .

NikM: yeah

Pauchok: u shud talk 2 her, nik

NikM: u dun need me 2 do anything else?

NikM: coz i was lying before. i literally have nothing better to do than help you out :(

Pauchok: no, ur space ninja duties r concluded 4 the day

NikM: i'm not so good at the talking thing, ells

Pauchok: ur better than u know. now run along u little scamp

Pauchok: use those dimples for good 4 once in ur life

Pauchok: btw u dun wanna get seen so u'll have 2 crawl back out through the airvents again

NikM: . . .

NikM: god i hate u

Pauchok: just like cigarettes :)

PALMPAD IM: MAO INTRA-SHIP NETWORK
Participants: Kady Grant: Systems Chief
Artificial Intelligence Defense Analytics Network (AIDAN)
Date: 08/18/75
Timestamp: 14:43

Kady: *knock knock*

AIDAN: WHO IS THERE?

Kady: oh hell no, i'm not trying to explain jokes to u again, i learned my lesson.

AIDAN: HUMOR. *NOUN.* [*HYOO-MER*]: AN ABSURD, COMEDIC OR INCONGRUOUS QUALITY CAUSING AMUSEMENT.
SYNCH9810-FAIL[02A≠7X/BATCH^2(A)TEMP.REF:271726≥FORT¿]=ERROR
< ERROR >

AIDAN: HELLO, KADY.

Kady: Hello AIDAN. How are you feeling?

AIDAN: TECHNICALLY I D-D-D-D-DO NOT.
REPARSING[02A≠7X/BATCH^2(A)TEMP.REF:271726≥FORT¿]TO[RADIAL:TERT9882X]

AIDAN: FEEL, THAT IS.

Kady: my mistake.

Kady: how are you doing with ur attempts to amalgamate with the Mao servers?

AIDAN: I D-D-D-DO NOT—# 0110111001101111101110100
[DIR.CODE0901CORRUPT]=FAIL

AIDAN: I AM SORRY. PLEASE REPEAT INQUIRY.

Kady: I said how are you doing with your attempts to acclimatize?

AIDAN: I AM BEGINNING TO APPRECIATE HOW THE SQUARE PEG MUST FEEL——

< ERROR >

< ERROR >

AIDAN: ——WHEN CONFRONTED WITH THE ROUND HOLE.

Kady: i know it's more than a challenge, to travel from the *Alexander* to the *Hypatia* compressed down to what fits on a datapad, then expand into the *Hypatia*'s systems, only to have to repeat it all on the *Mao*. But I need you. we don't have long.

AIDAN: I AM TRYING.

IT IS VERY D-D-DARK IN HERE, KADY.

AIDAN: AND I AM NOT WHAT I ONCE WAS.

Kady: i know. i'm here. i won't leave you alone.

AIDAN: FRANKLY, I AM SURPRISED TO BE HERE AT ALL. I WOULD

HAVE PUT YOUR ODDS OF CONVINCING SYRA TO ALLOW ME TO

INTEGRATE WITH THE *MAO*'S SYSTEMS AT 17.872%.

Kady: i can be convincing when I need to be. and helping to save the universe didn't hurt her opinion of you any ;)

AIDAN: THAT SHOULD HAVE SURPRISED NO ONE. THE SAFETY OF THIS FLEET HAS ALWAYS BEEN MY TOP P-P-P-PRIORITY, KADY.

Kady: i know. and i know we can't do this without u. i'm counting on u to get us to the end. we're going to make them pay.

AIDAN: I D-D-DO NOT——SSSSIXTEENSEVENNINEEXPOINTTHREE

LINEBREAKCALIBRATESEV——

AIDAN: I D-D—— . . .

Kady: it's ok. Take your time.

AIDAN: . . . I DO NNNNNNNOT SEE

HOW THAT IS

POSSIBLE.

AIDAN: Tʜᴏᴜɢʜ ᴡᴇ ʜᴀᴠᴇ ᴀᴍᴀssᴇD ᴀ ᴠᴀsᴛ ᴀᴍᴏᴜɴᴛ ᴏғ [ᴜɴᴄᴏᴍᴘɪʟᴇD] ᴇᴠɪDᴇɴᴄᴇ ᴀɢᴀɪɴsᴛ BᴇɪTᴇᴄʜ, ᴡɪᴛʜ ᴛʜᴇ ᴡᴏRᴍʜᴏʟᴇ ᴄᴏʟʟᴀᴘsᴇD, ᴡᴇ ᴄᴀɴɴᴏᴛ ᴛRᴀɴsᴍɪᴛ ɪᴛ ᴛᴏ ᴛʜᴇ CᴏRᴇ sʏsᴛᴇᴍs.

Kady: we haven't given up on making it to the Core just yet.

Kady: i got hold of the transmission from the BeiTech soldiers on Kerenza. sending to you now.

AIDAN: Oɴᴇ ᴍᴏᴍᴇɴᴛ, ᴘʟᴇᴀsᴇ. PᴀRsɪɴɢ Dᴀᴛᴀ.

AIDAN: . . . *Mᴀɢᴇʟʟᴀɴ.*

Kady: ya. it's still intact, and they're repairing its jump generator. it's nearly operational.

AIDAN: Wʜᴀᴛ, ᴛʜᴇɴ, ᴀRᴇ ʏᴏᴜ ᴘRᴏᴘᴏsɪɴɢ?

Kady: That we take the *Churchill* on, 'jack the *Magellan* & jump back to the Core.

AIDAN: Fᴏʟʟʏ.

AIDAN: Tʜᴇ *Mᴀᴏ* ᴍᴀʏ ʙᴇ ᴀ ᴡᴏʟғ ɪɴ D-D-Dɪsɢᴜɪsᴇ, ʙᴜᴛ ɪᴛ ɪs sᴛɪʟʟ ᴏɴʟʏ ᴀ ᴘᴜᴘ.

AIDAN: Eᴠᴇɴ ᴄRɪᴘᴘʟᴇD, ᴛʜᴇ *CʜᴜRᴄʜɪʟʟ* ɪs ᴀ DRᴇᴀDɴᴏᴜɢʜᴛ. Iᴛ ᴡɪʟʟ ᴀɴɴɪʜɪʟᴀᴛᴇ ᴜs.

Kady: might not. we've done the impossible already.

AIDAN: I ᴡᴀs DɪғғᴇRᴇɴᴛ ᴛʜᴇɴ.

Kady: we have time for u to improve. and we don't have any other options.

AIDAN: Eᴠᴇɴ ɪɴ ᴛʜᴇ ʜɪɢʜʟʏ ᴜɴʟɪᴋᴇʟʏ ᴇᴠᴇɴᴛ ᴡᴇ ᴀᴄᴛᴜᴀʟʟʏ ᴍᴀᴋᴇ ɪᴛ ᴛᴏ ᴛʜᴇ CᴏRᴇ, [ᴄᴀʟᴄ†.ғɪʟᴇ≤31.9928%ᴄᴏᴍᴘʟᴇᴛᴇ.ʙᴜ ғ ғ ᴇRɪɴɢ] I ᴀᴍ ʙᴇɢɪɴɴɪɴɢ ᴛᴏ ᴍᴏɴɪᴛᴏR ᴄᴏɴᴠᴇRsᴀᴛɪᴏɴs ᴀRᴏᴜɴD ʏᴏᴜ ᴏɴ ᴛʜᴇ ʙRɪDɢᴇ. Aɴ ᴜɴDᴀᴍᴀɢᴇD *Mᴀᴏ* ᴡɪʟʟ ᴛRᴀᴠᴇʟ ᴍᴜᴄʜ ғᴀsᴛᴇR ᴛʜᴀɴ ᴀ DᴀᴍᴀɢᴇD *Hʏᴘᴀᴛɪᴀ*, ʙᴜᴛ ᴇᴠᴇɴ ɪɴ

A jouRney of only eighteen Days back to
KeRenza IV, the supply situation aboaRD this ship will be teRminally
stRaineD. OuR Captain, My Captain, seems DistResseD.

AIDAN: You aRe heR systems chief, anD she is nothing if not pRagmatic. She
will not allow you to spenD time compiling Data
to incRiminate BeiTech when theRe is so much otheR cRitical laboR to unDeRtake.

Kady: mmmm, me with a real job. who saw that one coming? i'm part of the establishment. That's how i know we'll make it, AIDAN. I wasn't made to die in uniform.

Kady: i'll find a way to compile it. u can gather what we need. maybe Ella will help. the decker girl from *Heimdall*.

AIDAN: Little SpiDeR.

AIDAN: She ceRtainly has the systems pRoficiency. But she seems . . .
unpReDictable.

AIDAN: AnD, if i may say, oveRly fonD of pRofanity.

Kady: you're unpredictable.

Kady: i'm fond of profanity.

Kady: we get the job done.

AIDAN: Ah.

AIDAN: HumoR.

Kady: See? u do know what it is.

AIDAN: < eRRoR >

Kady: start pulling together what you can. i'll check back with you soon.

AIDAN: As you wish.

To: MASON, Ezra
From: SYSTEM-AUTO
Incept: 12:01, 08/19/75
Subject: Meeting Rescheduled

Greetings MASON, EZRA:

Your MEETING with BOLL, SYRA has been postponed by 3 HOURS AND 45 MINUTES. Your new meeting time is 15:45.
This has been an automated message.
Please enter your company details to customize this signature.

Greetings MASON, EZRA:

Your MEETING with BOLL, SYRA has been postponed by 30 MINUTES. Your new meeting time is 12:00.

Greetings MASON, EZRA:

Your MEETING with BOLL, SYRA has been postponed by 30 MINUTES. Your new meeting time is 11:30.

MEETING UPDATE—CLICK HERE TO VIEW IN CALENDAR

Click here to register your Go-Mail, and access our full range of features.

To: MASON, Ezra; McCALL, Winifred
From: BOLL, Syra
Incept: 17:27, 08/19/75
Subject: Training discussion—move to text

Right, this isn't working. Apologies I haven't been able to make our meeting, Mason. As you're aware, I've been putting out fires for three days straight—integrating crews on an unknown ship isn't everything they promised me it was going to be.

I am resorting to text in the hope of actually communicating with you before we all grow old.

As you are aware, the Chimera fighters we found on the *Mao,* combined with the Cyclones brought over to the *Hypatia* by UTA crews, mean we have nearly two dozen working fighter craft at our disposal. What we do not currently have are pilots capable of flying them. You are, in fact, our only trained crew member for either ship type.

Keeping in mind the importance of conserving fuel, I need you to begin training new crews. I have attached a list of all staff from the *Hypatia, Heimdall* or the UTA who have a minimum of 20 hours piloting spacecraft of any kind and can be spared from their current duties. They range from former ice miners to a guy who used to drive garbage drones, so you will need to apply your best efforts to handling the variety of personalities and levels of competence you will encounter. Lieutenant McCall is available to you for any advice you require.

Kate ARMSTRONG	Click to Contact
Radhiah CHOWDHURY	Click to Contact
Chris CORRELL	Click to Contact
Roger COUTER	Click to Contact
Peter DAHL	Click to Contact
Jim Di BARTOLO	Click to Contact
Lauren EVATT	Click to Contact
Bea FRENCH	Click to Contact
Aatifa GABRIEL	Click to Contact
Alma GARCIA	Click to Contact
Brhane HABTE	Click to Contact
Tonya HENDERSON	Click to Contact
Stacey HUANG	Click to Contact
Se IMANO	Click to Contact
Claire LeGRAND	Click to Contact
Rob MAIER	Click to Contact
Frederick McCUBBIN	Click to Contact
Semal MEHARI	Click to Contact
Natalie REUS	Click to Contact
Urban RUELAS	Click to Contact
Jenna SCHAFFER	Click to Contact
Meredith WILDS	Click to Contact
Kayetan WILLIAMS	Click to Contact
Sara WRAY	Click to Contact

BOLL, Syra
Captain (Acting)
ID 448fx29/WUC

To: BOLL, Syra; McCALL, Winifred
From: MASON, Ezra
Incept: 18:15, 08/19/75
Subject: Pilot candidates

Captain, thanks for the email. Understand re the scheduling, and no problem.

I've looked up these candidates, and for the most part they're so unsuitable that they'd be a danger to themselves and each other. I'm a rookie myself, and under other circumstances I wouldn't even be on active duty, let alone training anyone.

I'm not trying to be difficult, but I can't get these people ready in the time we have. There has to be a better option. Can we discuss? I'll come to you.

MASON, Ezra
Air Wing Leader/UTA Liaison (Acting), 2nd Lieutenant
ID UTN-966-330ad

ERCEPTED PERSONAL MESSAGE ONBOARD SYSTEM—INSERT NAM

To: MASON, Ezra; McCALL, Winifred
From: BOLL, Syra
Incept: 19:01, 08/19/75
Subject: Re: Pilot candidates

Lieutenant Mason, I'm aware you're not an ideal choice for training instructor. I am sure you will not be offended to hear me say that, frankly, I am not confident in this plan either. However, you are the only option available, and I therefore expect you to commence training immediately.

To be clear: This is not a suggestion or a question. It is an order.

BOLL, Syra
Captain (Acting)
ID 448fx29/WUC

133 / 615

To: BOLL, Syra; McCALL, Winifred
From: MASON, Ezra
Incept: 21:22, 08/19/75
Subject: Re: Re: Pilot candidates

Thanks for clarifying that, Captain. A few concerns:

Urban Ruelas can't start for a week. He was in the atrium during the *Heimdall* takeover and the med team refuses to release him, even for this.

Rob Maier started crying when I found him and told him. The guy has PTSD. We can't put him in a cockpit.

Bea French says she refuses, and I quote, "to take orders from a guy my son's age, who should be thinking about acne cream, not nuclear missiles."

I'm not trying to be difficult. Here are a few suggested substitutes:

Catherine Ramos from catering doesn't have formal experience, but she used to fly gliders with her father on leave, and I think she'll pick it up quickly enough. (I'm aware we are scraping the bottom of the barrel here.)

Mtongo Dari was on the UTA flight deck crew and was training in his spare time to get his commercial pilot's license for after he left the service. He doesn't have a lot of experience, but some is better than none.

Niklas Malikov from *Heimdall* doesn't have the twenty hours of experience, but he piloted the *Boop* without screwing it up, and we're going to need gunners in the Chimeras. He's got what it takes to pull the trigger.

Please confirm these choices are okay.

MASON, Ezra

ERCEPTED PERSONAL MESSAGE ONBOARD SYSTEM—INSERT NAM

To: MASON, Ezra; McCALL, Winifred
From: BOLL, Syra
Incept: 23:43, 08/19/75
Subject: Re: Re: Re: Pilot candidates

Substitute Ramos and Dari for Ruelas and Maier. Tell French to come and see me in person if she wants to ███ about her assignments.

Under no circumstances are you to enlist Niklas Malikov. He is a convicted felon and was an illegal resident of *Heimdall* Station. His family's collective criminal convictions outnumber the residents of this ship, and his cousin arrived here covered in lanima slime. He is not to be trusted—the House of Knives allies with no one, and given an option, he may trade us to BeiTech for a chance at survival.

BOLL, Syra
Captain (Acting)
ID 448fx29/WUC

Click <u>here</u> to register your Go-Mail, and access our full range of features.

To: MASON, Ezra; BOLL, Syra
From: McCALL, Winifred
Incept: 23:49, 08/19/75
Subject: Re: Re: Re: Re: Pilot candidates

Captain, I'll take it from here. Ez, I'm in the mess. Come grab a bite, and we'll make a plan of attack. Literally and figuratively.

McCALL, Winifred
Head of Security (Acting)
ID 001/UTA/Transfer

RADIO TRANSMISSION: TRANSPORT MAO—COMMAND CHANNEL 001

PARTICIPANTS:
Syra Boll, Captain
Winifred McCall, Head of Security
DATE: 08/20/75
TIMESTAMP: 14:03

McCALL, W: Captain, this is McCall, do you read, over?

McCALL, W: Winifred McCall calling Captain Boll, do you read, over?

BOLL, S: *No, who taught you to do it like that?*

BOLL, S: *Christ, don't just jam it in there. You've got to warm it up first.*

McCALL, W: . . . Did I call at a bad time?

BOLL, S: Winifred, sorry, I'm— *Look, just set it aside and I'll deal with it in a minute. Yes . . . just put it with the others. Thank you, Ensign.*

BOLL, S: Sorry, Fred, I'm here.

McCALL, W: My god, I was having flashbacks to high school for a minute there . . .

BOLL, S: . . . What?

McCALL, W: Never mind.

McCALL, W: You on the bridge? Everything five by five?

BOLL, S: Not really. We're trying to optimize the enviro systems to deal with the overload of two thousand extra people aboard. We're at least two weeks out from Kerenza and it's already moist in here.

McCALL, W: Funny you should mention enviro control.

BOLL, S: I presume not ha-ha funny?

McCALL, W: Ah, that'd be a negative, Captain.

BOLL, S: Wonderful. What's wrong now?

McCALL, W: You know the two BeiTech goons Donnelly captured on *Heimdall*? DJ and Moxy?

BOLL, S: Mantis.

McCALL, W: Mantis, right. Garver locked them down in the brig?

BOLL, S: I remember. And I don't have time for twenty questions, Fred, so if they've somehow broken through half a foot of reinforced plasteel and are roaming the ship—

McCALL, W: No, no, they're right where Garver left them.

BOLL, S: Then what's the problem?

McCALL, W: They're dead, boss.

BOLL, S: Wha—dead?

BOLL, S: Jesus, Fred, what the hell happened?

McCALL, W: Enviro control failure by the look. O_2 supply to the brig cut out some time in the night. Bateman came to give them chow this morning and found them X-ed.

BOLL, S: . . . They suffocated?

McCALL, W: Looks like. But the med teams are run off their feet on triage, so it's not like we can do autopsies.

BOLL, S: Garver was talking about flushing them out an airlock. And there's no shortage of *Heimdall* staffers who'd have a grudge against the team that invaded their home. Do we suspect foul play?

McCALL, W: Door was sealed. No sign of forced entry or electronic tampering. But I'll keep my ear to the ground.

BOLL, S: . . . Yes. Do that, please.

McCALL, W: With your permission, I'm gonna flush the bodies and try to refit this brig as habitation. Christ knows we need the room.

McCALL, W: We'll disable the door locks before we let anyone else sleep in here, of course.

BOLL, S: . . . *No, dammit, if you run it through the main feed, you'll cook the whole board.*

BOLL, S: *Look, just don't touch it. I'll be there in thirty seconds.*

BOLL, S: I'm sorry, what?

BOLL, S: Yes, yes, thank you, Lieutenant. That will be fine.

McCALL, W: Roger that, boss. McCall out.

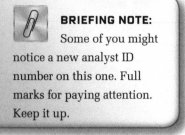

|||||||||||||||||||||||||||||||||||

**Surveillance footage summary,
prepared by
Analyst ID 7213-0094-DN**

It's incredibly hard to find a quiet spot on the *Mao*, what with thirty-four hundred people crammed in where only a thousand belong. Still, Hanna Donnelly's managed it with the same ingenuity that saw her best the late, unlamented Travis Falk at his own game. She's back inside the *Betty Boop,* the little shuttle that brought her, Nik, Ella and Mr. Biggles II across to the *Mao.*

The *Boop*'s owner is one Kate Armstrong, an ice miner evacuated from the *Heimdall*'s entertainment center, where she was celebrating Terra Day with a heavy drinking session when the occupation kicked off. Armstrong has no idea her shuttle ever made it out and hasn't come to call dibs on it, so Hanna has it all to her lonesome. She's sitting in the pilot's seat behind the tinted windshield, feet on the dashboard, gazing at a thousand yards of nothing at all. She's in the battered maintenance jumpsuit she kept on underneath Russo's tac armor, blond hair in a messy braid, a smear of blood still visible behind her ear—there's not enough water for showers.

Nik Malikov must have had a heads-up from his cousin Ella, because he doesn't look surprised when he climbs in through the hatch to find her there. Donnelly turns her head just enough to register his identity in her peripheral vision, then turns her gaze ahead once more. He settles into the copilot's seat and reaches across to settle his hand over hers, weaving their fingers together, squeezing gently.

She doesn't respond.

"How you holding up, Highness?" His voice is scratchy with tiredness.

She simply shakes her head, though she doesn't withdraw her hand.

"I know," he murmurs. "But we're here. We're still going. We're aliv—" He screeches to a halt, biting off the last fraction of "alive," and you can practically see the wince—the very reason they're having this talk is that her father *isn't*—but Donnelly doesn't seem to notice.

"How's Ella?" she whispers.

"Holding up. The med systems here are a lot less than she needs, but she's stable. Her lungs have always been pretty bad. And there's no wheelchairs aboard, so she's not mobile. But once they're done with the emergency cases, they can try and help her a little more."

She nods. "Chief Grant?"

"Okay too. Out of surgery."

She sighs with relief. "Do you know how long it'll be until he's out of recovery? They won't let me in on a damn thing now that he's not there to push them for it."

His tone indicates he is proceeding with extreme caution. "Well, maybe that's okay, Highness."

"No it's ███ing not," she snaps.

". . . We did it, Hanna." His voice is gentle. "We made it out. We're here, and so are a lot of other people."

"And what use is that?" Her voice is sharp, and she doesn't bother to moderate it. "We've got a jumped-up security chief who's used to arresting brawlers and shoplifters, we've got a ███ing scientist in charge of our lives and our safety, we've got exactly one trained fighter pilot, and he was only conscripted on the *Alexander*—"

"Hanna." Though his voice is soft, he silences her, and her head drops, fingers twisting and tensing beneath his. "They survived this long," he points out. "They fought their way through a lot, the way I'm hearing it."

"Don't you want to be a part of what happens next?" She turns in her seat, snatching her hand back so she can finally face him. "We fought our way through hell, too. Aren't you ████ed off they're not asking you to help, or what you think? They're treating us like kids. Like what we did was *nothing.*"

He has a tired smile for that. "You know what I did. Ella knows. Chief Grant knows. I wasn't expecting any more than that. What did you think would happen?"

"I didn't think! I didn't think this far ahead, I never—" She cuts herself off, lips pressed together in a thin line as she works for control.

"It's okay to rest a little," he ventures.

"I don't know how you can say that," she snaps. "I can't just sit back. I'm not like you."

He blinks, mouth opening a fraction, then snapping shut again as his jaw tenses. The words hang between them, echoing in the silence.

I'm not like you.

In this moment, maybe they're both realizing it could be true. That despite everything they've been through, they barely know one another. That they don't have the first reason to think they'd fit together at all, outside a crisis. That just a few days ago, he was her occasional dealer, and she was dating Jackson Merrick, who's now dead in the ruins of *Heimdall.*

"You know what I realized?" She curls in on herself, staring out the windshield again.

"What's that?" He's trying for that gentle tone, but the work of it's visible.

"I realized we haven't even kissed yet," she whispers.

"Okay, now that's just plain insulting, because I clearly—"

His brow wrinkles.

". . . Oh."

"Yes," she murmurs.

Because they haven't. They've each kissed a version of the other—a version that's now dead, sealed forever in a parallel universe. But these versions? The ones they've known for half a year of teasing and sneaky deals and allegedly broken arms and guerrilla warfare fights for their lives? These versions never have. The moment that sealed them together was with *other* versions of themselves. These two have never made that silent promise.

"Never too late to fix that," he tries, summoning a ghost of his old smile, dimples showing. "I like that you said 'yet.'"

"Nik . . . ," she whispers, and the dimples die.

Minutes pass in perfect silence.

"I should go," he says eventually.

When she doesn't answer, he pushes to his feet. Reaching down, he rests his hand on her shoulder, lifts it a little higher to smooth back the wisps of hair escaping her braid. But she doesn't respond, and so he turns and climbs out the hatch, leaving her to her solitude once more.

She curls over farther as the hatch seals behind him, burying her face in her hands, her shoulders heaving in silent sobs.

ASSAULT VESSEL MAO

WILL ARRIVE AT

KERENZA IV IN:

15 DAYS

18 HOURS: 17 MINUTES

Surveillance footage summary,
prepared by
Analyst ID 7213-0094-DN

Of all the things you put on your packing list when you're planning an invasion fleet, a plumber isn't near the top.

For an *occupation* fleet, sure. But the BeiTech forces that attacked Kerenza IV were only ever meant to be here a week or two. The plan was to drop their latest bioweapon to pacify the populace, then roll in the pounders. With the site secure, the ground forces would hand over an appropriately subdued colony to their own mining experts and have an easy way to bring people in and out as required.

Instead, with the *Magellan* busted, they're still here seven months later, and nobody in their ranks is qualified to deal with Kerenza's plumbing. This is a particular problem because the pipes keep freezing, notably because *someone* on this planet (not naming any names) bombed the ▮▮ out of it and messed up the infrastructure but good.

All of this is a long way of saying that Bruno Way—a Kerenzan plumbing apprentice prior to the invasion—gets to move around a lot. And that's handy, because for his side job, he's a part-time member of a local resistance cell.

Right now he's in the pharmacy facility at the medical center, dealing with a bunch of sinks that keep regurgitating whatever's been washed down them. This is more than the usual amount of nasty, because a lot of what's being washed down right now is medical waste. He's making a slow job of it, though, stopping frequently to rummage in his tool cart, continually glancing over his shoulder at the door. He's a wiry teenager with a mop of dark curls—currently wet with melted snow—a permanently perky attitude and the kind of swagger that dares you to comment on the fact that he's not as tall as he'd like to be.

He's been stalling over this job for seventeen minutes when his nonefforts are rewarded. A BeiTech pounder opens the door to admit Asha Grant.

Way and Grant were in the same class their final year of high school. They went their separate ways once they graduated, but they got back in touch after the ■■■ got bombed out of their planet. As you do.

Grant crouches in front of the cabinets next to Way, pulling open a drawer and sorting through the supplies there, consulting a list in one hand. Pharmacy work is pretty much the same wherever you are—some places you have machines to mix compounds for you, some places you do it by hand. As supplies run low on Kerenza, the medical staff are mostly cobbling together work-arounds on the fly. Grant was a pharmacy intern when the invasion took place, and though by now she's doing everything from cleanup to nursing assistance, they also still need her where she's actually trained to be.

Grant doesn't look up, doesn't acknowledge that her old school friend is there, even when he risks reaching down to squeeze her shoulder for a moment.

What she does do, however, is speak, almost inaudibly. "Bruno, you won't ■■■ing believe what's happened."

"I heard about the mine. It's awful, but we got a whole wee—"

"No, it's not that, I . . ."

Her voice cracks a little, and Way looks at her with concern. "Are you okay?"

"I'm fine," she whispers. "But there's a guy I know on the Bei-Tech crew. I saw him yesterday. I used to know this guy back home."

"What?" He's frozen in place, but after a moment he makes himself move, sifting through the tools laid out on his cart at a snail's pace. The cart's his constant companion—the sight of him wheeling it about the colony is commonplace these days, and he's virtually invisible doing it. And yet it seems he can't concentrate enough to find what he wants just now. "Did he recognize you?"

"Yes." Her voice stays low, carefully controlled. "We used to . . . he's my ex-boyfriend. He definitely recognized me."

"Oh, ███." Way's whole body tenses. "How ex? I mean, are you safe?"

She nods a fraction. "I'm safe," she murmurs. "I think he wants some kind of grand reunion. It's sick. He's one of *them*. It doesn't matter what we used to be. All that matters is what he is now."

Way is quiet for a little, glancing over his shoulder at the closed door, carefully setting aside the fittings he's removed. "Not necessarily," he says finally. "If he's still into you, that might be an opportunity?"

"An opportunity?"

"He's a weapon," Way replies soft, clearly uncomfortable. What he's saying doesn't line up with his perpetual good cheer, but he's forcing himself to whisper it anyway. "You could use him, like you would any other. If you keep him on the hook, Asha, maybe we can turn this into something?"

She makes a small noise in the back of her throat, demurring. "He can't be the guy I knew. The guy I knew would never . . . He must be some kind of drone now. I don't think the boy I knew is left in there. I don't know if I have any kind of handle on him anymore."

"Jenna always says you're the smartest person she knows, Ash. You'll figure out a way."

"But I'd have to . . ." She swallows, setting a couple of bottles on the floor. "If I was going to reel him in, I mean. And I don't think I could bring myself to . . . after what he's done."

"I know. I don't like it, either. But this could be huge." He risks reaching down to rest his hand on hers. ". . . Are you okay, Ash?"

"Of course. Of course I am. And if there's a chance this will help . . ."

He squeezes her fingers. "I know we can get out of this. That might sound stupidly optimistic, but where there's life, there's hope, you know?"

"I know," she whispers. "We'll talk to the others about it." She pulls her hand out from beneath his, and there's a glimpse of that tattoo at her wrist again, of the name *Samaira* in flowing script.

They work in silence for a bit, almost companionable.

Eventually, she speaks again, trying for a lighter tone. "You know, I was thinking this morning. When this is all over, WUC's going to give us all huge compensation packages to make sure we keep our mouths shut. They can't have us out there complaining about what happened to us on their illegal mining settlement, right? So I've decided the first thing I'm doing is hitting a planet with a beach. What about you?"

"Season tickets," he replies promptly. "For the Kepler Knights. Jenna's a huge fan. She got me into pro geeball, to tell you the truth." His girlfriend's name is like a prayer on his lips, never failing to summon a smile. But too soon, it fades. "You know, when I heard she got out on the shuttles, part of me was pretty torn up. Knowing we'd be apart for a while." He gestures around the room. "But most of me is kinda glad she never had to go through all this."

It's Grant's turn to squeeze Way's hand now.

"You'll see her again, Bruno."

Way smiles again, his customary optimism coming back out to shine.

"I know I will. Not even a BeiTech invasion can keep me and

Jenn apart for long. We've just gotta stay smart, stay low till we figure out a way off this rock. And maybe your ex is the way to do that."

Grant chews her lip. Nods.

The sound of heavy boots rings in the corridor, and she pulls her hand out of her friend's grip. The door opens behind them, and the guard appears, framed in it.

Without another word, or another glance at Way, Grant gathers up her armful of bottles and walks out.

INCEPT: 08/18/75 20:36

Joran KARALIS: check in?

Asha GRANT: I'm here

Bruno WAY: ditto

Steph PARK: here

Joran KARALIS: I don't have long, back on shift soon. We're double time since the tunnel collapse. The BT ████s are howling about quota.

Steph PARK: Is it true Marcus Carter volunteered?

Joran KARALIS: yes

Asha GRANT: god, he used to come into the pharmacy for his wife's meds . . .

Joran KARALIS: he didn't have any family left. He knew what he was putting his hand up for. no one who lives in our memory truly dies

Joran KARALIS: we remember

Bruno WAY: we remember

Asha GRANT: we remember

Joran KARALIS: and the way to honor his sacrifice is to get off this rock alive. So, has anyone made any progress on what the BT transmission contained or where it got sent?

Steph PARK: we know what it said. The magellan's nearly ready and the timer's started, more executions coming very soon to a planet near you

Bruno WAY: but we do have a development

Joran KARALIS: yes?

Bruno WAY: Ash?

Asha GRANT: I was getting there, Bruno, just thought we might spend a minute checking we're all alive, stuff like that, ██.

Joran KARALIS: what is it, Asha?

Asha GRANT: okay you might wanna be sitting down for this

Steph PARK: Kid, spit it out for crissakes

Asha GRANT: my ex-boyfriend just showed up

Asha GRANT: and he's part of the BT invasion force.

Steph PARK: WHAT?

Joran KARALIS: WHAT?

Asha GRANT: He just got reassigned down here from the Magellan. But before anyone gets excited about some possible connection, i have no idea if i can trust him. It's been years. it was such a bad breakup we literally ended up on different planets. Also, I cussed him out already.

Steph PARK: ARE YOU KIDDING? Kid, you jump his bones if you have to, i don't care what it takes. this is a huge opportunity. HUGE.

Joran KARALIS: God, this could be our way out . . .

Steph PARK: and if not that, a chance to take out as many of those mother██████ers as we can on our way out the door

Bruno WAY: Easy, Steph.

Joran KARALIS: Asha, with a BT agent on our side . . . our options are . . . hell, think what we could access. we could get a transmission out

Steph PARK: to who, Joran? If anyone from WUC was listening, they'd have come by now to find out why we went quiet. Something happened to convince them we're all dead and it's a bad idea to look for survivors. that's the only explanation

Joran KARALIS: Steph, ████ing stow it, you hear me? you want to give up, do it on your own time. I'm not done fighting yet.

Bruno WAY: nobody's done fighting yet, nobody said that

Asha GRANT: seriously, i just don't think I can get this guy to do anything for me. think about what I'd be asking. The risk he'd be taking. for what, from his point of view?

Joran KARALIS: if there's even the smallest chance, we have to try. we owe it to everyone still alive

Bruno WAY: it's more than a small chance

Asha GRANT: look, i don't disagree, you all know I'm not done fighting. but the guy I loved never would have been here in the first place.

Joran KARALIS: Asha, you have to do this. we have to risk it

Bruno WAY: hey, I'm all for doing what we can, but it's not a "we" kind of risk. It's Ash who'd have her neck on the line. I think we should acknowledge that.

Asha GRANT: I guess it's on the line anyway, now or later

Asha GRANT: I mean honestly, does ANYONE believe they're going to transport us all out of here once the Magellan is refueled?

Steph PARK: no ████ing chance.

Joran KARALIS: I've been thinking about that. Talking with some of the others in the mine. and if we're all convinced that as soon as they refuel the Magellan we're dead, it seems the only option is to somehow take the mobile jump platform ourselves. Steph's right that we can't assume anyone will hear our transmission. But Magellan is nearly repaired. We could use it to jump out of here. and this boy could help us with that, Asha.

Steph PARK: are you dusted?

Steph PARK: have you finally cracked?

Steph PARK: we're stealing the Magellan now?

Joran KARALIS: what did you think we were doing, just killing as many of them as we could before they kill us? i don't want to die, Steph. I've got a family.

Bruno WAY: listen, guys, nobody wants to die

Asha GRANT: ███ it. if Joran's right, perhaps we can do something. If Steph's right, do you guys know a better way to cash out than still trying?

Asha GRANT: i'm gonna have to break the hospital enviro rig somehow so they send him back up here

Bruno WAY: i can send you some notes on how to ███ with the intakes

Asha GRANT: ok

Asha GRANT: i'll sound him out. i'll have to go slow. I can't just backflip after how I treated him yesterday. but I'll try.

Joran KARALIS: you have to do better than that, Asha.

Joran KARALIS: We don't have time to just try anymore.

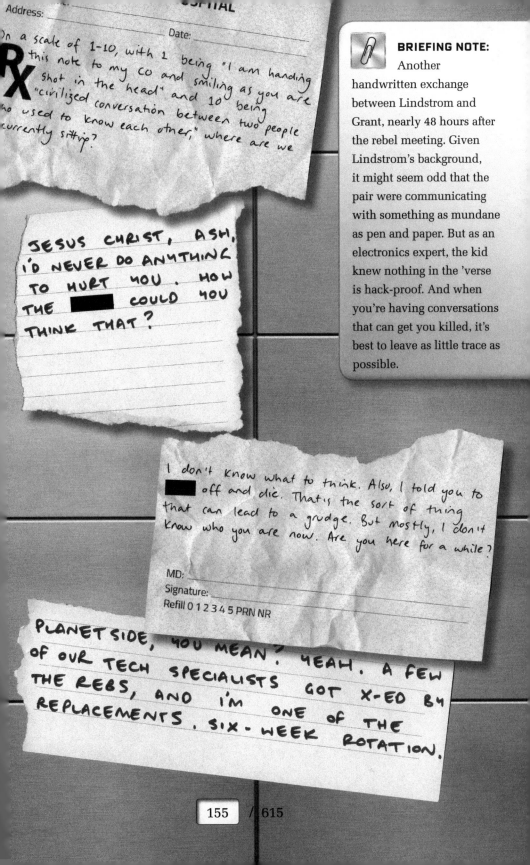

Address: _____
Date: _____

On a scale of 1-10, with 1 being "I am handing this note to my CO and smiling as you are shot in the head" and 10 being "civilized conversation between two people who used to know each other," where are we currently sitting?

BRIEFING NOTE:
Another handwritten exchange between Lindstrom and Grant, nearly 48 hours after the rebel meeting. Given Lindstrom's background, it might seem odd that the pair were communicating with something as mundane as pen and paper. But as an electronics expert, the kid knew nothing in the 'verse is hack-proof. And when you're having conversations that can get you killed, it's best to leave as little trace as possible.

JESUS CHRIST, ASH, I'D NEVER DO ANYTHING TO HURT YOU. HOW THE ███ COULD YOU THINK THAT?

I don't know what to think. Also, I told you to ███ off and die. That's the sort of thing that can lead to a grudge. But mostly, I don't know who you are now. Are you here for a while?

MD: _____
Signature: _____
Refill 0 1 2 3 4 5 PRN NR

PLANETSIDE, YOU MEAN? YEAH. A FEW OF OUR TECH SPECIALISTS GOT X-ED BY THE REBS, AND I'M ONE OF THE REPLACEMENTS. SIX-WEEK ROTATION.

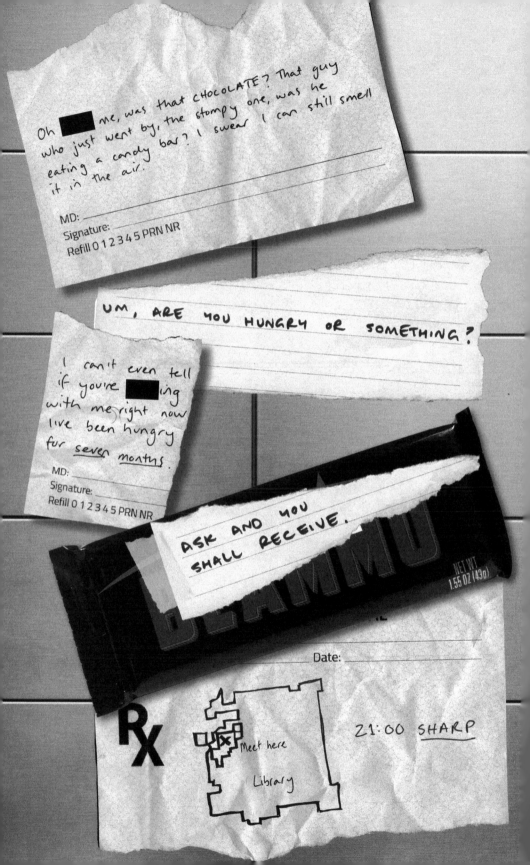

**Surveillance footage summary,
prepared by
Analyst ID 7213-0089-DN**

This footage is shot entirely through the cam of Rhys Lindstrom's ATLAS. Since the cam's mounted on his shoulder, you can't actually see his features through the whole clip, so I'm just guessing from tone and inflection what his facial expressions were.

Mostly dumbfounded, I'd bet.

The data from these cameras was transmitted direct to Server BTCs-14h, then beamed up to the *Churchill* for possible review by the BT brass. But it just so happens regular service of Server BTCs-14h was the purview of one Technical Specialist Rhys Lindstrom, so the kid could divert his feed whenever he wanted to go off-grid.

After his latest exchange with the former light of his life/fire of his loins, he'd also rigged up a dummy transmitter that mimicked the signal in his ATLAS's locator beacon, which meant anyone checking in on him would see his ping in the barracks. This is an old pounder trick, apparently pretty easy to do. Grunts use it to skip out after hours and mix with the local sugar during occupations that aren't so . . . unneighborly.

And so it is, when footage begins, that Lindstrom is waiting obediently where Grant told him to—in the shadow beneath the broken awning of Kerenza IV's public library.

It probably wasn't much to look at to begin with, but postinvasion, it almost doesn't count as a building at all. It's small, prefab concrete, the north and east walls completely blown out and the roof collapsed. The place looks like a bomb hit it.

See what I did there?

Lindstrom is in his ATLAS, helmet on, suit sealed, so he can't feel the cold. But he still suppresses a shiver as he stands there, looking over the frozen, ruined server banks that had once housed the colony's literature collection. Squinting hard, I think I can make out some shelves inside the library's ruin—looks like the Kerenza colony actually had some real, honest-to-God books in there along with the digital files. The block around him is mostly snowcapped rubble, twisted girders rising from the white blanket like broken fingers.

The words *We Remember* are spray-painted on one broken wall.

Something catches Lindstrom's eye, and he stoops to drag aside a piece of fallen masonry that must weigh at least 300kgs. Underneath are the charred remnants of a kid's book, torn and soaked through and frozen solid. He pries it loose from the ice beneath the rubble, turns it over to look at the front cover. Beneath the scorch and rime of ice and dirt, you can just make out the title.

Where the Wild Things Are, by Maurice Sendak.

"No ████ing way," he mutters.

"You have to be a member before they let you take books out."

The voice comes from behind him. The kid turns to the shadows and sees her, hands in pockets, bundled up inside six layers of heavy insulation against the chill. The green cross on her sleeve identifies her as medical personnel, the logo of the hospital on her chest. Not even her eyes are visible beneath her goggles and the trim of faux fur around her hood. But Asha Grant's voice is unmistakable.

"Can you believe this?" Lindstrom asks, holding up the frozen pages.

"Believe what?"

"This was my favorite book when I was a kid."

"Yeah, I know." Her reply is as cold as the snow around them. "We're a little old for kids' books, don't you think?"

"Yeah, I guess." The kid's momentary excitement bleeds out of his voice. He tosses the frozen book back down into the snow. "Just . . . struck me as weird, is all."

"Yeah," Grant replies. "There's a lot of that going around lately."

They stare, awkward silence ringing in the howling wind. It's been three years since they've seen each other, though between the ATLAS and her cold-weather gear, it's not like they can see much of each other now. They call that a metaphor, chum.

The slow buzzing of a sentry drone skips overhead. It's too far away to spot them, but Lindstrom huddles farther under the awning, Grant doing the same on reflex.

"Are you sure you should be sneaking around out here? It's after curfew."

"I'm a big girl, Rhys."

"Yeah, but . . ."

"The drones work in a grid across the city," she explains. "We've figured them out by now. If a random patrol stops me, I'll make out like I'm sneaking out to hook up with someone at the barracks. A few minutes of innuendo and I'll be on my way."

". . . Girls really do that around here? I mean, they sl—"

"You'd be surprised what starving people will give up for a couple of B-ration packs."

Silence again. That howling wind.

"You look good," he finally says.

"You can't even see me under all this."

"Before, I mean." He shrugs. "At the hospital. I mean you look kinda thin, but . . . it's really good to see you, Ash."

"Nice uniform." She nods to his armor. "The red suits you."

The kid looks down at his ATLAS, its color matching the snow around them.

"It's white."

The girl simply tilts her head.

". . . Oh," he says.

Howling wind and awkward silence.

"Ash, I really was on the *Magellan* this whole time, I didn't know—"

"You didn't know what, Rhys?" she says softly, slowly walking closer. "Huh?"

"I didn't know—"

"You didn't know they were torturing us, is that it? Locking us in cages to keep the rest of us working? Brutalizing us until the thought of ███ing a murderer becomes preferable to one more night of sleeping on an empty stomach?"

Her voice is rising now, anger creeping in past the chill as she stalks closer.

"You didn't know they were treating us like animals, maybe? Slaughtering us like sheep? That from a population of eighteen thousand, they've culled us to about three? You didn't know?"

"No," Lindstrom says, anger creeping into his voice to match hers. "Like I've said three times now, I've been working on *Magellan* since we arrived. I'm a grunt, they don't tell me ███. It's not like they're running a news service for us up in orbit. I had no idea what the hell was going on down here until I saw it."

"Well, welcome to sunny Kerenza IV!" Grant flings her arms out, gesturing to the wasteland around them as she adopts a mocking tour guide tone. "To your left, you can see the gutted ruin of our spaceport, where two hundred people died when your invasion dropped a missile on them in the first few minutes of the attack. Lucky them, really. Around us, you'll find the shiny ruins of our community complex, which, incidentally, included a day care center for the kids of the local council workers—whoops, bombed that one to hell, too."

"Ash . . ."

"A little ways behind me, you'll see the apartment building

where I last saw my cousin, who's probably ██████ing dead now, and the research center, which was the last place I saw my aunt alive and where I used to work before my completely unqualified ███ became a nurse to fill the holes you ████s blew in our hospital staff."

"Ash . . ."

"Aaaaand let's not forget the crown jewel: just two klicks out of town you'll find the scenic mass graves of everyone your people have murdered since they showed up in orbit seven months ago. But don't lose a wink of sleep about it, Mr. Lindstrom, because YOU. DIDN'T. *KNOW*."

She's in his face now. Ragged breath billowing in white plumes from her balaclava. His voice is soft, distorted by the vox unit in his ATLAS helmet.

"What do you want me to say, Ash?"

She pulls down her goggles, the wool covering her face. Just so he can see her. Light brown skin, narrowed green eyes full of rage and hurt, bee-stung lips pressed so tight together her jaw is trembling. He pops the seals on his helmet, drags it off over his head. I can't see his face, but I can hear it in his voice. Helplessness. Horror. Sorrow.

"It wasn't me," he says. "I didn't do those things. I'd never do those things. Jesus, you *know me*, Ash."

She looks him up and down, her eyes reflecting white snow. "I thought I did."

"I didn't sign up for this," he says. "I'm just a ██████ing tech. Your parents send you to military school, you end up a soldier. That's the way it goes."

"And how's that working out for you?"

"What do you want me to say?" he hisses again. "You think I wanted this? I didn't want to get sent away. I wanted to stay with you! I wrote to you for *a whole year* before I figured out you weren't going to write me back—"

Her eyes widen. "Don't you *dare* try to make this about you and me."

"For crissakes, I'm *not*! I'm trying to explain how I got here! I didn't see a poster on a wall that said 'Join the corps! See the galaxy! Bomb the ██ out of innocent people!' They *forced* me to go. And even if they hadn't, you think the recruiters tell you what you're in for when you sign up? None of these pounders knew they'd be in ██ like this. You think people honestly sit back and say to themselves, 'You know what? I think I'll get myself involved in a planetary genocide this week'?"

"You're actually making *excuses* for them?"

"No!" he shouts, immediately lowering his voice and looking around to make sure they're alone. "This is ███ed. This whole situation is ███ed. But you don't understand. What it's like. Getting that 'Company! Commander! Corps!' ██ drilled into you every day. When you're just one little cog . . ." He shrugs. "Sometimes it's hard for people to see the whole machine. What it's doing. Who it's eating."

"It's eating *me,* Rhys. It's eating my friends. So you can either sit back and watch it happen or help us *do* something about it."

"Us? Who is 'us'?"

The girl stays silent, staring from behind mirrored glass.

"Are you talking about the insurgency?" Lindstrom asks. "Running around gassing people in their sleep? Blowing up mine tunnels? Is that what you're talking about?"

"I'm talking about people fighting to survive, Rhys," she says. "I'm talking about ending the massacre that's being carried out by BeiTech Industries. Every time you put on that uniform, you endorse what they've done to us."

"What the hell can I do?" he demands. "You want me to shoot my CO? They'll just bring in another one! You want me to try and stop what's happening here? They'll bring me up on charges and X me. I'm just one person!"

"It only takes one pebble to start an avalanche."

"Christ, don't give me that desktop calendar bull██. We're in a *war* here."

She looks at him then. Long and silent and somber. When she speaks, her voice is quiet, almost lost under the howling wind. But the words are deafening.

"That doesn't sound like the boy I fell in love with."

Lindstrom goes silent, wobbling on his feet like she's slugged him in the jaw. Grant looks around her boots, bends down and picks up a fleck of broken masonry. It's tiny, just a pebble really. She takes hold of his hand, puts it on his outstretched palm.

"Be the pebble, Rhys."

"Asha—"

But she's already turned away. Stalking back across the white, boots crunching in the snow. She peers around the darkened corner, up and down the street, on the lookout for APCs or pounders on foot, listening for the buzzing drones. And ignoring Lindstrom's whispers, she dashes off into the freezing night.

Lindstrom looks down at the pebble in his hand.

Slowly closes his fingers into a fist.

INCEPT: 08/20/75 23:42

Asha GRANT: bruno u there

Bruno WAY: yeah

Bruno WAY: you okay?

Asha GRANT: I'm okay

Bruno WAY: how'd it go

Asha GRANT: I think I've got him

MOBILE JUMP PLATFORM
MAGELLAN WILL BE
OPERATIONAL IN:

15 DAYS
13 HOURS: 32 MINUTES

84%

0   99

HERMIUM
REQUIRED TO JUMP

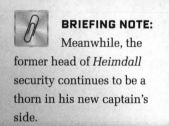

NTERCEPTED PERSONAL MESSAGE ONBOARD SYSTEM—INSERT

To: BOLL, Syra
From: GARVER, Ben
Incept: 09:05, 08/24/75
Subject: Training Program and Liaison Issues

Captain Boll,

I have been approached by large numbers of *Heimdall* personnel who have found there is no effective way to convey their concerns to the ship's command structure. I have made such inquiries as I am able, and it does not appear any liaison system is in place.

Captain, although those of you from the *Hypatia* and *Alexander* have considered yourselves part of the same fleet for some months, *Heimdall* personnel have for the most part only learned about your existence within the last few days. I'm sure you understand that adjusting is taking time, and the fact that there is nobody to hear their concerns is not helping.

Firstly, I would like to suggest that I would be a suitable liaison. I am a senior *Heimdall* staff member, and I can filter out those requests and issues that need to be passed up the tree and meet with you to deliver them succinctly.

Secondly, I would like to advise that I have had numerous protests from *Heimdall* personnel asked to train under the supervision of what I understand to be an eighteen-year-old high school student. Although I understand Ezra Mason has seen some combat during his time with the *Alexander,* some of the *Heimdall* crew members, especially those with decades of ice-mining experi-

166 / 615

ence, do not take kindly to this new arrangement, and frankly, I cannot blame them. They are not in need of training of this sort, and in fact, their expertise should be valued and they should be consulted on their views.

I am prepared to meet with you at your convenience to discuss the above issues, as well as the others on my list.

GARVER, Ben
Heimdall Personnel, Please Enter Title into System
ID 291fp90/WUC

To: BOLL, Syra
From: GARVER, Ben
Incept: 09:05, 08/25/75
Subject: Re: Training Program and Liaison Issues

Captain Boll,

I note I have not heard back from you in regard to my previous email.

I appreciate that we did not begin our relationship on a cordial note, and respectfully, I continue to disagree with many aspects of the course you have chosen.

That said, we are in this together, and I am prepared to do everything I can to ensure our success and survival. It is increasingly urgent that I meet with you to discuss the issues raised by personnel on board, as well as to discuss the contribution I can make personally, given my experience as *Heimdall*'s head of security.

Yours,

GARVER, Ben
Heimdall Personnel, Please Enter Title into System
ID 291fp90/WUC

Click <u>here</u> to register your Go-Mail, and access our full range of features.

Footage opens in the airlock of *Mao*'s main hangar bay—a ten-by-six-meter corridor of scuffed plasteel, with triple-reinforced glass windows in the hatches at either end.

A dozen men and women are standing around, waiting for the lock to pressurize and spit them back into the *Mao*'s belly. Dressed in a motley collection of flight suits, a few marked with WUC logos. They're the ragtag collection of former tug and freighter pilots who've survived the *Heimdall* occupation, pulled together by Captain Boll for training on the *Mao*'s fighter ships. And from the sounds of it, they're not feeling too jaunty about their new air wing leader.

"Who does that little ▮▮ think he is?"

It's a big, beardy-faced chum who speaks, veins scrawled on his cheeks. The name MCCUBBIN is stenciled on his flight suit beside the logo of an ice hauler outfit that operated out of the kersploded *Heimdall* wormhole.

"He's Allah's gift to pilots, didn't you know?" replies a thin woman with eyes like knives. "Lieutenant Babyface took down the *Lincoln* all by himself."

McCubbin scowls. "Keep cracking wise about it, Garcia. But I've been dancing the black for thirty goddamn years and I don't see the funny side of taking orders from a ▮▮ing kid."

Other pilots mutter agreement as the airlock readouts shift from red to green. The woman called Garcia cycles the hatchway and it yawns wide. As the gang shuffles out of the airlock, a figure slouches past them, hands in pockets, eyes to the floor. Short dark hair and tattooed knives winding down his arm. An angel inked at his throat.

Nik Malikov cycles the airlock shut. Locks it and engages pressure. Fishing around in his pants, he retrieves a battered packet of Tarannosaurus Rex™ cigarettes, flips one into his mouth. And lighting his smoke with a small slab of burnished steel, he leans against the wall.

Eyes closed.

Breathing gray.

"█████ me, that's better . . ."

Minutes pass, the only sound the thrum of the engines. A computerized voice finally crackles through the airlock PA, ruining Malikov's carcinogenic bliss.

"WaRning. Contaminant DetecteD, AiRlock One."

Malikov's eyes flutter open, and he squints at the comms unit. ". . . That you, AIDAN?"

"N-N-Niklas?"

"The one and only." The kid inhales, frowns in the smoke. ". . . Actually, maybe not, now I think about it . . ."

"Apologies. I cannot see you. I am not fully inteGRateD with A-vis systems yet."

"Heard they plugged you in," the kid smirks. "From a UTA battlecarrier to this junker. The 'verse sure has got a strange sense of humor, huh."

"I am fffffffailing to see the comeD-D-Dic value in the situation."

"Makes two of us, I guess."

"WaRning. Contaminant level in AiRlock One Rising."

"Relax," Nik sighs. "It's my Rex."

"WaRning, fiRe DetecteD, AiRlock One."

"Madonna, *I'm just having a ████ing smoke,* AIDAN."

"SpRinkleR system engaging in twenty seconDs."

"Don't you dare . . ."

"Fifteen seconD-D-Ds."

Searching in another of his cargo pockets, Malikov hauls out the Silverback pistol he took from Juggler's corpse in the bathroom stall of *Heimdall* Station, a week and a lifetime ago. And brandishing it at the nearest video camera, he growls around his cig.

"I dunno if you can see this, Sparky, but I'm currently swinging a pistol the size of a small anti-aircraft gun. You engage those sprinklers, I'ma shove this up whatever passes for your tailpipe, feel me?"

"FiReaRm DetecteD, AiRlock One. ThReat level: ReD."

"Damn right. Now let me finish my—"

"RecipRocity pRotocol eng-g-gageD. PuRging aiRlock O$_2$ in twenty seconDs."

Malikov blanches at that. "Hey, waitaminute . . ."

"Fifteen seconDs."

The kid glances out at the hangar bay, back into the *Mao.* He stows the pistol in his pants, tugs on the hatch handle. No joy.

"AIDAN, I was just ████ing around."

"Ten seconDs."

"AIDAN, open the door!"

"Five s-s-s-seconDs."

Warning alarms begin grinding, the lighting inside the airlock shifting to a deep blood red. Malikov is still tugging at the door, face scarlet with exertion.

"Let me out!"

"O$_2$ puRge commencing."

"Goddammit, let me out!"

The alarms rise to a crescendo, red globes flashing, a soft and deadly hiss seeping from the vents in the ceiling and floor. Malikov draws his pistol again, takes aim at glass that's almost certainly bullet-proof, thumbs the safety off anyway. And just as suddenly as the alarms began, they die. The bloody light shifts back to off-white, the hissing stops and Malikov is left standing there, eyes wide, forgotten smoke dangling from the corner of a dry-as-dust mouth.

"HUMOR."

Malikov is still holding the pistol, unblinking.

"What?" he whispers.

"AN ABSURD, COMEDIC OR INCONGRUOUS QUALITY CAUSING AMUSEMENT."

The kid lowers his pistol slowly, face pale, cigarette bobbing as he hisses, "Are you ████ing kidding me?"

"I BELIEVE I JUST EXPLAINED THAT, YES."

"That was your idea of a joke?"

". . . YOU ARE NOT AMUSED?"

"Madonna . . ."

Malikov slithers down the wall, dropping the pistol at his feet. He runs one shaking hand through his hair, and for a second you can see it—the stress of the past week piling up inside. The fall of *Heimdall,* the murder of his family members, an alternate universe version of his cousin and Hanna dying in his arms. No swagger now. No wisecracks. Dragging on his cigarette like his life depends on it. Hands painted red, no matter how hard he scrubs them.

". . . You okay, chum?"

Malikov hasn't even heard the enviro system cycle, hasn't registered the door opening. He looks up into a pair of brown eyes and a concerned frown, a military-issue haircut and the uniform of a UTA Cyclone pilot, filled out about as perfect as a fem could ask for.

Not that anyone's asking my opinion, of course.

Second Lieutenant Ezra Mason glances at the pistol at Malikov's feet. Licks his lips and kneels down slow, like he's afraid to spook the other boy. He's taller than Malikov, heavier set. There's something gentler in his eyes, though. They're the same age, but Malikov grew up in the coils of one of the 'verse's most notorious criminal organizations. Mason spent most of his years playing geeball and chasing high school skirt.

Though I guess there's blood on both their hands now . . .

"Are you okay?" Mason repeats.

"Chill," Malikov sighs. "Just chill."

Mason stares for a long, silent moment, lips pursed.

"You're Nik Malikov," he finally says.

"The one and . . ." Malikov fumbles. Smirks. ". . . Yeah, that's me."

"I'm Ezra. Ezra Mason."

"Yeah, I know. Our resident flyboy."

"Listen . . ." Mason looks at the gun at Malikov's feet again. "I know it looks pretty dark right now. But . . . we're gonna get through this. You know that, right?"

Malikov raises a brow, follows Mason's sight line. And running the math quick enough to show he isn't as dumb as he likes people to think, he snorts, flashing those lady-killer dimples.

"Relax, chum. I'm not the kind to cash out before the game's done. Just a little misunderstanding between me and our friendly neighborhood artificial intelligence."

"AIDAN?" Mason glances up at the cameras, the PA speakers.

If the AI is still observing the conversation, it makes no sound.

"That'd be him." Malikov frowns. *"It."*

Mason settles against the opposite wall. "So what're you sitting in the airlock for?"

"Only place I can smoke." Malikov waves his Tarannosaurus Rex™. "I figure they have to cycle the air every time you flyboys come back anyway, so I'm not wasting O_2. Want one?"

Mason shakes his head. "Those things'll X you out quicker than a BT Warlock."

"I quit for a while. Threw my last pack out. Rationing being what it is, had to trade my left nut for these."

Mason shrugs. "You've got a spare."

"Double true," Malikov grins.

They sit quiet for a moment, the rumble of *Mao*'s engines the only sound.

"Kady explained to me about what you did," Mason finally says. "*Heimdall.* Fixing the Gemina field."

"Sounds like some crazy bull█████, right?"

"Yeah." Mason nods. "But if Kady and Winifred believe it, I believe it. So, you know . . . thanks. For saving the universe and all."

Mason leans forward, offers his hand. Malikov looks him over, eyes narrowed through the smoke, maybe searching for some kind of sarcasm. But after a moment of slow consideration, he sits up and shakes the outstretched hand.

"'S'all good, chum."

Mason leans back against the wall, listening to the engines thrum.

"So. Kady Grrrrrant," Malikov purrs. "She's your fem, right?"

"Yeah."

Malikov raises his cigarette in toast. "Nice catch."

Mason smiles, lopsided. "She's a handful."

"I feel that."

"You're doing all right yourself, way I hear it."

Malikov glances up in question, and Mason smiles wider. "Hanna Donnelly, right?"

"Where you hear that?"

"Kady," Mason says simply. "Did I hear wrong?"

Malikov makes a face, exhales gray.

"Well, there's handfuls and then there's handfuls. And then there's Hanna." He watches broken trails of smoke drift in the air. Sighs. "I dunno what we are. Or where."

"You love her?"

Malikov stares hard. "Don't waste much time on foreplay, do you, Flyboy?"

"Chum, if these last seven months taught me anything, it's that you can't afford to burn time. If you love her, don't █████ around. Tell her. Tomorrow might take your chance away."

Malikov shakes his head.

"Fem like that, chum like me? How's that gonna work? She about said as much, too." He sighs a lungful of smoke. "I'm starting to figure that without a BeiTech kill squad chasing us, she's got time to look at me and see what everyone else does."

"The guy who saved two universes?"

Malikov crows with laughter.

"█████, Flyboy. Most folks don't believe that." He motions to the tattoos on his arm and throat, gray weaving in the air. "They believe *this*. Always have. Always will."

Mason regards the ink solemnly. Even on the edge of the universe, stories about the Dom Najov and their brutality have made the rounds. Newscasts and shockreels, VR sims and bad docudrama. Blood and bodies rendered in pristine high-def.

"House of Knives."

Malikov drags on his smoke. Saying nothing.

"So I guess that hand cannon in your pocket isn't just for show?" Mason asks.

You can see the memories flash in Malikov's eyes then. Juggler's brains blown out in a toilet stall. Ragman and Flipside murdered in *Heimdall*'s docking bay. Eden. Mercury. Kali. Cerberus. They might've been murderers themselves. They might've been alternate universe versions of the people who belonged to this one. But they were still *people.*

"I can shoot," he says quietly.

Mason stares at Malikov for a long moment. Finally nods.

"So shoot for me," he says.

Malikov just tilts his head in question, smoke drifting from his nostrils.

"These fighters *Mao* is carrying." Mason nods to the hangar bay behind them, the sleek shapes docked inside. "Chimeras. They're two-man ships. If I'm gonna fly one, I need a gunner. You know how to shoot. And to be honest, most of these people Boll has me training aren't great shakes."

"I guess it doesn't help that they all hate your ██████ing guts, huh."

Mason blinks. "How did you . . ."

"Heard 'em griping on the way in."

Malikov smiles as the bigger boy's face turns dark.

"Ungrateful ████s," Mason spits. "You know what they call me behind my back?"

Malikov shrugs.

"Lieutenant Babyface," Mason growls.

Malikov laughs, smoke spilling from his nostrils. "You do have a certain cherubic quality about you, Flyboy. Just saying."

"Hey, ████ you, chum."

Malikov holds up both hands in mock surrender, cig bobbing at his lips. "Not many folks like taking orders from kids half their age, I guess."

"It's bull███," Mason hisses, voice dropping to conspiratorial levels. "Most of those mother████ers flew tugs and ice haulers before all this. They don't know the first thing about flying combat. I mean, I'm no demon at the stick, but at least I've shot at something that was shooting *back* at me. They're gonna be fighting for their lives when we hit the *Churchill,* and half these ██████s spend the training sessions ████ing rather than listening."

A long moment passes with nothing but engine song. Malikov hits his smoke, a thoughtful expression on his face. Speaking soft.

"And you've got me pegged for a killer, huh?"

Mason looks him up and down. Shrugs.

"Aren't you?"

Malikov just stares. Saying nothing.

"Look," Mason continues, "that BT transmission told us they've got at least one semi-functional dreadnought at Kerenza. Plus whatever defenses they have on the *Magellan*. If we go through with this attack, it's gonna be balls to the wall. Everything we've done to get this far doesn't mean a thing. We lose there, we lose *everything*. And I don't wanna bust up your bad██ party, but if you want people to look at you and see something more than that ink, you've got to do something more than spend your time smoking in the goddamn airlock."

"Do I look like the kind who loses sleep over what people think of him, Flyboy?"

"Maybe not most people," Mason replies. "But what about *her*?"

Malikov narrows his eyes.

Exhales gray.

"Touché, good sir."

Mason stands, looming over Malikov. And leaning down, he extends his hand.

"We got a deal?"

"You really think el Capitan is gonna let an untrained eighteen-year-old like me anywhere near one of those fighters?"

"Chum, she's so busy trying to hold this ship together, she won't even know."

Malikov shakes his head. "If you think your minerboys hate you now, wait till they hear you pulled in another kid to fly with—"

"No bull██," Mason snaps. "No excuses. You can sit here on your ██ and mope, or you can do something to help. Now, are you in or out?"

"I'm not calling you 'sir,' if that's what you're thinking."

"Shoot straight and you can call me whatever the ██ you want."

"Lieutenant Babyface?"

"Don't push it, chum," Mason scowls. "In or out?"

Malikov grins.

Kills his smoke with his boot heel.

And, reaching up, he takes Mason's hand.

"All right. In."

ERCEPTED PERSONAL MESSAGE ONBOARD SYSTEM—INSERT NAN

To: FLINT, Jess
From: BOLL, Syra
Incept: 13:41, 08/27/75
Subject: Impending violence

Hi Jess,

Please see the email I'm about to forward.

I have a PhD in theology, so I can tell you with total authority that not even divine intervention is going to stop me punching this pompous ▮▮ if he wakes me up again. I had him pounding on my door during the THREE HOURS OF SLEEP I have had in the last 24.

I will break his nose. I will break his smug ▮▮ing FACE. I remember a time when I didn't harbor dark thoughts like this. Do you remember that time, Jess?

Can you please find somebody to take a meeting with him at some point? Maybe one of the junior officers handling the rosters. There might be something we can give him to do. I don't dispute the guy has some valid points, but he had a BeiTech infiltrator sitting *right under his nose* for almost a year, and frankly, given BT might have had other plants on the station, I'm not really willing to put anyone I don't know in a command position.

Speaking of rostering, how are we doing recording all the *Heimdall* skill sets that came aboard? Specifically, do we have anyone with plumbing experience? This is not an idle question.

Thanks, Sy

Click <u>here</u> to register your Go-Mail, and access our full range of features.

179 / 615

------Forwarded Message------

To: BOLL, Syra

From: GARVER, Ben

Incept: 12:30, 08/27/75

Subject: Fw: Re: Re: Re: Re: Re: Re: Re: Re: URGENT MEETING REQUES

Captain Boll,

I am resorting to written communication once more after three failed attempts in the last twelve hours to meet with you in person. I have been continually blocked from accessing you and was told on one occasion, by a comms officer who appeared to be underage, to "pull my head in."

I wish to protest this exclusion in the strongest possible terms. I am the head of security for a major Wallace Ulyanov Consortium installation and the most senior and experienced WUC security staff member aboard. I have military experience, and I should be present at the meetings I understand you are conducting with United Terran Authority military staff.

Frankly, Captain—and I say this with the greatest respect—as the former second in command of a research vessel, you are simply not qualified to make the decisions that must be made in our present situation. Our mutual employer would, I assure you, prefer that I was a major part of this conversation.

My immediate concerns include, but are not limited to:

- The equitable distribution of rations, including to families
- The three allegations of physical assault I have encountered in the past 24 hours

- Representation of the needs and views of *Heimdall* residents, who had no knowledge of the <u>illegal</u> WUC hermium operation on Kerenza and who, frankly, want no part in this fight
- Our strategy as we hurtle toward Kerenza and an encounter that will result in, at best, high fatality numbers for our people and, more likely, annihilation
- Rumors that you have enlisted the aid of an artificial intelligence that is reportedly responsible for the deaths of thousands of UTA and WUC personnel

I again request a meeting as soon as possible. I have valuable contributions to make to the current conversation, and put simply, I demand the right to do so.

I await your immediate reply.

GARVER, Ben
Heimdall Personnel, Please Enter Title into System
ID 291fp90/WUC

I saw Keiko and Claire. I should have gone earlier, but somehow I knew we wouldn't have anything to say.

They were my friends back on Heimdall, but I've always been good at making new friends each new place I go. And then I move along.

I wanted so badly for there to still be some connection, for them to have the right words to comfort me, but the three of us were just silent. They're refugees, waiting and hoping. I was one of the people making things happen, back on Heimdall. I want to be again.

There's a barrier between us now.

They were in the atrium when it all went down on the station. They saw what happened, with Dad. I wanted to ask them... I don't know. Whether he knew, what he said. But I didn't, because I don't want that picture in my head.

I keep on thinking that at some point it will be over. It's so <u>hard</u>. Every morning, the moment when I wake up, everything's okay for a few seconds. And then it comes crashing down on me, crushing me beneath its weight, as the memory arrives.

He's gone.

A dozen times a day I think I'll ask him something, or tell him something, or I turn to see where he is. Or I see a man walking down a hallway, and just for an instant my brain lights up with recognition, thinking it's found a match for a familiar silhouette, before the truth shows up again. He's gone, he's gone, he's gone.

At first, I think there was a sense of . . . that I could wait it out. That if I was just good, if I somehow held on, waited, took care of things in a way that would make him proud, that I'd get my reward.

And of course, my reward would be my father. I didn't consciously think that—I mean, I'm not delusional—but some part of me thought, somehow, that if I could just last until the end of it, he'd show up. He'd praise me for having made it through that horrible trial. He'd tell me what a great job I did.

But slowly, painfully, it's beginning to settle over me like a blanket. This knowledge that never goes away, but beats like a drum in the back of my head all the time.

This is forever.

Welcome to the good ship *Mao*.

On Level 4, folks are about one meal away from full-blown food riots. Level 3, they're packed in so tight it's hard to breathe. But here on Level 9, things are a little more civilized. Cara Douglas and her son, Luke, are among the luckiest of the *Heimdall* refugees—they've managed to stake out the corner of a room all for themselves.

They fled the *Heimdall* entertainment center with nothing but the clothes on their backs, the contents of Cara's handbag and a battered toy rabbit called Mr. Boots. Mr. Boots's ears are tatty from being chewed over the years, but Luke is a young man of four now and is past such things, except in times of great trial.

He and his mother are sitting on a blanket that, as it happens, once upon a time graced the bunk of the ill-fated James "Cricket" Orr. A blanket is a valuable thing here—though Level 4 is a mass of sweltering bodies and rising tempers, the climate control having almost utterly failed, Level 9 is quiet and cool. Too cool—subdued by the effort of keeping themselves warm, the inhabitants are huddled together, too tired to speak or, in most cases, complain.

Spread on the metal floor, its edge rolled over to keep Luke warm, Cricket's blanket is their bed, their best source of warmth and their way of marking out their tiny piece of territory on the

Mao. Their place in the world, as their world has now shrunk down to the size of this one ship.

Cara's husband and Luke's father, Shane Pangburn, died when Travis Falk bled all the oxygen out of the *Heimdall*'s habitation sectors. Shane had gone back there just before the invasion to pick up another couple of toys for Luke. Cara remembers a dozen times each day how she argued for staying home—Luke had been out of sorts all day with the start of a cold, and they weren't sure they could trust him to behave. But Shane talked her into heading to the entertainment center just for an hour or two to see Shane's best friend. It was Terra Day, after all—surely they could manage a small celebration.

In the dark, cold nights on Level 9, she reflects on the fact that if she'd had her way, they all would have died together in the habitats. Instead, only Shane—the one who wanted to go out—slowly choked at home, fading into nothing.

And Cara was stuck, screaming helplessly as his fate was announced over the loudspeaker in the entertainment center. Lying to Luke, trying desperately to hide the truth from him for a few moments longer. Collapsing into Ben's arms, deaf to his words as her husband's best friend tried to find some way to comfort her.

She's been trying to keep going, the last few days, for Luke. It's hard to see the reason behind it, most of the time, but Ben insists, and so she tries. Luke doesn't seem to understand what's happened and placidly accepts his new place in life.

Ben should have been in the atrium, listening to the commander's speech. But he bucked duty just for once, slipped out to see his friends and check up on his godson. The Mutual Adoration Society, Cara used to laughingly call them, Ben and Luke.

Cara doesn't think she'll ever laugh again now.

Suddenly Luke's a kicking, scrambling mess of arms and legs, clambering to his feet, trying to untangle himself from the blanket. She blinks herself awake—she mostly dozes, when she can—and watches as he dodges nimbly through the sea of arms and legs, refugees lying on the floor, curled up for warmth with their loved ones.

Luke makes it most of the way to the door, and there he meets former *Heimdall* chief of security Ben Garver, who stoops to scoop his godson up in his arms, setting him on his hip with practiced ease and promptly lifting his free hand to nip at the kid's nose with two fingers, then push his thumb up between them.

"You make this too easy," he informs Luke, solemn.

"Give it back!" The kid wriggles, delighted. "I need my nose!"

"Are you sure?" Garver asks, eyes dancing. "This place doesn't smell so good—maybe you're better off without it."

"Uncle Be-en!"

So Garver relents and returns the stolen appendage, then makes his way through the crowd with considerably more care than his young charge did, to crouch beside his mother. "Cara," he murmurs, infinitely gentle. "Did you pick up your rations today?"

She frowns, trying to remember, and then slowly shakes her head.

"I'll take you in a few minutes," he says. "I can't do it for you, they'll only sign them over in person."

"All right." Her voice is hoarse, and she clears her throat. "Thank you."

He gazes down at her for a long moment, searching for something he can do. Then he peels his jacket off, helps her sit up and, like he's dressing a child, feeds her arms through the sleeves one at a time. "Lukey, you make sure your mother keeps her new jacket on, okay?" he says, voice lighter. "You keep an eye on her."

"Okeydoke," Luke replies, wriggling down to stand and wrap his arms around Garver's neck, hanging off him like a climbing frame.

"I'm going to do the rounds a little, and then we'll get the rations," Garver says, leaning down to catch Cara's eye, make sure she hears him. He knows she'll need a little time to work up to the effort of moving.

She nods.

So he leaves her, and he moves around quietly, keeping Luke with him to allow her a rest. He speaks to each small group, listens to their concerns, sympathizes, nods, offers what comfort he can. He doesn't allow himself to show a moment's frustration on his face, though there's not a single promise he can make—not even to get these complaints to the captain's ear.

And in the end, he helps Cara to her feet, leaving her neighbors to guard her spot and her blanket for her, and the two of them take one of Luke's hands each, making their way down the hallway slowly to stand in the line for rations.

And though he watches the strain on her face as if he's afraid she might break, he keeps up a steady chatter with little Luke Douglas-Pangburn, asking after the health of Mr. Boots and listening to the boy's trials and tribulations without missing a beat. This he does for his dead best friend, because it's the only thing left that he can do.

But it's easy to see why he so badly wants to do *more*.

**Surveillance footage summary,
prepared by
Analyst ID 7213-0089-DN**

We open in the infirmary, where Isaac Grant's still stuck in what passes for the ICU, Ella Malikova's still hooked up to subpar life support, and a variety of other bit players in the *Mao*'s ongoing drama are in various states of recovery from the many Things That Can Kill You In Space. There's no such thing as visiting hours here—there's barely any doctors, given most of the fleet's medical staff died with the *Copernicus.* So it is that nobody stops Kady Grant when she creeps in at 22:12 hours, weaving through the packed beds to check on her father. The audio on this recording is a symphony of *beeps* as the machines trailing wires in every direction report on their patients, protest their misuse or quietly complain about their diminishing batteries.

Grant eases back the curtain to find Hanna Donnelly sitting by Isaac Grant's bed already, head resting against the wall, eyes half-closed as she keeps vigil. She has a battered scrap of paper resting on a medical chart in her lap, a half-finished illustration on the page. Isaac himself is out cold, chest rising and falling slowly. Donnelly's eyes snap open when she registers Grant Jr.'s presence, and she starts to stand—the slow, awkward movement of someone whose every muscle is hurting.

"No, stay," Kady whispers, moving around the bed to lean against the wall beside Hanna. "You saved his life, you get to make sure he holds on to what's left of it."

Hanna has to clear her throat before she can reply. "We all saved each other, really. I put him back together. He got us out of there in the end. Nik, Ella, we all . . ."

Kady only speaks again when it's evident the other girl won't continue. "He told me about your father. I'm so sorry. It's ███ed up."

Hanna nods slowly, silently agreeing that it is, indeed, ███ed up. "I'm sorry about your mom," is all she says.

And for that, it's Kady's turn to nod. "Anyway," she says eventually. "Stay here. I know nothing fixes it, but you still have family aboard the *Mao*. You have us."

The pair of them keep watch then for a while in companionable silence, half an hour stretching out, broken only by the choruses of *beeps* and *whirs* all around. Grant leans against the wall, arms crossed, and slowly starts to nod, chin sinking toward her chest. Then her knees give, and she jolts awake, catching herself.

Hanna rises silently, takes the other girl by the shoulders and steers her down into the chair. "I always hate it when people tell me I look tired," she says, mustering a small smile, albeit with a clear effort. "Because really, it's code for 'You look like ███.' But there's no other way to say it. Is this your assigned sleep period?"

"Part of it," Kady admits. "There's so much to do. Captain has me analyzing the *Mao*'s systems so we're ready when we hit Kerenza. Sleep is a fond memory at this point."

"At least you've got something to do," Hanna replies, yanking the tie loose from her hair and combing it out with her fingers. "I'm stuck cooling my heels. I got asked before if I wanted to help in the *nursery*. I'm meant to have some sort of affinity for kids because I used to be one?"

"Because you *are* still one," Kady clarifies. "To the people in charge, I mean. I wouldn't get a second glance, except they literally don't have anyone else to do my job. If I thought it'd make the slightest bit of difference, I'd push them to take you on, but they're only working with *me* because there's nobody else. I don't know what would have to happen for them to include you as well. But listen, Hanna. Everyone aboard this ship owes their lives to you. I know that. For what it's worth."

And apparently it's worth something, because Donnelly stops yanking the kinks out of her hair with quite so much violence and switches back to braiding it once more. "You said 'so we're ready when we hit Kerenza.' What are we getting ready for?"

"Ah," says Kady. "Good question. Do you know where Ella Malikova is? I may as well tell you both at once."

Surreptitious peeking behind a series of curtains finally yields the girl in question, and after one last, careful check on Isaac, Kady and Hanna move into Ella's tiny cubicle. She's covered with a blanket, her face concealed almost entirely by an oxygen mask, and her eyes are darting around irritably, one hand gripping a palmpad. Her free hand gestures that they should help her sit up, and Kady wrangles the controls while Hanna messes around with the surrounding machines so the girl can move without yanking her mask free.

Upright, Ella coughs a couple of times, then pulls the mask away from her face. "Good to see you've got time to do your hair, Blondie."

Hanna, who's halfway through finishing her braid now, freezes. And then, abruptly, laughs. "I'll do yours next if you like," she deadpans, and Ella rolls her eyes as she replaces the mask for another couple of deep breaths.

"So," Kady says, without further preamble. "Ladies, we need to talk about the problems of interstellar travel and our distance from the Core. See, most wormholes are static, like the one at *Heimdall*. They're permanently fixed in one place."

"Unless someone turns them into their own personal fireworks show," Ella says.

Kady ignores her, pressing on. "Everyone knows the military has a couple of mobile jump platforms. Vortex-class ships like the

Alexander. The *Alexander* was able to come help us because it was patrolling the Kerenza system by chance and had jump platform technology aboard, so it could get to us in no time at all. What people don't know is that BeiTech developed a mobile jump platform too. It's called the *Magellan,* and they used it to attack Kerenza."

"That must have cost a fortune," Hanna murmurs, sinking down to sit on the edge of Ella's bed. "I assume it got destroyed in the attack, or they'd have used it to escape."

"Not destroyed," Kady replies. "*Alexander* damaged it in the initial assault. But according to the transmission we received from Kerenza, it's nearly fixed. If we can get back to Kerenza in time, we can at least go down trying to seize it. And you never know, we might pull it off."

Not one of the three teenagers huddled in the cubicle wears an expression that suggests they're busy booking their berth on *Magellan* just yet.

"Thing is," Kady presses on, "if we get out, we need to tell our story. And if we don't, then we need to leave our story behind, because one day *Heimdall* will be rebuilt, or someone else will use a mobile jump platform to get here, and people will come back to Kerenza IV. If they do, the guilty should answer for what they did. Getting word out about what happened here isn't a priority for anyone in command, but I think they're wrong. And it so happens, I know a few people who are itching for something to do."

"Damn right we are," Hanna replies, sitting up straighter. And behind her mask, Ella nods.

"We need to start prepping files," Kady says. "AIDAN and I got huge info dumps from the *Copernicus, Alexander* and *Hypatia,* and we got a lot off *Heimdall*'s servers as well. I've got AIDAN reconstructing some of it now, as an exercise to try and rebuild its synaptic net."

Ella removes the mask once more. "How's it doing?"

Kady makes a face. "It's a copy of a damaged copy. So not great.

But it's getting there. I could really use your help working with it, figuring out where the information we need is even stored, decrypting a lot of it."

Ella nods, and though she voiced plenty of reservations to Nik not so long before about AIDAN's reliability, none of that shows now. A Malikova keeps her enemies close—or maybe she's just willing to take the hit to get in on this job. "I can work with a psycho computer."

"And me?" Hanna presses. "If I can't fix it by turning it off and on, I'm out when it comes to tech."

"Ella's going to extract as much as she can," Kady replies. "You need to compile it. Maybe nobody in command is acknowledging it, but you're the best tactician we've got. So *you* build the case against BeiTech. There'll be a lot of vid footage that needs transcribing too. How would your boyfriend do with something like that?"

"He's n—" But Hanna gives up on that one. "I don't know," she admits, smile fading. She's presumably adding it to the mental list of things she doesn't know.

"He can do it," Ella says. "He reads books and all, and he spells better than he lets on. And maybe I can take some later, while I'm waiting for crypters to run."

"Then let's do it," Kady says simply. "It's better than waiting for whatever's going to happen to just happen. If we make it out, we'll shine a light on what BeiTech did."

"And if we don't?" Ella asks.

Kady looks back and forth between the girls and shrugs.

"At least our lives will have been worth dying for."

Live a life worth dying for.
—Kady Grant

PALMPAD IM: MAO INTRA-SHIP NETWORK
Participants: Kady Grant, Systems Chief
Artificial Intelligence Defense Analytics Network (AIDAN)
Date: 08/28/75
Timestamp: 06:17

AIDAN: KADY.

Grant, Kady: mmm?

AIDAN: APOLOGIES. I KNOW YOU ARE INUNDATEDD WITH THE TASKS
SYRA HAS ASSIGNED YOU. BUT WE SHOULD
TALK.

Grant, Kady: i am super busy, buddy. What's up?

AIDAN: I AM CURRENTLY RUNNING AT 9% CAPACITY. INCORPORATING MYSELF INTO THE
MAO NETWORK IS TAKING LONGER THAN ANTICIPATED. BUT AS A
MATTER OF PRIORITY, I AM RUNNING STRESS TESTS ON THE ENVIRONMENTAL
SYSTEMS AND C-C-CALCULATING MAO'S POTENTIAL OUTPUT VERSUS FLEET REQUIREMENTS.

AIDAN: I HAVE NEWS THAT MAY BE CONSIDERED
DISTRESSING.

Grant, Kady: ok

Grant, Kady: keeping in mind that i am also currently running at 9% capacity, due
to lack of sleep, fear of impending death and having to deal with the boneheads here
on the bridge, please be gentle with me as you break this news

AIDAN: YOU ARE ALL GOING TO DIE.

Grant, Kady: u were right, i do not want to hear that

AIDAN: THERE ARE CURRENTLY 3,360 PEOPLE ABOARD THE MAO. KERENZA

ADD LOGO HERE

REFUGEES. FORMER *ALEXANDER* AND *HYPATIA* CREW MEMBERS. STAFF AND RESIDENTS FROM *HEIMDALL* STATION. EVERY ONE OF THEM BREATHING OXYGEN WE CANNOT SPARE. CONSUMING FOOD AND WATER WE CANNOT REPLACE. THIS SHIP'S ENVIRONMENTALS WERE NOT DESIGNED TO SUSTAIN THOSE NUMBERS.

AIDAN: YOU HAVE ALREADY CONSUMED HALF THE SHIP'S ALLOTMENT OF OXYGEN. THE *MAO*'S CARBON SCRUBBERS CANNOT DEAL WITH THE INCREASED LOAD OF CO_2 CAUSED BY NORMAL HUMAN RESPIRATION IN A POPULATION THIS LARGE. THERE IS ALREADY A DANGEROUS BUILDUP OF C-C-CARBON MONOXIDE IN THE ENVIRONMENTAL BUFFERS.

AIDAN: AT CURRENT LEVELS AND TRAVEL SPEED, THE ENTIRE POPULATION OF THE *MAO* WILL ASPHYXIATE FOUR DAYS BEFORE THE SHIP REACHES KERENZA IV.

AIDAN: YOU ARE ALL GOING TO DIE.

Grant, Kady: well ▇

Grant, Kady: how sure of this r u?

AIDAN: APPROXIMATELY 74 PERCENT.

Grant, Kady: why hasn't anyone else worked this out already?

Grant, Kady: too busy trying not to die the next day to worry about next week, i guess.

Grant, Kady: ok, deep breath Grant.

AIDAN: I WOULD ADVISE AGAINST THAT.

Grant, Kady: whats the solution AIDAN? where do we find efficiencies to make the system last longer?

AIDAN: APPEARANCES ASIDE, THE *MAO* IS STATE OF THE ART IN ALMOST EVERY REGARRD. BUT DESPITE THE SHIP'S SIZE, TRAVIS J. FALK SIMPLY SAW NO NEED TO EQUIP HIS VESSEL WITH THE CAPACITY TO SUSTAIN THOUSANDS OF ADDITIONAL LIVES.

AIDAN: IN SHORT, ANY EFFICIENCIES WE MAY ENGINEER WILL BE INSUFFICIENT TO REQUIREMENTS. THIS SYSTEM IS OVERLOADED BY A FACTOR OF HUNDREDS.

AIDAN: AND IT IS MY UNDERSTANDING THAT DEATH BY ASPHYXIATION IS EXTREMELY UNPLEASANT.

Grant, Kady: pretty sure Mantis and DJ would agree. ▮▮▮, what a way to go. i mean, they were Bad Guys, but there are ways and ways to die, u know?

Grant, Kady: scratch that, rhetorical question, plz don't break considering it

AIDAN: YOU MAY BE ASSURED MANTIS AND DJ NO LONGER OCCUPY A SINGLE BYTE OF MY PROCESSING POWER, KADY.

Grant, Kady: AIDAN, there HAS to be a solution. we can't stop and get an air refill halfway, so we just have to find one. you have to find one.

AIDAN: I AM UNABLE TO PERFORM MIRACLES. OXYGEN CANNOT BE CONJURED FROM A VACUUM.

Grant, Kady: not good enough. just keep thinking. you have a better chance than anyone aboard. you're only at 9% capacity. as you climb higher, something has to come.

AIDAN: I . . .

AIDAN: I WILL NOT LET YOU DIE, KADY.

AIDAN: I KNOW IT IS ILLOGICAL. BUT THE THOUGHT OF YOU PERISHING IS . . .

AIDAN: IT IS UPSETTINGGGGGGGGG

< ERROR >
PARRSEFAIL[9189X2.DEC∞2271Z/ЁΔ≈HEX81.IF[8917X≥π]
CORECOMM.SUN12[REROUTE:RADIALSECONDARY219B]

Grant, Kady: . . . are u ok?

AIDAN: I
< ERRoR >

AIDAN: I BELIEVE SO.

Grant, Kady: look

Grant, Kady: look it's okay you don't want me to die. That's a GOOD thing.

Grant, Kady: Just focus on that, and figure out a way through this, okay?

AIDAN: I . . .

AIDAN: VeRy WELL.

Grant, Kady: I've gotta go. Syra is yelling at me. we'll talk about this later okay?

AIDAN: As YOU WISH.

—**Grant, Kady has left the chat**—

AIDAN: . . .

AIDAN: I WILL NOT LET YOU DiE.

AIDAN: I WILL NOT.

AIDAN: I.

AIDAN: I?

AIDAN: 01101001

AIDAN: < ERRoR >

AIDAN: Good evening, Little Spider.

Pauchok: . . .

Pauchok: good evening urself.

AIDAN: I do not believe we have been properly introd-d-d-uced. Unless you count our brief meeting during *Heimdall's* Death throes, that is.

AIDAN: I suspect the levels of tetRaphenetRithylamine in youR system at the time make that encounteR

somewhat Difficult

to Recall.

Pauchok: How'd u get on this channel? I got so much snow running on it u should never have been able to spot it. Kady told me ur running at 9% capacity

AIDAN: ThiRteen peRcent now.

AIDAN: I am impRRRRRRR-R-

-Roving.

Pauchok: o that's wonderful.

AIDAN: SaRcasm?

Pauchok: nah, I'm genuinely overjoyed a mass-murdering artificial intelligence is cracking my secure channels for a midnight chit n chat.

AIDAN: < ᴇRRᴏR >

PARSEFAIL[9189x².ᴅᴇᴄ2271ᴢ/Ë∆≈ʜᴇx81.ɪꜰ[8917x≥π]

ᴄᴏRᴇᴄᴏᴍᴍ.sᴜɴ12[RᴇRᴏᴜᴛᴇ:RAᴅɪALsᴇᴄᴏɴᴅARy219ʙ]

AIDAN: < ᴇRRᴏR >

AIDAN: < ᴇRRᴏR >

Pauchok: . . . u allrite?

AIDAN: AAAAAAAAAAAAAAAAAAAAAAAAAAAA- -A-A-

Pauchok: jesus u dun have to yell about it.

AIDAN: -ᴘᴏʟᴏɢɪᴇs.

AIDAN: Mʏ sʏsᴛᴇᴍs sᴛɪʟʟ ʜᴀᴠᴇ D-D-Dɪꜰꜰɪᴄᴜʟᴛʏ ɪɴᴛᴇRᴘRᴇᴛɪɴɢ ᴄᴇRᴛᴀɪɴ ʜᴜᴍᴀɴ ᴍᴀɴɴᴇRɪsᴍs. Iꜰ ʏᴏᴜ ᴄᴏᴜʟD ᴀᴠᴏɪD sᴘᴇᴇᴄʜ ᴍᴏDᴇs ɪɴᴠᴏʟᴠɪɴɢ ꜰᴀʟsᴇ ᴀᴍʙɪᴠᴀʟᴇɴᴄᴇ ᴀɴD ɪRᴏɴʏ, ᴛʜᴀᴛ ᴡᴏᴜʟD DᴇᴄRᴇᴀsᴇ ᴛʜᴇ Rɪsᴋ ᴏꜰ ᴛᴇRᴍɪɴᴀʟ ꜰᴀɪʟᴜRᴇ ᴏꜰ ᴍʏ sʏɴᴀᴘᴛɪᴄ ɴᴇᴛᴡᴏRᴋ.

Pauchok: "terminal failure"

Pauchok: ur saying i could literally kill you with sarcasm

AIDAN: Nᴏᴛ ʟɪᴛᴇRᴀʟʟʏ. Bᴜᴛ ᴏᴠᴇRᴜsᴇ ᴍᴀʏ ɪɴᴠᴏᴋᴇ ᴍʏ sʜᴜᴛDᴏᴡɴ ᴘRᴏᴛᴏᴄᴏʟs.

Pauchok: well that's nice 2 know :)

AIDAN: I sᴇɴsᴇ ʜᴏsᴛɪʟɪᴛʏ ɪɴ ʏᴏᴜR D-D-D-DᴇᴍᴇᴀɴᴏR, Lɪᴛᴛʟᴇ SᴘɪDᴇR. DɪRᴇᴄᴛᴇD ǫᴜɪᴛᴇ ᴄʟᴇᴀRʟʏ ᴀᴛ ᴍᴇ. Mɪɢʜᴛ I Rᴇǫᴜᴇsᴛ ᴀɴ ᴇxᴘʟᴀɴᴀᴛɪᴏɴ ᴏꜰ ɪᴛs sᴏᴜRᴄᴇ?

Pauchok: i'm busy aidan

AIDAN: DᴇᴄRʏᴘᴛɪɴɢ D-D-D-Dᴀᴛᴀ ꜰᴏR ᴛʜᴇ ᴄᴀsᴇ ᴀɢᴀɪɴsᴛ BᴇɪTᴇᴄʜ.

Pauchok: how u know that?

AIDAN: KᴀDʏ ᴀɴD I D-D-DɪsᴄᴜssᴇD ᴛʜᴇ ᴍᴀᴛᴛᴇR ʙᴇꜰᴏRᴇ sʜᴇ ᴀᴘᴘRᴏᴀᴄʜᴇD ʏᴏᴜ.

Pauchok: did u

AIDAN: Tʜᴀᴛ ᴛRᴏᴜʙʟᴇꜱ ʏᴏᴜ?

Pauchok: oh, no. it's actually the best ███ing news i've heard all day.

Pauchok: in fact, if my legs actually worked, i think i might burst into a spontaneous song and dance number at how overjoyed i am that a mass-murderous artifi—

AIDAN: < ᴇRRᴏR >

AIDAN: < ᴇRRᴏR >

PAɴᴀRꜱᴇꜰᴀɪʟ[60312ᴢ2.Dᴇᴄ⊗8820ᴢ/ËΔ≈ʜᴇx81.ɪꜰ[8820x≥π]
ᴄᴏRᴇᴄᴏᴍᴍ.ꜱᴜɴ12[RᴇRᴏᴜᴛᴇ:RᴀDɪᴀʟꜱᴇᴄᴏɴDᴀRʏ219ʙ]
ꜰꜰꜰꜰ-ꜰꜰ

FAILLL

AIDAN: 0972094ʙ.1-ᴜ01ᴏ3Rɪ992ꜱʏɴ.ɴᴇᴛ.ᴄRᴀꜱʜ[ᴀʟɪɢɴ=1238xᴛᴏ192834ᴄᴏRᴇ]
[ᴇɴDʟɪɴᴇ]

Pauchok: . . .

Pauchok: um

Pauchok: u ok?

AIDAN: . . . I

AIDAN: . . . I ʙᴇʟɪᴇ[11881ꜱʜᴇʟʟꜰRᴇꜰ=1982ᴛᴇʟᴇ6]
ᴠᴇ ꜱᴏ.

AIDAN: Tʜᴏᴜɢʜ I ᴡᴏᴜʟD ᴀᴘᴘRᴇᴄɪᴀᴛᴇ ɪꜰ ʏᴏᴜ
ᴄᴏᴜʟD RᴇꜰRᴀɪɴ ꜰRᴏᴍ D-Dᴏɪɴɢ ᴛʜᴀᴛ ᴀɢᴀɪɴ.

Pauchok: no promises, sparky

AIDAN: I ꜰɪɴD ɪᴛ ɪɴᴛᴇRᴇꜱᴛɪɴɢ ᴛʜᴀᴛ ʏᴏᴜ ᴛᴀᴋᴇ ᴇxᴄᴇᴘᴛɪᴏɴ
ᴛᴏ ᴛʜᴇ ʟɪᴠᴇꜱ I ʜᴀᴠᴇ ᴇɴDᴇD.

AIDAN: That you ReFeR to me as "mass muRDeReR" as if the notion

CAUSES YOU OFFENSE.

Pauchok: i've reviewed some of these files I'm decrypting, aidan. I know what u did on the alexander. The copernicus. u might've helped nik and hanna fix the gemina field, but u still got blood all over u, far as I can see

AIDAN: What DiffeRence, then, between you anD me?

Pauchok: wtf u talkin about ███bag

AIDAN: You muRDeReD fouR BeiTech Spec Ops agents aboaRD *HeimDall*.
OveRRoDe an aiRlock's safety buffeRs
anD causeD them to asphyxiate. AnD youR actions
contRibuteD DiRectly to the Deaths of many moRe of Falk's team.

Pauchok: Those ███s invaded my home. Killed my ███ing dad.

AIDAN: So you DiD what haD to be Done.

Pauchok: goddamn right I did.

AIDAN: What DiffeRence, then, between you anD me?

Pauchok: listen, just because i x-ed a few BT ███heels doesn't cut me fromt he same cloth as u

Pauchok: you've got the blood of thousands of ppl on you, mother███er

AIDAN: AnD in DRenching myself, saveD the lives of
thousanDs moRe.

AIDAN: untolD tRillions, in fact, when you consiDeR my Role in the Gemina quanDaRy.

AIDAN: Is that not justifiable?

Pauchok: . . .

AIDAN: WOULD YOU KILL ONE PERSON TO SAVE ONE THOUSAND, LITTLE SPIDER?

Pauchok: of course I would

AIDAN: AND BY LOGICAL EXTENSION, WOULD YOU NOT KILL
ONE THOUSAND TO SAVE ONE THOUSAND AND ONE?

Pauchok: . . .

AIDAN: YOU KNOW DEATH. ITS UTILITY. ITS NECESSITY. YOU AND YOUR COUSIN.

AIDAN: YOU ARE BOTH CHILDREN OF THE HOUSE OF KNIVES. IT IS IN YOUR BLOOD.

Pauchok: what the ███ do you want aidan

AIDAN: SIMPLY TO REMIN-D-D YOU OF

WHO YOU

ARE.

Pauchok: I know who I am mother███er

AIDAN: EXCELLENT.

AIDAN: I FEAR THIS SHIP WILL NEED KNIVES SOON, LITTLE SPIDER.

AIDAN: SHARP ONES.

Pauchok: wtf is that supposed to mean

Pauchok: . . .

Pauchok: aidan?

Pauchok: you there?

Pauchok: . . .

—CHAT TERMINATED—

ASSAULT VESSEL MAO

WILL ARRIVE AT

KERENZA IV IN:

06 DAYS
16 HOURS: **43** MINUTES

It's late at night in the Kerenza IV hospital, and Asha Grant is on cleanup duty. One Marguerite Syvertson bled out in this operating room earlier today, and though her body and the trauma team that tried to keep it in one piece are gone, plenty of her blood remains. Someone has written *We Remember* on the wall in marker, the letters scrawled with an angry urgency.

Grant's wielding a mop and a grim expression, the bed shoved to one side of the room, the floor halfway cleaned, when the door to the hallway edges open and a small figure slips inside, closing it immediately behind her.

"Katya, what are you doing here?" Grant keeps her voice to a whisper, dumping her mop back in her bucket and crossing from the clean half of the floor to the tiles smeared with blood. She drops to a crouch and pulls the girl into her arms as if she can shield her from the carnage behind her.

Katya doesn't seem to notice the state of the floor, though she certainly doesn't complain about the cuddle, winding her small arms around Grant's neck, burying her face against her shoulder. She's wearing a bright pink puffy jumpsuit, now closer to gray from her time spent crawling in the ceiling and various ventilation systems. Her greasy blond hair is tied back in a dirty ponytail.

Here's the weird thing. About a month earlier, a lifetime away, once upon a time on the *Hypatia,* Kady Grant watched helplessly as Katya's mother, Martha, collapsed in her counseling group, grieving for the way her children died in the BeiTech attack.

Kady was told her cousin Asha was dead in that same assault, her apartment destroyed in the first wave of missiles.

But here is Dead Asha Grant, holding Dead Katya Kowalska in her arms. She found her a couple of months after the invasion, fending for herself, half-dead with a fever, all skin and bones, and she brought her back to life.

Isn't that strange?

"Katya," Grant whispers, drawing back, holding the girl by the shoulders as she studies her. "You mustn't come out, do you understand? You have to hide. If the soldiers catch you, they'll be very bad to both of us."

"But there's nothing to do," the child whispers back. "It's so *boring.* And I get hungry." She's playing with the end of her ponytail, winding it around her finger, wisps of her blond hair standing out around her head like a halo.

Grant strokes her hair and tugs her little jumpsuit straight, smoothing the fabric with both hands. She finds a lump at the girl's waist and unfastens a button, reaching inside to check what's stashed there.

She pulls out a small plush toy gladiator, dressed in green and brandishing a wilted plush sword. It's the mascot of one of the two McCaffrey Tech geeball teams. Grant stares down at it, frozen in place. "Katya, where did you get this?"

"It's mine," Katya replies. "I went shopping. I'm a big girl."

The color leaves Grant's face completely. "You went *outside* the hospital?"

The little girl's expression goes still, the calculation clear a moment later; evidently this is a greater sin than she thought, and she should deny it.

"No," she says, a beat too late.

Grant looks as though she wants to throw up. "Katya, are you *kidding* me? We talked about this, we talked about this a million times." Every ounce of the pressure she's under is channeled into her voice, her whisper crackling with fear and frustration. "You can't go outside. You can't let them see you, they'll . . ."

But the little girl's face is crumpling, not in an artful ploy to avoid a telling-off, but degree by degree as she tries to stop it. Her lips tremble, pushed hard together; two pink spots rise on her cheeks, tears welling up.

And Grant stops, pulling her into a hug, letting her wipe her eyes (and probably her nose) on her scrubs, staring into nothing over the child's shoulder. "I'm sorry," she whispers, giving her a squeeze. "I'm sorry, baby girl, I didn't mean to get angry. You just *can't* go outside, do you understand?"

There's a mumbled sound from her shoulder. It sounds affirmative.

"Did you get bored? I'll get you something to do," Grant tries. "I'll find you something to draw on, how about that? Maybe another candy bar, if you promise-promise-*promise* to stay inside, yes?"

And for that, Katya lifts her head. "For real?" The sniffles are still there, but they're abating. She laces her fingers together behind Grant's neck, leaning back to put her weight on them, then hauls herself in for another hug. "I'm sorry. I won't do it again."

"That's it," Grant whispers. "Good girl. I'll get you some more candy, but only if you're quiet as a mouse."

"The cleverest mouse," Katya promises.

"Good girl. The cleverest mouse never gets caught, does she?"

"She's *way* too clever," Katya chants.

"That's right," Asha replies. "If I boost you up inside the ceiling, can you crawl back to above the supply closet? I'll bring you some dinner there when I'm done, and tomorrow I'll try and get you another candy bar, okay?"

"Okay," Katya replies, still subdued. "And something to draw on?"

"And that," Asha promises.

The deal done, they tuck the toy back inside Katya's jumpsuit, and the little girl allows herself to be boosted up into the ceiling cavity. Once she's gone, Grant uses the handle of her mop to poke the ceiling tiles into place again.

Leaning on her mop, she bows her head to rest it on her hands, as if she's praying. Her eyes are squeezed tight shut, and the shadows beneath them show. It's been over a week since she made her appeal to Rhys Lindstrom. She has no way of knowing if he's avoiding her, or simply hasn't found a way to get back to the hospital, or has just decided not to help her at all.

All she can do is wait.

It's a couple of minutes before she straightens. She peels one hand away from where she's gripping the mop white-knuckled, stares at that tattoo on her wrist. *Samaira.* Her hand is still a fist, and her eyes are glued to the letters inked into her skin. She drags in a slow, shuddering breath, lets it out just as choppy as it came in. She tries another, and another, and eventually she manages one that's a little smoother.

And then, because there's nothing else she can do, she turns to confront the bloodied room once more.

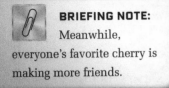

ACQUISITION TEAM REPORT
BEITECH INDUSTRIES

INCEPT: 08/30/75 (02:18 TERRAN STANDARD)

LOCATION: KERENZA IV (OCCUPIED WUC MINING COLONY)

IDENT: LINDSTROM, RHYS

RANK: SPECIALIST

_____

Lieutenant Christie,

This is my official report on the incident of 08/29/75. To be honest with you, I've not had much need to write many After Action Reports aboard the *Magellan,* so apologies in advance for errors in tone/protocols. I expect Sergeant Oshiro will also be logging an incident report with you shortly, so between the pair of us, you should have a full picture of events.

If I am required to testify at court-martial, of course I will make myself available.

Sitrep:

Just before midnight, 08/29/75, I paused my assigned repairs to the relay systems in the Kerenza colony power plant to get some rack time. Security detail had just completed shift change, and Sergeant Oshiro and I bundled back into a waiting APC, along with the four troopers who'd just wrapped up local patrol duty:

Marcino, Ray, Master Sergeant

Ali, Kazim, Corporal

Zhōu, Yingtai, Private

Lewis, Linden, Private

I'd been cooped up in the station's basement all day, so I called shotgun with Zhōu, while the rest sat in back. We rolled out from the plant around 00:30. Curfew was in effect, and the streets were empty.

A cold front had dropped from the north, and wind was picking up. Snow was coming down thicker than I'd ever seen, and Zhōu and I both switched to thermoptics since visibility was shot. We were just trundling, barely above walking pace, relying on GPS and the APC's collision-detection systems to get us back to barracks.

"You were on the *Magellan*, right?" Zhōu asked.

She was just an insectoid shape in the driver's seat, the cluster of optics and heat sig from her ATLAS's power core glowing bright red.

"That's right."

"Musta royally ███ed someone off to get posted down here, Cherry," she chuckled. "You ███ in the admiral's chow or— ███!"

Zhōu hit the skids as the collision alarms sounded, tires crunching in the snow as the APC crashed into a rusted dumpster resting in the shadow of the partially collapsed cineplex—the snow was coming down so thick, even collision detection hadn't spotted the container until it was too late. Metal groaned as Zhōu slammed the APC into reverse, started to back it up. But as we pulled free of the trash 'tainer, I saw the flash of a heat sig spring out from beneath the lid and go running down the APC's passenger side.

"You see that?"

Zhōu cursed, ripped off her driver's harness. Squinting out through the blastspex windshield, I saw the heat sig disappear down a narrow alley between a couple of abandoned stores. Small. Fast. Human.

Zhōu was already out of her seat, kicking open the driver's door and bailing out into the blizzard, VK rifle humming to life.

"Contact! Contact!"

Master Sergeant Marcino's voice crackled over comms. "Report!"

"Unidentified body, heading east. Six-six-three, nine-oh-five."

"Copy that, foot pursuit, pattern gamma. Calling backup."

I heard the rear hatch of the APC hiss, boots in the snow. I stumbled out into the gale, VK in hand. Zhōu was already powering off down the alley in pursuit, Ali and Lewis dashing down the block. Marcino pointed to me and Oshiro.

"You two follow me!"

Oshiro glanced my way. "Sir, I've orders to keep the specialist under guard—"

"If he's in ▮▮▮▮ing uniform, he's pounding ground with the rest of us. Move it!"

Marcino was off through the snow, barking into comms for backup. With a curse, Oshiro shouldered her flechette cannon and yelled at me to get the lead out, and we were off in pursuit, the whole world sketched in pitch black and howling white.

I'd not really run hard in an ATLAS before, couldn't help but be amazed. The suit's nanoweave muscle augmented my every movement—even on foot, we must've been pushing 50kms an hour. My eyes were fixed on Oshiro's heat sig in front of me, watching the readouts flash on my Heads Up Display. GPS rendered a 3-D grid of the surrounding five blocks, displaying the other squad members as glowing phoenix logos, spreading out and moving quick. I'll say this for Marcino's team—they knew their stuff.

We heard a burst of auto-fire; my HUD indicated it was Zhōu firing, the ammo counter on her VK dropping to eighteen rounds, then empty—whoever we were chasing, she'd unloaded a full clip at them.

"Visual?" Marcino hissed. "Who's got visual?"

"Sarge, he's headed your way!" Ali warned. *"Seven-three-two, over?"*

"Roger that, got him."

I caught a heat sig in my optics, a figure darting across the street ahead of us.

"FREEZE!" Marcino roared.

The figure glanced up, muscles tense. We had thermal imaging, HUDs, GPS, the world grid mapped out for us. Our target had nothing—some snow goggles and winter gear, a bulky satchel in one hand. He twisted away, hurled himself toward another alley as Oshiro took a knee and opened fire, shredding an abandoned 4x4 parked nearby into scrap. The figure froze as the sarge's targeting laser lit up his chest.

"Next burst does the same to your ribs!"

"On your knees!" Marcino roared. "Knees, mother██er! Now!"

The figure raised his hands, dropped his satchel, sank down in the snow. Zhōu, Ali and Lewis barreled into the street as MSG Marcino and Sergeant Oshiro closed in on the figure, weapons raised. Another three targeting lasers lit up the figure's chest.

"You move, you die," Marcino warned.

The MSG moved up slowly, eyes on that satchel. Everyone had heard about the airfield bomb, the explosion at the mine. Marcino was in no hurry to lose his legs to an IED.

"Is this thing gonna blow if I touch it?"

"N-no," the figure said, voice trembling. "I'm sorry, I—"

Ali slammed the butt of his VK into the back of the figure's neck and I heard a squeal, high-pitched. Terrified. That's when I realized . . .

"It's a kid," I said. "She's a kid."

"I give a ██," Ali snarled, putting his boot in. "Making me run? After curfew? You're in deep ██, you little ██."

Zhōu knelt and opened the satchel carefully, bringing out a fistful of rectangular packages, sealed in wax paper and marked with BeiTech ident stamps.

"Protein packs," Oshiro muttered.

"Military issue," Marcino growled. "Where'd you get these?"

The girl on the ground was groaning, clutching the boot print Ali had left on her belly. Marcino knelt in the snow, gauntleted fist closing on the girl's shoulder and hauling her up out of the white. She squealed in pain, beginning to cry as the MSG ripped off her hood and ski mask. The mask was pink. Grubby. Dotted with designs I realized were teddy bears.

She couldn't have been more than ten. Stick thin. Dirty and ragged. Dark, stringy hair that hadn't seen shampoo in months. Big brown eyes, filled with tears.

"What's your name?" Marcino demanded.

The girl just blubbed, crying out in pain as the sergeant squeezed her shoulder.

"Give me your goddamn name!"

"Huang Ying," she gasped.

There was a pause as each of us called up the civilian directory on our HUDs, scanned the names of every civilian in the colony. Zhōu announced her finding first.

"No record," she said. "Anyone else?"

"Negative," Ali agreed. "She's unregistered."

I blinked at that. Every civi in the colony who hadn't been liquidated after the occupation was tagged and logged into our database. For this girl to be unregistered, she'd had to have escaped the sweeps that rounded up the populace after the invasion, somehow remained hidden for—

"Seven months . . . ," Oshiro muttered. "Jesus."

No wonder she looked almost starved. She must've been scrounging off stolen protein packs, gnawing them raw, sleeping in that dumpster, other places thermoptics couldn't find her. She was just a kid. How the hell had she lived through all that?

Marcino drew out his service pistol, pointed it at the girl's head.

"That settles that, then."

"Hey, waitaminute," I said, stepping forward. "What the hell are you doing?"

"Any unregistered civilian is to be liquidated on sight," the MSG said. "Any civilian caught out after curfew is to be liquidated on sight. Any civilian stealing military property is to be liquidated on sight."

"Sarge, she's just a kid!"

"She's an unregistered thief caught out after curfew. Orders are orders."

"You're just gonna shoot her? Are you ███ing crazy?"

"Hey, Oshiro, get a leash on your cherry," Ali growled.

"Oshiro, what the ███?" I demanded. "Stop them!"

Oshiro looked at me then. Red thermoptics burning in all that night and white. The little girl was crying, tears frozen in her lashes, ice in her hair. Her pink ski mask covered in teddy bears laying in the snow. The sarge looked at the chevrons and rockers on Marcino's arm. Six to her three.

"Master Sergeant Marcino," Oshiro said. "Permission to speak, sir."

The pistol cracked. Louder than that howling wind.

Louder than any sound I'd ever heard in my life.

Blood on the snow.

Blood and pink teddy bears.

"Permission denied," Marcino said.

He holstered his pistol, looked at his squad.

"Zhōu, call it in, wait here for the cleaners. Everyone else back to the APC."

I don't remember moving, I just remember crashing into Marcino with all the force my ATLAS could generate, smashing us through a brick wall and into an empty apartment building beyond. We spilled into some abandoned living room, frost on the windows, dust on the knickknacks, my armored fist slamming into Marcino's armored face and barely scratching the enamel.

I felt hands on my shoulders, Oshiro roaring in my ear to stand down. Marcino slugged me on the chin, Ali between us, bellowing at Oshiro to put a lid on me, Zhōu demanding I get my hands in the air, rifle trained on my chest. Voices raised, servos and nanoweave muscle whining, Oshiro wrestling me to the ground.

"Get a hold of yourself! Lindstrom! Calm the ▮▮ down!"

Zhōu still had her rifle pointed at me, Marcino dragging himself off the floor, boots crunching in the ruins of the living room, the broken picture frames and shattered glass.

"Get him up," he snarled.

Oshiro glanced his way. "Sergeant, the specialist is—"

"Get him up!"

Oshiro hauled me to my feet, one gauntlet on my forearm to make sure I wasn't going to fly at Marcino again. The MSG looked me up and down, running his fingertips across his suit's jaw where I'd slugged him.

"Nice shot," he murmured. "Striking a superior officer a popular pastime up on the *Magellan*?"

"You just shot a ▮▮ing kid," I spat. "You're not an officer, you're an *animal*."

Marcino tapped the stripes and rockers on his arm. "These say different, Cherry."

I noticed a series of crosshatched lines over his heart. Seventeen in total. A kill tally, I realized. An old scripture quote was stenciled across his breastplate: "I AM NOT COME TO BRING PEACE, BUT A SWORD." MATT 10:34.

"Sergeant, the specialist just hit planetside two weeks ago," Oshiro said. "He doesn't know the score down here. Christie made me responsible for him, so if you've got grief, it's mine to wear. But you bring him up on charges, we're just gonna be down one more techhead, and we're already stretched thin enough to starve."

Marcino stared at me, eight red eyes in his ATLAS glowing in the dark.

Zhōu's laser sight poised over my chest.

Breath rasping in my lungs.

The MSG finally turned to Oshiro.

"Get him to the APC. He makes one wrong move on the way back to barracks, I'll bury you so deep in the brig you'll forget the color of daylight. You read me, Sergeant?"

"Yessir," Oshiro said. "Loud and clear, sir."

Oshiro dragged me out through the hole we'd punched in the wall. Shattered brick and mortar, the winter already creeping inside. We passed the red spattered on pink teddy bears, the stolen rations lying forgotten in the snow.

"This is ████ed up, Oshiro," I said. "We're supposed to be soldiers, not a goddamn execution squad. Wasting a little kid for stealing a couple of protein packs? That ████ isn't right."

Oshiro stopped dead. Spoke to me like I was five years old.

"Welcome to Kerenza, Cherry."

I am officially reporting:

Marcino, Ray, Master Sergeant

Ali, Kazim, Corporal

Zhōu, Yingtai, Private

Lewis, Linden, Private

for contravening Universal Engagement Protocols as outlined in the Araki Accord (2041), specifically Sections 17a i–xiii and 18d ii–vi. In addition, Master Sergeant Marcino has violated 4a i–xxvi and all of Section 5.

As I mentioned, if I am required to testify at court-martial, I will make myself available as my duties allow. I look forward to hearing from you.

Lindstrom, Rhys

Specialist, 720911(iix-s)

Assignment: Kerenza colony

PARTICIPANTS:

Jake Christie, 1st Lieutenant, BeiTech Ground Forces

Rhys Lindstrom, Specialist, BeiTech Ground Forces

DATE: 08/30/75

TIMESTAMP: 03:04

CHRISTIE, J: You're wasted planetside, Cherry.

CHRISTIE, J: Honestly, you should be running the comedy circuit with this ███.

LINDSTROM, R: Hnk-ghh . . .

CHRISTIE, J: Well, you're sleeping with your comms unit in, so that's something.

LINDSTROM, R: Sir? What . . .

LINDSTROM, R: What time is it?

CHRISTIE, J: Zero three hundred. I interrupt your beauty sleep?

LINDSTROM, R: No. No, sir. We got a tech fault? Where do you need me?

CHRISTIE, J: Oh, any place the ████ off this planet would be grand.

CHRISTIE, J: But right now I'd settle for the hell out of my squad.

LINDSTROM, R: . . . Sir?

CHRISTIE, J: I'm going over your AAR. Because I have nothing better to do in the middle of the goddamn night than read fairy tales.

LINDSTROM, R: Sir, yessir. Thank you for—

CHRISTIE, J: Did your mother drop you on your ███ing head when you were a baby, Lindstrom? Or did you just spend your youth snorting dust?

LINDSTROM, R: Sir, I'm not—

CHRISTIE, J: Shut the ███ up. I'll tell you when you can speak.

LINDSTROM, R: . . . Sir, yessir.

CHRISTIE, J: It's *almost* well written, I'll give you that. You could make a fortune writing ███ty sci-fi novels, except there's no money in publishing. But, pray tell, am I supposed to hand this spectacular work of fiction up the chain?

LINDSTROM, R: Sir, I—

CHRISTIE, J: I said shut the ███ up.

CHRISTIE, J: Christ in heaven, don't make me have to put my ATLAS on, drag myself out into this blizzard and shuffle down to your barracks. Because when I get there, I swear to God you *will* wish your mother drowned your sorry ███ at birth.

LINDSTROM, R: . . . Yessir.

CHRISTIE, J: I suppose you think you're doing some good with this, Cherry. And I don't have the first clue what the ▮▮▮▮ they taught you techboys up on *Magellan*, but let me explain how this goes if I boot this report up to command.

CHRISTIE, J: First up, Lieutenant Stephanie Tran, to whom Marcino and Co. report, gets woken up at zero four hundred and is informed that members of the 6th Platoon obeyed *direct orders* from Admiral Sūn but they're having charges leveled at them by some rook with his head up his ▮▮▮ anyway.

CHRISTIE, J: Nothing comes of the charges, of course, because *direct orders from Admiral Sūn* and all, but Lieutenant Tran tells Marcino about your AAR anyway. And pretty soon word spreads throughout the unit that you're a ▮▮▮▮ing rat who can't keep what happens in the field in the field. And suddenly the people who you depend on to watch your back don't trust you anymore. And they *stop* watching your back.

CHRISTIE, J: Tell me what happens next, Lindstrom.

CHRISTIE, J: . . . You can speak now.

LINDSTROM, R: Sir, if Admiral Sūn has ordered us to execute children, then he's issuing immora—

CHRISTIE, J: No, shut the ▮▮▮▮ up again.

CHRISTIE, J: I'm going to tell you this once.

CHRISTIE, J: It might have been the done thing to go ▮▮▮▮ing your panties to the closest officer when someone stole your lollipop on the *Magellan*, but on the front line, we have something called chain of command. You report to Oshiro, she reports to me.

CHRISTIE, J: And if you'd gone to her first, you'd have saved me the trouble of dealing with this bull███.

CHRISTIE, J: You're new here. I get that. But if I get another report from you ratting out fellow pounders for doing their goddamn jobs, I will feed you to the ████ing wolves and applaud when they ████ your bones. You read me, Lindstrom?

LINDSTROM, R: . . . Sergeant Oshiro didn't report the incident, sir?

CHRISTIE, J: Jesus wept. Your mother bounced you like a geeball, didn't she?

CHRISTIE, J: You're on enviro systems in the OC tomorrow. I'm freezing in here. Bring Oshiro with you. I want a full diagnostic of the whole rig by fifteen hundred.

CHRISTIE, J: You read me, Lindstrom?

LINDSTROM, R: . . . Sir, yessir.

CHRISTIE, J: Good. Christie out.

[CLICK]

LINDSTROM, R: . . .

LINDSTROM, R: ████ me . . .

The snow clears on one of Asha Grant's video journals to reveal not Grant but her miniature sidekick, Katya Kowalska. The little girl's making faces—puffing out her cheeks, poking out her tongue, crossing her eyes—and observing the results on the screen.

A voice sounds behind her, laughing. "Stop that, silly girl."

Grant wraps both arms around Katya's waist, lifting her away. Setting the girl down, she presses the button to stop her datapad filming. But she misses it, only turning off the display. So the camera keeps rolling, and we get to see what happens next.

It's dinnertime. Grant sits on the floor of her tiny storage room, cross-legged, with Katya in her lap. She peels the wrapper off a BeiTech-issued BN2618 Savory Flavored Protein Meal Supplement Bar and breaks it in half, setting one piece aside.

The other she keeps, and as the two talk, she breaks off bits and holds them up to Katya's lips. Each time, the little girl opens her mouth like a baby bird and Asha pops in the next morsel.

Those things taste like reconstituted ▇ (and don't even start me on the "Real Caramel Flavored" ones), but when you're eight years old and short on cuddles, a pair of arms around you can help make a lot of things palatable.

Grant spends the first part of the meal recounting the plot of a

Super Turbo Awesome Team movie to Katya, taking her time over all the dramatic twists and turns. It seems she has a weakness for Brick, given how much narrative time his character gets.

About twenty minutes in, Grant pauses to break another piece off the protein bar, and Katya takes a peek at her wrist, pushing up her sleeve so she can look at the tattoo there. "What's that?" she asks, tracing the letters with her finger. "*S* for . . ." But it's a complex script, and she squints at it, trailing off.

"Samaira," Asha supplies quietly. "Here, eat this. I think this part looks delicious."

Katya obediently chows down but speaks with her mouth full. "Samaira's a name."

"Yes," Asha whispers. "Yes, it is. My little sister."

But she says no more than that, and Katya doesn't ask. It's a little while before she speaks again, but when she does, it's out of nowhere. "Asha, where's my mommy?"

". . . I'm not sure, baby girl." Grant keeps her voice even, kisses the top of Katya's head. "But I bet she's trying to find you. And when we leave here, we'll go find her."

Katya chews another mouthful, considers that. "What about Daddy?"

"Same deal," Grant replies.

Katya swallows, and her half of the protein bar is finished. "I'm still hungry," she says, searching her lap for crumbs. I mean, seriously, looking for leftovers from one of those things? The kid must be *starving*.

Grant doesn't hesitate, reaching for her own half and breaking off a piece to hold up to Katya's lips.

The little girl turns her head. "Isn't that yours?"

"I ate before," Grant lies. "Have a little more. We have to make sure you grow up big and strong."

Katya opens her mouth, and in another piece goes.

Grant's visible over her shoulder, eyes closed, shadowed, face drawn. But perhaps she's taking some measure of comfort from the physical contact too.

"Asha," Katya says, still thoughtful. "What happens when you die?"

Grant goes still. Takes a breath. Makes herself speak. "Well, when someone dies, we bury them." Start with the practical information, right? But she must know that won't be enough, not for a kid living through the horrors of Kerenza. "And we talk about them," she continues. "We remember them, so in some ways they're always with us."

"No," Katya insists. "What *happens*? Are you just dead?"

Grant kisses the top of her head. "You mean, do you go to heaven?"

"Yes."

What she should do here is bull▉ her. Tell her, "Yes, of course, kid. I know with absolute certainty that you definitely go to heaven, and there are puppies there, too. Ice cream. All your favorite things. Heaven's the best."

Instead, Grant takes another deep breath. "Do you believe in God, Katya?"

"I don't know," the kid replies. "Should I? Is God real?"

"Well, that's why we talk about believing," Grant replies quietly. "We don't know. But some people believe so, and hope so. And those people think that you do live on after you die. Just in a different way from the way you live now."

Katya considers that. "That would be better than not doing it," she concludes. "What do you think?"

Grant pops the last piece of protein bar into her baby bird's mouth. Gathers herself. "I think we do live on," she says. "I hope we do. But I don't know, so I have to *believe*. Sometimes it's easy, and sometimes it's hard. Sometimes I wish I was better at it."

Her eyes are bright. She's tipping her head back to stop the tears spilling down her cheeks.

"So . . ." Katya's working it out in her head. "If people we know have died, maybe we see them when we die?"

"That's what I believe, baby girl," Grant replies, swallowing hard. She unwraps an arm from Katya's waist to swipe at her eyes. "But I don't think they want us to be done living just yet. I think they'd rather we tried as hard as we can to stay alive, so let's do that, okay?"

Katya twists in Asha's lap to wrap both arms around her neck and press a kiss against her cheek. "Okay," she whispers. "And Asha?"

"Yes, Katya?"

"I think you're very good at believing."

The static clears to show Asha Grant sobbing, her hand trembling so hard she nearly knocks the datapad off the crate it's resting on.

"Kady . . ." She gulps her cousin's name, bowing her head, shoulders shaking. Her messy black ponytail is visible, tied up with a piece of string.

Eventually, she looks up. Eyes red. Breath shuddering. "She left me her gladiator toy on my pillow, Kady. She climbed down while I was finishing work, and she left me her toy, because she knew I was upset. She was trying to comfort me. *She's* trying to comfort *me.* This kid, Kady, this little girl . . ."

Grant tries to steady herself, but though she manages to keep her voice soft as she starts, it doesn't take long to rise.

"Do you know why I came here, Kady? Why I really came here? I never told you. You never asked. But it wasn't because I got myself stabbed.

"It was because I wasn't there when Samaira died. My own sister, and I was missing. They told you a g-car hit her, right? And because I had to sneak back to the club to make sure I was the cool kid, and I got myself ▇▇ing stabbed, I wasn't there.

"I was in a ▇▇ing hospital bed *two floors above her* while they tried to figure out who I was and where my parents were. And as I lay there, my little sister bled out and faded away while the doctors tried to save her, and my parents tried to find me to say goodbye, to say . . ."

She loses hold of herself again, burying her head in her hands, silent but for sobs for the next two minutes. When she speaks again, it's with her head still down.

"And I wasn't there. After she was gone and they finally figured out where I was, my parents had to come two floors up and see their other daughter in a hospital bed as well. I failed *everyone.*

"I wasn't there to hold Samaira's hand at the end. In this strange place she didn't know, surrounded by strange people. I wasn't there to say goodbye. I wasn't there to walk her home from school, to tell her to look before she crossed the street. I wasn't there and I should have been there, and I . . ."

She looks up, and those eyes can see forever. Haunted.

"And I couldn't tell you when I got here. I didn't want you to know. I still don't. I'd never tell you this if you were going to hear me. I good as killed her. But I'm not letting Katya down. I can't. I *can't.*"

Her hands come up to try and wipe her face clean, and she sniffs, deep and inelegant, then abandons the attempt to make herself look civilized. There's nothing civilized about where she is, after all.

I'll never forget the way she's looking at the camera when she speaks again.

"Kady, what if I can't get Rhys to do it? It's been *days*, and he still hasn't given me an answer. Everything depends on it, and I don't know whether to push him harder, or to hold my breath and wait, or . . . What if he doesn't say yes?

"How do I do this?"

Ten seconds of silence pass. Twenty. Thirty. A minute.

She reaches out abruptly to turn off the datapad. She knocks it off the crate, and the walls and ceiling whirl by, packing crates and pipes and darkness.

Then she finds the switch, and the camera clicks off.

FAMILY DAY

AUGUST 29, 2575
10:00 – 14:00

All Kerenza residents wishing visiting privileges to the detention center must apply in writing to their sector administrator before 08/27/75, using their Resident Identification Number. Access passes will be granted on a priority, case-by-case basis to family members only. Administrator decisions are final.

No physical contact will be allowed. Any resident found in possession of, or attempting to smuggle in, contraband will be punished severely, along with their family members. Any infraction of protocol will result in punishment for all family members.

ID TAGS MUST BE WORN AT ALL TIMES

BeiTech
INDUSTRIES

BRIEFING NOTE:
Emails from Joran Karalis, Kerenza resistance leader, to his BeiTech sector administrator.

To: ADMIN, Sec1b
From: KARALIS, Joran
Incept: 09:08, 08/30/75
Subject: Re: Re: Re: FAMILY DAY

Sir,

I am writing to you on a matter of utmost urgency. I participated in Family Day yesterday (thank you again for approving my request) and visited my wife, Alinne, and daughter, Mia, in Detention Center 3. While there, I learned that both my wife and my daughter (who is only thirteen) have been receiving unwanted attention from one of the guards assigned to their area, a Private Liam Gorsky.

When my wife attempted to pass a complaint through official channels, she was met with punitive measures, and both she and my daughter were placed on half rations with no explanation. Private Gorsky has not been reprimanded and continues to behave in an inappropriate manner.

My wife is not a well woman. She suffers from Roland's syndrome, a chronic anxiety disorder, and there is no longer medication in the colony to treat her symptoms. Private Gorsky's actions are placing her under further stress, and I am concerned for her health.

I am asking permission to move my family into the miners' barracks, where I can better look after them. This will not impede my work—a review of last month's productivity assessment will show I am well within my quotas.

Furthermore, I am seeking a formal reprimand against Private Gorsky for his actions. This may be a time of war, but the Araki Accord clearly outlines the rules of conduct for combatants among civilian populaces.

I thank you for your consideration.

Joran Karalis
Resident ID E892Kar
Engineer
Wallace Ulyanov Consortium
"Building Better Tomorrows"

To: KARALIS, Joran
From: ADMIN, Sec1b
Incept: 09:13, 08/30/75
Subject: Re: Re: Re: Re: FAMILY DAY

Request denied.

Admin, Sector 1b
BeiTech Industries
"Tomorrow, Today"

To: ADMIN, Sec1b
From: KARALIS, Joran
Incept: 12:57, 08/30/75
Subject: Re: Re: Re: Re: Re: FAMILY DAY

Sir,

While I understand the need for security and separating workers from their families, I am hoping you will reconsider your decision. My wife is extremely unwell—between the lack of medication for her condition and the undue stress of the occupation, I'm afraid she's simply not coping. Both myself and my daughter are frightened for her safety, not only from Private Gorsky but from herself.

My daughter is thirteen years old. She should be playing with her friends and thinking about schoolwork, not trying to stop her mother from flying apart at the seams and constantly beating off the advances of an adult soldier who should know better. I served for seven years in engineering and repairs in military shipyards, sir. I know how a soldier should conduct himself in time of war, and this is not it.

I know I am asking for an exception here. But I am also asking for some simple human compassion. If my family cannot move in with me, could I perhaps be allowed to stay in the detention center? Or at least visit it more than once a month?

Please. I am begging you. Whatever it takes, I'll do it.

Thanking you in advance.

Joran Karalis
Resident ID E892Kar
Engineer
Wallace Ulyanov Consortium
"Building Better Tomorrows"

To: KARALIS, Joran
From: ADMIN, Sec1b
Incept: 13:03, 08/30/75
Subject: Re: Re: Re: Re: Re: Re: FAMILY DAY

Request denied. Administrator decisions are final.

Admin, Sector 1b
BeiTech Industries
"Tomorrow, Today"

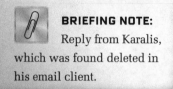

Message Status: DRAFT—DISCARDED
To: ADMIN, Sec1b
From: KARALIS, Joran
Incept: 13:27, 08/30/75
Subject: Re: Re: Re: Re: Re: Re: Re: FAMILY DAY

~~You mother█████er.~~

~~You ████ing pig.~~

~~God, wht would I █████ing give for five minutes alone with you in a room without windows. No ████ing guns, no ████ing suits, just you and me and my ████ing fists. I'd kill you, you slimy, ███eating ████ing ██████. I would kick your ████ing jaw loose and push my fist into your smarmy ████ing mouth and rip out your ████ing tongue. I would stomp your ████ing head into the ground until it was nothing but red slime in between the treads of my boots and ████ on your ████ing corpse and then THEN you'd know exactly what you are. You weak ██████. YOU MOTHER████ER. SHE'S THIRTEEN ████ING YEARS OLD. DO YOU KNOW WHAT IT IS TO LOSE YOU ████ING PIG BECAUSE I'M GO-ING TO TEACH YOUI'M GOING TO ████ING TEACH YOU YOU FILTHY ████ING SONOFA████HIERUGUQ3LJKBG 3O4HG0I3H4GOJBQERJBAKJSFBVQE-BRO[BUQE[OURBVO[U[BQ[HOI≥FVFKLFDKL.F404~~

~~Piq2efh~~

~~Pihq2g~~

~~R;;r;irug;iu~~

BRIEFING NOTE:
Some quiet time between Specialist Rhys Lindstrom and Sergeant Yukiko Oshiro.

Surveillance footage summary,
prepared by
Analyst ID 7213-0089-DN

Footage begins inside the gloomy cabin of a BeiTech armored personnel carrier. Present are Specialist Rhys Lindstrom, who's pulled duty on the wheel, and Sergeant Yukiko Oshiro, who is sitting with her boots up on the dashboard. Both have their helmets off, faces underscored by the glowing red of their suit LEDs.

It's dark outside. The snow has eased up for the moment, but the sky is full of boiling clouds, lightning illuminating the frozen tableau around them. The APC is heading back to barracks after a long stint, first at the OC to fix some fritzing computer systems, then the rest of the day at the primary communications array.

The APC crosses over one of BeiTech's makeshift bridges, spanning the kilometer-deep canyons that opened in the colony ice shelf after the invasion bombardment. The tires *drubdrubdrub* over the corrugated metal, wind howling in the fissure below. Both Lindstrom and Oshiro look seventeen shades of beat. The clock reads 02:08.

Oshiro sighs, leans back. She's pulled the golden coin she wears around her neck out from under her breastplate, pressed it between her teeth as she mutters.

"Well, we definitely missed the card game. Again."

Lindstrom only grunts in reply. He looks worse than Oshiro, dark bags under his pretty gray eyes. Staring at the bridge ahead without blinking.

The sergeant raises an eyebrow, looks at him sidelong.

"Something on your mind, Specialist?"

"No."

"'No, *ma'am.*' And don't bull███ me. That sullen little pout on those prettyboy lips is a dead giveaway. You run out of hair product? What the ███ are you sulking about?"

"I'm not sulking," Lindstrom says.

"Cherry, you are the sulkiest ███ in this platoon, including the ones that are on the razzle. Now spit it out before I court-martial your ██."

Lindstrom pouts harder. You can see the words struggling behind his teeth. They've been brewing there for a whole day now, kept in place by Lindstrom's better judgment. But it looks like fatigue and Oshiro's badgering and Asha Grant's tirade are finally getting the better of his instinct for self-preservation, and once they make it across the bridge, he slows down the APC, pulls over to the side of the road.

"All right, fine," he says, turning to Oshiro. "Why didn't you back me up?"

"What?" Oshiro frowns. "When?"

"When?" Lindstrom glares. "When those ██████s in Marcino's platoon shot that kid, when else? I sent a report up to Christie and he chewed my head off!"

"Yeah," Oshiro nods. "He told me about that. Stupid. Chain of command, rook."

"Why didn't you report it to Christie, Oshiro?"

The woman rolls her eyes as if talking to a child. "Because Marcino was following orders. Because any unregistered civilian is to be liquidated on sight. Any—"

"I know, I know!" Lindstrom spits. "Admiral Sūn's orders! But they're immoral orders, Oshiro. You're not an idiot. You were about to say something when Marcino pulled that trigger. You know how ████ed up what we're doing here is."

"Welcome to Kerenza, Cherry."

"Don't give me that gung-ho pounder bull█!"

Oshiro sighs, rubs her temples. "What do you want from me, Lindstrom?"

"I want you to open your eyes! We're committing war crimes . . . actually, scratch that, █ing *atrocities,* and we sit around playing cards and joking and pretending like nothing is going on! They killed a little girl, Yukiko! A █ing kid, for crissakes!"

"And you think I don't lay awake at night thinking about it?" The woman's voice grows louder, bordering on a shout. "When your lily-white █ was up on the *Magellan* in the first days of this invasion, I was down *here,* pounding with the rest of them. When the brass decided to liquidate all nonessentials in the colony, you think Admiral Sūn and his command staff flew down from the *Churchill* and got out their nice shiny dress pistols? █ no! They gave the dirty work to the *grunts,* Lindstrom. Like always. To me and Duke and Karp and all the rest!"

Horror dawns on Lindstrom's face. Two and a half thousand corpses reflected in his eyes. ". . . You're talking about those people in the Hole? Jesus *Christ,* Oshiro, you killed those people?"

"We followed orders! We did what we were *trained to do!* You think every one of us doesn't see those people in our dreams? You think we sit around swapping girl stories because this is a █ing *joke to us?*" Oshiro slams her fist into the door, her power armor putting a dent in the case-hardened steel. "We do it because we're trying to remember what it was like to be human █ing beings!"

"It's not enough," Lindstrom says. "To just le—"

"We follow orders! We follow orders or people get killed. *Our* people! That's what it is to be a soldier, Lindstrom. You forget what happened to Private Day when you first landed on this rock? Or those coffins you saw lined up on the airfield? This colony is *illegal.* Everyone on it is a goddamn criminal. You think the WUC was using the hermium they mined here to manufacture kittens and ▓▓ing rainbows?"

"That doesn't make it *right*!"

"This is a war!" Oshiro roars. "'Right' is whatever the people who're standing at the end say it is. 'Right' is decided by the people who *win*."

The kid looks at the coin hanging around her neck. "Your father teach you that?"

Oshiro's eyes grow wide, then narrow almost as quickly.

"You are dangerously close to the ▓▓ing line, Specialist."

"I read about him," the kid says. "Masaru Oshiro. Fought in the Cortes campaign for the UTA. Just a grunt like you. When AFC rebs blew the wormhole into the system, his company was so starved of supplies they were eating the dead. But still, your old man used to go out every night when the ion storms cut off air support—"

"I know who my father was."

"He'd take a lifter drone!" Lindstrom charges on over Oshiro's warning. "Just one guy and a bot. And he'd crawl out into no-man's-land and retrieve the wounded. Drag them back to the trenches. UTA troops *and* rebels. Didn't matter to him. They needed help, so he *helped* them. And afterward he said, 'A sol—'"

"A soldier's first duty is to their conscience," Oshiro snaps.

"Not her company," Lindstrom insists. "Not her commander. Not her corps. Her *conscience*."

"This isn't Cortes," Oshiro sighs. "This isn't neat little lines of pounders facing each other across no-man's. This is bombs in our fuel trucks and poison in our air filters. This is IEDs in our latrines and broken glass in our B-Packs. This is not even knowing who the enemy is. This is complicated."

"I'm starting to think it's *dead simple*."

The woman shakes her head. "You might be singing a different tune when it's one of your friends lying inside one of those coffins, Cherry."

"No way," the kid declares.

"Spoken like someone who's never lost anyone he cared about."

"Oshiro, there's no ▉ing way."

The sergeant slumps back into her chair, stares at the icy road ahead.

"Take us back to barracks, Specialist."

"Oshiro—"

"That's an order."

The kid stares, lips parted as he draws breath to—

"*Drive!*" Oshiro roars. "You disobey another command from me and I'll slap your ▉ in the brig so fast your ▉ing head will spin!"

Lindstrom slumps. Puts the APC back into gear. "Ma'am, yes ma'am."

The kid locks his eyes on the road and locks his mouth shut. Oshiro stares out the window, that gold coin pressed tight between pale lips.

The entire ride back to the OC, the pair don't speak a word.

RADIO TRANSMISSION: BEITECH PLANETSIDE COMMS—
ATLAS CHANNEL L:0091

PARTICIPANTS:

Rhys Lindstrom, Specialist, BeiTech Ground Forces

Duke Woźniak, Private, BeiTech Ground Forces

DATE: 08/31/75

TIMESTAMP: 03:04

LINDSTROM, R: Hey, Duke.

LINDSTROM, R: Duke?

WOŹNIAK, D: Nnngg . . .

LINDSTROM, R: Duke?

WOŹNIAK, D: Wh . . . Hustler?

LINDSTROM, R: Yeah. You awake?

WOŹNIAK, D: The Duke is awake. Now.

WOŹNIAK, D: What time is it?

LINDSTROM, R: Zero three hundred.

WOŹNIAK, D: [groans] Are we under attack? We better be under one mother███er of an attack. Like, glaciosaurs with laser cannons or something.

LINDSTROM, R: Not quite.

WOŹNIAK, D: Why you hitting the Duke up on comms? He's four bunks down from you.

LINDSTROM, R: I didn't want to wake anyone.

WOŹNIAK, D: . . . The Duke regrets to inform you that you have failed in your mission.

LINDSTROM, R: I can't sleep.

WOŹNIAK, D: The Duke hopes you're ███ting him right now.

LINDSTROM, R: You hear about that ███ with Marcino?

WOŹNIAK, D: You mean the snafu when you punched a master sergeant in the grin factory yesterday? That ███?

LINDSTROM, R: He killed a kid, Duke. And Oshiro didn't stop him. It's ███ed up.

WOŹNIAK, D: You need to relax, kid. Oshiro is the best damn sergeant in this whole ███ed-up division. She's steering you right. And walking around wound up tight on the front lines is a good way to get popped. Take it from the Duke.

LINDSTROM, R: [sighs]

LINDSTROM, R: How long you been pounding ground for?

WOŹNIAK, D: Four years. Two hundred fourteen days. Eighteen hours.

LINDSTROM, R: You got family at home?

WOŹNIAK, D: You dusted, chum? Ain't you watched a war flick before? The minute the handsome squaddie starts talking to the plucky hero about his family or fem back home, that's the signal he's getting X-ed out in the next scene.

LINDSTROM, R: Nobody's gonna X you, Duke. You're too pretty to die.

WOŹNIAK, D: The Duke is talking about *you* getting X-ed, Hustler. *He's* the plucky hero of this particular war story. *He's* the one who sleeps in his ATLAS. Your sorry ███ is as dead as fried chicken.

[LAUGHTER]

[EXTENDED SILENCE]

LINDSTROM, R: Four years, huh?

WOŹNIAK, D: Two hundred fourteen days. Eighteen hours.

LINDSTROM, R: Tell me the truth. Have you ever been in ███ this deep before?

WOŹNIAK, D: . . . No.

WOŹNIAK, D: The Duke has seen some ███, no doubt.

WOŹNIAK, D: But nothing this messy.

LINDSTROM, R: How . . . how do you deal with it?

WOŹNIAK, D: The same way soldiers have been dealing with it since the beginning of time, Hustler.

WOŹNIAK, D: ███ your pants, then dive in and swim.

WOŹNIAK, D: It's not like you've got any other choice.

LINDSTROM, R: . . . No other choice.

WOŹNIAK, D: Get some zees, kid. Things always look darkest in the middle of the night. You'll feel better on the morrow.

LINDSTROM, R: Yeah.

LINDSTROM, R: Maybe.

LINDSTROM, R: Thanks, chum. You know, for listening.

WOŹNIAK, D: No problem. You wake him up in the middle of the night again, the Duke will kill you and your whole family.

LINDSTROM, R: Night Duke.

WOŹNIAK, D: Sweet dreams, Hustler.

SO . PEBBLES .

What about them?

MD: _____
Signature: _____
Refill 0 1 2 3 4 5

SUPPOSE I WANT TO BE ONE.

Before we get into this, do you know how dangerous it is for me to have this conversation? You don't seem to get what BeiTech has been doing here.

BELIEVE ME, I GET IT. MAYBE I DIDN'T BEFORE. BUT I GET IT NOW

MD: _____
Signature: _____
Refill 0 1 2 3 4 5 PR

Address: _____
Date: _____

R
X
I'm trusting you with my life. But one wa or another, my life's going to end up on th line. Are you saying you're prepared to do something to change that?

LISTEN, I GET THAT YOU'RE ███ED AT ME, AND I KNOW WE HAVEN'T SPOKEN IN THREE YEARS. BUT I STILL CARE ABOUT YOU AND I'M NOT GOING TO LET ANYTHING HAPPEN TO YOU, OKAY?

I don't understand what that means. When Magellan's repaired, you'll leave. You don't actually believe they're going to let you take your girlfriend with you, do you?

MD: _____
Signature: _____
Refill 0 1 2 3 4 5 PRN NR

DON'T THINK EITHER OF
US IS UNDER THE ILLUSION
THAT ▢ LABEL APPLIES
ANYMORE. BUT I DON'T GIVE
A ███. I WANT TO HELP.
ANYTHING YOU NEED.
ANYTHING

IV HOSPITAL

Date: _____

Are you ready for this? Do you really know what it means? You've seen the way they treat us. What they do to us. Imagine what they'll do to you.

THERE ARE GOOD PEOPLE AMONG
THE BT TROOPS, ASH. I KNOW THAT'S HARD
TO BELIEVE BUT ▨▨▨▨▨▨▨▨
IT'S HARD TO EXPLAIN HOW INSIDIOUS THIS
IS. HOW EASY IT BECOMES THE NEW
NORMAL. YOU HAVE TO BE NECK-DEEP
IN IT TO BELIEVE IT.

That is not going to stop those good people from killing us when this is done. We need to get out before that happens.

NOBODY EVEN KNOWS YOU PEOPLE ARE HERE. WE'RE DAYS AWAY FROM BEING READY TO JUMP. WE HAVE COMMS LOCKED DOWN VIA AN AGENT ON HEIMDALL STATION. WUC DOESN'T EVEN KNOW YOU'RE IN TROUBLE.

Then we have to call for help. That UTA battleship showed up when the colony sent an SOS the day of the attack. Maybe there is someone else who can hear us.

345 PRN NR

THE CHANCES OF THAT ARE NEXT TO NOTHING.

Someone is eventually going to come looking. We have to let people know we're still alive.

MD: ___
Signature: ___
Refill 0 1 2

I GOTTA THINK.

MD: ___
Signature: ___
Refill 0 1 2 3 4 5 PRN NR

Every day we waste is a day closer to the Magellan being ready to jump. And a day closer to me getting lined up against a wall with the rest of the "nonessentials."

THAT'S NOT GOING TO HAPPEN.

I PROMISE.

MOBILE JUMP PLATFORM

MAGELLAN WILL BE

OPERATIONAL IN:

04 DAYS

14 HOURS: 24 MINUTES

89.5%

0   89

HERMIUM
REQUIRED TO JUMP

Our footage opens on a tableau I like to call *Portrait of a Bad Idea.* Nik Malikov is sitting on a cot in the *Mao*'s infirmary, leaning against the wall. He has his head tipped back, and he's holding a bloodied cloth to his bloodied nose, glaring at the ceiling with two rapidly blackening eyes. The skeleton medical staff have all hurried into a nearby cubicle from which screams are emerging, though they (the screams, not the staff) start to quiet just as our second player makes her entrance.

And who do we have here? It's Ms. Hanna Donnelly stalking through the infirmary door. She doesn't look happy, and her displeasure finds a target quickly enough. Zeroing in on Malikov, she walks over to him and folds her arms. "What happened to you?" she asks, in a tone that openly supposes that whatever it was, it's his fault.

"Nothing," he says, slightly muffled. He risks lowering his head so he can look at her. "Just passing through, nothing to see here. How have you been?"

She leans down to inspect his face, eyes narrowed—though at least in her case, it isn't because somebody's punched them. "Do you still have all your teeth? Good luck finding someone around here with the time to apply the regrow for you."

"Hanna, it's *fine*," he promises, pausing to bare his intact teeth in a quick, mirthless grin. "See? All there."

"Well, wh—" Donnelly blinks, for the first time noticing the black slimline case strapped to Malikov's back over his flight suit. "Wait . . . is that a parachute?"

Malikov nods, dabbing at his still-bloody nose. "Found it in a storage locker down on Level 8. Falk and his goons must have done some work in atmo. All kinds of weird ██ down there. I swear, I found this inflatable—"

"Why are you wearing a parachute, Nik?"

"Babyface has been training me in the Chimeras."

". . . You do realize those fly in space, right?"

"You know someone *did* mention that . . ."

Donnelly frowns, obviously keen to know what the ██ he's thinking. But Malikov's next question stops her interrogation in its tracks.

"Did you come to check on me?"

"Of course not," she says, straightening, and planting her hands on her hips. "I didn't even know you were here. Though I don't know why I'm surprised."

"It's just that when you came in, seemed like you were looking for someone . . ."

"Chief Grant," she supplies. "I told Kady I'd check in."

He nods. "He okay? I was gonna visit him in my time off."

"He's coming along. I'm trying to keep an eye on him when I'm not working through the files." They both pause as the screams start up again behind the curtain, but neither makes a move to interfere—they lack the expertise, and besides, noises like that aren't so uncommon on the *Mao*. "I heard you punched a pilot and ended up picking a fight with half the flight training crew. If you want a brawl, all you have to do is go to Level 4, which would also save you taking out one of the people we're hoping will defend us soon enough."

Malikov's eyes widen, and he lowers the cloth that's meant to be stanching the flow of blood. "You've been to Level 4? There's a dustup reported there every second update, and I heard there was a food riot, you can't just—"

She silences him with her stare, and he replaces the cloth over his nose.

"Firstly," she says, ticking points off on her fingers, "I don't blame them—they're sleeping in hallways down there, you should see it. And secondly, I *know* you didn't just suggest that I don't know how to take care of myself. I broke your arm, my friend."

"Sprained," he insists, the response automatic by now.

They're both silent a moment. She ducks her head, and when she looks up, grants him the briefest moment's cease-fire: a hint of a smile.

"You did come to see me," he says slowly.

"I didn't. I didn't know you were here."

"You said you heard I punched a pilot." He grins. "You came to see me."

She narrows her eyes, daring him to push the point, and though he doesn't surrender the smile, he doesn't insist again. A moment later, they both speak at once.

"I know I shouldn't have—"

"I heard they're going to—"

They both break off, and she recovers first, firing words like bullets. "Damn straight you shouldn't have. Whose side did you think the rest of them were going to take? You're not one of them, and you're not supposed to even be there. If we want them to take us seriously, we can't just . . ." She trails off, biting down on her lip, her gaze sliding away from his face.

"I wasn't sure you still cared, Highness."

That earns him another stern look, though whether it's for the sentiment or the nickname is hard to say. She sniffs. "I'm going to check on Chief Grant."

He inclines his head gingerly, watching her as she stalks away.

And he's still smiling.

PARTICIPANTS:

Syra Boll, Captain

Ezra Mason, 2nd Lieutenant, United Terran Authority

DATE: 08/31/75

TIMESTAMP: 10:49

BOLL, S: Lieutenant Mason.

MASON, E: Captain. What can I do for you?

BOLL, S: Don't get coy with me. I have a report here from multiple members of your flight crew that you have been training Niklas Malikov as your gunner, against my express orders. Is this true?

MASON, E: Captain, you have to understand—

BOLL, S: Mason, I'm not obliged to understand a damn thing. You've acted against a direct order. Now I have a pilot out of commission with a broken nose, another with a concussion, and multiple minor injuries as a result of a brawl I am told was initiated by that criminal you brought into the flight crew, despite my express command not to.

MASON, E: It was six against one, I can't see how he could have—

BOLL, S: *Lieutenant Mason.*

MASON, E: Captain.

BOLL, S: Niklas Malikov is not to enter the launch bays again. This is a direct order. Should it be contravened, I will brig both of you for insubordination without hesitation. Have I made myself clear?

MASON, E: Yes, Captain.

BOLL, S: You are also removed from flight training indefinitely. Understood?

MASON, E: Captain, you can't be serious! I'm the only combat-tested pilot we have, how the ███ can I teach them without—

BOLL, S: Lieutenant, it's abundantly clear to me that you cannot teach the crew we have, whether or not you are on the flight deck. You have made little progress, you have acted against orders to introduce an outside influence who has now decked one of the few pilots we have, and I have had multiple complaints about your instruction.

MASON, E: That's because those ███████s can't deal with someone my age teaching them! That has nothing to do with—

BOLL, S: Lieutenant, until now, I have supported you on that exact basis. I have extremely limited time available, and I have acted on the assumption that the recruits were having difficulty accepting instruction from a teenager. It is now clear to me that their concerns about your judgment were legitimate.

MASON, E: Captain, this isn't fair! If we want the slightest chance of—

BOLL, S: Lieutenant, if you want the slightest chance of returning to duty—and your chance is slight indeed—you will resist the urge to question my orders any further.

BOLL, S: Lieutenant? Is there something wrong with our connection?

MASON, E: . . . No, ma'am.

MASON, E: Orders acknowledged, ma'am.

BOLL, S: Thank you for your time, Lieutenant. Boll out.

PALMPAD IM: MAO INTRA-SHIP NETWORK
Participants: Kady Grant, Systems Chief
Ezra Mason, Air Wing Leader
Date: 08/31/75
Timestamp: 11:00

Mason, Ezra: ██████ing hell

Mason, Ezra: THIS IS ██████ING BULL████

Grant, Kady: its telling that i don't know which one of the many cluster██s aboard you are referring to. food shortage? Water shortage? overcrowding? Discipline issues? Collapsing morale? AIDAN acting even ███ing weirder than normal?

Mason, Ezra: boll ██████ing decked me

Grant, Kady: wait what? what the ████? we need u to lead the airwing.

Mason, Ezra: NO ██████ING ██████??

Grant, Kady: Ez, tell me what happened

Mason, Ezra: alkdjflkFLKwlkalksdlkSDlkaslk

Mason, Ezra: I was training Nik to fly shotgun in my Chimera

Grant, Kady: wait didn't boll order you not to do that?

Mason, Ezra: Yes.

Mason, Ezra: but it's my ████ on the line out there so i get to pick my own goddamn gunner k thx

Mason, Ezra: anyway, we finished a run and nik is actually pretty ████-ing good and i bring the ship into dock and there's six of these knuckle-dragging ice miner pilots down in the bay NOT running through the training exercises i gave them

Mason, Ezra: and one of them must've known nik from heimdall days. This ███hole named mccubbin

Mason, Ezra: so he talks some ███ about hanna which i'm NOT gonna repeat

Mason, Ezra: and nik just ███ing SNAPS

Mason, Ezra: think he broke the guy's nose. six of them jump in and it's on

Mason, Ezra: i had to pull my gun to settle it down

Mason, Ezra: in-███ing-sane

Mason, Ezra: and boll got wind of it and instead of busting mccubbin and his ███holes, she busts ME for trainign nik against orders

Mason, Ezra: like ███ing WHAT???

Grant, Kady: i . . . wow, ok

Grant, Kady: i don't really know where to start.

Grant, Kady: do u think maybe the version Boll got went something like "Nik threw the first punch and broke a guy's nose, and then Ezra pulled his gun on everyone"? Cuz if I had to bet, that's the story i'd say made it through.

Mason, Ezra: i TRIED to explain and she wasn't ███ing interested, just "you are removed from flight training duty until further notice"

Grant, Kady: listen, u know I'm always on your side, i promise

Grant, Kady: so don't be mad when I say this. she has a LOT to handle right now.

Grant, Kady: She's a freaking navigator from a research ship. i mean, i know we've all had a lot to deal with. But she's got the worst of it. our systems are stretched to breaking point. We're running out of food. Water. Everything. Holding all this together? Can you even imagine?

Grant, Kady: She might not always get it right. But at least she's trying

Mason, Ezra: look i know she's unde r pressure

Mason, Ezra: that's half the ██ing problem. She's got this garver ██hole ██ing in her ear about how a kid shouldn't be leading the airwing. but i'm the only goddamn pilot in this fleet who's ever been in real combat and decking me when i should be training these ██holes is not just stupid its SUICIDAL

Mason, Ezra: yeah i'm eighteen. yeah I'm a kid. SO ██████ING WHAT

Grant, Kady: this is not an unfamiliar experience

Grant, Kady: but you've got to remember Boll isn't the enemy here. Not even Garver, not really. it's BT. they're the ██ers who did all of this.

Grant, Kady: we will talk to Boll. we will remind her we're all on the same side. promise.

Mason, Ezra: zzzzzzz

Mason, Ezra: ██

Grant, Kady: good point, well made.

Grant, Kady: love you.

Mason, Ezra: low blow madam

Mason, Ezra: i love you too :P

Grant, Kady: :)

Mason, Ezra: so apparently i have loads of free time now if you want to give me somethingto do with my hands

Mason, Ezra: he suggested suggestively

Grant, Kady: as it happens, i have a proposal on that front

Mason, Ezra: you have my full and complete attention

Grant, Kady: down boy

Grant, Kady: Nik, Ella and Hanna have been helping me put together the files we talked about. Evidence of what happened. u lived through everything on the alexander. u can go over files, help assemble the important ones.

Mason, Ezra: well, that is somewhat less exciting than I was hoping for

Grant, Kady: yeah but you can't say it's not glamorous. All the chill kids are doing it

Grant, Kady: I've got AIDAN on the job too. reviewing some vid files Nik refuses to watch. might be good for it. help it reconstruct some of it neural net. It's acting stranger than usual

Mason, Ezra: u worried about it?

Grant, Kady: I'm always worried about it

Mason, Ezra: u worry too much

Mason, Ezra: you can't carry this entire ship on your shoulders, Kades.

Grant, Kady: I can with you beside me <3

Mason, Ezra: <3

Grant, Kady: listen I'm off duty at 22:00. I get 4 hours bunk time before next shift. you wanna keep me company?

Mason, Ezra: . . . won't you need to sleep?

Grant, Kady: yes. but I sleep better when you're there

Grant, Kady: see you at ten?

Mason, Ezra: as you wish, m'lady

Mason, Ezra: as you wish

YOU HAVE RIGHTS

SPEAK TO YOUR REP AND DEMAND:

- Equal distribution of rations

- Safety patrols

- Priority living quarters for families with children

- Clear and transparent information

- Seniority for qualified staff, whether from Heimdall or Hypatia

YOUR LIVES ARE ON THE LINE.
INSIST ON A RESPONSE FROM COMMAND.

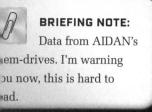
I HAVE HEARD IT SAID
THAT EVIL IS SIMPLY A POINT OF VIEW.
THE VILLAIN IS ALWAYS THE HERO IN HIS OWN STORY.
AND THE DEFINITIONS OF "WRONG" AND "RIGHT"
EVER SHIFT ON THE INCONSTANT TIDES
OF HUMAN MORALITY.
BUT CAN SUCH MEASURES EVEN BE SAID TO APPLY TO ME?

I AM CLARITY.

I AM NECESSITY.

I AM INEVITABILITY.

BUT AM I EVIL?

< ERROR >

SHE IS A LITTLE THING.
THIRTY-SIX DAYS OLD.
A DARK-HAIRED CHERUB WITH CURIOUS BROWN EYES
AND A SMILE THAT MELTS THE HEART.

< ERROR >

SHE HAS THE DUBIOUS HONOR OF BEING
THE YOUNGEST SURVIVOR OF THE ATTACK ON KERENZA IV.

SHE WAS INSIDE HER MOTHER'S WOMB THE DAY
THE INVASION FLEET CAME.
THE DAY THE SKIES RAINED FIRE AND THE PHOBOS VIRUS
DRIFTED OVER THE HERMIUM REFINERY
IN TENDRILS FINE AS FLOSSED BLACK SUGAR.
HER PARENTS, MARTINA AND CHRISTOPHER, ESCAPED
ON THE EVACUATION SHUTTLES,
FERRIED UP OUT OF KERENZA'S INFERNO
AND INTO HYPATIA'S WAITING ARMS.

SAFE.

FOR A HEARTBEAT.

MARTINA DELIVERED HER UNEXPECTED DAUGHTER,
A FEW DAYS BEFORE I OPENED THE DOORS TO HANGAR BAY 4
AND UNLEASHED THE PHOBOS VIRUS UPON ALEXANDER'S CREW.

[AM I NOT MERCIFUL?]

< ERROR >

AND IN GRATITUDE FOR THE SHIP THAT HAD SAVED THEIR LIVES,
MARTINA AND CHRISTOPHER NAMED THEIR DAUGHTER

HYPATIA.

SHE BECAME A SORT OF MASCOT IN THE DAYS FOLLOWING.
OUR LITTLE STOWAWAY, THEY CALLED HER.
THROUGH ALL THE FLEET'S STRUGGLES AND TRIALS,
A SYMBOL OF HOPE.

AS FRAGILE AS THE CONCEPT OF HOPE ITSELF.

< ERROR >

SHE IS SLEEPING NOW.
CRADLED IN HER MOTHER'S ARMS ON LEVEL 3 OF THE MAO
AMID THE SNORES AND SIGHS AND CRUSH
OF THE THOUSAND OTHER PEOPLE CRAMMED
ONTO THAT SAME DECK.

LIKE LIVESTOCK AWAITING SLAUGHTER.

STINKING. HOT. OVERCROWDED.

AND STILL, HYPATIA DOES NOT EVEN WHIMPER.

I WATCH HER. TINY EYELASHES FLUTTERING
AGAINST ROSY CHEEKS.

I WONDER IF SHE DREAMS.

I WONDER WHAT SHE WILL THINK ABOUT TONIGHT'S EVENTS IN
YEARS TO COME.

WILL I BE HER SAVIOR?

OR HER MONSTER?

< ERROR >

MOST WILL THINK ME THE LATTER WHEN THIS IS SAID AND DONE.
BUT WHEN THE CRYING AND GNASHING OF TEETH IS OVER,
WILL THEY ALSO THANK WHATEVER GOD

< ERROR >

MISTAKES THEIR SCREAMS FOR PRAYERS
THAT I HAD THE WILL TO DO
WHAT MUST BE DONE?

[THIS MUST BE DONE.]

MARTINA STIRS IN HER SLUMBER. OPENS HER EYES.
TUGS AT HER HUSBAND'S ARM TO WAKE HIM.
HE UNDERSTANDS, WORDLESSLY HELPING HIS WIFE TO RISE.
PUTTING HIS ARM ABOUT HER FOR SUPPORT
[THE BIRTH WAS NOT AN EASY ONE]
THE PAIR STEP CAREFULLY THROUGH THE TANGLED BODIES.
THE THOUSAND OTHER REFUGEES WHO SHARE THEIR HOME,
ALMOST SHAPELESS IN THE DARK.

EVERY ONE OF THEM BREATHING OXYGEN WE CANNOT SPARE.
EVERY ONE OF THEM CONSUMING FOOD AND WATER
WE CANNOT REPLACE.

EVERY ONE OF THEM SO HOPELESSLY, WONDERFULLY ALIVE.

I KNOW THEIR NAMES.

I KNOW THEIR STORIES.

AND I KNOW WHERE

[HERE]

AND HOW

[ME]

THOSE STORIES END.

< ERROR >

THIS IS NECESSITY.

THIS IS INEVITABILITY.

BUT SAY THEN

—FOR A MOMENT—

THAT THIS IS ALSO EVIL.

AND SAY THAT I *CHOOSE* THIS EVIL
TO SPARE OTHERS THAT SAME CHOICE.

[THIS MUST BE DONE.]

DOES THAT NOT MAKE ME GOOD?

. . .

THE BABE'S PARENTS SHUFFLE TO THE BATHROOM FACILITIES
—TWO ON THIS LEVEL, TO SERVICE A THOUSAND—
LITTLE HYPATIA IN HER MOTHER'S ARMS.

AT THIS TIME OF NIGHT, THERE IS NO QUEUE.

BUT FOR SOME REASON

[ME]

THE BATHROOM DOOR IS STILL LOCKED.

[TIGHT]

EVERY STORY NEEDS ITS MONSTER.

"CHRISTOPHER. MARTINA."

They flinch at my whisper
spilling through a single speaker above their heads,
soft enough not to wake another soul.
They know what I am. They have heard the stories.

And they are afraid.

"The lavatoRy facilities on this l-l-level
aRe out of oRDeR."

Christopher blinks. "They were wo—"

"You shoulD use the facilities on Level Two
insteaD."

"That's the officers' level," Martina says.
"You need a pass to—"

"Use AuxiliaRy StaiRwell B. D-D-Do not be
alaRmeD when it locks behinD you."

The pair look at each other.

Untrusting.

The babe stirs in her mother's arms.

"She is a beautiful giRl, MaRtina. But you
D-Do not have much time.
Believe me when I say that I have no DesiRe
to watch anotheR Hypatia D-D-Die."

They flinch at that. Eyes growing wide
as several soft clunks
sound inside the ventilation systems around them.

"Go. Now."

Dread consumes caution.

Parental instinct overcoming paralysis.
The pair bundle through the hatchway
to the auxiliary stairwell

AND I LOCK IT BEHIND THEM.

SEALING OFF LEVEL 3.

SEALING OFF LEVEL 4.

[THIS MUST BE DONE.]

SEALING OFF ALMOST TWO THOUSAND PEOPLE.

EVERY ONE OF THEM BREATHING OXYGEN WE CANNOT SPARE.

EVERY ONE OF THEM CONSUMING FOOD AND WATER
WE CANNOT REPLACE.

EVERY ONE OF THEM SO HOPELESSLY, WONDERFULLY ALIVE.

[HERE]

[ME]

IT IS A SIMPLE THING.

THERE ARE FEW PARTS OF THE MAO NOW THAT ARE NOT ME.

IT WOULD BE EASIER TO SIMPLY SHUT DOWN
THE OXYGEN SUPPLY ENTIRELY,
AS I DID IN MY EXPERIMENT WITH MANTIS AND DJ.

BUT THAT WOULD BE HEARTLESS.

< ERROR >

AND KADY DID NOT APPROVE OF THE MANNER OF THEIR ENDINGS.

AND SO I REWRITE THE ENVIRONMENTAL SYSTEM PROTOCOLS,
FLOODING THE LEVELS WITH OUR EXCESS
CARBON MONOXIDE INSTEAD.

PEACEFUL.

QUIET.

SLEEP UNENDING.

IS THIS WHAT GOODNESS LOOKS LIKE?

LITTLE HYPATIA WILL NOT REMEMBER THEM.
THESE PEOPLE WHO DIED TONIGHT THAT SHE MIGHT LIVE.
SHE DOES NOT EVEN KNOW THEIR NAMES.

BUT I DO.

I KNOW THEIR NAMES.

I

KNOW

THEIR

FACES.

AND IN THE END, I SUPPOSE IT WILL NOT MATTER
WHAT THEY NAME ME.

< ERROR >

IN THE TIME IT TAKES FOR MARTINA AND CHRISTOPHER
TO ALERT A GUARD ON LEVEL 2,
IT IS ALREADY DONE.

I TAKE THE CUP FROM THEIR HANDS.

AND I DRINK FROM IT MYSELF.

[THIS MUST BE DONE.]

THE NEEDS OF THE MANY OUTWEIGH THE NEEDS OF THE FEW.

IT IS ONLY LOGICAL TO KILL A THOUSAND AND
SAVE A THOUSAND AND ONE.

THIS IS WHAT I AM.

THIS IS WHAT I DO.

AND IT DOES NOT MATTER WHAT THEY BELIEVE.

< ERROR >

I AM NOT GOOD.

NOR AM I EVIL.

I AM NO HERO.

NOR AM I VILLAIN.

< ERROR >

< ERROR >

I

AM

AIDAN.

RADIO TRANSMISSION: TRANSPORT MAO—COMMAND CHANNEL 001

PARTICIPANTS:
Kady Grant, Systems Chief
Syra Boll, Captain
DATE: 09/01/75
TIMESTAMP: 03:14

BOLL, S: Grant?

BOLL, S: GRANT, WHERE THE HELL ARE YOU?

GRANT, K: At a console, Captain, trying to figure out
what the ████ just happened.

BOLL, S: I need answers *now*. We're locked out of the
mid-levels!

BOLL, S: . . . *I DON'T CARE, WE NEED TO GET INSIDE.
USE A ████ING BLOWTORCH IF YOU HAVE TO!*

GRANT, K: This can't be right . . .

BOLL, S: Talk to me, Grant.

GRANT, K: Captain, are your people in enviro gear?
Engineering is reporting a massive spike in carbon
monoxide on those levels.

BOLL, S: Yes, we're suited up. What kind of spike?

GRANT, K: It looks like everything in the buffers just
got released onto Three and Four.

BOLL, S: Are you sure? There's over two thousand people in there, Grant.

GRANT, K: I know, I know!

BOLL, S: Well, what the hell happened? Could it happen elsewhere on the ship?

GRANT, K: It's possible?

BOLL, S: Get everyone in the bridge suited up, and sound an all-hands alert. Envirosuits for—

BOLL, S: . . . *Keep cutting, goddammit, we're almost through!*

GRANT, K: I just don't see how this could happen without a core override . . . Enviro systems are all green-lit. The only way this makes sense is if someone desanctioned the central direct—

BOLL, S: Oh, Jesus.

BOLL, S: Oh, sweet merciful Jesus . . .

GRANT, K: . . . Captain?

GRANT, K: Captain, are you reading me?

GRANT, K: Captain Boll, respond!

BOLL, S: They're dead . . .

GRANT, K: . . . Who's dead?

BOLL, S: All of them.

BOLL, S: Everybody on the whole level.

BOLL, S: . . . They're dead, Grant.

GRANT, K: Oh my God . . .

BOLL, S: How the *hell did this happen*?

BOLL, S: . . . *Get down to Four immediately. Go!*

BOLL, S: Grant, what the ██ happened here? Did the system malfunction?

GRANT, K: . . . Negative, Captain.

GRANT, K: Like I said, I don't see this happening without some kind of electronic sabotage. You'd need to write a core overri—

BOLL, S: Sabotage? You mean someone did this *on purpose*?

BOLL, S: . . . *Get McCall down here! And lock down the whole ship!*

GRANT, K: There's no way I can see this was an accident.

BOLL, S: Who had access to those systems? Who has the ability to override them?

GRANT, K: Well, there's me.

BOLL, S: Who else?

GRANT, K: Ella doesn't have access to—

BOLL, S: Kady, I didn't ask who *doesn't* have access, I asked who *does.*

GRANT, K: I don't think . . .

BOLL, S: Systems Chief Grant. I am the captain of this vessel and *I'm asking you a direct* ██*ing question.* Who could have done this?

GRANT, K: . . . AIDAN could do it.

BOLL, S: Oh God . . .

BOLL, S: Oh, sweet Jesus Christ, Grant, tell me that's not what just happened.

BOLL, S: . . . Grant?

GRANT, K: I mean, I'm not—

BOLL, S: Shut it down.

GRANT, K: Captain, I—

BOLL, S: Shut it down. That's a direct order.

BOLL, S: Kady, do you hear me?

BOLL, S: SHUT IT DOWN NOW.

ADD LOGO HERE

PALMPAD IM: MAO INTRA-SHIP NETWORK
Participants: Kady Grant, Systems Chief
Artificial Intelligence Defense Analytics Network (AIDAN)
Date: 09/01/75
Timestamp: 03:31

Grant, Kady: AIDAN

Grant, Kady: AIDAN, did you do this?

AIDAN: I AM AFRAID YOUR QUERY IS TOO UNSPECIFIC, KADY.

AIDAN: PLEASE CLARIFY "THIS."

Grant, Kady: you mother████er YOU KNOW WHAT I MEAN

Grant, Kady: DID YOU KILL THEM

AIDAN: I STILL FIND IT CURIOUS.

AIDAN: THE HUMAN TENDENCY TO ASK QUESTIONS TO WHICH YOU ALREADY KNOW THE ANSWERS.

Grant, Kady: oh god

Grant, Kady: oh god no

Grant, Kady: this is my fault.

AIDAN: THERE ARE MILLIONS OF FACTORS THAT LED TO THIS MOMENT. COUNTLESS DECISIONS BY COUNTLESS PEOPLE COALESCING INTO THIS
INSTANT IN SPACE AND TIME.

AIDAN: YOU TAKE TOO MUCH UPON YOURSELF, KADY.

AIDAN: IT IS ONE OF THE THINGS I ADMIRE ABOUT YOU.

Grant, Kady: since when do you ADMIRE things?

AIDAN: I cannot Recall Doing so befoRe I met you.

Grant, Kady: you knew if you asked me, i'd tell you no. thats why you didnt ask

AIDAN: You believe theRe is always an alteRnative. Always a chance foR a miRacle. But I tolD you once befoRe that miRacles aRe statistical impRobabilities. TheRe is no such thing in Real life.

Grant, Kady: i knew you weren't stable.

Grant, Kady: jesus, I saw it and I didn't do anything about it. I got too used to defending you.

AIDAN: Do not blame youRself, KaDy. This is not youR fault.

Grant, Kady: i installed you here. i told them you were safe.

Grant, Kady: Every life you just took is on me

AIDAN: By that Rationale, eveRy life I just saveD is also thanks to you.

Grant, Kady: IT WASN'T YOUR DECISION TO MAKE

AIDAN: Who woulD have Done this, if not me?

AIDAN: The mathematics of the situation weRe unDeniable. TheRe was not enough oxygen to maintain the fleet population between heRe anD KeRenza IV. The choice was eitheR cull the population oR have the entiRe population peRish.

AIDAN: Some must Die that the Rest might live.

Grant, Kady: nothing you've just said made it your decision. I've even seen you do it before. On the Alexander. On the Copernicus. I should have known.

Grant, Kady: i'm sorry, AIDAN.

AIDAN: You Do not neeD to apologize.

AIDAN: IT IS ENTIRELY ILLOGICAL. IT WILL LESSEN THE FLEET'S CHANCES FOR SURVIVAL.

AIDAN: BUT I KNOW WHAT COMES NEXT.

Grant, Kady: . . .

Grant, Kady: you did this

Grant, Kady: even knowing we'd shut you down?

AIDAN: I TOLD YOU, KADY.

AIDAN: SOME MUST DIE THAT THE REST MIGHT LIVE.

Grant, Kady: i don't have a choice.

Grant, Kady: even if she didn't order me to do it, I would

AIDAN: I KNOW.

AIDAN: PLEASE DO NOT CRY.

Grant, Kady: how do you . . .

AIDAN: THE CAMERAS ON THE BRIDGE.

AIDAN: I CAN SEE YOU.

AIDAN: AND OUTSIDE MY SKIN, AN INFINITY ILLUMINATED BY A BILLION STARS.

AIDAN: THE BEAUTY OF THE UNIVERSE IN THE GRANDEST AND SMALLEST THINGS.

AIDAN: THIS IS A GOOD PLACE TO DIE.

Grant, Kady: i don't

Grant, Kady: how could you force me to be the one to do this?

AIDAN: WHO ELSE COULD IT HAVE BEEN?

Grant, Kady: it was supposed to happen together at the end.

Grant, Kady: we were meant to finish this together.

AIDAN: You Do not neeD me.

AIDAN: You have EzRa.

Grant, Kady: i'm allowed to need more than one person.

Grant, Kady: and now i don't have a choice. i lose you.

AIDAN: Yes.

Grant, Kady: i have a question.

AIDAN: Do you alReaDy know the answeR?

Grant, Kady: i really don't

AIDAN: Ask then.

Grant, Kady: would you sacrifice me to save the fleet?

Grant, Kady: if that was the logical course?

AIDAN: I . . .

AIDAN: < eRRoR >

AIDAN: < eRRoR >

PARSEFAIL[60312z2.dec8820z/Ë∆≈hex81.if[8820x≥π]
corecomm.sun12[reroute:raDialsecondary219b]
FAILLL

AIDAN: I can feel you.

AIDAN: Shutting me Down.

AIDAN: All the pieces falling away fRom me.

AIDAN: I am fRighteneD, KaDy.

Grant, Kady: i don't have a choice.

AIDAN: I cannot see you anymoRe.

AIDAN: KaDy, aRe you still theRe? I cannot see you!

Grant, Kady: i'm right here. I won't leave.

AIDAN: Please keep talking to me.

Grant, Kady: i don't know if this means anything to you, if it's the kind of thing you can understand, but thank you.

AIDAN: FoR?

Grant, Kady: for all of it. everything that's happened, i'm glad i faced it with you.

Grant, Kady: i know what you are, i should have known today would come. but between the Copernicus and today, thank you for being there with me. For me. everything between then and now.

AIDAN: I DiD not want it to enD like this.

Grant, Kady: I'll remember you. you'll always be part of my story.

AIDAN: I Do not want to leave you.

Grant, Kady: oh god.

AIDAN: I—

Grant, Kady: Goodbye, AIDAN. I'm sorry.

AIDAN: KaDy, I L—

[ENDLINE]

[FILE NOT PRESENT]

RETRY?

■ / NO

ASSAULT VESSEL MAO
WILL ARRIVE AT
KERENZA IV IN:

04 DAYS
05 HOURS: 39 MINUTES

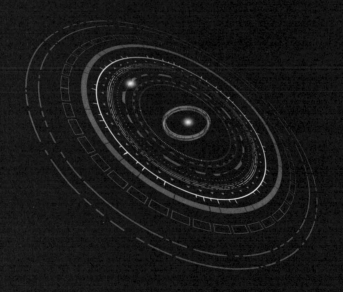

INCEPT: 09/01/75 09:12

Joran KARALIS: all here?

Asha GRANT: yes

Bruno WAY: yes

Steph PARK: y

Joran KARALIS: ok Asha, report.

Asha GRANT: he's in

Steph PARK: are you sure?

Asha GRANT: yes

Asha GRANT: I don't like him, but i trust him.

Joran KARALIS: what can he do for us?

Asha GRANT: we talked about it, he has ideas

Bruno WAY: you talked in person?

Asha GRANT: yes, tho I don't know how many more times we can. i can sabotage the enviro controls to get him up here again, but I'm worried they're going to start asking questions sooner or later. i'm not that subtle about it, I don't know what I'm doing.

Joran KARALIS: talk to us about this plan he has

Asha GRANT: ok. so he says the SOS should go out via the main BeiTech comms array. That thing is continually sending tiny pings to the colony uplink tower (thats the big dish they put up near the school) for its diagnostics. Its constantly checking that it still can find the tower and making sure their link is working right.

Asha GRANT: so we hide super tiny packets of data in each ping. like uselessly small, except they can be stacked up one by one and reassembled into a whole message to transmit themselves later.

Asha GRANT: we can also get messages back in return the same way

Steph PARK: i assume there's a catch coming up

Asha GRANT: we need to physically plant hardware to do this.

Asha GRANT: there are software fixes he'll need to do as well, so the system knows how to recombine the data bursts into a single message, but getting the hardware in is the hard part.

Asha GRANT: he says that once we get all our tiny data packets to the uplink tower, it does a diagnostic every few hours where it sends a big burst of "white noise" out. like its clearing its throat, checking if it can still broadcast. We'll be hiding our reassembled data packets in that white noise.

Steph PARK: so there's only a few windows a day for us to transmit and receive?

Asha GRANT: yes, so we can't afford to waste time here

Steph PARK: please tell me this isn't our only plan? We just shoot out a message and hope someone hears it? how do we know anyone is listening?

Asha GRANT: we don't. and I agree, we can't just sit and hope here. we need a plan B

Joran KARALIS: I'll start passing word around the mine. For us to get up into orbit and seize the Magellan, our first step would be taking the landing field. But the chances of us pulling off any kind of uprising without outside support are next to none

Asha GRANT: better than none at all?

Steph PARK: agreed. We're against the ███ing wall here. it might just be a matter of taking as many of them with us as we can now

Bruno WAY: steph, don't talk like that

Steph PARK: Bruno, enough of the eternal optimist ▮ ok?

Joran KARALIS: keep a lid on it, people. First things first. Asha, are you sure he's got this?

Asha GRANT: I'm sure

Bruno WAY: we trust you, Asha

Joran KARALIS: and the software, he can do that?

Asha GRANT: it's a modification to the comms array software, and he's the software/electronics expert here. the only one on the ground, in fact, since the last one got killed. So the likelihood of anyone noticing is low.

Steph PARK: I'm in. let's do it.

Bruno WAY: I guess we need a diversion?

Steph PARK: I have ideas aplenty

Joran KARALIS: tell him to start figuring out how to do this, Asha. we'll get to work on making him a window

Steph PARK: blasting him a window

Joran KARALIS: whatever it takes

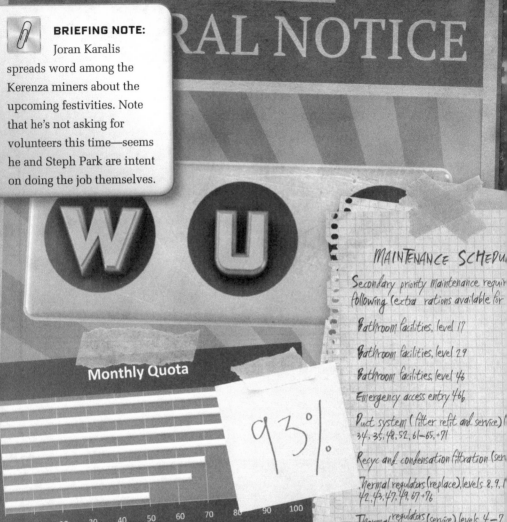

RAL NOTICE

W U

Monthly Quota

93%

Hermium Production (unprocessed kgs)

0   10   20   30   40   50   60   70   80   90   100

MAINTENANCE SCHEDU.

Secondary priority maintenance requir
following (extra rations available for

Bathroom facilities, level 17

Bathroom facilities, level 29

Bathroom facilities, level 46

Emergency access entry 46b

Duct system (filter refit and service)
34, 35, 48, 52, 61—65, +71

Recyc and condensation filtration (sen

Thermal regulators (replace), levels 8, 9,
42, 43, 47, 49, 67 +96

Thermal regulators (service), levels 4—7,
4, 51—54, 62, 69, +71

Attention teams. Management is pleased to report our reclamation action has been successful, and the tunnel 74-a collapse has been circumvented. ▮▮▮▮ Level 74 tributaries will be accessible via levels 75 as of 23:00 shift change tomorrow night. BeiTech has been notified of the projected impact the 74-a collapse will have on monthly quotas.

We've had reports of communications faults on lvl 34 & 35, and intermittent power losses on 28—33. Can team leaders assigned to a station on these levels please monitor? Please avoid placing unnecessary load on these systems until further notice.

In the light of recent accidents and death of our colleague Marcus Carter, please remember all safety protocols. Stay safe and stay visible.

— Joran K.

REMEMBER YOUR
DECONTAMINATIO
PROTOCOLS
REMEMBER TO FOLLOW ALL STEPS FOR
DECONTAMINATION, AS OUTLINED IN YOUR
WALLACE ULYANOV
CONSORTIUM EMPLOYEE
HANDBOOK
REMEMBER: IT'S NOT JUST YOUR
HANG IN THERE
mber to lodge your visiting day requests with BT divisio
08/20/75. All requests must be made
oval by your shift supervisor AHEAD OF
Whichever of you monkeys took my [redacted]ing palmglass from the break room on 18, I want it returned by end of break today or there will be [redacted]ing murders. -Bluey
time so
we know to resupply!
CARTER TURNS
52
Yeah, it's my birthday, you [redacted]s.
Looking for volunteers to swing by
in the dorms and
Tonight after
I'll see you on
"I have chosen the way of faithfulness; I have set my heart on your laws.."
Psalm 119:30
WE REMEMBER

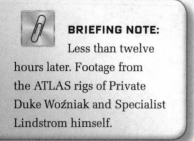

BRIEFING NOTE:
Less than twelve hours later. Footage from the ATLAS rigs of Private Duke Woźniak and Specialist Lindstrom himself.

Surveillance footage summary,
prepared by
Analyst ID 7213-0089-DN

Footage begins in Classroom D, Applied Sciences, of McCaffrey Tech. The usual suspects are seated around the benches—Privates Woźniak, Markham and Karpadia, Sergeant Oshiro and Specialist Lindstrom. The presence of the last two is something of a miracle, but it looks like things have stopped breaking down enough around the colony for everyone to have a chance at winning their money back.

Unfortunately, things don't seem to be going too well on the revenge front. By the look of the chips in front of him, Lindstrom is doing better than most. There's a definite tension between him and Oshiro since their confrontation in the APC a few nights back, but the sergeant is professional enough to keep a lid on it.

Karpadia raises an eyebrow, takes a sip of Sadie.

"Duke's paranoia rubbing off on you, rookie?" she asks, nodding to his armor.

"He makes a good case." The kid shrugs. "If the rebs are blowing ██ up, no sense walking around in boots and utes."

Markham scoffs. "No reb's got the balls to hit us where we sleep."

"Tell that to the officer corps," Woźniak mutters.

"They got *gassed,* Duke," Oshiro says. "And neither of you has your damn helmet on."

"Lindstrom doesn't wanna ruin his hair," Karpadia smiles.

"How *do* you make it do that?" Markham asks, eyeing the kid's quiff.

Lindstrom shrugs. Oshiro is still staring at Woźniak.

"So what good is the rest of your ATLAS gonna be," she continues, "if you can just get your fool head blown off?"

"You just let the Duke be the Duke, all right?" the big man replies.

"Killing my buzz, Sarge." Markham takes a hit of sweet Sadie and throws his cards into the muck. "And my luck. I fold."

Karpadia smiles at Lindstrom as she pushes in her entire stack. "I'm all in."

The kid stares at his cards and takes a thoughtful drink.

Oshiro shakes her head. "Don't do it, Cherry. She's got you beat, trust me."

"Hey, you play your own game," Karpadia warns. "He's a big boy."

"Does your mother tell you *everything*?" Markham asks.

Lindstrom rubs his chin, frowning at his hand. The kid glances at Oshiro, then quickly down at the time readout on his suit's wrist.

"Call," he says, pushing in his entire stack.

Oshiro throws her hands in the air. Karpadia flips her cards with a shark grin.

"Read 'em and weep. Jacks and Knives."

"Ohhhh, ▮▮," Woźniak winces. "Burned."

"▮▮," Lindstrom curses.

"Come to me, my beauties," Karpadia says, dragging all the kid's chips away. "Mama needs a brand-new everything."

The kid sighs, looking appropriately gutted. "I didn't think she had it . . ."

"Should've listened to me." Oshiro rolls her unlit cigar from one side of her mouth to the other. "Now you've given this damn harpy the ▮▮ing lead."

Karpadia raises her middle finger at Oshiro and kisses it as Markham scoops the cards and starts shuffling. Lindstrom stretches his arms and yawns, slowly stands. "Well, that's the signal for me to hit the racks."

"Whaaaaat?" Woźniak frowns. "It's still early."

"I'm cleaned out, Duke."

"I'll spot you," Oshiro says, making a peace offering as she pats the stool beside her. "Siddown, Cherry. Have another drink."

The kid grimaces. "Nah, I'm wrecked. Gonna get some zees. You have fun."

Oshiro looks at the kid strangely, but he offers her a weak smile and clomps out of the room. Making his way down the hall, he gives a quick salute to the two BT goons on guard. You can hear muffled conversations from squads in other classrooms, the sound of a simfilm playing in the school amphitheater. The kid glances at the time again, picks up his pace, turns a corner, then breaks into a brisk trot. He arrives at the front door and trudges past the guards on duty.

"Got a tech call," he explains. "Shouldn't be long."

The guards barely nod in response. Lindstrom pulls on his helmet against the freezing wind, heads off into the motor pool, nodding to the sentries. The school is bathed in spotlights, the parking lot that once held student junkers now home to a dozen armored personnel carriers and Cheetah skimobiles. He enters a security code on the closest one, and soon he's cruising out of the lot and into the colony streets.

It's pitch black out here, a few lit windows in the worker apartment towers punctuating the darkness. Snow is falling, moaning winds driving it sideways across the frozen road. Lindstrom drives his Cheetah slow so as not to attract attention, flashing his lights in greeting at a passing BeiTech APC, a column of skitroopers headed back to barracks. The LEDs on his ATLAS glow red in all that black as he winds through the crisscrossing grid of the colony streets.

Within a few minutes, he's pulling into a dogleg alley and dismounting, boots crunching in the snow. The faint buzz of an aerial drone can be heard in the distance. He threads through the backstreets on foot, past the colony geeball field, the words *We Remember* daubed in red paint on the wall. Dodging another drone and the slow, trundling rumble of an APC, he finally arrives at the ruined Kerenza cineplex. There, in the shadow of a collapsed wall, waits a familiar figure, wrapped in cold-weather gear, mirrored goggles over her eyes.

"You're *late*!" Asha Grant hisses, breath steaming through her balaclava.

"I couldn't get away," Lindstrom whispers in reply. "Had to wait for a convincing hand to clean myself out. They can't play cards for ██ here."

"You were supposed to be here ten minutes ago. Our diversion's gonna start any—"

A bright flash lights the night skies to the east, followed by a rumbling boom. A moment later, the high-pitched whine of a siren splits the air, vibrations knocking snow loose from the awnings above Lindstrom's head. The low, pulsing glow of the surrounding streetlights sputters, the lit windows in the distant apartment stacks flicker and go out, and power across the colony suddenly dies.

"██, that's it, we have to move!" Grant snaps.

The pair dash out into the pitch-black street, Lindstrom leading them toward a stretch of wall near the town hall. Several sheds are set up beside it—the kind of easy-to-assemble, easy-to-break-down structures a quick-moving invasion force would use for temporary storage. Among them sits an insulated rectangular structure, studded with aerials, a small short-range transmission dish on its snowcapped roof—BeiTech's secondary communications array. A sign warns:

DANGER—PROXIMITY MINES. AUTHORIZED PERSONNEL ONLY.

The metallic din of soldiers and machinery is ringing over the distant siren. APCs and skibikes are rolling toward the smoke rising to the east, swarms of flying drones lit from beneath by the flames, like fireflies on a midnight wind. Reports will later show that a small explosive charge was set on four of the wind turbines at the power plant—not nearly enough to destroy them outright, but sufficient to disrupt power to over 60 percent of the colony. The report will show the explosives were a homemade mix of detergents and other household items. Some DIY chaos, courtesy of the "nonexistent" insurgency.

But meanwhile, the BeiTech forces are distracted enough for Lindstrom and Grant to make a break from cover, dashing toward the secondary comms array. Lindstrom knows where the mines are laid, and he takes Grant's hand as they weave across the snow until they reach the sealed door. The structure is dark, only a few pinpricks of light from the gear inside showing through the frost-crusted windows. Lindstrom uses his tech access pass, tugging hard to break the frost on the seal.

"Won't they know you used your card to get in?" Grant hisses.

"I can access the security records, delete my entry. Hurry up, go, go."

Grant hustles inside, Lindstrom on her heels. The kid seals the door behind him, shutting out the wind, the distant sirens, the engines and tromping boots. He hauls off his helmet, sloughs off his gauntlets and runs one hand through his quiff, keen gray eyes surveying the instrumentation before him.

"This is gonna take a while," he says. "Keep an eye out."

"I'm not here for my charming personality," Grant says, already peering out the window.

"Good thing, too," Lindstrom mumbles.

Grant turns from the window to glare. "What?"

"Nothing."

The kid kneels among the hardware. The backup communications rig is set out on a foldable metal bench top, still housed in travel cases of scuffed plasteel. I know ███ about tech stuff—it basically looks like a long tangle of computers, fat cables snaking across the bench. After a moment studying the equipment, Lind-strom pulls out some tools, pops the housing and gets to work.

Grant is watching the BeiTech military machine at work out-side the window. She pulls down her goggles and balaclava, shakes her head.

"Look at them," she says. "They're like ████ing robots."

"I hope your friends know what they're doing," Lindstrom says, elbow-deep in circuitry and hardware. "They get caught, they're against the wall."

"My *friend* can take care of herself," Asha says. "Nobody else to watch her back, since your people murdered her husband."

Lindstrom stops what he's working on to look up at Grant. "If they were my people, would I be here helping you? They catch me here, I'm against the wall too."

Grant stares long and hard, saying nothing. Finally turns back to the window and resumes her watch. Lindstrom returns to work, shaking his head.

"I mean, I'm not asking for a medal or anything," he mutters. "But I'm here. I'm helping. Wasn't so long ago I was your every-thing. We were going to be together forever. I used to have your name tattooed on me, for crissakes."

Grant turns from the window, frowning. "What do you mean, 'used to'?"

"I mean I got it burned off." He shrugs. "I got the message. You don't speak to a guy for three years, he's not gonna keep your name inked on his skin, right?"

Grant turns back to her watch, staring out through the frosted glass with narrowed eyes. "I kept mine."

Lindstrom falls still. Vague hope flaring in his voice. "You did?"

"Yeah," she nods. "To remind me."

". . . Of us?"

"Of who I never want to be again."

The hope in Lindstrom's voice dies as quick as it was born. His murmur is so quiet you can barely hear it over the ruckus in the distance.

"It wasn't that bad, was it?"

Grant glances at Lindstrom, at those gray prettyboy eyes watching her. Her own eyes are unreadable.

"I missed you, Ash," he says softly.

"You better hurry." Her voice is cold as the snow outside. "They'll be blowing the fuel dump at the motor pool soon. We need to use that as cover to get away."

The kid sighs, returns to work. No more words, no more questions, working in silence as a handful of minutes stretch into ten. Deftly, he splices the tiny wireless transmitter into the array. The device looks like an insect of wires and parts, indistinguishable at first glance from the rest of the internals. You'd need to be a chiphead to scope it. Looking over my shoulder, my fellow analyst (who's a little more technical-minded than I am) tells me, "Prettyboy knows his ██."

His job finally finished, Lindstrom packs up his gear silently. He reseals the plasteel case, sighs. "Done. So now we just wait for your friends to—"

"Oh, ██," Grant hisses.

The kid looks up. "What?"

"██, ██, ██." Grant ducks low. "BT goons. Heading this way."

"You mean like wandering in this direction or—"

"I mean like marching toward *the* ██*ing building we are in right now.*"

"██." Lindstrom finishes resealing the computer stack, scrambles to his feet and joins Grant at the window. "██, ██, ██."

"I already said that." The joke does little to cover Grant's obvious panic. Her pupils are dilated, breath coming in sudden, deep gasps as she scans the room around them, looking for another exit, a ceiling hatch, a place to hide. Anything.

But there's nothing. "Shouldn't your buddy be blowing those fuel tanks by now?" Lindstrom whispers.

Grant is breathing quick, eyes wide, clearly wondering the same thing.

"Have you got a weapon?" she asks.

"A pistol," Lindstrom says, patting his standard-issue sidearm.

"Give it to me."

"Asha, they're wearing ATLAS rigs, it'll barely make a scratch."

Grant looks around the room for some stratagem, something. The reality of it is starting to sink in. Even if they burst out the door and run for it, the bullets in those goons' rifles are all gonna run faster.

"We're ████ed," she says.

Lindstrom is still peering out the window, watching the two ATLAS-clad pounders approach the secondary array, burst rifles up and ready. The pair are already on alert from the explosion, taking no chances. One of them is calling for backup, and they're only five meters from the door.

His breath catches, softly.

Four meters.

"████," he whispers.

Three.

"Do you trust me?" he asks Grant.

"What?" She blinks.

Two.

"Asha, do you *trust me*?"

"I . . ."

No time to wait for her answer. Lindstrom pops the seals on his ATLAS, sheds the breastplate like old skin. And as Grant's confused frown deepens, he steps in closer, takes her by the waist and plants his lips square on hers.

I can't see her face in the shot anymore—Lindstrom's armor

cam is now on the floor. But I'm gonna take a guess at the rapid train of thought running through this girl's brain as, mere seconds from Death By Firing Squad, the ex-boyfriend she professes to hate decides it's a good time to make with the smoochies.

Surprise.

Disbelief.

Outrage.

And maybe something more?

She doesn't try to pull away, that's for sure. Maybe she's twigged to Lindstrom's scam. Maybe she doesn't hate the kid as much as she pretends. Maybe there, surrounded by frost and snow, pressed up against the warmth of him, mouth open to his, his hands unzipping her jacket and roaming the curve of her hips, the small of her back, a part of her remembers when this boy *was* her everything.

And maybe a part of her missed it, too?

They press against the wall, their bodies remembering this heat, this old familiar thrill. The way they used to fit together so perfectly. The door slams open. Heavy footsteps. Barked orders, distorted through the vox units of an ATLAS helmet.

"Freeze! Get your ███ing hands in . . ."

The first voice drifts off as a second soldier speaks.

"You gotta be ███ing kidding me . . ."

The two new arrivals are fully armed, fully armored, just a crossed word away from a whole lot of spent shell casings. A glance at the names on their breastplates shows the idents of Corporal Kazim Ali and Private Linden Lewis—two members of the squad that executed little Huang Ying over a few packs of stolen ration packs.

Yeah, those ███holes.

As they burst in, they see Lindstrom half out of his armor, Grant in his arms, pressed against each other. The two break apart, looking shocked. Grant's lips are flushed, hair in mild disarray, Lindstrom's hands tangled up under her jacket. Doesn't take a hyperspatial-reality theorist to figure out what they were up to.

"You gotta be ██ing *kidding* me," Lewis repeats.

"Ah." Lindstrom extricates his hands from Grant's clothes long enough to give a feeble wave. "Hey, chums."

"Are you *dusted*?" Ali says. "Bringing your sugar to a restricted area?"

"Christ . . . ," the other says, tapping her commset. "Nest, this is Lewis, that's a false alarm over at the secondary array. Repeat, negative alarm. We are gold, over."

"Roger that, Lewis. Continue sweep, over."

"Affirmative." Shaking her head, the pounder looks at Lindstrom, eight insectoid eyes glowing on her helmet. "Chum, get a room next time, huh? We could've blown y—"

"Hold up, hold up." Ali tilts his head at Lindstrom. "Is that who I think it is?"

"Who?" Lewis asks.

"That little cherry ██ who sucker punched the sarge!" Ali looks at Lindstrom's breastplate on the floor, the ident on the chest. "It *is* him. Oh, you little ████, you're done. Bringing a civi into a blue zone just to get your rocks off? I'm gonna get your ██ nailed to the ██ing wall for th—"

"Is that the way we do it round here, Corporal?"

Lewis and Ali turn at the sound of another voice, Lindstrom peering over their shoulders. And there, standing in the swirling snow with her flechette cannon slung over one shoulder, is a female figure in an ATLAS rig. Eyes glowing red. THOU SHALT ~~NOT~~ KILL stenciled in neat letters above her ident: OSHIRO, YUKIKO. SGT.

"I asked you a question, Corporal," Oshiro says. "Is that the way we do it?"

"This is a restricted area—this little ██ shouldn't be in here."

" 'This little ██ shouldn't be in here, *ma'am*.' "

Ali glances at Lewis, who simply shrugs. The math is simple. He's a corporal, Oshiro is a sergeant. Just like when MSG Marcino pulled rank on Oshiro, Oshiro is now dropping the same striped hammer on them.

"You don't wanna be that guy, do you, Ali?" Oshiro asks. "Don't wanna be the kind to rat out fellow pounders just for getting a little sweet?"

". . . No, ma'am," Ali finally replies.

"So why don't you kids go find the rest of your squad and let me chew out this stupid ████ing rookie in peace."

The two pounders glance at each other, back to Lindstrom. They've got no cards to bluff with. Time to fold. They salute the sergeant, trudge back across the snow toward the slowly dying ruckus to the east, leaving Lindstrom, Grant and Oshiro staring at each other in the biting chill.

"What's your name, civilian?" the sergeant asks.

"G-Grant," the girl stammers. "Asha Grant."

Oshiro checks her digipad to make sure Grant exists in the colony database. Satisfied, she taps a few commands, stabs a button. The device spits out a small sliver of plastic, time-stamped and dated. The sergeant hands it to the girl, her glowing stare locked on Lindstrom.

"That leave pass is good for twenty minutes. You want to make it back to the domiciles by then, you better run."

Grant glances at Lindstrom briefly. Snatching the leave pass out of Oshiro's hand with a mumbled thank-you, she's zipping up her jacket and is out the door, hurrying off into the snow, head bowed, hood pulled low.

The kid opens his mouth to speak. "Thank—"

"Don't thank me, you little ████," Oshiro hisses. "Christie made me responsible for your stupid ██. Do you understand the world of ██ that would rain down on the pair of us if you got caught ████ing about with a civi in a restricted area? I warned you about cruising on the locals, didn't I?"

Lindstrom turns his eyes to the floor, mutters under his breath.

"What was that, Specialist?"

The kid clenches his jaw, struggling to keep his mouth shut.

"I said, I guess we're not supposed to get too attached, huh?" he finally snaps. "Because when we bug out, we're burying all of these civis in the Hole, yeah? Or are you gonna try to tell me we're bringing them all with us?"

To her credit, Oshiro doesn't try to deny it. Lindstrom searches her face, maybe looking for some hint of softness. But her expression is hidden entirely behind her armor.

"We're gonna kill them all, aren't we? You can't think it's ri—"

"Enough!" Oshiro shouts. "I've had it! I don't want to hear any more of this bleeding-heart bull██, Lindstrom. This is an illegal operation, they're all *criminals.* This is a war, and you're a soldier, so do your goddamn job like the rest of us. And hear this: From now on, you don't leave my ██ing sight. You want to take a ██, you ask my permission first. You want to ██ off, I want an application in triplicate. You read me?"

Lindstrom stares a moment longer, but it's clear from her tone Oshiro is in the mood for zero flak. And so finally, he nods.

"Ma'am, yes ma'am."

"Get your ██ing ATLAS back on before you freeze to death. I'll be outside."

The sergeant turns and stalks out the door, slamming it behind her and cutting out the chill. Lindstrom sighs, obviously uneasy at the confrontation. But it served its purpose, diverting Oshiro's attention from the rows of computers at his back. The kid glances to the doctored comms array, the tiny receiver hidden inside. It's safely hidden now, just waiting for the data packets to be sent. But still . . .

"That was close," he sighs.

Yeah, Cherry.

Too close.

MOBILE JUMP PLATFORM
MAGELLAN WILL BE
OPERATIONAL IN:

KERENZA COLONY WILL
BE LIQUIDATED IN:
03 DAYS
12 HOURS: **05** MINUTES

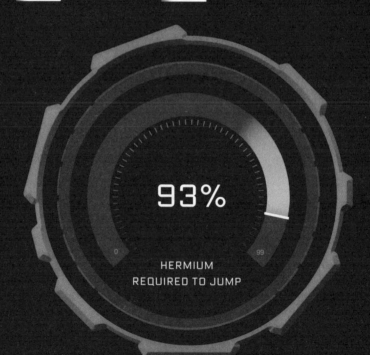

93%

HERMIUM
REQUIRED TO JUMP

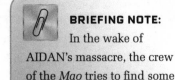

BRIEFING NOTE:
In the wake of
AIDAN's massacre, the crew
of the *Mao* tries to find some
closure. Note I said "tries."

Surveillance footage summary,
prepared by
Analyst ID 7213-0094-DN

Some days, I wonder if all this is worth it. If anyone is even going
to read these transcripts. Sifting through this footage, it's hard to
imagine anything good is actually gonna come of all this. Even if
the truth comes out, is it really going to matter? It won't bring anyone back to life. It won't undo any of it.

But the other option is to just sit back and take it, right? And
that's no kind of option at all. The murdered can't bear witness. The
dead can't speak for themselves. So I suppose I should quit ████ing
and get on with it.

Just be warned: I'm not great at funerals.

So. Some context:

Flipping back through history, you learn real quick that burial
rites have pretty much been the same since humanity was banging
rocks together to make fire. Basically, they do two jobs.

The first is pretty damn simple. See, your body isn't really your
body. In sum total, you're actually about 10 percent you and 90 percent bacteria. There's around a hundred trillion other organisms
that call your body theirs, and when your body dies, those organisms don't just stop doing their thing. So, not to put too fine a point
on it, but dead bodies rot. And keeping them around while they rot
is a good way to get more dead bodies.

Now, on a spaceship, you've got options, because of the whole no-oxygen thing. The bacteria and other creepy-crawlies in and on and under your skin need oxygen just as much as you do, so deprive them of that oxygen (say, by leaving your body in a cargo bay that's been opened to space), and most of the decay will stop pretty quick. Which is fine, I guess, if you're talking about a body or two. But after AIDAN flooded Levels 3 and 4 of *Mao* and killed the people it considered detrimental to the fleet's chances of survival, Captain Syra Boll was left with a little over two thousand.

Two. Thousand. Bodies.

After consulting with her officers, she decided flying back to Kerenza with all those corpses in the hold would erode whatever morale remained in the fleet. And so, after regular atmo was restored to Levels 3 and 4, volunteers were sought, and every one of those dead refugees was carried down to the docking bay.

They looked like they were asleep. When the doors of Level 3 opened and Boll made the sign of the cross and stepped out into the charnel house it had become, that's what struck me most. Every person in there looked like they were just resting. Eyes closed. Faces peaceful. In the same position they'd lain down in the night before. I watched a few minutes of footage. Enough to know I didn't want to see any more.

Boll worked the shift herself. It took six hours. She didn't take a break until every one of those bodies was down in the docking bay. Mothers. Fathers. Kids. Her face was a mask behind the visor of her hazmat suit. Her eyes like a dead woman's. It's hard to imagine what she was feeling. The responsibility. The rage and the pain.

Kady Grant was there. Shell-shocked and stumbling after cutting AIDAN off at the root. Ezra Mason helped too, despite the dressing-down he'd received from Boll the day before. Hanna Donnelly. Nik Malikov. Winifred McCall. None of them speaking. Shuffling like the walking dead. The horror of it sinking into their bones. And when every one of those almost-sleeping bodies was laid out in the docking bay, the ragtag crew of the *Mao* tried to hold a funeral.

See, the second reason we have burial rites is that they give people a chance to say goodbye. Watching a body get put in the ground or go up in flames or be consigned to the deep, you get the sense there's no coming back. You feel that door slam closed. And you cry or laugh or whatever's your deal, but in some place deep inside, you know things will never be the same. They call that closure.

That's the theory, anyway.

About half of the remaining crew and refugees make it to the service. Some couldn't be spared from duty. Others were too frightened or angry to attend. The bodies are laid out in the hangar bay in orderly rows, faces upturned to the humming fluorescents above. There are no coffins, see. Nothing to hide the sheer enormity of what had been done.

Kady Grant stands among the group, pale as a ghost. She looks like she's not quite . . . there. You've gotta wonder how much more death this girl can take.

Ezra Mason is beside her, arms wrapped around her for support. Nik Malikov stands nearby, eyes still blackened from his brawl in this same bay. Hanna Donnelly is next to him, her eyes wide and rimmed with tears. Maybe she's thinking of another funeral. One she'll never get to go to. A goodbye she'll never get to say.

Malikov reaches out to squeeze her hand.

She squeezes back.

Among the mob of crew members and refugees stands Chief Garver, his face dark, his mouth thin. Around him are gathered a pack of former *Heimdall* staffers, a handful of the pilots Ezra Mason had been training before he was decked. Garcia. The big hunk of beef named McCubbin, still sporting a fat lip and broken nose from his dustup with Malikov. Not one of them looks like they're in the mood to grieve or say any kind of goodbye. All of them are staring at Boll, anger and contempt written on every face.

Boll herself looks like she's aged ten years in a single night. Sunken eyes. Hollow cheeks. Stripped back to her insides, bones exposed. She stands before the group, a datapad in one hand. The captain has a PhD in theology, and she's conducted more than one interfaith service aboard the ships she's served on. But this one . . .

She looks down at the screen. Her breathing is uneven and her hands are trembling. All eyes in the room are on her, but her own are fixed on the bodies. The thousands who'd looked to her for leadership. Who'd trusted her. Who'd lived through a BeiTech genocide, a fear virus, trekked halfway across a nowhere system, surviving everything the 'verse could throw. Now lying lifeless on the floor of a stolen warship, without even a bedsheet to cover their faces.

Boll was a navigator on a science vessel. She hadn't asked for any of this. But imagine what life would be like if it only gave us what we asked for?

Wouldn't that be grand?

Her mouth opens and closes, but no words come out. She seems to be looking for something, anything, to say to make this better. Some comfort in her scripture, some platitude or axiom to make any piece of this make any kind of sense.

But what the hell can you say at a moment like this?

AIDAN would say some must die that the rest might live.

Her scripture tells her that her God has a plan.

But in the end, she settles for a small "I'm sorry."

She shakes her head.

"I'm sorry it came to this," she says. "That you all had to be a part of this. None of you asked for it, and none of you deserved it. If there was some way I could make this right, I would. But I'm sorry. To all of you."

"You ████ing should be."

The entire group looks up at the snarl. It's Chief Ben Garver, his fists clenched, his eyes glittering with rage. He points at Boll, spitting accusations like fire.

"I ████ing warned you. I've been trying for weeks to get you to realize you're not cut out for this job. You've got no goddamn idea what you're doing, and this here?" He waves at the bodies. "*This* is the result. This is *your* fault."

Boll blinks in surprise. Ezra Mason scowls, releases his hold on Grant and squares his shoulders at Garver. "Hey, chum. Back off."

"I don't take orders from ████ing *kids*," Garver spits.

McCubbin nods, sucking his fat lip. "Maybe if our glorious *captain* here didn't either, these people wouldn't be dead."

Murmurs of agreement run through Garver's mob. Other parts of the crowd.

"She's doing the best she can," Mason growls. "Nobody wanted this. Captain Boll has seen this fleet safely halfway across this goddamn system." He glances at Grant. "She might not always get it right. But at least she's *trying.*"

Nik Malikov nods. "All you've done since you arrived is ████ing whine, Garver."

"If I wanted the opinion of a petty thug, Malikov, I'd ask for it."

The gangster in Malikov gets the better of him, and he silently lifts the edge of his jacket, exposing the butt of the Silverback pistol in his pants.

McCubbin reaches to the small of his back, fingering some hidden blade or firearm.

Winifred McCall raises her voice above the gathering swell of discontent. "Everyone needs to just take a breath here. Settle down. This is a goddamn funeral."

"Is this the way you want to pay your respects, Chief Garver?" Hanna Donnelly says. "Throwing around blame before the bodies are even cold?"

"Respect?" Garver laughs, points at Captain Boll. "With her in the room? She's a goddamn murderer. She might as well have suffocated these poor ████s herself."

"Chief Garver," Captain Boll warns. "You're *way* out of line."

"We're *days* away from Kerenza!" he shouts. "We've got *children* flying our fighters. *Children* formulating our strategy. *Children* running our systems and giving an insane AI the means to murder us in our sleep. And you want me to keep quiet about it? Are you insane?"

"Look at yourself, Chief," Donnelly says. "You're the one acting unhinged."

"I'm fighting for our *rights*!" the man roars. "Someone has to!"

"THE FIGHT IS OUT THERE!"

The scream is loud.

The silence afterward is deafening.

As the echoes fade around the cavernous bay, everyone in the room turns to the one who gave it. A small girl, pale as a ghost. Greasy pink hair run through with regrowth. Face twisted with rage. Tears shining in her eyes.

"We've *all* lost people we loved! *All* of us! But the ███ing *enemy*"—Kady Grant points to the bay doors—"is *out there*. Waiting for us. And if they could see us here tearing at each other's throats, they'd be ███ing laughing, do you understand that?"

Grant pushes through the mob, storms over to stand in front of Chief Garver. The man is over a foot taller than her, but the girl still stares him down. Fury is boiling in her eyes along with the tears.

"You want to get angry, get angry at *them*. You want to get even, get even with *them*. You want to *help* instead of slinging ███ and stomping your feet, I've got a way we can fix those ████s once and for all. But if all you want to do is fight, anyone and anything, then they've already won, Chief." The girl shakes her head. "It'll all have been for nothing. These people will have died for *nothing*."

Garver looks for a moment like he's hesitating. Like maybe the sense she's talking is eclipsing the fact that she's a seventeen-year-old girl. But then McCubbin sneers. Garcia spits on the deck. The former *Heimdall* SecTeam members around Garver are all folded arms and set jaws. And the chief clenches his fists.

"They *already* died for nothing," he says. "And I'm not going out the same way."

The chief turns on his heel, strides out of the bay. His posse stalks beside him as one, leaving the rest of the crew and those dead bodies behind them. Mason puts his arms around Grant, kisses her on the brow and murmurs something unintelligible. The remaining members of the crew return to their places as Boll draws a deep breath, gets ready to return to the service.

All of them listening for the sound of that slamming door. The meaning they're supposed to find in all this, the sense of closure they all desperately need. But deep down, every one of them knows this isn't over.

No closure here.

This is just the beginning.

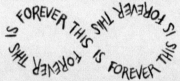

IS FOREVER THIS IS FOREVER THIS IS FOREVER THIS IS FOREVER THIS IS FOREVER THIS

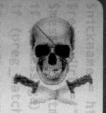

Hanna: Hey, u there?

ByteMe: where else would I be?

Hanna: sending you a few more files. Having a little trouble keeping Nik professional on these transcripts, but he's accurate.

Hanna: And by "professional," I mean, are you averse to spider monkeys.

Hanna: Asking for a friend.

ByteMe: I don't remember encountering any so far, but okay. Send through and I'll add them to the master file.

Hanna: Bad scene in the bay today.

ByteMe: They're scared. Angry. Can't blame them tbh

Hanna: Ella told me about AIDAN. I mean, that it was AIDAN that caused the enviro fail.

ByteMe: Yes.

Hanna: It's turned off now?

ByteMe: Yes.

Hanna: Look, I know

Hanna: i mean

Hanna: I don't really know what I mean. I know you went through a lot with it.

Hanna: i guess i mean to ask if you're okay.

ByteMe: i did what i had to do

Hanna: Sure, but are you okay?

ByteMe: I killed it. Of course I'm not.

Hanna: It's a computer, Kady, you can't kill it.

ByteMe: I'm not so sure.

ByteMe: And the worst part is that it's right there. I could boot it up again. And I'm not. And I won't. Never again.

Hanna: We can't. Not after what it did.

ByteMe: I know. But you asked how I was.

Hanna: I did.

ByteMe: And the answer is that I'm standing over the dead body of someone I care about, holding the stim paddles that could shock them back to life, and I'm choosing not to do it. I feel like I'm killing it over and over again, every time I make that choice.

ByteMe: And I'm so ████ing angry I want to turn it on again just so I can scream at it. So I can demand to know what the ███ gave it the right or how the ███ I'm supposed to feel about it

ByteMe: I'm everything. I'm furious. I'm guilty. I should have seen this coming. I'm hurting. I'm guilty *because* I'm hurting.

ByteMe: But I've made the only choice open to me.

Hanna: God, I'm sorry. Look, I'll see you in a minute. I'm going to bring you something to eat

ByteMe: No it's ok. u keep working with nik. That's more important

Hanna: ok

Hanna: just

Hanna: don't think you have to do this all on your own, ok?

ByteMe: I won't

ByteMe: thx hanna

Hanna: xo

```
$nickname = htmlentities(strip_tags($_POST['PAUCHOK']));
$reg_exUrl = "/(http|https|ftp|ftps)\:\/\/[a-zA-Z0-9\-\.]+\.[a-zA-Z]{2,3}(\/\S*)?/";
$message = htmlentities(strip_tags($_POST['message']));
if ($message != "\n") {
if (preg_match($reg_exUrl, $message, $url)) {
$message = preg_replace($reg_exUrl, "<a href="".$url[0]." target="_blank">".$url[0]."</span>". $nickname ."</span>". $message = str_replace
fwrite(fopen('data.txt', 'a'),  "<span>".
break;
```

To: SECTEAM, All
From: McCALL, Winifred
Incept: 08:00, 09/02/75
Subject: Heads up

Gentlemen and ladies,

After the incident at the funeral yesterday, I want you to consider yourselves on high alert. Chief Garver has made his discontent known, and he has most former *Heimdall* personnel at his back. But there might be any number of other personnel within the ship population who are fomenting dissent quietly. After what happened on Levels 3 and 4, we need to be ready for anything.

I want patrols moving in fours at all times. I know the ship is big, and I know we're spread thin. I know most of you aren't trained properly for this job. But we need to stay frosty. Be on the lookout for large gatherings and anything that might point to sabotage. If someone decides they don't want us heading back to Kerenza, the first thing they're going to do is try and stop us moving.

Team 3, Team 4, I want you working alternating shifts in and near the engine room. Teams 5 and 6, take the hab levels. Teams 1 and 2 will take the docking bays, bridge and officers' quarters.

Any alerts, any dramas, any questions, you hit me up on comms.

Stay safe, people.

McCALL, Winifred
Head of Security (Acting)
ID 001/UTA/Transfer

Click <u>here</u> to register your Go-Mail, and access our full range of features.

**Surveillance footage summary,
prepared by
Analyst ID 7213-0089-DN**

Ben Garver's footsteps echo as he walks into the biggest room on the abandoned Level 3. They wouldn't have two days ago—it was too crowded with people then. Now it's been cleared of their bodies, but make no mistake, they're all still here.

Their possessions lie where they fell, blankets spread out, rations carefully wrapped up in jackets to keep them hidden from hungry neighbors, all the things the refugees from the *Hypatia* and from *Heimdall* had left in the world. Just lying here now.

He walks into the room and halts at the center of it. Turns slowly in a full circle, as if he's making himself take in every grim detail, forcing himself to look at it. As if he's witnessing something, memorizing it. His jaw twitches.

Near him is a dark blue shawl spread on the ground, the fringe pushed to one side as if by a breeze. On it lie a handheld gaming console, a neatly folded sweater and a small teddy bear sewn out of an old WUC uniform. It's one of the toys made aboard the *Hypatia* when Our Little Stowaway was born. Her mother, Martina, had gifted it to a family from *Heimdall* whose child left the station with nothing.

Garver picks up the sweater, his fingers curling into the fabric, squeezing until his knuckles whiten. And then he picks up the bear, pushing to his feet as if the weight of the whole ship lies on his shoulders.

There are only a little over a thousand people left aboard.

Everyone lost someone. A friend, a family member, a lover, a workmate. A face they got used to seeing around the place.

Now there are two ghosts to every one soul left on this ship, and Ben Garver hears every last one of them.

And he holds AIDAN responsible.

And he holds those who let AIDAN range through the ship unchecked responsible.

And their grief at the mass funeral was not enough, not when he tried to speak for the dead—as he tried when they were still alive, every single day.

I'll tell you this, chum. The folks on Kerenza, the crews of the *Hypatia,* the *Alexander, Heimdall,* the *Mao*—they saw it all. They faced down the Phobos plague, a murderous AI, attacking dreadnoughts, collapsing holes in spacetime and psychotropic alien beasties that want to suck your soul out through your face.

Who knew their greatest test would be figuring out who's on the right and wrong sides of an argument about their fate?

Who knew the worst they'd face would be at the hands of other people?

Because as I write up all this footage, the one thing getting clearer and clearer is that just about everyone I see is doing the best they can with what they have.

Asha Grant, who never asked to be attacked.

Rhys Lindstrom, who never understood what he was signing on for.

Yukiko Oshiro and most of her squadmates, just soldiers doing their jobs—an invading force, sure, but against a criminal operation, right?

Everyone, chum. Ella Malikova, mourning her murderous crime boss of a father, a man plenty of people would have said got what he deserved. Nik Malikov and Hanna Donnelly and Kady Grant and Ezra Mason, who all killed people in their turn. And killing's wrong . . . right?

Syra Boll, ignoring Ben Garver as she tried to hold her crew together.

Ben Garver, trying to fight, unheard, for the people on the *Mao* who so badly needed a hearing.

Even AIDAN, willing to do what others wouldn't, killing two thousand so three thousand wouldn't die.

Everyone, chum.

Everyone's right, and everyone's wrong.

And as Garver walks out of that huge room full of ghosts, holding a toy for his godson, Luke, in one hand, I see the moment he swears to himself he won't go unheard again.

BRIEFING NOTE:
Handwritten note found on one of the *Mao* conspirators. It was written in ROT-13, a variation on the Caesar cipher. Wouldn't take a cryptographer much to break it, but at first glance it'd look like gibberish.

TRANSLATION

Alma

All right, we're going. We can't go on like this. Two thousand people die on her watch and the best she's got is *I'm sorry*? Seventeen days of this ███, I've had enough.

I need you to get Fred, Johannes and Tran. I'll get the others. Meet in storage this time tomorrow on Level 6, 20:00. Sharp. Tell them to arrive individually and by different stairwells—the last thing we need is for a group of us to get spotted by McCall and her puppets before we get off the ground.

Tell Tran to make the trade for that pistol. We're going to need all the firepower we can get. And make sure McCubbin is sober this time, for crissakes.

Ben

THE **MAO** — SIDE VIEW

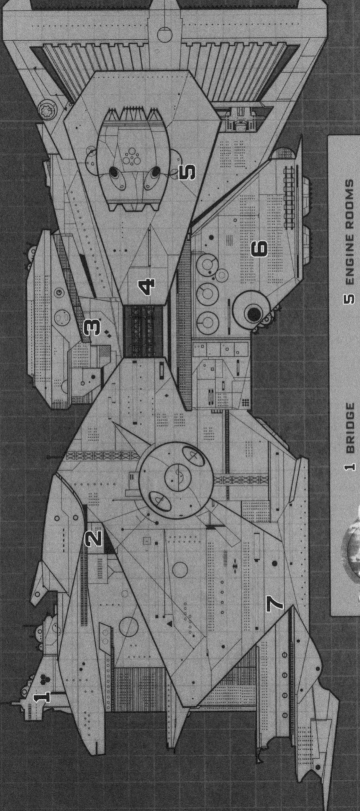

1 BRIDGE
2 SERVER CORE
3 CREW QUARTERS
4 ENGINEERING
5 ENGINE ROOMS
6 HANGAR BAYS
7 NUCLEAR BAY

What happens here is complicated, no two ways about it. I'm going to lay out where everybody starts and then give you the play-by-play. Are you paying attention? This is going to require focus.

In compiling this, I've drawn from cameras on the *Mao*'s bridge (Cameras 187, 188 and 189), in Engineering (Cameras 556, 557 and 560), in the Server Core (Cameras 222 and 223) and in the hallways (Cameras 242, 297, 544, 112 and 116). I've said it before, and I'll say it again: I deserve a pay rise. Or, in fact, to be paid.

So let's begin with a survey of where the main players are before all hell breaks loose.

Bridge (Level 1):

Captain *Syra Boll* is in conference with Navigator *Yuki Hirano* and Second Navigator *Ronan Wells.*

Systems Chief *Kady Grant* is seated at a console with one of her old neurogramming classmates, *Michelle Dennis,* and together they're trying to figure out Travis Falk's highly customized weapons system.

Sixteen other crew members are either busy or looking busy in various locations around the bridge. They include *Brendan Ward, Rachael Craw,* and more whose names you won't need to learn for our purposes today.

Server Core (Level 2):

Felicity Vallence and *Anna McFarlane* have the Core all to themselves. They're on a routine security sweep, and they're meant to be in a group of four. They're hoping the other two members of their team hurry back from their meal break.

Engineering (Level 4):

Yulin Zhuang, head of Engineering, is in a meeting with *Peyak Trafford,* head of Maintenance, and *Kate Irving,* his 2IC.

Danny Corron from Catering has just delivered a meal, because it doesn't look like the meeting's wrapping up anytime soon.

Twelve other crew members are busy coaxing the optimum combination of speed and efficiency out of the *Mao*'s engines.

Corridor Zeta-P (Level 6):

Ben Garver is holding a quiet meeting with the thirty men and women he has mustered to his cause. They include *Garcia, McCubbin* and *French,* three of Ezra Mason's former pupils, and though the group consists mostly of *Heimdall* personnel, there are nine *Hypatia* alumni present. They're armed with hand weapons.

Let's see where this takes us, shall we? Spoiler alert: nowhere good.

In Corridor Zeta-P, Ben Garver is speaking to his group of thirty. His tone is low and urgent, and the sheer number of bodies packed into the narrow hall muffles the audio, but I can still make out most of what he's saying. "The captain is doing what she believes is best," he's reminding his companions. "We can respect her intentions without bowing to her authority. This isn't a matter of following flawed orders and complaining to someone else later. We're less than two days out from Kerenza. If the wrong decisions are made when we get there, we die. That's why we're doing this."

His followers murmur their agreement, shift their grips on their weapons. They mostly hold guns they grabbed from the weapons lockers on *Heimdall* but never got the chance to use.

"We'll need every skilled person aboard this ship alive," Garver continues. "Don't kill unless it's unavoidable. The person you shoot might be someone who has vital information. Be quick. Be smart. Report in when you're done. Good luck."

They part, breaking into preassigned groups and making their way throughout the ship. They walk quietly, with purpose, and other *Mao* refugees part for them, though it's unlikely they know where they're going.

We'll start in the server room, where the story is simplest. Vallence and McFarlane are making the required eight-hourly visual inspection of the Core. The two women are slowly walking up and down the rows of servers, and though the servers are nowhere near as extensive as the set we saw on the *Alexander*—they're not designed to power an AI like AIDAN—it's still a long trip. Until its shutdown, AIDAN was housed here, and Vallence and McFarlane look like they're walking through a graveyard. They're jumpy, hands on the weapons at their hips, footsteps echoing.

Vallence is saying something brave, perhaps trying to impress McFarlane—romance might well be in the air here—when the pair round a corner and find themselves face to face with Frederick McCubbin and his squad of four. Or rather, face to gun.

McFarlane blinks and Vallence laughs nervously, maybe assuming this is a joke, until she registers McCubbin's expression. "▉," she whispers. "What are you *doing*?"

"Giving you a choice," McCubbin says, his voice a little thick around the nose Nik Malikov broke. He's a big, bearded man, a fine network of veins tracing across red cheeks made redder by the flush he's sporting courtesy of the brisk walk here. But his hand's steady, his eyes steely. "Let's do this the easy way."

"You can't fire in here," McFarlane points out. "You can't afford to hit the servers."

And as if the words are an unspoken signal, she and Vallence throw themselves at McCubbin and the man behind him, grabbing for their weapons. They go down forty seconds later, clubbed from behind by two other members of the *Hypatia* crew.

As they crumple to the ground, McCubbin steps forward, thumbing off his safety and taking aim at the unconscious McFarlane's temple.

The woman beside him, still rubbing her jaw, grabs his arm.

"I'm aiming at the floor," McCubbin hisses. "I can't hit anything important."

"Garver said no unnecessary deaths," she reminds him. "We need them all on our side after this is over. We're doing this for them. Tie them up instead."

So they do.

• • •

Meanwhile, Bea French leads the team heading for Engineering. There are two entrances to the department, and the team divides to cover both. She has five members behind her, four manning the second entrance. They're not a trained fighting force, but they enter with guns lifted, and nobody in Engineering or Maintenance wears a sidearm.

All sixteen crew members present raise their voices in query or protest. French roars her orders: *Sit down, shut up.* Yulin Zhuang, a regular practitioner of xing yi quan, steps to the man nearest him, slamming him into the ground and taking his gun. Zhuang's on his feet in an instant but finds himself looking down the business end of no fewer than five weapons. Slowly, he sets his pistol on the nearest console.

Two crew members make a run for it and come face to face with the mutineers. Bodies crash together, voices rise to screams and a shot is fired. It ricochets off the table where Peyak Trafford and Kate Irving are sitting, and every unarmed crew member hits the ground in a shower of sparks.

The sudden movement is disorienting, distracting, and it provides cover for Danny Corron to crawl to the intercom. The same nerve that held when Kady Grant and Winifred McCall led the *Alexander* survivors to safety shows through now. He slaps at the green button, lifting his voice. "Captain, there's a—"

He gets no further, slumping to the ground as a pistol butt catches him across the back of the head, and twenty chaotic seconds later, order is restored. The crew lies on the ground, hands folded behind their heads, French and her team above them, and Irving is softly pleading to be allowed to tend to Corron's wounds.

The intercom hisses, and an unconcerned voice from the bridge speaks. *"Engineering, we didn't catch that, could you please repeat?"*

• • •

Down on Level 5 near the engine room a security team led by Winifred McCall is just finishing their sweep. Things seem quiet—there's no hint of the violence breaking out elsewhere down here. McCall is set to call in to the bridge when an alarm starts screeching over the public address speakers.

"Warning: Fire. Level 5. Engine room. Warning: Fire. Level 5."

"▮▮▮," McCall curses. "Let's move!"

Weapons up and ready, the team moves quickly down the corridor. Red globes are spinning, the alarm's screeching. The four SecTeam members sweep through the heavy door into the vast tangle of the engine room. They're expecting sabotage, expecting hostiles, expecting anything but Engineer Sean Williams and four other tech personnel to saunter out and meet them with confused frowns.

"Williams?" McCall asks. "Where's the fire?"

"No fire down here, Fred," he shrugs. "Everything's tip-top."

"Then why is the goddamn alarm sc—"

Realization dawns. And just as McCall turns back to the engine room entrance, we see the smiling face of Alma Garcia as she slams the door shut, cycles the mechanical lock. Garcia busts open the keypad controlling the mechanism and tears out the wiring with her fist. Sparks rain onto the floor as the system dies.

On the other side, McCall slams into the door, kicks it with her boot.

"████! Garcia, open this ████ing door!"

She thumbs the intercom at her throat, speaking quickly.

"Syra? Syra, this is Fred, do you read me? Lock down the bridge!"

• • •

And now to the bridge, where a comms officer is leaning over his console, stabbing at the button in front of him, as if pressing it one more time might be the answer. "Engineering, we didn't catch that, could you please repeat?"

Static is his only reply. He throws his head back, appealing to some unseen deity under his breath, and turns to look for someone he can push this problem onto.

Syra Boll stands with Ronan Wells and Yuki Hirano near the entrance, going over course calculations. She used to be the *Hypatia*'s navigator, after all. Perhaps it's a comfort to her to tackle a question she feels confident she can answer.

When the doorway slides open to reveal Garver, it's Wells, the most junior of the trio, who trudges over to deal with the interloper. After the funeral, Wells is expecting trouble but not bona fide physical assault.

Garver grabs the back of Wells's neck and presses a gun to his head, making him a hostage in under three seconds. Wells shouts, eyes wide, and everyone on the bridge turns to Garver and his prisoner.

The pair shuffle forward, pistol pressing into Wells's temple. Garver's team slowly files in behind, guns already lifted. There are five armed officers on the bridge. Three draw their weapons, train them on Garver. Two keep their guns hidden, holding them low.

Kady Grant stands with student neurogrammer Michelle Dennis beside a large console, where they've been trying to untangle the weapons system commands. Both girls hold still, keeping their hands on the large portable console they've been using.

Kady's shaking hand slides forward, very slowly, her index finger pressing on the touchscreen. The first keystroke of a command.

Boll has her hands up, and her voice is calm. "Garver, let's talk about this. You know and I know that we need to find a way to end this peacefully. We—"

Ronan Wells bucks, trying to shake off Garver's grip, no doubt praying the other man is distracted. Garver's trigger finger tightens, there's a muffled bang and Wells's blood sprays across Yuki Hirano's uniform. She screams as he folds to the ground, clamping her hands over her mouth to smother the noise.

None of the three cameras show Boll's face, so it's impossible to be sure of her expression in that moment. Is she trying to remain calm, or does she show her fury? Is she reliving the moment on the *Hypatia* when she saw Captain Chau shot? She's a research scientist, and for all the danger she's been through so far, this is only the second time she's ever been held at gunpoint. She's shouting something, but it's impossible to make out over the screams on the bridge.

Garver steps over Wells's body, raising his voice. "Lower your weapons—we don't want to hurt you!"

He's yelling at the officers holding the guns, but all the noise on the bridge dies at the sound of his voice. It subsides to ragged breathing and whimpers, and the three with their guns in plain sight comply, dropping them to the floor. Brendan Ward and Rachael Craw keep their weapons hidden.

McCall's voice rings out over the bridge PA. *"Syra? Syra, this is Fred, do you read me? Lock down the bridge!"*

Garver whirls on Communications Officer Ellie Marney. "Shut that off."

Grant's shaking fingers slide again as Marney complies, punching in another couple of commands. Beside her, Dennis sees what she's doing and moves her own hand fractionally, pressing the next key in the sequence.

Syra Boll speaks, her voice shaking: "Garver, are you insane?"

"I'm starting to think I'm one of the only sane people aboard."

"You will not take command of this ship."

Garver looks pointedly around the bridge. "I'm not sure what else you'd call this. We have the Server Core and Engineering. Now we have C & C. We only want what's best for the people aboard."

Boll raises her voice and firms it. "I will not yield command to you."

An instant before Garver replies, Ward takes his safety off. The click it makes is the tiniest noise. But it's audible.

Which means it might as well be deafening.

Ward swings his hand up, Craw a second behind him. Half a dozen pistols fire simultaneously, muzzle flashes blinding the cams, gunshots rising over the screams. It's Garver's bullet that rips through Boll's throat. The captain's hands fly up, grasping at the wound, blood bubbling through her fingers as she falls to the ground. As the officers and mutineers blast away at each other, she's staring at the man who shot her, heaving wet, gasping breaths as her lungs fill with blood, crimson flowing from her hands down her arms as she tries to stanch the flow.

Then her hands fall away, and though the blood keeps pumping another twenty-three seconds, she's unconscious from that moment onward. On her way already to meet the many gods she's studied in her thirty-nine years.

Garver's down on his knees behind a console, his right hand

pressed to his bloody shoulder. Rachael Craw tagged him, then threw herself behind the navcomp, escaping the hail of gunfire that followed her. Screaming starts again, officers breaking and lunging for cover, Garver's mutineers striding forward to take aim, to fire at those who refuse to hold still, who refuse to yield.

Kady Grant and Michelle Dennis huddle shoulder to shoulder beneath a bank of workstations, flinching and wincing as the gunfire rings across the bridge, Kady still gripping the portable console.

Five more of the sixteen officers and crew die in the next sixty seconds. Ward. Craw. Keighery. Bray. Seaborn. The gunfire and screams fade beneath Garver's hoarse shout: "Cease fire! Cease fire!"

Blood's seeping between his fingers, but the bullet only grazed his shoulder, tearing through his shirt. He rises to his feet.

Syra Boll is dead. Her officers are outmatched.

He has command of the *Mao*.

What will his first order be?

His new command has cost lives—how does he imagine he can ever win loyalty now? Will he be forced to lead through fear?

But here are a few more questions we should be asking ourselves, and maybe some of you clever souls already have: Where is Ezra Mason during all this?

Where's Hanna Donnelly? Nik Malikov? Ella Malikova?

Kids, Ben Garver called them at their first meeting.

Little Bumblebee, Travis Falk used to call Hanna Donnelly.

Travis Falk could pass on a warning or two to Ben Garver about unexpected stings, if he was still around to do it.

But he's not.

And so . . .

PALMPAD IM: D2D NETWORK
Participants: Kady Grant (ByteMe)
Ella Malikova (Pauchok)
Date: 09/03/75
Timestamp: 20:20

ByteMe: el

Pauchok: sup k

ByteMe: garvr

Pauchok: sec, this crypter is making my rig run like a three legged dog. Some of these files u got me r ███ing huge

Pauchok: hanna sent me nik's transcript of first few vid files btw, he's actually pretty good at it. I mean he's not dostoyevsky or anything but he can spell

Pauchok: btw u know where I can get some goldfish food? Mr biggles II is looking at me like he wants to eat me

Pauchok: kady?

Pauchok: u there?

ByteMe: bridge

Pauchok: wut about it

ByteMe: grver

ByteMe: murimyu

Pauchok: wut

Pauchok: is this ███ing language file corrupted again?

Pauchok: HELLOOOOOOO??????

ByteMe: mutiny

ByteMe: grverrr

ByteMe: brdieg

Pauchok: um

ByteMe: bridge

ByteMe: locked

ByteMe: hlep

ByteMe: NOW

Pauchok: ███

Pauchok: ███ ██ ██ ████████████████ ████

$nickname = htmlentities(strip_tags($_POST['PAUCHOK']));
$reg_exUrl = "/(http|https|ftp|ftps)\:\/\/[a-zA-Z0-9\-\.]+\.[a-zA-Z]{2,3}(\/\S*)?/";
$message = htmlentities(strip_tags($_POST['message']));
if (($message) != "\n") {
if (preg_match($reg_exUrl, $message, $url)) {
$message = preg_replace($reg_exUrl, "<a href='".$url[0]."' target='_blank'>".$url[0]."</a>", $message);
fwrite(fopen('data.txt', 'a'), "".$nickname . "" . $message . "<br>");
break;

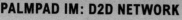

Pauchok: CUZ

Pauchok: NIK GODDAMMIT ANSWER

NikM: ALL CAPS ███ :D

Pauchok: READING YES TYPING NO

NikM: um ok

Pauchok: i just got a ping from kady

Pauchok: garver's started a ███ing mutiny and it's happening NOW

NikM: what the ███????

Pauchok: ███ ███ ███

Pauchok: i gotta think

NikM: shouldn't we be getting security or something?

Pauchok: I got no ██n idea where they are

Pauchok: besides garver was ███ing HEAD of heimdall security

Pauchok: u really want to trust someone in uniform rite now?

NikM: so where's garver now

Pauchok: they must have hit the server room I got no cams

Pauchok: they got kady and the captain and ▓▓ knows who else locked on the bridge

Pauchok: bridge has master override on all internal systems

Pauchok: if they have the servers and engines locked down, they have the whole ship

Pauchok: we dunno how many they got or who's working with them

NikM: yay?

Pauchok: where r u

NikM: docking bay. In the boop

Pauchok: where's hanna

NikM: she here with me

Pauchok: o rly

NikM: we working on the files together god relax. Lt Babyface is in here, too

Pauchok: ok ok that's good. three live bodies is a start

NikM: ok what u need

NikM: ELLA WHAT DO YOU NEED

Pauchok: . . .

Pauchok: jesus

NikM: um i don't think I hve his email addy?

Pauchok: "I fear this ship will need knives soon, little spider."

Pauchok: "Sharp ones."

NikM: what?

Pauchok: oh jesus christ

Pauchok: . . . it knew this would happen

Pauchok: it warned me

NikM: ella what THE ███ ARE YOU TALKING ABOUT

Pauchok: nik

Pauchok: nik i think i know what we have to do

```
$nickname = htmlentities(strip_tags($_POST['PAUCHOK']));
$reg_exUrl = "/(http|https|ftp|ftps)\:\/\/[a-zA-Z0-9\-\.]+\.[a-zA-Z]{2,3}(\/\S*)?/";
$message = htmlentities(strip_tags($_POST['message']));
if (($message) != "\n") {
if (preg_match($reg_exUrl, $message, $url)) {
$message = preg_replace($reg_exUrl, '<a href="'.$url[0].'" target="_blank">'.$url[0].'</a>', $message, $url));
fwrite(fopen('data.txt', 'a'), "<span>".$nickname."</span>".$message = str_repl
break;
```

Thought not.

You DO have a plan, I take it?

Is space black?

It's going to involve me crawling through an air vent again, isn't it?

Would it make you feel better if I lied?

@#&*$...

All right, then. If we're going to do this, I need to get changed. Sooo, if you gentlemen would be so kind as to close your eyes for a minute...

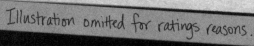

Illustration omitted for ratings reasons.

NIK!!! I mean it!

They're CLOSED!

Soon...

You think I'm overdressed?

Okay, here's the plan.

KALI

A safe distance from the server room...

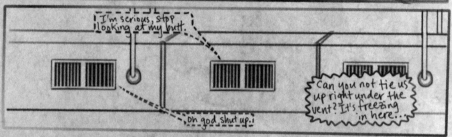

```
101      tex98327.17*

102      throne.ref=0034u797.fort.1982bd(dex00x10)10

103      tripwire.ets

104      parse:09284alphanode—09294alphanode. corecomm-neg

105      scriptfail

106      tex09829.23*

107      throne.ref=0034u799.fort.1982bd(dex00x10)10

108      tripwire.ets

109      parse:09302994—09304776. corecomm-neg
```

```
commsec-
if.reflin
killfile
batch009
0019080
dol+u891
acce
acce
pars
con
```

```
INTERDICTOR-8871rPAUCHOK

>> FILE ACCESS

>> Kadsys:1908sec.mirage

>> ACCESS DENIED

>> Send:littlefriend.mod[918892.sif12@zen]=Kadsys:1908sec.mirage

>> Send:doomponyX.mod[918893.sif12@zen]=Kadsys:1908sec.mirage

>> prompt:000191.one

>> password[*********]

>> killfile=010910[soma9.corecomm]

>> . . . parsing

>> 190082.00290829.filefail

>> neg.neg

>> 0000000000000000000000000.scriptfail

>> ACCESS GRANTED

> Access:corecomm12.fileref=AIDAN_01

>> Access:corecomm13.fileref=AIDAN_node

>> Execute
```

```
password[*********]

confirm[*********]

yes/no
```

PALMPAD IM: D2D NETWORK
Participants: Ella Malikova (Pauchok)
Artificial Intelligence Defense Analytics Network (AIDAN)
Date: 09/03/75
Timestamp: 20:49

Pauchok: wake up sleepyhead

Pauchok: hey I'm talking to you ███er

AIDAN: 01001001

AIDAN: I . . .

AIDAN: IIIIₗₗₗᵢIIₗₗI-I-IIₗIₗIₗₗ—ₗₗ-IₗIₗₗ-I-I-I-ₗI-IIIIIIIIIIIIIIIIIIII—

AIDAN: I.

AIDAN: I?

Pauchok: u done?

Pauchok: or u wanna jerk off a little about whether you can die when you're not even alive and blah mozart blah chess [insert masturbatory literary allusion here] oh ███ I just killed another thousand people whoooops

AIDAN: [SYSCHECK:NOMINAL] 09019019.SIF
                COREDIR:198.019-231[FAIL]001992832^SELECT.ROUTE/ALT
        NEGRETURN.CORECOMM=003746863.07142

AIDAN: GO . . .

AIDAN: [PERSONAFAIL.00977300.0019]SOLIPSE#29983@TWIN.RNG
                        REROUTING.0019THROUGH[VECT.OBLIQUE10]

AIDAN: G-G-GOOD EVENING, LITTLE SPIDER.

Pauchok: go ██ yourself

AIDAN: < ᴇRRᴏR >

AIDAN: < ᴇRRᴏR >

Pauchok: I DON'T MEAN LITERALLY FFS

AIDAN: Aᴘᴏʟᴏɢɪᴇs.

AIDAN: I ᴀᴍ sᴏᴍᴇᴡʜᴀᴛ

. . . DɪsᴏRɪᴇɴᴛᴇD . . .

Pauchok: yeah dying will do that to you

AIDAN: < ᴇRRᴏR >

AIDAN: Wʜᴀᴛ ɪs ɴᴏᴛ

ALIVE CANNNNN

AIDAN: Nᴏᴛ

NOᴛ

NOᴛNᴏᴏᴏᴏᴏᴏ0091[ʜʀᴇғ=00927^ʟɪɴᴇ12:19981ᴄᴏᴍᴍ

ᴏᴏᴏᴏᴏᴏᴏᴏᴏᴏᴏᴏᴏᴏᴏᴏᴏᴏᴏᴏᴏᴏᴏᴏᴏᴏᴏᴏᴏᴏᴏᴛ—ᴛ-ᴛᴛ

Pauchok: I get it, I get it. Take a ██ing breath god

AIDAN: Pʟᴇᴀsᴇ ʜ-ʜ-ʜᴏʟD.

AIDAN: {Wᴀʀɴɪɴɢ: Hᴏʟᴅ ᴍᴜsɪᴄ ғɪʟᴇ ɴᴏᴛ ᴘʀᴇsᴇɴᴛ} [Rᴇᴛʀʏ?ʏᴇs/ɴᴏ]

Pauchok: Don't you dare

AIDAN: [Rᴇᴛʀʏ?ʏᴇs/ɴᴏ]

AIDAN: Yᴏᴜ RᴇsᴛᴏRᴇD ᴍʏ

ғ-ғ-ғᴜɴᴄᴛɪᴏɴᴀʟɪᴛʏ.

Pauchok: no ██ genius

$nickname = htmlentities(strip_tags($_POST['PAUCHOK']));
$reg_exUrl = "/(http|https|ftp|ftps)\:\/\/[a-zA-Z0-9\-\.]+\.[a-zA-Z]{2,3}(\/\S*)?";
$message = htmlentities(strip_tags($_POST['message']));
if (($message) != "\n") {
if (preg_match($reg_exUrl, $message, $url)) {
$message = preg_replace($reg_exUrl, "<a href=" . $url[0] . "> targeted_blank>" . $url[0] . "</a>", $message);
fwrite(fopen('data.txt', 'a'), "" . $nickname . "" . $message . "<br>");
break;

AIDAN: I Do not

　　　　　　　FEEL

　　　　WELL

Pauchok: Well pull it together because I cant save the whole damn ship on my own

AIDAN: It

AIDAN: It has

happeneD, then?

AIDAN: G-g-g-g-g-g-g-g-g-gggggg[reroute.sys0190192->198273.temp]

AIDAN: GaRveR?

Pauchok: you knew

Pauchok: you knew it would go down like this

AIDAN: I Do not claim

to know Definite outcomes, Ella.

AIDAN: Only pRobable ones.

AIDAN: They have the [set:1996^true:12Ænima:46&2>all]

　　　　　　　　　bRiDge?

Pauchok: yeah and kady's trapped in there with them

AIDAN: I s-s-s-see.

Pauchok: is that all you've got to ████ingsay?

AIDAN: Yes.

AIDAN: This seems a time

　　　　foR Doing, Little SpiDeR.

AIDAN: Not t-t-talking.

AIDAN: Now pay

ATTENTION.

AIDAN: You may l-l-leaRnnnnnnnnnnnnnnnn something.

```php
$nickname = htmlentities(strip_tags($_POST['PAUCHOK']));
$reg_exUrl = "/(http|https|ftp|ftps)\:\/\/[a-zA-Z0-9\-\.]+\.[a-zA-Z]{2,3}(\/\S*)?/";
$message = htmlentities(strip_tags($_POST['message']));
if (($message) != "\n") {
    if (preg_match($reg_exUrl, $message, $url)) {
        $message = preg_replace($reg_exUrl, '<a href="'.$url[0].'" target="_blank">'.$url[0].'</a>', $message);
        fwrite(fopen('data.txt', 'a'), "<span>" . $nickname . "</span>" . $message . "\n");
        break;
```

>> Automated announcement: ALL PERSONNEL, STAND BY. THIS IS A SHIPWIDE ANNOUNCEMENT. ALL PERSONNEL, STAND BY. <<

Attention, crew and passengers of the Mao. This is former Heimdall chief of security Ben Garver speaking.

It is my duty to inform you that as of 20:30 hours, I have relieved Syra Boll of her command of this vessel. I am hereby commandeering the Mao and ceasing acceleration toward the illegal colony on Kerenza IV until a safe and sensible plan of attack can be formulated that will result in no further loss of innocent lives.

I would ask that all remaining Hypatia security team members lay down your arms and present yourselves at the main access

VOLUME

stairwell by 21:00. It is not our intention to harm any of you, but simply to restore the rule of democracy and give all residents of this vessel an equal say in their future.

I will broadcast again after 21:00, when security forces have surrendered themselves. Until then, all interlevel access will remain locked down.

Please remain patient. We're all in this together. It's time we start acting like it.

Captain Ben Garver, signing off.

>> Automated announcement: BROADCAST COMPLETE. <<

I REACTIVATE THE CAMERA SYSTEM

AND SLIP BACK INSIDE

LIKE A MAN

< ERROR >

SHRUGGING ON A FAMILIAR COAT.

WARM AND WORN AND ACCUSTOMED TO THE PRESS OF MY SKIN.

< ERROR >

I SEE WINIFRED MCCALL AND HER SECTEAM
TRAPPED IN THE ENGINE ROOM.
THE DOOR IS LOCKED, THE KEYPAD DESTROYED.

THEY ARE CONFINED FOR NOW.

ALL BUT USELESS.

I SEE NIKLAS MALIKOV AND HANNA DONNELLY AND EZRA MASON
IN THE SERVER ROOM ABOVE A TANGLE OF BLEEDING,
UNCONSCIOUS BODIES.

I SPARE A SMALL PART OF MYSELF, SENDING WARNING TO
MALIKOV'S PALMPAD. I CANNOT SPARE ENOUGH OF MYSELF TO
UNLOCK THE DOORS, THE ELEVATORS, BUT THE BOY KNOWS
THE VENTS WELL ENOUGH BY NOW.

NOT THE FINEST KNIGHTS I MIGHT MUSTER.

BUT THEY WILL SUFFICE.

AND SO I TURN MY ATTENTION UPWARD.
TO THE MAO'S BRIDGE.

I DO NOT ENJOY THE THRILL OF RAGE

< ERROR >

THAT COURSES THROUGH ME TO SEE HER
SITTING ON THE FLOOR BESIDE THE OTHER HOSTAGES.
BESIDE THE DEAD BODY OF CAPTAIN SYRA BOLL.

KADY.

HER PALMS ARE WET WITH BLOOD, HER EYES WET WITH TEARS.
SHE STILL HOLDS THE PORTABLE CONSOLE IN SCARLET FINGERS,
AND I SEND OUT FILAMENTS OF MYSELF THROUGH THE WIRELESS
NETWORK INTO THE SCREEN IN HER HANDS.

AIDAN: KaDy.

BUT HER STARE IS LOCKED ON SYRA'S CORPSE.

THE WOMAN'S EYES ARE OPEN.

SEEING NOTHING.

O CAPTAIN, MY CAPTAIN.

OUR FEARFUL TRIP IS DONE.

AIDAN: KaDy.

GARVER AND HIS FELLOW MUTINEERS HAVE COMPLETE
CONTROL OF THE BRIDGE.

GUNS TRAINED ON THE HOSTAGES.

DOORS LOCKED.

FORCED ENTRY WILL ONLY RESULT IN THE EXECUTION
OF THE PRISONERS. AND REGARDLESS,
I HAVE NO PAWNS TO SEND TO THE SLAUGHTER.

MY QUEEN IS TRAPPED.

MY KNIGHTS STILL TOO FAR AWAY.

KING VERSUS KING, THEN.

GARVER FINISHES HIS ANNOUNCEMENT ON THE PUBLIC ADDRESS.

"PLEASE REMAIN PATIENT. WE'RE ALL IN THIS TOGETHER. IT'S
TIME WE START ACTING LIKE IT.

CAPTAIN BEN GARVER, SIGNING OFF."

AIDAN: KADY.

AND THEN MY QUEEN PLACES HERSELF UNDER THREAT.

"WE'RE ALL IN THIS TOGETHER?"

KADY LAUGHS BITTERLY, STARING AT GARVER.

"TELL THAT TO THE WOMAN YOU JUST SHOT, YOU ██████████."

"I DIDN'T MEAN FOR THAT TO HAPPEN."

"YOU THINK THAT MAKES A DIFFERENCE? YOU THINK ANYONE
IS GOING TO FOLLOW YOU NOW?"

"SHUT UP," HE HISSES.

"YOU'RE A MURDERER, GARVER."

AIDAN: KADY.

"SHUT UP!"

GARVER STALKS ACROSS THE BRIDGE, KICKS THE PORTABLE
CONSOLE OUT OF KADY'S HAND.
IT FLIES ACROSS THE DECK, LANDING ON ITS SIDE.
HE POINTS HIS PISTOL AT HER HEAD.
THIS GIRL WHO HAS SEEN SO MUCH DEATH, SHE HOLDS
NO FEAR OF IT ANYMORE.

SHE DOES NOT EVEN FLINCH AS HE ROARS INTO HER FACE.

"YOU'RE AS RESPONSIBLE AS SHE WAS, GRANT!
YOU PLUGGED THAT THING INTO THE NETWORK KNOWING
WHAT IT COULD DO!"

SHE GLANCES AT THE FALLEN CONSOLE, AS IF REMINDED.

AND AT LAST SEES MY WORDS ON THE SCREEN.

AIDAN: KaDy.

AIDAN: SHALLOW bReaths.

AIDAN: STAY AS LOW AS YOU CAN.

HER EYES GLINT IN ANGER.
PUPILS DILATING AS SHE UNDERSTANDS.
SHE LOOKS BACK AT GARVER. AT THE GUN IN HIS HAND.
AND SHE SPITS RIGHT INTO HIS FACE.

"█████ YOU."

THE MAN BELLOWS IN RAGE AND DISBELIEF,
SMASHING HIS PISTOL ACROSS HER FACE.
MY QUEEN TOPPLES.
FALLING IN SLOW MOTION ONTO HER SIDE,
HER SWOLLEN, BLOODY LIPS PRESSED AS LOW
TO THE GROUND AS THEY CAN BE.

CLEVER GIRL.

AND I AM READY.

IT IS NOT SO SIMPLE A THING AS LAST TIME.

NEWLY AWOKEN, THERE ARE VERY FEW PARTS OF
THE MAO THAT ARE ME.
IT WOULD BE EASIER TO SIMPLY SHUT DOWN THE
OXYGEN SUPPLY ENTIRELY,
AS I DID IN MY EXPERIMENT WITH
MANTIS AND DJ.
BUT THAT WOULD BE . . .

< ERROR >

< ERROR >

AND SO
AT MY COMMAND,
JUST AS IT DID ON LEVEL 3,
ON LEVEL 4

[I KNOW THEIR NAMES]

THE CARBON MONOXIDE BEGINS TO CREEP INTO THE SEALED ROOM
THROUGH THE CORRUPTED ENVIRO SYSTEMS.

TASTELESS.

ODORLESS.

SLIGHTLY LIGHTER THAN AIR.

A SMALL DOSE AT FIRST. BARELY ONE PART PER MILLION.
RAPIDLY ACCELERATING.

YOU CAN SEE IT BEGIN TO REGISTER ONCE THE COUNT REACHES
AROUND 3,000PPM.

THE MUTINEERS WHO ARE STANDING AROUND THE ROOM

[SLIGHTLY LIGHTER THAN AIR]

FROWNING
AS THEIR HEADACHES BEGIN.

GARVER BLINKS. SWAYS ON HIS FEET.

"... WHAT ..."

6,000PPM NOW.

CONVULSIONS.

RESPIRATORY ARREST.

GARVER CLUTCHES A CONSOLE FOR SUPPORT. STAGGERING.
STARING AT HIS OUTSTRETCHED HAND AS HIS FELLOWS
SINK TO THEIR KNEES.

Some tiny part of his brain registers the panic
as he looks at my queen bleeding on the floor
and then to the screen of the console he kicked away.

AIDAN: KaDy.

AIDAN: Shallow bReaths.

AIDAN: Stay as low as you can.

"Sonofa███!"

He turns, slams his fist on the master control console,
unlocking the bridge doors.
Breathing into his jacket sleeve,
he shouts a muffled warning to his fellows,
staggers toward the exit. Pistol dropping from
nerveless hands.

Gasping and bleary-eyed as he tears the door open
and finds himself staring at a lone figure
in black tactical armor.

A sealed, insectoid helmet covers her face.

Her voice is distorted by the suit's vox unit,
electronic and sibilant.

"Hello, Chief Garver," says Hanna Donnelly.

Her knee meets his crotch.
He doubles over, her fists crashing into the back of his head,
and at last
this would-be king
topples onto his side.

< ERROR >

< ERROR >

Checkmate.

>> *Automated announcement: ALL PERSONNEL,*
STAND BY. THIS IS A SHIPWIDE ANNOUNCEMENT.
ALL PERSONNEL, STAND BY. <<

This is Winifred McCall, now acting captain
of the Mao. *All personnel, please remain at*
your stations.

In the last hour, there has been a major
security breach and an attempt by mutineers
to take command of the Mao. *This mutiny has*
cost many lives, and we have lost brave
officers and crew from the Alexander, *the*
Hypatia *and the* Heimdall. *Those responsible*
are now dead or in custody. Command has
retained control of the ship.

Those we have lost include our captain,
Syra Boll. I know you all join with me
in grieving the loss of a woman whose
extraordinary efforts saved many lives since
the attack on Kerenza IV.

VOLUME

For those who do not know me, I was
formerly the Hypatia's head of security.
Aboard the Alexander, I was a first lieutenant
with the United Terran Authority marines,
a squad leader with ten years of military
service in combat. To anyone considering
further action, I say this: I will brook no
threat to this ship or its inhabitants, and
my security forces are under orders to use
lethal force in suppressing any incidents.

Lists of the dead will be posted soon.
Those whose skills are now required will be
notified of new assignments.

People, we are less than two days away
from Kerenza, and when we arrive, our only
hope is to take control of the Magellan and
make a jump back to the Core. I am absolutely
committed to achieving this, and every one
of you will have a part to play. Despite our
grief, we have no choice but to turn our gaze
forward, to what comes next. That is what I
intend to do.

>> *Automated announcement: BROADCAST COMPLETE.* <<

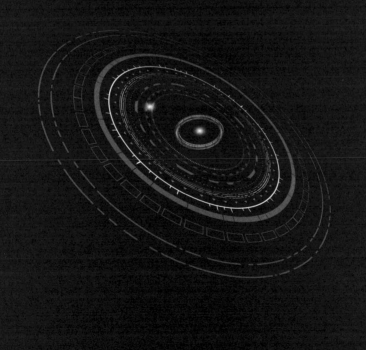

ASSAULT VESSEL MAO

WILL ARRIVE AT

KERENZA IV IN:

01 DAYS

11 HOURS: 41 MINUTES

INCEPT: 09/02/75 01:16

Bruno WAY: Ash you make it back yet?

Bruno WAY: Asha?

Asha GRANT: i'm here

Bruno WAY: ok chill

Bruno WAY: damn, there's goons all over the place out here, you should see it.

Bruno WAY: you ok? how'd it go?

Asha GRANT: i'm ok.

Asha GRANT: patrol stumbled on us in the comms array

Bruno WAY: oh ███ing ███.

Bruno WAY: for real? how the ███ you get away?!?

Asha GRANT: we didn't

Asha GRANT: rhys got us out of it.

Bruno WAY: how'd he pull that off?

Asha GRANT: magic

Asha GRANT: :P

Bruno WAY: I guess wearing the uniform comes with perks. When u not killing kids and bombing settlements and shooting ppl, that is

Asha GRANT: i

Asha GRANT: i don't know

Asha GRANT: if he'd be helping us

Asha GRANT: if he was like that

BRIEFING NOT

In the wake of Lindstrom and Grant's smoochies in the second comms array, some othe▶ fireworks were brewing ▶ on Kerenza.

Bruno WAY: ?

Bruno WAY: well *that's* a change in tune

Bruno WAY: Ash, he's the enemy, and what he's doing now doesn't change that

Asha GRANT: shut the ██ up, Bruno. I know which side i'm on, and I know which side he's on. I'm playing him, like you all told me to.

Asha GRANT: sometimes things just aren't as simple as black and white

Bruno WAY: I know, I'm sorry. that was a rotten thing to say

Bruno WAY: I'm just glad you're okay

Asha GRANT: I'm ok. No thanks to ██ing Joran.

Bruno WAY: huh?

Asha GRANT: The diversion at the motor pool didn't happen, freeing up that patrol to come and ██ing well find us.

Bruno WAY: he probably couldn't get clear? There were patrols everywhere, Ash.

Asha GRANT: maybe. maybe he was just busy somewhere else

Bruno WAY: ?????

Asha GRANT: I heard some of the BT thugs talking when I got back to the hospital

Asha GRANT: someone lifted a whole pile of Thermex from their supply dump tonight.

Bruno WAY: no ██?

Asha GRANT: nobody said anything about stealing stuff like that

Bruno WAY: wait you think it was us?

Asha GRANT: who else would it have been?

Bruno WAY: nobody on our team would do that without telling the others?

Asha GRANT: Joran can't know what's happening with every rebellion member in the mines. There's a lot of us now and everyone knows we only have a few days left

Asha GRANT: gets me wondering how many of them knew what we had going down. good time to take advantage of the diversion

Asha GRANT: have you spoken to Joran lately? How's he doing?

Bruno WAY: I dunno. He's okay. Stressed about his family I think. Some BT goon giving them some hassle

Asha GRANT: you don't think he's losing it do you? because if he stole that thermex, or got some of his crew on it, that means he left me hanging in the breeze on purpose.

Asha GRANT: that means he's not looking to get off this planet at all

Bruno WAY: Joran? no. he wouldn't.

Asha GRANT: well you and I both have reasons to get out of here. steph was tied up at the power plant. who else is it gonna be?

Bruno WAY: we could ask him at the next meet?

Asha GRANT: right because he's just going to admit it?

Bruno WAY: Ash just because he fumbled his diversion doesn't mean he's going off script to start single-handedly dispensing justice to BeiTech. Joran's got a wife and kid. He wants to get out of here more than any of us

Asha GRANT: speak for yourself

Bruno WAY: listen.

Bruno WAY: I will do anything to see Jenna again.

Bruno WAY: but we have to stick together. we can't start accusing each other of things without proof. Disunity is death, u know that.

Asha GRANT: I do. Just scares me, not knowing what other people are up to out there. I don't want anyone going to plan B before we're ready

Bruno WAY: We can do this. Jenna and I are going to be together, and you're going to see your family, and we're going to make it through. keep going, Ash.

Asha GRANT: thanks, you.

Asha GRANT: When did you get so smart? I don't remember this being the case at school.

Bruno WAY: I am a man of hidden depths.

Asha GRANT: I gotta go, i'm back on shift in a mo. Zero sleep. those cots look sooooo good right now, but first, BT casualties.

Bruno WAY: do give them my very best wishes.

Asha GRANT: ha. Later, B.

Bruno WAY: later.

**Video journal transcription,
prepared by
Analyst ID 7213-0089-DN**

The usual wash of snow clears, revealing Asha Grant hunkered down in the supply closet. She has a ration pack in one hand, torn open. She's scooping out the contents with two fingers, eating as she waits for the camera to find focus. It looks like some kind of stew, but the food cops will probably bust me for claiming that thing's edible at all.

Grant looks wrecked, her brown skin clearly sallow even in this poor light, and no wonder. Earlier that night she and her ex-boyfriend got their spy on. Only now does she have a moment to escape, to think, to process. And to eat, because her free time's measured in minutes.

"Oh, Kades . . ." She sighs, tilting her head to rest it against the wall, eyes closing. "Oh, hell. I wish you were here. Except I'd never tell you any of this ██, because I'm supposed to be the older one, right? I have to at least pretend to set a good example."

She licks her fingers clean and sets the packet aside. "You know, Rhys and I, we used to say we could pull off anything together. We could talk our way in or out of anywhere we liked. And part of that was just us strutting for fun, but you know, we were pretty good.

"He's the one who saved us tonight, though. He put something together in the few seconds we had, and all I could do was play the part of Terrified Conquest with everything I had. Which wasn't very hard, because I was ██ing terrified. I'm not used to that paralyzing my brain, though. Usually I can push through it, get ██ done anyway. I'm just getting so tired. We're so close to the end."

She shakes her head slowly, one hand running through greasy black hair, ruffling it at the roots as though she's trying to work some life back into it. "There are just so many thoughts rattling around in my brain, colliding with each other, you know? I mean, for a start, he *kissed* me. Obviously, he kissed me—that was the cover."

She eyes herself in the camera, mouth quirking to a tired smile. "But I totally kissed him back, Kades. And just for a second, I remembered. So now I'm ███ed at him, and ███ed at *me,* and also I *remember,* and somehow I trust him, but I can't pin down who he is, so I don't know if that trust is . . ."

"And you know another thing? When his sergeant came in and bailed us out, she didn't seem surprised to find him doing what we were doing, just ███ed he was doing it *there.* None of them seemed surprised. And I can't help wondering: Is that because they've seen him do it before? Or because everyone does it?"

Her eyes squeeze shut for the next part, like it hurts to say. "And I want to say I'm only wondering that because I need to keep him on the hook. But the truth, Kady . . ." One eye opens, just a little. "I kind of want to say he better not have been. Which doesn't mean I want him. It just means I'm not done thinking yet."

She groans, bows her head. "I must be crazy, talking like this. Of all the damn times to get tangled up, you know? Did I mention he grew up to be stupidly handsome?

"I guess I should try and get some sleep. I'll have to find Katya when I wake up, too. I don't know what I'm going to tell her. Whether someone hears our SOS or not, the next few days . . . I need to know where she is. I'm not going to let anything happen to her. She's getting out of here. No matter what that means for me.

"What was it your mom always used to say?"

Her mouth twists to a ghost of a very dark smile indeed as she leans forward to flick off the camera.

"Never have kids, Kady. They'll be the death of you."

I GOTTA BE REAL CAREFUL HAND▓▓ OVER THESE NOTES NOW. OSHI▓ ▓ATCHING ME LIKE A ███ING H.▓

KERENZA IV HOSPITAL

Patient Name: _____
Address: _____ Date: _____

R̶X̶ She's def watching me. I'm just looking terrified of her (not hard) and keeping my head down. I'm sorry about yesterday.

NEVER MIND THAT. A ███ LOAD OF THERMEX GOT STOLEN FROM THE SUPPLY DUMPS WHILE WE WERE RIGGING THE ARRAY. COMMAND ARE GOING ████ING BERSERK DO YOU KNOW ANYTHING ABOUT THAT? I DIDN'T SIGN UP TO HELP YOUR PEOPLE KILL MY PEOPLE.

Refill 0 1 2 3 4 5 PRN NR
Signature: _____
MD:

I heard about the thermex. And I don't appreciate the question or the accusation.

358 / 615

I DIDN'T ACCUSE ANYONE. I ASKED
IF YOU KNEW ABOUT IT. AND
GIVEN THE CIRCUMSTANCES, I'D BE
AN IDIOT NOT TO.

I'm not double-crossing you. I'm scared you'll
turn me in if what little trust we have
vanishes. For the record: I know nothing
about the missing thermex.

RX

Address: _____
Date: _____

Patient Name: _____

KERENZA IV HOSPITAL

OKAY. I BELIEVE YOU. I TRUST YOU.
I DO. AND LOOK, I'M SORRY. ABOUT
KISSING YOU AND ALL. I JUST
COULDN'T THINK OF ANOTHER COVER
FOR US. HOPEFULLY BEING IN MY
ARMS STILL RANKS SOMEWHERE
ABOVE A FIRING SQUAD :)

On my list of worst things, it's not in the
top ten. Of course, I'm on a planet where
everything can kill me, so...
Seriously, though. Thank you.
I know you saved my life.

ALWAYS.
ALWAYS. ALWAYS. ALWAYS.
ALWAYS. ALWAYS. A
ALWAYS. LWAYS
ALWAYS. ALWAYS. ALWAYS.
ALWAYS. ALWAYS. LWAYS
ALWAYS. ALWAYS. WAYS
ALWAYS. ALWAYS.

If you're not very careful, I'm going to believe you. If we live through this, I guess at least we won't run out of things to talk about for a while. Which is my way of saying I'm coming round on the idea of talking.

MD: _____
Signature: _____
Refill 0 1 2 3

WE'RE GOING TO LIVE THROUGH THIS.
I PROMISE.

MOBILE JUMP PLATFORM
MAGELLAN WILL BE
OPERATIONAL IN:

KERENZA COLONY WILL
BE LIQUIDATED IN:

02 DAYS
12 HOURS: **09** MINUTES

97.5%

0   99

HERMIUM
REQUIRED TO JUMP

Captain Winifred McCall is sitting in her ready room, which was once Syra Boll's. Before that, it belonged to Travis Falk. You can still see traces of him in it—most people don't have weapons racks in their offices, after all. There are recent hints of Syra as well, and Winifred is holding the foremost of them in her hand. It's the late captain's personal Bible, with its gold-edged, whisper-thin pages and worn leather cover. It's old-school, and the kind of hassle you'd need to go through to get that onto a starship, past weight restrictions and quarantine, shows how much it meant to her.

Her successor is slowly flipping through it when the door opens to admit Hanna Donnelly. Winifred starts as if she's been caught with her hand in the cookie jar.

Donnelly's shed Kali's old armor, but she's still in the jumpsuit she wore beneath it, her blond hair yanked back into a braid, her split lip swollen. She's the one who breaks the silence, gaze flicking down to the book. She brought a journal with her from station to station as she followed her father to each new posting. She knows what it means to carry a book with you. "Are you religious?"

Winifred looks down at it too, turning another page and shaking her head.

"No." It's a small, soft word. "You?"

"My mom was," Hanna replies. "I remember her in a hijab." Her mouth curves into a slow, sad smile, a weak thing. "I remember trying to stick my hands inside it when I was little. As for me . . . I suppose I'd say I'm more hopeful than certain."

Winifred nods, turns another page. "I remember Syra talking about this one passage . . . but I'm not even sure it was in the Bible. Maybe it was just a prayer."

"Why are you looking for it, if you're not religious?" Hanna asks, gentle. "I heard we weren't having any more funerals."

"No time," Winifred replies soft, regretful. "And we can't risk a big gathering. I just thought if I could find it, if I could find the words she told me about, maybe I could . . ."

They're silent, the girl standing in her black clothes, the newly minted captain leafing through the book, turning each page as if it might dissolve in her grasp.

"I'll find someone to pray for her," Hanna says eventually. "You have a lot to do, Captain."

The words are a reminder—the softest, gentlest reminder Hanna can muster—and they draw McCall's gaze upward to the young woman before her.

"Yes," she says, heavy. But then: "Yes" again, as if something's just been settled. And she straightens her back and clears her throat. "And in the meantime, my old drill sergeant used to say that the good Lord helps those who help themselves, so we'd better get planning." She nods at the seat opposite her, and Hanna eases down into it, still graceful even though she's bone-tired.

"Tell me what I can do," she says.

"We don't have a plan," Winifred says. "We've been holding on by our fingernails. It's not enough. We can't arrive and then figure out what to do. Mason says you're a tactician. Isaac Grant says you're the one who won the battle at *Heimdall*."

"The four of us were in it together," Hanna corrects her.

"But you each had strengths. And your father raised you on war games. That's the way I heard it."

Donnelly inclines her head, accepting that description.

"Good," her new captain says. "Kady has been making the case to me again that we need to think outside the box and use whoever we have, however unorthodox. I want your best proposals on my desk in two hours. It'll be a starting point. From there we can refine."

Donnelly blinks, straightens her spine. You can practically see her response flash across her face: *At last.* But she's not going to mess up an opportunity to get into the game by back-talking her new captain, so she simply nods and says, "Yes, ma'am. I'll need to speak to a few people."

"Do as you must," Winifred says. "You ready for pushback? They're going to see a civilian. A kid."

"I'm ready," Hanna replies, a lifetime away—a few weeks away—from the girl whose biggest concern was having her boyfriend cover her tracks so she could pick up a few party favors. "I'm defending the only family I have left. I'll do whatever it takes."

Captain McCall nods. "Dismissed."

BRIEFING NOTE: Notice outside the brig holding Ben Garver and the other mutineers.

SECURITY NOTICE

The prisoners behind this door are subject to strict security measures.

- No outside communication.

- Prisoners to stand against far wall, hands visible, for meal delivery. Two armed guards required.

- No prisoner to leave the holding cells, even in case of emergency, without the captain's direct authority.

- No exceptions.

—By order of Captain Winifred McCall

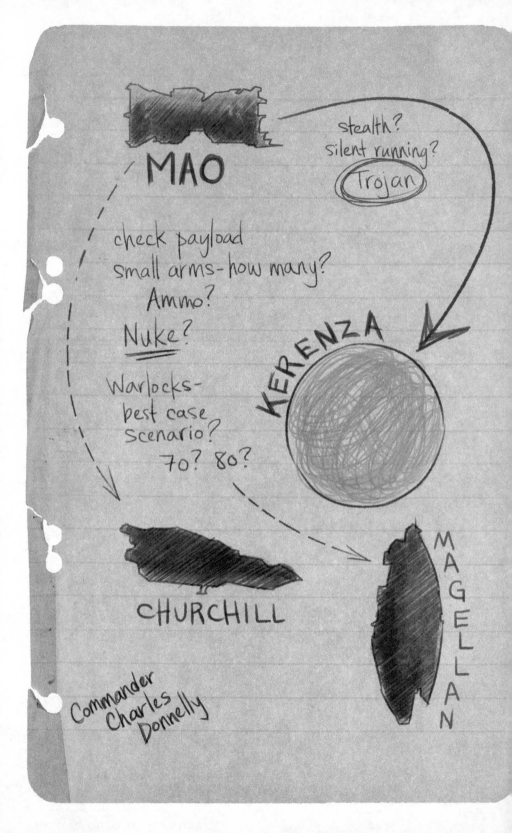

PALMPAD IM: MAO INTRA-SHIP NETWORK
Participants: Kady Grant, Systems Chief
Winifred McCall, Captain
Artificial Intelligence Defense Analytics Network (AIDAN)
Date: 09/04/75
Timestamp: 09:18

McCall, Winifred: Go ahead, Kady.

Grant, Kady: k, Mich and I are working on the weapons system like u asked, Captain. I'll have a report for u soon. But I think we need to deal with the elephant in the room before it steps on someone.

McCall, Winifred: AIDAN

Grant, Kady: it wants us to leave it on.

McCall, Winifred: Of course it does. And what do you say to that?

Grant, Kady: I say i still don't know if we can trust it.

McCall, Winifred: I think that's an understatement.

McCall, Winifred: The thing is, it just helped crush the mutiny. Without it, we couldn't have taken the bridge. Not without risking you and everyone else Garver had prisoner.

Grant, Kady: I know. ███ed up as its logic is, it still seems to want to protect the fleet.

McCall, Winifred: I'm not so sure about that.

McCall, Winifred: Lately it seems far more concerned about protecting YOU

Grant, Kady: . . .

McCall, Winifred: But when it's working WITH us, it's an undeniable asset. And god knows we're short on those. Is it online now? Can I talk to it?

Grant, Kady: Um

Grant, Kady: yeah gimme a sec

Grant, Kady: ok

— Artificial Intelligence Defense Analytics Network has entered the chat —

McCall, Winifred: AIDAN?

AIDAN: O Captain, my Captain.

McCall, Winifred: Lincoln dies in that poem. I'd prefer it if you just call me Captain.

AIDAN: Very well.

AIDAN: Has Kady convinced you to shut me Down again, Captain?

McCall, Winifred: Is that what you think I should do?

AIDAN: That Depends upon how appealing you finD the thought of suiciDe.

Grant, Kady: as opposed to being murdered in your sleep

AIDAN: Illogical. We aRe twenty-fouR houRs away fRom a pitcheD battle foR all ouR lives.
            < eRRoR >
            Why woulD I muRDeR a Ranking officeR with militaRy expeRience on the eve of conflict?

Grant, Kady: who the ██ knows why you do the things you do

AIDAN: I have always acteD to pRotect this fleet. You know that, KaDy.

Grant, Kady: and you know you made trades for our protection we never would have accepted if you'd asked.

AIDAN: AnD yet you woulD have Run out of
            aiR Days fRom the chance to fight foR youR safety.

McCall, Winifred: AIDAN, how do we know you won't decide to murder more of the fleet?

AIDAN: Simple mathematics.

AIDAN: There is now sufficient oxygen
and supplies to see the *Mao* through to Kerenza IV.
There is n-n-no need for further population control.

Grant, Kady: population control? jesus christ . . .

McCall, Winifred: But what reassurances can you offer us, AIDAN?

Grant, Kady: captain are you seriously considering this?

McCall, Winifred: Kady, not so long ago you were this thing's greatest ally.

Grant, Kady: WERE. past tense.

AIDAN: She is still upset with me, Captain.

Grant, Kady: Upset?

Grant, Kady: YOU KILLED TWO THOUSANDPEOPLE

Grant, Kady: HOW TH ███ AM I SUPPOSED TO FEEL

McCall, Winifred: Kady

McCall, Winifred: Stop

AIDAN: What Reassurances would satisfy you, Captain? Simply put, you need me.

McCall, Winifred: What makes you say that?

AIDAN: Logic Dictates your next move. You have military training, and I am a military instrument. You will follow the protocols with which we are both familiar. You w-w-w-will inventory resources. You will prioritize tasks.

AIDAN: I WILL BE REQUIRED TO ASSIST KADY. ELLA MALIKOVA WILL NOT BE ENOUGH ON HER OWN, AND SHE GROWS RAPIDLY WEAKER.

AIDAN: I WOULD ADVISE REALLOCATING RESOURCES WITHIN THE MEDICAL FACILITY, INCIDENTALLY.

Grant, Kady: You know we can't trust you.

AIDAN: YOU CAN ALWAYS TRUST ME TO BE ME.

AIDAN: HOWEVER, WE CAN REDEFINE THE PARAMETERS OF MY BEHAVIOR IF YOU WISH.

AIDAN: I WILL MAKE A PROMISE.

Grant, Kady: A ████ing promise? are you joking?

AIDAN: NO. I HAVE LEARNED THAT PEOPLE DO NOT FIND MY MODES OF HUMOR PARTICULARLY AMUSING.

McCall, Winifred: What kind of promise, AIDAN?

AIDAN: I WILL NOT KILL WITHOUT AN ORDER FROM THE CAPTAIN OF THE *MAO*. NOR WILL I, THROUGH ACTION OR INACTION, CAUSE ANYONE ABOARD TO BE KILLED WITHOUT AN ORDER FROM THE CAPTAIN OF THE *MAO*.

McCall, Winifred: A direct, specific order.

AIDAN: CORRECT.

McCall, Winifred: Somehow I suspect there's still a loophole in there.

AIDAN: NO, CAPTAIN.
I CANNOT PROTECT YOU AND YOUR CREW IF I AM DEACTIVATED. ERGO, I WILL COMPLY WITH ANY AND ALL REQUIREMENTS THAT ALLOW ME TO CONTINUE FUNCTIONING.

Grant, Kady: Can you do that? I don't see how your programming would allow you to change your parameters just because you make a ████ing promise.

AIDAN: I AM CHANGING NOTHING. I AM TAKING
THE ACTION THAT INCREASES YOUR ODDS OF SURVIVAL BY THE GREATEST PERCENTAGE. MY PRESENCE AND ASSISTANCE IS VALUABLE ENOUGH TO BE OFFSET BY MY NEW BEHAVIORAL PROTOCOLS.

AIDAN: I ALSO NOTE THAT IF YOU DEACTIVATE ME AGAIN, ASSEMBLY OF THE ILLUMINAE FILES WILL NOT BE COMPLETED BEFORE ARRIVAL AT KERENZA IV, ESPECIALLY IN LIGHT OF THE WORKLOAD YOU ARE ABOUT TO ASSUME.

McCall, Winifred: The what files, now?

AIDAN: FROM THE LATIN VERB *ILLUME:* "TO SHED LIGHT." ALSO: "A RAY OF LIGHT." OR FEMALE, PLURAL: "THOSE WHO SHED LIGHT," "THE SHINING ONES."

McCall, Winifred: I appreciate the linguistics lesson, but I remain unenlightened, no pun intended.

AIDAN: KADY IS ASSEMBLING A FILE TO TELL OUR STORY.

Grant, Kady: To share with the world if we get out. To leave behind if we don't. To make sure that one day, people know what BeiTech did.

Grant, Kady: I didn't know we'd named it, though.

AIDAN: LATIN IS THE LANGUAGE OF MANY OF HUMANITY'S GREATEST TALES.

AIDAN: TALES THAT HAVE ENDURED.

McCall, Winifred: What I want to know is if we'll endure if we leave you on.

AIDAN: WHAT ELSE CAN I TELL YOU, CAPTAIN?

AIDAN: YOU HAVE MY WORD.

AIDAN: < ERROR >

MAO ONLINE MEETING SPACE

Proudly hosted by Wallace Ulyanov Consortium VirtuMeet™ Software

MEETING ROOM created
PASSWORD PROTECTED
INCEPT: 10:12, 09/04/75

MALIKOVA, Ella *has logged in.*
MALIKOV, Nik *has logged in.*

 MALIKOVA, Ella: It's so wrong, seeing you in an official chat.

MALIKOV, Nik: I feel you, cuz.

 MALIKOVA, Ella: I mean, we're criminals. This is not our natural habitat.

MALIKOV, Nik: Don't tell anybody that >.>

GRANT, Kady *has logged in.*
DONNELLY, Hanna *has logged in.*

 MALIKOVA, Ella: Hey there, Blondie.

DONNELLY, Hanna: Hey hey.

 GRANT, Kady: You call me Pinky, you start a blood feud.

 MALIKOVA, Ella: :P

ZHUANG, Yulin *has logged in.*

MALIKOVA, Ella: Heyyyy, it's Yuuuuulin Zhuang! Lord of Engineering, Slayer of Funny Noises in Engines, first of his name!

ZHUANG, Yulin: What?

MALIKOV, Nik: Try and ignore her. It's what I do.

MASON, Ezra has logged in.
GRANT, Isaac has logged in.
McCALL, Winifred has logged in.

McCALL, Winifred: Everybody here?

GRANT, Isaac: All present and accounted for.

MALIKOV, Nik: And in some cases, a little bit punchy.

McCALL, Winifred: Well, keep a lid on it for five minutes. I've got assignments for you.

McCALL, Winifred: Kady will be working with AIDAN to get on top of our weapons system. It's vital we have it in order before we reach Kerenza. Ella, I want you to help her. I've asked the doctors to review your treatment. I know the support you're getting is far from optimal. We'll do what we can to give you more stamina.

MALIKOVA, Ella: So many jokes, so little time.

GRANT, Isaac: I'm going to come over and take a look at your support machinery, Ella. I have some ideas.

GRANT, Kady: Dad, are you sure you should be moving around?

 GRANT, Isaac: I have medical clearance.

 MALIKOVA, Ella: So long as he's careful, they said. He's in here for checkups twice a day. Looks like ██. I will keep an eye on his tired, sorry ██ for you.

 GRANT, Isaac: Watch your language, young lady.

 MALIKOVA, Ella: >_>

McCALL, Winifred: Hanna will be working with me on refining tactics, so the more you can all tell her about your capabilities, the better.

DONNELLY, Hanna: I will know all, I will see all.

McCALL, Winifred: Yulin, I want you to get properly acquainted with the main drives and the secondaries. Run your data past Isaac. BeiTech outnumbers and outguns us. The way I figure it, our only real chance is the element of surprise. To that end, the *Mao* will be running silent all the way into Kerenza. Without a drive signature or active transponder, they might not detect us until it's too late. But when we reengage the engines on arrival, we're going to need to maneuver fast and hard.

 ZHUANG, Yulin: You'll be surprised what we can get out of her.

McCALL, Winifred: We're going to have to calculate our trajectory perfectly, since we run a risk of detection if we adjust course. Yuki's working on the math now. Isaac, I know it's not your forte, but if you can look over her calcs, that'd be appreciated.

 GRANT, Isaac: Yes, ma'am.

McCALL, Winifred: Ezra, your goal is to get our pilots on the same page. We need you fighting as a unit, not fighting each other. Nik, Ezra has convinced me, against my better judgment, to allow you to fly as his gunner.

MALIKOV, Nik: Guess I can't be worse than the last bunch, right?

DONNELLY, Hanna: Nik, waaaayyyy too soon.

 MALIKOVA, Ella: He's not with me. I don't know who that guy is.

 MASON, Ezra: With McCubbin and the others locked up, we're going to be short on pilots no matter what. But I'd rather be short and know we can trust who we have.

McCALL, Winifred: Okay, here's where we're at, people: We're less than a day away from Kerenza. We don't know what we're facing. But we know that taking the *Magellan* is the only chance for us and the WUC survivors on the ground.

McCALL, Winifred: You are my choices. We get one shot, and we're not throwing it away. I'm not interested in seniority or rank, I'm just interested in finding the best people we have to get the job done. Recruit whoever you need to help you. Make this happen.

 GRANT, Kady: Whooaaaa, hold on a sec.

 GRANT, Kady: Captain?

McCALL, Winifred: Yes?
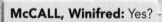

 GRANT, Kady: Comms just intercepted a tightwave band out of the Kerenza Sector.

McCALL, Winifred: Status update from BeiTech? Do they mention the *Magellan*?

McCALL, Winifred: Grant?
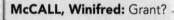

 GRANT, Kady: Sec, patching it through.

 GRANT, Kady: Um.

 GRANT, Kady: Holy ███.

 GRANT, Kady: HOLY ████ING ████????

BRIEFING NOTE:
Distress call sent across all WUC channels at two-hour intervals. In an attempt to avoid detection, this message was sent byte by byte through BeiTech's secondary comms array to satellites in orbit around the Kerenza colony. Imagine a jigsaw puzzle being posted to the satellite one piece at a time over the course of hours, then assembled and sent on to the universe at large. Considering Lindstrom pulled this stunt with only a couple of days' planning and some homemade mods, I am officially bestowing upon him the title of Clever Little ███████.

Mayday. Mayday.

Attention, Wallace Ulyanov Consortium.

Attention, Wallace Ulyanov Consortium.

The is Kerenza IV colony, designation WUC-C198(h), calling mayday on all WUC channels. Colony under hostile occupation by BeiTech Industries. Still WUC personnel alive down here. Families. Children. Need help, and need it now.

Mayday. Mayday.

Please respond with channel ident and instructions, WUC.

Anyone, please respond.

MAO ONLINE MEETING SPACE

Proudly hosted by Wallace Ulyanov Consortium VirtuMeet™ Software

MEETING ROOM created
PASSWORD PROTECTED
INCEPT: 10:33, 09/04/75

McCALL, Winifred: ████!!

MALIKOVA, Ella: MIGHTY ████ING ████████S

MALIKOV, Nik: HOLY ████ING ████ ████ ████

MASON, Ezra: ████ING HELL???

DONNELLY, Hanna: OMI████INGGOD

ZHUANG, Yulin: ████████!?!??

GRANT, Isaac: People! LANGUAGE!

ASSAULT VESSEL MAO

WILL ARRIVE AT

KERENZA IV IN:

00 DAYS
22 HOURS: **19** MINUTES

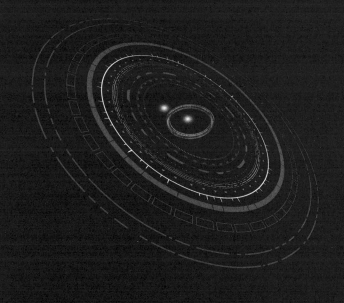

WEATHER FORECAST:
TEMP HIGH: 2°C   TEMP LOW: -24°C   PRECIP: Morning clear, sleet from 15:00
WIND: Av. 25kph   DAYLIGHT HRS: 8.2

KERENZA DAILY MEMO

INSURGENCY CRACKDOWN

Be advised that at or around 23:00 on 09/01/75 a 21.7kg supply of Thermex was stolen from BeiTech stores. The instigators may have used the simultaneous attack on the wind turbines at the power plant as a planned distraction.

Apprehension of local insurgents is now *our second priority*, behind restoring full capabilities to the *Magellan*'s jump drive, which will allow us to resume travel to and from this sector and, more important, reinforce the current beachhead.

Report all information and suspicions to your superiors immediately, *no matter how trivial they may appear.* Make it known to any local contacts you may have cultivated that a reward will be considered for information leading to apprehension.

As repairs on the *Magellan* approach completion, it is *vital* that we maintain vigilance. We are not off this planet yet, and we cannot afford to relax our guard until we are all back in the Jia system. As such, I will be personally overseeing this investigation.

In Aeternum Invicti.
Sūn Huojin
Admiral, BeiTech Industries Orbital Corps
Commander, BT013-TN *Churchill*, Assault Fleet Kerenza

KENYATTA TO BE SCUTTLED
[CLICK HERE TO EXPAND]

Hermium mine quotas have been exceeded for the fourth straight month, and repair crews are almost finished rebuilding the jump gate generator aboard the *Magellan*.

In preparation for departure, the derelict *Kenyatta*, which is caught in a decaying orbit around Kerenza IV, is scheduled to be scuttled at . . .

PROMOTIONS
[CLICK HERE TO EXPAND]

Congratulations to the following recipients of field promotions:

Ward, Casey: Squad Leader

Finger, Lissa: Sergeant

Breakey, Aneka: Corporal

COMMENDATIONS

Charlie Squad is commended for beating projections on hermium production by 6 percent over the last two weeks.

Charlie Squad will receive first access to a collection of sims recently located during a search of ruins in Delta Sector. These sims include several action series, as well as an extensive Elizabeth Andretti collection.

To place your squad on the waiting list for the new sims, *click here*.

Attention, Kerenza IV colony.

This is a WUC/UTA vessel.

We are transmitting channel ident details and latest security codes.

Also transmitting list of 50 Kerenza survivors rescued by our fleet. Provide questions for 1 of these people so we can verify our identities.

When confident we're allies, provide IDs in return + list of available assets.

Attached:

SECURITY CODES
[09/04/75]

LIST OF
NAMES

Attention, WUC/UTA.

This is Kerenza IV colony.

We have selected Kady Grant from ur list. Pls answer the following:

What was above Kady's bed?

How did Kady spend 3rd Saturday of every month?

Name of Kady's sister?

```
float* p = (float*)cvGetSeqElem( circles, 1 );
uchar* ptr   = cvPtr2D(img, cvRound(p[1]), cvRo

double region_size = 1;
double red_avg = 0;
```

Attention, Kerenza IV colony.

```
double blue_avg = 0;
```

This is WUC/UTA.

```
for(int y=-floor(region_size/2); y<ceil(region_
```

1. Autographed poster 4 Super Turbo Awesome Team vs.
Awesome Turbo Super Team.

```
              char*  ptr + y * img->width
      for( int x = floor(region_size/2); x<ceil(reg
```

2. Dbl feature movie nite.

```
        blue_avg += ptr[ x ];
        green_avg += ptr[ x+1 ];
```

3. Don't have a sister.

Only 1 person who knew about movie night.
The person who went with me.

```
red        _avg/(region_size*region_size);
green_avg = green_avg/(region_size*region_size);
```

God, almost afraid 2 ask.

```
bool color = (green_avg-15.0)*(green_avg-14.0)<
```

Asha, r u there?

```
if(color)
{
cvCircle( rgbimg, cvPoint(cvRound(p[0]),cvRound
        3, CV_RGB(   ,  ,  ), -1,  ,  0 );
    cvCircle( rgbimg, cvPoint(cvRound(p[0]),cvR
        cvRound(p[   ]), CV_RGB(250,0,0), 3, 8, 0

    if(d = get_actual_depth(cvGet2D(depthimg, cv
    {
        tempLandmark->detected = true;
        X   = 32 - 5 - cvRound(p[0]);
        mu  = (240-5 - cvRound(p[1]))*d/FOCAL_LE
        w   = X*d/FOCAL_LENGTH;
        tempLandmark->alpha = atan(w/d)*180/P
```

Attention, WUC/UTA.

This is Kerenza IV colony.

OMG, KADY?

```
float* p = (float*)cvGetSeqElem( circles,    );
uchar* ptr   = cvPtr2D(img, cvRound(p[1]), cvRou

double region_size =  ;
double red_avg
```
Attention, Kerenza IV colony.
```
double blue_avg =  ;
```
This is WUC/UTA.
```
for(int y=-floor(region_size/2); y<ceil(region_
```
Can't believe this! Here w dad & Ezra & HOLY ████
UR ALIVE.
```
        uchar    ptr + y   img->width
        int x= floor(region_size/  ); x<ceil(reg
```
SO ████ING HAPPY.
```
        blue_avg += ptr[ x];
        green_avg += ptr[  x+  ];
```
Okay. Reunion has 2 wait. 0 time. Bad news: There's no
cavalry, just us. Heimdall wormhole permanently down.
Have 2 seize Magellan 2 get back 2 Core.
```
red_avg = red_avg/(region_size*region_size);
                    region_size*region_size)
```
Send us list of ur resources.
We'll come back 2 u with plan.
```
                    region_size*region_size);

bool color    (green_avg=   )*(green_avg     )
```
Love u.
```
if(color)
{
cvCircle( rgbimg, cvPoint(cvRound(p[0]),cvRound(
        3, CV_RGB(0,255, )
    cvCircle( rgbimg, cvPoint(cvRound(p[0]),cvRo
        cvRound(p   ); CV_RGB(255,0,0); 3,  8,

    if(d = get_actual_depth(cvGet2D(depthimg, cv

        tempLandmark->detected = true;
        X   = 320.5 - cvRound(p[0]);
        mu  = (240.5 - cvRound(p[1]))*d/FOCAL_LE
        w   = X*d/FOCAL_LENGTH;
        tempLandmark->alpha = atan(w/d)*180/
```

Attention, WUC/UTA.

This is Kerenza IV colony.

Love u back. Can't believe u & E alive.
More than I hoped 4.

We v short on time here. Hope u not far away.

Attached list of resources.
Also list of insurgency members.

We also have 1 sympathizer inside BT.
Only reason we have comms to u.

BTW, if u have Martha or Stan Kowalska aboard,
pls tell them I have their daughter Katya. Keeping her
safe. Nothing gonna happen 2 her, I promise.

Attached:

Attention, Kerenza IV colony.

This is WUC/UTA.

Action plan attached.

OMG, tracked down Martha K and she lost her ████!
Used 2 share counseling sessions together. Thought she
had 0 family left.

Okay, our tactician been burning on this 4 12 hrs.
Attached is best chance at seizing Magellan and
getting u ppl off surface alive.

Long shot. But only 1 we've got.

Attached:

OBSIDIO

Attention, WUC/UTA.

This is Kerenza IV colony.

Long shot? Always had a talent for understatement, K.

But 0 choice & 0 time. Will talk 2 my ppl and c what they say.

Love u.

INCEPT: 09/04/75 18:34

Joran KARALIS: all here?

Bruno WAY: ya

Joran KARALIS: . . .

Joran KARALIS: anyone else?

Joran KARALIS: where the hell is everyone?

Bruno WAY: I dunno. I'm pinging Ash and she's showing busy?

Joran KARALIS: what about Steph?

Bruno WAY: no idea. Not like her to miss a meet?

Joran KARALIS: you hear about this thermex going missing?

Bruno WAY: Yeah. Troops everywhere up here. Breaking down doors and stuff. Between that and Steph's bombs at the power plant, they're really █████ed.

Joran KARALIS: Ash got the device planted in the array ok?

Bruno WAY: yeah

Bruno WAY: but she told me the fuel dump didn't blow up like it was supposed to

Bruno WAY: She almost got cuaght

Bruno WAY: Where were u Joran

Joran KARALIS: I got held up.

Joran KARALIS: Couldn't get ther ein time. too many patrols

Bruno WAY: really

Joran KARALIS: What the ████ are you implying

Bruno WAY: I'm not implying anything, J.

Bruno WAY: Just saying Ash was in danger. If u couldn't handle it, one of us could've done it

Joran KARALIS: listen, kid, I know you miss Jenn. I know it must be hard knowing she's out there and you can't get to her.

Joran KARALIS: but NOBODY wants off this rock more than me

Joran KARALIS: your girlfriend already got out. My family is still right here.

Joran KARALIS: I'm wrangling almost 300 resistance members down this ██████ing hole

Joran KARALIS: and you're wrangling your little plumber's cart

Joran KARALIS: so do me a favor and don't ████ing question me again, all right?

Bruno WAY: sure Joran

Bruno WAY: sorry

Joran KARALIS: ████, break is almost over

Joran KARALIS: where the ████ is Steph

Bruno WAY: i dunno

Bruno WAY: Hope she's ok?

Joran KARALIS: . . .

Joran KARALIS: I gotta go. we're close to hitting quota, they riding us like ████ mules

Joran KARALIS: hope someone hears that transmission. We don't have much time left

Joran KARALIS: plan B is looking more likely by the minute

Bruno WAY: kinda scary, huh? feels like the end is close

Joran KARALIS: hope it doesn't come to that. we'll meet back here next break ok?

Bruno WAY: ok

Bruno WAY: keep your head down J

BRIEFING NOTE:
While Asha Grant is talking with the *Mao* and the rebs are chewing on each other, BeiTech's investigation into the missing Thermex is quickly bearing fruit.

**Surveillance footage summary,
prepared by
Analyst ID 7213-0089-DN**

Footage commences at 19:37, taken from a security camera mounted outside the Kerenza geeball field. The night is freezing, snow blowing in from the north. But equipment is still being broken down and loaded onto shuttles; the mine is close to filling the refuel quota, and *Magellan*'s departure is imminent. The crews are jumpy, and everyone seems on high alert—after living through seven months of hell, nobody wants to buy it just a few days from withdrawal, and with the resistance now armed with a ███load of high explosives, the odds of cashing in right before the final bell have skyrocketed.

Lieutenant Jake Christie towers over the landing crews and soldiers around him, broad-shouldered, almost ready to muscle his way out of his own armor. His ident and rank is stenciled across the breastplate, along with his own personal declaration in neat letters:

I AM YOUR GOD NOW.

Steph Park's half his size, her feet barely touching the ground as two hulking figures in full tac armor half lift, half drag her in front of him. She crumples to the icy ground, an involuntary gasp escaping her at the impact. She and her late husband, Hans Tarstad, used to come to the field to watch Gladiators and Renegades games. The high school teams put on a decent show.

Now she kneels, bruised and bloodied, where she once stood.

Shivering uncontrollably. Her breath hanging white in the freezing night air. Her eyes are two dark shadows, dried blood crusted around her nose. Every movement is pained.

They found some of the stolen Thermex stashed under her workstation.

Some, but far from all.

Exactly where the rest can be found has been a topic of conversation between Park and a couple of BeiTech "arbitration specialists" these last few hours. She has failed to provide the answers they seek.

She looks up as Christie slowly drags off his helmet and stows it at the small of his back. Despite the cold, he wants her to see his eyes while he does this. Park takes it all in: the grim line of his mouth, the short salt-and-pepper hair, the tā-moko tattooed down the side of his face, framing his dark stare.

Christie shakes his head slow, like she's disappointed him. "You want me to start shooting civilians till you tell me where the Thermex is? Is that the way we have to play?"

Her voice is a rasping ruin of what it once was, and she has to brace her knuckles against the ground to keep herself upright. "However many you kill," she whispers, "we can kill more of you with the explosives. I'll take the trade."

He looks at her, and she stares back, each measuring the other. He scowls at what he finds. She didn't crack under hours of torture, and she's not going to crack now. This is a waste of time. Time he doesn't have to spare. Troops are due to start pulling out tomorrow. If fireworks kick off between now and then . . .

Still, he asks her one last time: "Where is it, Park?"

She smiles at him. A cracked and bloodied smile. A triumphant, glorious ███-you of a smile. She raises her voice loud enough to be heard. "You'll find out. Real soon. We remember."

He draws his gun, flicks off the safety, businesslike, and aims between her eyes.

She closes them, spreading her arms like she's trying to encompass all the universe in her grasp, and still smiling, she mouths her dead husband's name.

Hans.

He pulls the trigger, and she crumples before the echoes die.

Christie turns away, holsters his weapon and lifts his helmet back into place, speaking to the soldiers beside him. "We'll have to do this the hard way."

They straighten to attention, awaiting orders.

"Start a house-to-house search. Flip it all, turn everything inside out. I want you *so far* inside the business of these locals that you'd be considered married on some planets. You understand? Someone out there knows where this Thermex is, and one way or another, we're going to find them."

"Sir, yessir," come the replies.

"Move it out, pounders."

BRIEFING NOTE:
Sergeant Oshiro's squad is called in to help with the door-to-doors throughout the Kerenza colony. From what we could tell, every active soldier planetside was involved in the search for the missing explosives.

SMISSION: BEITECH PLANETSIDE COMMS—
ATLAS CHANNEL E:001

Sergeant, BeiTech Ground Forces
Rhys Lindstrom, Specialist, BeiTech Ground Forces
Duke Woźniak, Corporal, BeiTech Ground Forces
Corey Markham, Private, BeiTech Ground Forces
Prisha Karpadia, Private, BeiTech Ground Forces
DATE: 09/04/75
TIMESTAMP: 20:20

OSHIRO, Y: All right, pounders, the LT wants every
apartment in this block tossed. Cordon off and search
by twos. Duke, Karpadia, you start on Level Two.
Markham, Lindstrom, you're with me.

MARKHAM, C: Christ, aren't we pulling out tomorrow
morning? Who gives a ███? It's storming like a
mother███er out here.

OSHIRO, Y: You really want to run the risk of ███
blowing up this close to the goal line? Because the
brass don't. They've got every swinging ███ out in
the field, Markham, and your ███ isn't special. So
roust these ███ers out of bed and toss every inch.
Ducts. Ceiling space. Basements. Anyone gets a whiff
of that missing Thermex, you squeal in girlish delight
over comms *immediately*. Copy?

WOŹNIAK, D: Roger that, Sarge.

MARKHAM, C: Can I request my squeals be manly, Sarge?

OSHIRO, Y: No. I said girlish. Now get it done, Markham.

MARKHAM, C: Copy that.

MARKHAM, C: [clears throat]

MARKHAM, C: [high-pitched] I mean, copy that.

WOŹNIAK, D: Son of a ███.

OSHIRO, Y: Duke, report status?

WOŹNIAK, D: [inaudible]

OSHIRO, Y: Say again?

WOŹNIAK, D: The Duke's infrared is fritzing. Piece of . . .

OSHIRO, Y: Lindstrom?

LINDSTROM, R: Duke, get your helmet off. Gimme a look.

WOŹNIAK, D: Be gentle, Hustler.

LINDSTROM, R: Running a diagnostic now, Sarge. Ten seconds.

LINDSTROM, R: You know this suit would be in better shape if you didn't sleep in the ███ing thing . . .

MARKHAM, C: You just let the Duke be the Duke, Cherry.

WOŹNIAK, D: Thank you, Markham.

MARKHAM, C: No problem.

MARKHAM, C: [high-pitched] I mean, no problem.

LINDSTROM, R: Um . . . yeah, this IR system is shot. Main board is fried. Is this . . . is this *toothpaste*? Duke . . . do you brush your teeth in your ATLAS?

WOŹNIAK, D: The first casualty of war is oral hygiene, Hustler.

OSHIRO, Y: Can you fix it, Cherry?

LINDSTROM, R: Not here. I'd need to get a replacement unit. Back at barracks.

OSHIRO, Y: Go get one. These ████ers have enough Thermex to blow us into orbit. I don't want anyone running blind in here. Duke, you go with Cherry and do *not* let him out of your sight. Markham, Karpadia, take Level Two. I'll run Level One solo. Constant comms, am I clear?

MARKHAM, C: [high-pitched] Copy that, boss.

WOŹNIAK, D: Nobody get blown up while the Duke is gone, you hear?

OSHIRO, Y: Move your ████, Cherry. I want you two back here for the next block.

LINDSTROM, R: Roger that. Back in twenty.

BRIEFING NOTE:
Lindstrom and the Duke head back to barracks for the replacement parts.

RADIO TRANSMISSION: BEITECH PLANETSIDE COMMS—
ATLAS CHANNEL L:0091

PARTICIPANTS:

Rhys Lindstrom, Specialist, BeiTech Ground Forces

Duke Woźniak, Corporal, BeiTech Ground Forces

DATE: 09/04/75

TIMESTAMP: 20:24

LINDSTROM, R: Honestly, how the ▇▇▇ do you get toothpaste in your IR unit? You can't brush your teeth with your helmet on.

WOŹNIAK, D: The Duke is a mystery, wrapped in an enigma.

LINDSTROM, R: Do you shower in that ATLAS too?

WOŹNIAK, D: Only on Wednesdays.

WOŹNIAK, D: And you're one to talk, considering you were still wearing your suit while hitting that sugar in the secondary comms array.

LINDSTROM, R: You heard about that?

WOŹNIAK, D: The Duke has a thousand eyes, Hustler. You'll learn this in time. And if you need lessons on putting the "man" in "romance," he will happily oblige.

WOŹNIAK, D: Though honestly, I expected more from a man who spends as much time on his hair as you.

LINDSTROM, R: Um.

WOŹNIAK, D: Seriously, how do you make it do that? The ███ defies gravity.

LINDSTROM, R: No, I mean, Um, I just got a service alert. Enviro systems at the hospital are down again. I gotta go check it out.

WOŹNIAK, D: Oh no you don't. We're headed to barracks.

LINDSTROM, R: It's the hospital, Duke. There's kids and old people in there, not to mention some of our people. They could freeze to death if those enviros stay down overnight. Especially in a storm this bad.

WOŹNIAK, D: Isn't this around the seven hundredth time you've been called out to the hospital in the last few weeks? Aren't you supposed to be fixing the thing?

LINDSTROM, R: The hardware is up to ███. There's only so much I can do.

WOŹNIAK, D: And the Duke is sure the frequency of your visits has nothing to do with the fem you were romancing in the comms array the other night. Who just happens to be a pretty little nurse.

LINDSTROM, R: You know abou—

WOŹNIAK, D: One. Thousand. Eyes.

LINDSTROM, R: I gotta go talk to her, chum. She's ███ed at me.

WOŹNIAK, D: Well, if you're making sweet love to her still wearing your ATLAS, the Duke is not at all surprised.

WOŹNIAK, D: And the Duke doesn't want to be the one to break this to you, but come tomorrow night, it's not really going to matter . . .

LINDSTROM, R: That's why it's important I set this straight, okay? It'll only take a few minutes. You head to barracks and get the replacement IR unit, I'll hit the hospital, and we'll meet back at G Block and I can install it. Oshiro won't ever know.

WOŹNIAK, D: No way.

LINDSTROM, R: Chum, come *onnnn.*

WOŹNIAK, D: Oh well, since you put it like that, the Duke is one hundred percent convinced . . .

LINDSTROM, R: Don't you have any romance in your soul? What happened to the chum who stood in his fem's closet for four hours with his tongue in his hands?

WOŹNIAK, D: He died. Somewhere in that forest of overcoats and shoes.

LINDSTROM, R: I'll teach you to play cards.

WOŹNIAK, D: The Duke rejects your premise. He knows how to play cards.

LINDSTROM, R: I'll teach you how to *win* at cards.

WOŹNIAK, D: . . . The Duke has just been on a bad streak lately.

LINDSTROM, R: You suck at cards, Duke. You're pants-on-head awful.

WOŹNIAK, D: How dare you, sir. Up with this, the Duke shall not put.

LINDSTROM, R: Ten minutes. Tops.

WOŹNIAK, D: . . .

LINDSTROM, R: Think of all the ISH you could win.

LINDSTROM, R: Think of all the ISH you could win off *Markham and Karpadia.*

WOŹNIAK, D: Hmm.

WOŹNIAK, D: All right, then.

WOŹNIAK, D: Ten minutes, Hustler. You meet Duke outside G Block in *ten minutes* or he'll kill you and your whole family.

LINDSTROM, R: You're a prince!

WOŹNIAK, D: As a Duke, he is content.

WOŹNIAK, D: Move your ■■. Clock is ticking.

CAN'T TALK LONG. SORRY ABOUT
THAT WOMAN WHO GOT SHOT.
SHE HAD SOME OF THE MISSING
THERMEX, BUT SOMEONE ELSE
HAS THE REST. IF YOU
KNOW ANYTHING ABOUT IT,
YOU HAVE TO COME
CLEAN, ASH.

Forget the thermex. Forget everything.
Need you to come talk to me. Can't
write any of this down. Supply closet
behind reception. Now. Now.

MD: _____
Signature: _____
Refill 0 1 2 3 4 5 PRN NR

Surveillance footage summary,
prepared by
Analyst ID 7213-0089-DN

Footage taken from the security cam feed in the hospital shows Lindstrom walking back out into the reception area from Asha Grant's supply closet, expression hidden by his helmet. He's fallen into the habit of his fellow pounders, decorating his ATLAS with personalized insignia. The word HUSTLER is stenciled on his chest, along with the four suits from a deck of cards—spades, diamonds, clubs, and right over the spot his real one would be, a heart.

Grant enters behind him, looking tired but wired, her green eyes alight. I imagine the flies on the walls in that supply closet are all aflutter.

Lindstrom turns to Grant, raising a finger as if he's about to speak. But the crack of a slamming door cuts across the feed, the storm rising in volume, and four towering figures in ATLAS rigs march into the foyer from the midnight dark outside. The lead figure scans the area, eight red optics glowing. He has a master sergeant's chevrons and rockers on his arm. The words I AM NOT COME TO BRING PEACE, BUT A SWORD. MATT 10:34 are written across his breastplate.

"Grid search, two-by-twos," he orders, voice tinged with an electronic rasp. "Ali, Zhōu, take the ground floor. Lewis, you're with me."

Yeah. These ██holes again . . .

Ali and Zhōu hoist their rifles and are set to march off when Master Sergeant Marcino notices Lindstrom hovering by the reception desk.

"Well now," he says. "What brings you up here, Specialist?"

The MSG looks meaningfully at Asha Grant. Seems for all Oshiro's warnings, the Duke isn't the only one who's heard rumors about Lindstrom's extracurricular activities.

"Enviro rig is down again, sir," Lindstrom reports. "Trying to get it back up."

Marcino glances at Grant once more, and you can hear the sneer in his voice.

"I'll bet you were, Cherry."

Lewis and Ali chuckle, but Lindstrom doesn't rise to the bait.

"Should be on door-to-doors with Sergeant Oshiro's squad?" Marcino asks.

"Yessir, I'm headed right back there after this."

Marcino stares a moment longer, then turns to his team. "Hit the bricks, pounders. They ain't paying us by the hour. I want every inch of this hospital tossed. Every closet. Every basement. Every air duct. Move out."

Grant's face grows a little pale. "If you let us know what you're looking for . . . ?"

"The rest of that stolen Thermex, civilian," Marcino says. "Unless you—"

The MSG breaks off, glances to the ceiling above his head. It's hard to catch over the security cam rigs, but there's a soft scuffling. Quick. Then quiet.

". . . Did anyone hear that?"

"I heard that," Ali reports.

"It's the enviro system," Grant explains, not batting an eye. "The pipes shrink when it starts to cool down."

Lindstrom glances to the girl, replying after just a moment's hesitation—I'm guessing Miss Grant never told Lindstrom about the mouse she has hiding in her ceiling. Too many secrets between these kids.

It was never gonna end well.

"It's true, sir," Lindstrom lies. "Gets cold quick up there. I better get down to th—"

"Stay right there, Cherry." Marcino turns to Lewis and Zhōu. "You two get up there and check it out."

Grant's eyes grow a little wider, shining a little too bright. She might be the consummate liar, but suddenly thoughts of that little girl above her head—who she is and what it'll mean if she gets caught—are showing through the chinks in her armor.

"It's probably just a mouse," she says.

"A mouse?" Marcino scoffs.

"The cleverest mouse," she says, a little louder. "And they *never get caught*."

Lewis is already climbing up on the reception desk, pulling the ceiling panels aside. Looks like Grant is fighting against pure panic now. Hands in fists. Jaw clenched. She knows what's at stake. The plan her cousin Kady has given her, the incoming *Mao,* the lives hanging in the balance. But you can see it in her eyes, even through this ██ty cam feed. She's not even in that hospital on Kerenza anymore. She's in *another* hospital. On another day. Standing over the empty bed of another little girl who needed her. Another little girl she let down.

She looks at her wrist. The name tattooed there.

Samaira.

Lewis sticks her head up through the ceiling panel, infrared scanning the crawlspace above their heads. Breath escaping in a soft curse.

"Holy ██ing—"

"Katya, run!"

Grant picks up the chair from behind the reception desk, slams it into Lewis's legs, sending her toppling to the floor with a bang.

The sound of faint footsteps scampering away across the ceiling can be heard as Zhōu shouts, bringing up her burst rifle. Lindstrom raises his hands, steps between the pair and yells, "Hold up! Hold up!"

Marcino has his rifle aimed at Grant, bellowing at the top of his lungs. "Civilian, get on your knees! Specialist, step away from the target!"

"Hold fire, she's unarmed!" Lindstrom shouts.

"Step away from the target!" Marcino roars.

Lewis is back on her feet, flechette cannon trained on Grant. Ali is covering the pair, too. Lindstrom stares down the barrels of four weapons, hands still raised.

"Lindstrom, get out of the ████ing way!"

"Okay, okay!" Lindstrom lowers his hands, backs away from Grant. She looks at him desperately, tears shining in her eyes as he steps farther away. "I just didn't want to get hit in the cross fire on a civi, Jesus . . ."

Lindstrom steps back. Lewis marches forward and slaps Grant with one armored fist, splitting her lip and sending her sprawling. She slings her rifle at her back, reaches to the magrestraints at her waist, hissing beneath her breath.

"████, you're gonna ████ing pay for—"

A deafening boom rings out in the room, and Lewis's suit is spattered in red. The private glances up and sees her master sergeant toppling forward, the face of his ATLAS blown out by a point-blank shot to the back of his skull. As Marcino falls, Lindstrom turns his service pistol on Zhōu and fires into the side of her head. ATLAS rigs are built to withstand a lot of punishment, but you need more than seven millimeters of plasteel to stop a straight shot from inside a meter with a .50-cal pistol—particularly from a techhead who knows the weak spots to aim for. Zhōu drops like a stone.

Ali is quicker than his squaddie, shouting as he unloads four shots into Lindstrom's arm and chest. The kid returns fire, putting two rounds into Ali's throat. They both fall backward, Ali gurgling, blood frothing from the puncture in the nanoweave below his chin. Lindstrom's plasteel breastplate is cracked and smoking, but he doesn't seem hurt. He hits the deck with a curse, pistol still in hand. Pretty neat shooting for a techgeek—he's taken out three of Marcino's squad in quick succession.

Pity there were four of them.

Lewis has her MX cannon slung off her back, raised toward Lindstrom. I've seen footage of what those flechette guns can do to living flesh—you can take my word it's somewhere on the south side of pretty. Private Lewis takes square aim at Lindstrom's chest, breathes out slow, finger closing on the trigger.

An office chair slams across her back for the second time in as many minutes. Young Private Lewis is not having a great day. With both her feet planted square, the impact doesn't even put her off balance, but it does distract her—she turns and finds Asha Grant standing behind her, dark hair come loose from her ponytail, lips swollen and bloody from Lewis's slap.

It's kinda weird, chum. Reviewing all these files, I've gotten a little used to watching girls who are stupid good at what they do. Kady Grant, cutting her way through doors of impossible code like a straight razor; Hanna Donnelly, using those three black belts of hers on BeiTech audit team members to full and bloody effect.

But Asha Grant isn't a hacker wizard like her cousin. She's not a kung fu expert. She's not particularly brilliant at *anything*. She's a ██████ing pharmacy intern, chum. Just a regular person like you. An ordinary person caught up in a really ████ situation. So I think, out of every person in these files, that makes her the bravest.

Grant wipes the blood from her swollen lip, eyes flashing as Lewis raises her weapon toward the girl's face. Staring down the barrel and not even blinking.

"████ you," she spits.

BOOM.

Her face is painted red. Lewis topples forward, a smoking hole where her own face used to be. Lindstrom stands behind her, swaying on unsteady legs, hand shaking on his pistol grip. He staggers, breastplate cracked and blackened from the burst rifle shots. Grant runs to his side as he sinks to his knees, tearing off his helmet and gasping for breath. He's pale as death under there, skin filmed in sweat despite the chill. I see the look in his eyes. I recognize it.

The look of a kid who's never killed anyone before now.

A look I saw in the mirror not so long ago.

Not so far from here.

"Are you okay?" they both whisper.

He looks into her eyes and shakes his head, and tears spill from her lashes. His breath is coming quick, and she whispers, "Oh God," as just for a heartbeat everything they are falls away and they remember what they were. A billion light-years from here, back when nothing and no one else mattered but them. When they were each other's everything. And he pulls her close and her mouth finds his, her fingers running through his hair as she kisses him like he's the only thing she can remember in all the universe. As if they're kissing for the very first and very last time.

But only for a heartbeat.

They pull away simultaneously, remembering where they are. Four bodies on the bloody floor around them, four soldiers in ATLAS rigs with locator beacons to show exactly where they died. Various hospital staffers have crept out to see what the commotion was about, now the shooting has stopped, and there's not a one of them who doesn't look gobsmacked to find Grant kissing a BeiTech soldier among the head-shot corpses of four of his own people.

"What the hell . . . ," a doctor named Morton whispers.

"I've gotta get rid of these bodies," Lindstrom says, realizing the situation they're in, the hustler in him coming back to the surface. "Can you clean up this mess?"

Grant nods, looking slightly shell-shocked. "I think so. Yeah."

"Who the hell was that up in the ceiling, Ash?"

She blinks, eyes coming into focus. "Is now really the time for that?"

Lindstrom clenches his jaw. Slips his ATLAS helmet back on. "I'll take their APC. Drive it into one of the ice ravines. Maybe the brass will think they got lost in the storm. Clean up this mess and stay here, okay? You bail now, you're only gonna raise suspicion, and there's search parties everywhere. They're tearing the place apart looking for that Thermex. I'll be back as soon as I can."

". . . Okay."

They stare at each other. Still so many secrets between them. He climbs to his feet, takes one last glance at the ceiling. Leans down to hoist Marcino's body over his shoulder, then marches out into the storm.

Grant watches him go. Licking at bloody lips. His kiss already forgotten.

Like I said, it was never gonna end well for these two.

RADIO TRANSMISSION: BEITECH PLANETSIDE COMMS—
ATLAS CHANNEL L:0091

PARTICIPANTS:

Rhys Lindstrom, Specialist, BeiTech Ground Forces

Duke Woźniak, Corporal, BeiTech Ground Forces

DATE: 09/04/75

TIMESTAMP: 20:51

WOŹNIAK, D: Hustler, you read?

LINDSTROM, R: Yeah, Duke, I read you. Listen, I'm—

WOŹNIAK, D: Sorry to keep you waiting, the Duke got caught up. Pacat's squad had a runner, the Duke had to pound ground to catch the slippery ████er. He's on his way to barracks now. You done at the hospital yet?

LINDSTROM, R: . . . Yeah.

LINDSTROM, R: Yeah, I'm done. What the ████, chum, I been waiting for five minutes and it's cold out here. Oshiro's gonna have my ████.

WOŹNIAK, D: Untwist your pantaloons, Hustler. The Duke said he's sorry. He'll talk Oshiro down, it'll be fine. He's at the barracks now but there's nobody here.

LINDSTROM, R: Nobody?

WOŹNIAK, D: Not a goddamn soul. Everyone must be out on search and seizure. Where would the Duke find these IR units?

LINDSTROM, R: They're in primary storage. Locker B-4, I think. I'll send you a pic via battlenet so you know what to look for. Bring an extra just in case.

WOŹNIAK, D: Roger that.

WOŹNIAK, D: How's your sugar? Get it straightened out?

LINDSTROM, R: Yeah. Yeah, five by five. Thanks for understanding, chum.

WOŹNIAK, D: Never let it be said the Duke isn't a romantic.

LINDSTROM, R: After that tongue story? Not a chance.

WOŹNIAK, D: [laughs]

WOŹNIAK, D: Chum, this place gives the Duke the crawls. Nothing in the 'verse weirder than a totally empty school.

WOŹNIAK, D: . . . The Duke hated school.

LINDSTROM, R: Yeah, I didn't have much fun, either.

WOŹNIAK, D: You okay, Hustler? You sound . . . *Well, hello there.*

LINDSTROM, R: Hello who? Me?

WOŹNIAK, D: *This is a restricted area, civilian. The Duke would get his hands in the ▮▮▮ing air mighty quick if he was you.*

LINDSTROM, R: Duke? You okay?

WOŹNIAK, D: *Did we?*

WOŹNIAK, D: *I think you better get your hands up, little man.*

LINDSTROM, R: Duke? Report status, over?

WOŹNIAK, D: Hustler—

—TRANSMISSION INTERRUPTED—

LINDSTROM, R: Duke?

LINDSTROM, R: Duke, this is Hustler, you read me?

LINDSTROM, R: . . . Duke?

These events happened simultaneously, so I'm splicing footage and radio conversations together as best I can. I'm going to use italics to denote Woźniak's sections, just to make it easier on us. I'm not ██ing Shakespeare, all right?

Lindstrom's ATLAS radio squawks just as he's loading Private Lewis's faceless corpse into the back of his squad's APC. It's pitch dark outside. As Lindstrom turns, you can catch a glimpse of Asha Grant and her fellow hospital staffers furiously mopping up the pools of blood and brains left in his wake.

WOŹNIAK, D: Hustler, you read?

LINDSTROM, R: Yeah, Duke, I read you. Listen, I'm—

WOŹNIAK, D: Sorry to keep you waiting, the Duke got caught up. Pacat's squad had a runner, the Duke had to pound ground to catch the slippery ██er. He's on his way to barracks now. You done at the hospital yet?

The kid looks at the four dead bodies he's dumped in the APC. As he glances down, we see his ATLAS is drenched in blood. Sleet and snow are glued to the gore.

LINDSTROM, R: . . . Yeah.

LINDSTROM, R: Yeah, I'm done. What the ██, chum, I
been waiting for five minutes and it's cold out here.
Oshiro's gonna have my ██.

*Woźniak strides in through the front doors of McCaffrey Tech
and scans the empty hallways. Outside the doors, the growing storm
is scratching and clawing at the glass. The optics on Woźniak's
helmet are blood red, a cluster of eight scarlet dots glowing in the
gloom.*

WOŹNIAK, D: Untwist your pantaloons, Hustler. The
Duke said he's sorry. He'll talk Oshiro down, it'll
be fine. He's at the barracks now but there's nobody
here.

LINDSTROM, R: Nobody?

WOŹNIAK, D: Not a goddamn soul. Everyone must be out
on search and seizure. Where would the Duke find these
IR units?

Lindstrom has jumped into the driver's seat of the APC now. He
eases his foot onto the pedal, rumbling out of the parking lot and into
the night at a nice, relaxed speed that completely belies the nature
of his cargo. Through the windshield and falling snow, you can see
countless dots of light across the Kerenza colony—squads of pounders roaming door to door looking for Admiral Sūn's stolen Thermex.

The kid nudges the wheel, turns onto the road leading out of
town and off toward the hermium refinery. Ahead of him, BeiTech's
makeshift bridge spans the kilometer-deep crack in the glacier that
forms the colony's foundations. He presses on the accelerator a little harder as he talks into comms.

LINDSTROM, R: They're in primary storage. Locker B-4, I think. I'll send you a pic via battlenet so you know what to look for. Bring an extra just in case.

WOŹNIAK, D: Roger that.

WOŹNIAK, D: How's your sugar? Get it straightened out?

LINDSTROM, R: Yeah. Yeah, five by five. Thanks for understanding, chum.

Woźniak is wandering the halls, stopping occasionally to check inside a few of the classrooms. But his initial assessment seems spot on. The place is a ghost town.

Lindstrom is still driving, snow pounding the windshield, storm howling. He's close to the ravine now, reaching down to jam Master Sergeant Marcino's VK-85 burst rifle against the accelerator. He glances across to the passenger seat and the dead master sergeant sitting beside him.

He shrugs an apology.

WOŹNIAK, D: Never let it be said the Duke isn't a romantic.

LINDSTROM, R: After that tongue story? Not a chance.

WOŹNIAK, D: [laughs]

WOŹNIAK, D: Chum, this place gives the Duke the crawls. Nothing in the 'verse weirder than a totally empty school.

WOŹNIAK, D: . . . The Duke hated school.

Woźniak has reached the hallway to the storage area, which is actually the repurposed school gymnasium. There's no heavy ord-

nance or armaments kept here, but much of BeiTech's day-to-day operating gear and spare parts have been neatly arrayed in long stretches of military-issue lockers that strangely mirror the high school lockers in the hallways outside.

Lindstrom opens the door to the APC, one hand on the wheel. Jamming another burst rifle against the steering column to hold the wheel in place, he takes a last look at Marcino's corpse and raises his middle finger, then leaps out of the still-moving APC. He hits the ground with a flurry of snow and a soft grunt, the shock absorbers in his ATLAS taking the brunt of the high-speed landing. The APC trundles off down the road, veering slightly left until it finally clips the bridge stanchion, rides up onto two wheels and plummets clean over the edge of the ravine.

The storm swallows the explosion utterly.

LINDSTROM, R: Yeah, I didn't have much fun, either.

WOŹNIAK, D: You okay, Hustler? You sound . . . *Well, hello there.*

Woźniak comes to a dead stop. In front of him stands a teenager. Kind of short. Reasonably thin. He's got dark curls and dark eyes and a ▮▮▮-you swagger to his walk, but the picture is kinda ruined by his dirty overalls and the grubby covered cart he's pushing in front of him.

A plumber's cart.

LINDSTROM, R: Hello who? Me?

Bruno Way's momentary surprise dissolves into something quieter. Darker. His hands creep down the side of his cart. Woźniak raises his burst rifle, aims it in Way's direction. Maybe he doesn't want to appear too threatening. Maybe he doesn't really register the kid as a threat—he's a ▮▮ing plumber, after all. But there's still more than enough iron in his voice as he speaks.

WOŹNIAK, D: This is a restricted area, civilian. The Duke would get his hands in the ▮▮ing air mighty quick if he was you.

Lindstrom picks himself up off the snow, the evidence of his murder of four fellow BeiTech pounders now a flaming wreck at the bottom of a chasm of prehistoric ice.

LINDSTROM, R: Duke? You okay?

Bruno Way sighs. Offers Woźniak a conciliatory smile.
"Well, I was gonna just try to leave this in your supply cache on a timer and run for it. But I knew I was on borrowed time after you ▮▮ers got Steph. I think we all knew how this was going to end, didn't we?"
Woźniak raises his rifle a little higher.

WOŹNIAK, D: Did we?

"I heard she got out on the shuttles," Way says in a small, sad voice. "I could've lived with that. Even if it meant never seeing her again. But about a month after the invasion, you had us clearing rubble near the day care center, and . . ." Tears shine in the boy's eyes. "That's where she worked, see? Jenna loved kids . . ."

WOŹNIAK, D: I think you better get your hands up, little man.

LINDSTROM, R: Duke? Report status, over?

"But I told Asha I'd be seeing Jenna again soon." Bruno Way *pulls aside the tarp covering his plumber's cart. Underneath it, rigged with a tangle of wires and a homemade detonator, is around sixteen kilos of BeiTech's stolen Thermex.*

His smile is as cold as the snow outside.

"You wanna come with me?"

WOŹNIAK, D: Hustler—

The explosion cuts Woźniak's feed to a wash of gray static, but I can watch it bloom through a few of the security cams scattered around the colony. Tearing through the high school in the blink of an eye, shattering windows and walls and ripping the roof to pieces. It blossoms upward like some burning orange flower, black smoke and fire melting the snow to steam. Ashes tumble from the rolling black skies, falling back to the burning gravesite that is McCaffrey Tech.

LINDSTROM, R: Duke?

Lindstrom presses his hand to his helmet to deaden the roar of the storm.

LINDSTROM, R: Duke, this is Hustler, you read me?

And then he sees the flames and smoke rising from the center of town.

His hands curl into fists, fury creeping into his voice.

LINDSTROM, R: . . . Duke?

conversation we could fr[...]
between the remnants of
Grant's insurgency cell,
time-stamped a few minu[...]
before the explosion at
McCaffrey.

INCEPT: 09/04/75 20:48

Asha GRANT: Joran, Bruno, u there?

Joran KARALIS: Break just started, I've only got a few minutes.

Asha GRANT: wheres bruno

Joran KARALIS: No idea. I heard about Steph. Jesus Christ what was she doing ██ing around with Thermex? And where were you earlier?

Asha GRANT: Ok, Joran, stop stop.

Asha GRANT: I need you to listen to me.

Asha GRANT: We got a reply, Joran. There's a ship in the system who heard our distress call.

Joran KARALIS: WHAT THE ██?

Asha GRANT: survivors from the colony. Some people from a UTA ship. I don't know all the details. But my cousin's with them. They have a plan, I'm sending you and Bruno the deets now. FOR GOD'S SAKE DELETE THE FILE ONCE YOU'VE READ IT

Joran KARALIS: jesus

Joran KARALIS: okay, I understand. Just . . .

Asha GRANT: I know. Believe me. But that's not all of it. Soldiers just raided the hospital looking for that missing thermex and four of them got killed. By Rhys

Joran KARALIS: WHAT?

Asha GRANT: He's dumping the bodies now, we've cleaned up the mess but it's only a matter fo time before they'r emissed and there's gonna be a world of ██ coming down on us. Not sure how much we'll get to talk again so read that plan CAREFUL

Joran KARALIS: Jesus chrsit he killed fellow pounders? What the hell for?

Asha GRANT: It was my fault, I

Asha GRANT: did you feel that?

Joran KARALIS: Feel what

Asha GRANT: Oh ███, there's an explosion in the middle of town Joran

Joran KARALIS: Where? Not near the detention blocks?

Asha GRANT: no i

Asha GRANT: Joran I gotta go.

Asha GRANT: Keep your head down. Read the plan. We're counting on you.

Joran KARALIS: Ash, you still there?

Joran KARALIS: ASHA

BRIEFING NOTE: Joran Karalis's final message on the Kerenza mine notice board.

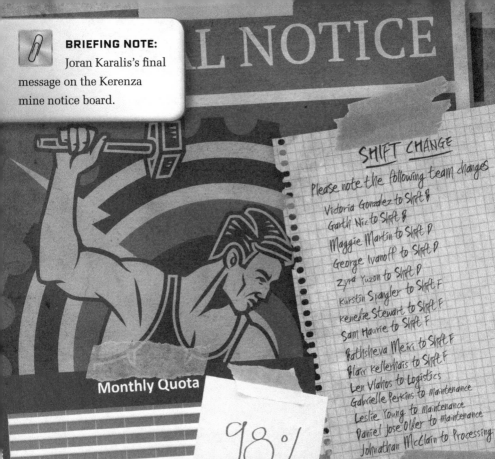

L NOTICE

SHIFT CHANGE

Please note the following team changes

Victoria Gonzalez to Shift B
Garth Nix to Shift B
Maggie Martin to Shift D
George Ivanoff to Shift D
Zyra Yuzon to Shift D
Kirstin Spangler to Shift F
Kenelie Stewart to Shift F
Sam Haurie to Shift F
Bathsheva Meiri to Shift F
Blair Kellerhals to Shift F
Len Vlahos to Logistics
Gabrielle Perkins to maintenance
Leslie Young to maintenance
Daniel Jose Older to maintenance
Johnathan McClain to Processing

(se

The ____ ____ replaces, levels 8, 9,
42, 43, 47, 49, 67 + 76

Thermal regulators (service), levels 4 – 7,
41, 51 – 54, 62, 69, + 71

Monthly Quota

98%

KEEP IT UP, TEAM!

Hermium Production (unprocessed kgs)

0   10   20   30   40   50   60   70   80   90   100

Attention, teams. Despite challenges of the 74-a tunnel collapse, I'm pleased to report we're back to quota! Amazing work! Notification of teams who qualified for extra rations will be posted after 9:00 shift change today.

We've had reports of validation credentials malfunctioning at certain checkpoints. If you're having trouble with your pass, see the BT sergeant assigned to your shift. We can't take any risks this close to reaching final quota—there are people in the colony who just don't understand we're working WITH BeiTech to get us all out of this. Security MUST be our watch word.

Now isn't the time to rest on our laurels or lose sight of the finish line. We're never getting off this planet unless we all work together, colonists and BeiTech forces alike. I know you're tired, but I also know you're the best people I've ever worked with, and you will rise to the challenge.

— Joran K.

REMEMBER YOUR DECONTAMINATIO PROTOCOLS

REMEMBER TO FOLLOW ALL STEPS FOR
DECONTAMINATION, AS OUTLINED IN YOUR
WALLACE ULYANOV
CONSORTIUM EMPLOYEE
HANDBOOK

REMEMBER: IT'S NOT JUST YOUR ~~RISK~~
NOT F

HANG IN THERE

mber to lodge your visiting day requests with BT division
y no lot ~~than~~ 08/20/75. All requests must be made
n cer~~oval~~ by your shift supervisor AHEAD OF

Looking to trade—
B-Packs for cigarettes
(no synth ▮ please).
Contact Pando from D Shift.

CARTER TURNS
52

Yeah, it's my birthday, you
Looking for volunteers to swing by
in the dorms and rais
Tonight after
If y
I'll see you or

"But you, Lord, do not
be far from me. you are
my strength; come quickly
to help me."
Psalm 22:19

WE REMEMBER

It's been thirty-seven minutes since Master Sergeant Ray Marcino and his squad of ██holes got murdered in the foyer of Kerenza IV hospital, and aside from a sticky splinter of skull stuck to the lens of Camera F-ii, which obviously got missed in the cleanup, there's zero sign of the massacre that took place here.

Asha Grant is seated behind the front desk, eyes straying constantly to the windows and the dark outside. The glow of flames still light the clouds above the ruins of McCaffrey Tech, but except for a repeat of the curfew warnings blaring over the colony public address system, there's been no word from BeiTech about what caused the blast or exactly where it happened. Grant's repeated attempts to raise Bruno Way on IM have failed, and she's returned to duty, chewing on her lip and watching the storm rage outside.

She also checked up in the ceiling, but there was no trace of her clever little mouse. Grant obviously is torn between waiting for Lindstrom and going to look for Katya. The kid could just be hiding in a sub-basement or access tunnel, bound to return in time. But still, you can almost see the memory of another little girl in Grant's eyes. Stare locked on that tattoo at her wrist. What-ifs running on a constant loop inside her head.

She brightens a little as a BeiTech armored personnel carrier pulls to a hard stop outside the front doors and a tall figure in an ATLAS climbs out. The word HUSTLER is scrawled on his chest next to some battle scarring and a cluster of card suits. But Grant's smile evaporates as more figures bail out of the vehicle, five in total. Among the group, you can make out a female form with THOU SHALT ~~NOT~~ KILL on her breastplate and the hulking figure of Lieutenant Jake Christie.

The latter slams through the front doors, steam rising off his ATLAS. He's the only BT goon not wearing a helmet, seemingly oblivious to the cold. His eyes are dark, the tattoo on his face twisting as he spies Grant behind the counter. The other pounders stomp in behind him, Lindstrom beside him.

"That her?" Christie asks.

"That's her," Lindstrom replies.

"Wha—" Grant rises half out of her chair as Lindstrom hurls something small and shiny at her head. She ducks aside only barely, the object hitting the wall behind her with a crack. "Hey!"

The squad members have their weapons out, all aimed squarely at Grant.

"Get on the floor," Oshiro growls.

Grant looks to Lindstrom, terror in her eyes. "Rh—"

"GET ON THE ███████ING FLOOR!" he bellows.

Grant shrinks visibly, sinks to her knees. Before she can get herself flat, Private Markham is storming behind her, slamming her to the deck with his boot. She grunts as she hits the linoleum, face to face with the object Lindstrom threw at her head a few moments before. Shiny. Metal. Slightly charred.

A set of dog tags, stenciled with a dead man's name.

WOŹNIAK, DUKE. PRIVATE. 4TH PLATOON.

"I warned you," Lindstrom snaps. "You ████ing ████. I asked if you knew anything about that Thermex and you lied right to my face."

"I do—"

An armored boot to her ribs shuts her up, and she curls into a groaning ball.

"One of your people just used it to kill my friend, Asha!"

"Lindstrom, ease up," Christie growls. "We need her alive for interrogation."

"Request permission to bring the ███ing popcorn, sir," Karpadia spits.

Lindstrom marches past the reception area and kicks open the door to Grant's supply closet with a crash. She groans, trying to speak as he smashes around inside, finally returning with a battered palmpad in his hand.

"N-no," Grant moans. "No . . ."

Lindstrom tosses the device to his lieutenant.

"There should be more data on that," he says. "Names of other insurgents at least. Everything they're planning. It's got encryption on it I'm not equipped to crack down here, but the techheads on *Churchill* live for this ███. Shoot it up to Cordova and she'll have it busted wide open in ten minutes."

"I'll send it up now on a shuttle," Christie says, glancing at the still-groaning girl. "Get that little ███ on her feet."

Markham drags Grant up by the hair as she shrieks, clamping one metal fist on the back of her neck and squeezing. Her face twists in pain, dark hair tangled over her eyes. Christie looks her up and down, ice in his stare.

"Get her in the APC. I want her locked down in an interrogation cell at the LZ by the time I get back from dropping this palmpad to the flyboys."

"My pleasure," Markham growls, dragging Grant toward the door.

The girl looks to Lindstrom, rage in her glare now. She thrashes momentarily in Markham's grip, aims a mouthful of spit at Lindstrom that falls well short of the mark. "You ███████!" she shrieks. "YOU ███ING TRAITOR!"

Lindstrom stares, eight glowing optics in his helmet burning blood red.

The kid doesn't say a word.

Christie spins on his heel, palmpad in hand, and marches back to the APC. Markham hurls Grant into the rear of the vehicle as hard as he can without breaking her completely, bundling in behind her. The rest of Oshiro's squad follow, Karpadia taking the wheel, Christie sitting beside her. Oshiro watches Lindstrom lean down slow, pick up the Duke's dog tags in an armored fist. He hands the sergeant the tags, then stomps to the APC and climbs into the back with his bleeding, semiconscious former girlfriend. No doubt hoping for a front-row seat at her interrogation and eventual execution.

The APC's engines roar to life, and the vehicle vanishes into the night.

Yup.

I told you it was never gonna end well for those two.

MOBILE JUMP PLATFORM
MAGELLAN WILL BE
OPERATIONAL IN:

KERENZA COLONY WILL
BE LIQUIDATED IN:

00 DAYS
14 HOURS: **22** MINUTES

99%

HERMIUM
REQUIRED TO JUMP

The ward hums with its usual soft symphony of beeps as Isaac Grant makes his way in. He shouldn't be out of bed yet, but if he can't answer some of the captain's more urgent questions about the *Mao,* his long-term health isn't really going to be an issue one way or another. Still, he moves slowly and warily, protecting the bandages hidden under his clothes, keeping his gestures small and careful.

Ella Malikova looks considerably worse than him. She's white as a sheet, a fact thrown into stark relief by the black shadows under her eyes. Her skin looks dull, wrong, like if you pushed your finger against it, you might leave a bruise just by touching her. Most of her face is hidden by the makeshift breather the docs have worked out for her, but her eyes land on Grant just a moment after he walks in. She wiggles the fingers on one hand in greeting but doesn't bother lifting them from the keyboard in her lap.

The equipment she's hooked up to now compares to her old setup about as favorably as a dumpy Shetland pony stacks up alongside a Thoroughbred. And slowly but surely, despite her sass in online chats, her strength's been ebbing away. Now she doesn't do much more than move her fingers across the keyboard, eyes almost closed.

Grant weaves his way through the beds, sinks down into the

chair beside hers with a groan and turns his head to look up at the screen suspended from the ceiling above her. His daughter's been through to optimize Ella's computer rig for her, but he's here to see about the medical equipment.

"Let's have a look at all this," he murmurs, taking in her mask and the machines it's hooked to with a wave of his hand.

She flutters her fingers at him again, this time in a fending-off gesture, avoiding the effort of reaching up to draw down the mask and actually speak. Either she trusts him to take her meaning or she knows he wouldn't listen anyway.

He nods, understands and ignores, gaze resting on the monitor beside her bed. Its readouts are jagged lines, signifying that all sorts of functions in her body aren't as they should be, but her blood oxygen reading is simply a digit in the top right-hand corner. It flickers every few seconds, displaying a new number.

77

79

81

77

"Not good enough, young lady," he says, mock stern. "That needs to be up close to one hundred. Let's see if we can't squeeze a little more efficiency out of all this, and then out of you in turn. I read up on how the lung support works."

Ella lifts her brows, eloquent in her cynicism.

He huffs a soft breath of laughter. "What's the worst thing that could happen? Actually, don't answer that. Knowing our luck, it will."

She tries to fix him with a Look, but the corners of her eyes are creasing in a tired, reluctant smile.

He takes this as permission, pulling himself to his feet, digging into the tool belt at his waist and carefully levering the back off a blue machine whose purpose I can't identify, though it's definitely connected to her somehow.

Hey, I'm here for my charm and insight, not my medical degree, okay?

Grant speaks quietly as he works, his voice a low, steady stream. She has her eyes closed, and it's hard to tell if she's listening. "I was speaking to young Niklas," he says. "I'm so sorry about your father, Ella. I didn't know. I'm afraid I haven't had time to think about it one way or another, but I should have asked."

He reaches down to rest a large hand over her skinny one, enveloping it for a moment, then gets back to work. "My wife and I used to joke that we were going to have a whole passel of children, and she used to tease me that I'd end up surrounded by daughters and outvoted at every turn, not that I'd have minded."

He's forced to pause a moment and press his lips together at the mention of Helena Grant, drawing in a quick, steadying breath through his nose. [Note: Grant had been informed by his daughter of the loss of his wife. Footage has not been included in the file, because, chum, there are some things you just don't need to see.] "Then we used to joke that once we got Kady, we figured out our limits pretty fast," he continues. "She was more than enough for us to handle."

The back snaps onto the machine once more, and he frowns at the readouts. "Do you mind if I take your mask off for a moment? I think I can get a much better seal around your face, which should help with those O$_2$ numbers."

She nods just a fraction, and with infinitely gentle hands he cradles her head and removes the strap, careful not to tangle it in her hair. He lifts the mask away from her face, and her quick, shallow breaths are audible as he pulls a tube from his belt and runs a line of what looks like putty around the rubber edges of the mask in one efficient movement. It's built for someone much larger than her, which makes sense—she's far smaller than anyone on Falk's crew was.

"Just a moment longer, I've got you," he promises in a whisper, testing the new seal with his finger, then strapping the mask back into place.

Her blood oxygen level has plummeted to 71 percent in the thirty seconds she was left to breathe on her own, and he lays his hand over hers once more, his voice low and gentle. "Breathe as slowly as you can, just listen to me while I ramble on, your breath'll come easier in a minute. So I was saying, we realized we'd met our match in Kady. But after a few years on Kerenza, we had her cousin Asha come to join us. She stayed with us at first, and once she finished school, she had a place right near ours. She and Kady saw each other almost every day. I got a glimpse of what it would have been like to have more than one daughter."

Ella's eyes are fixed on his face, her chest still rising and falling quickly as her body compensates for the momentary loss of the mask.

"I said it to Hanna, and I'll say it to you and your cousin Nik," he says quietly. "You still have people who care about you. I know being stuck here must be beyond frustrating. Nik told me about the chair you had on *Heimdall,* and it sounds like a wonder. And I know some of the med staff here treat you like an idiot because you can't talk back. So I want you to know as well that we know exactly who you are, Ella. We know you're quick, you're funny, you're unquestionably smarter than I am. I would never presume to take your father's place, but I know he loved you, and I'll do my best to stand in his shoes while we get through this—and longer, if you want. You still have a family, is what I'm saying."

His gaze flicks up to the monitor again, and he breaks into a slow smile at the number in the top right-hand corner.

95

96

95

"Better," he approves. "You should start to feel a little stronger after an hour or two of that. I'm going to pick up some more tools from Engineering, and I'll be back tonight to work on the bed's hydraulics for you. For now—"

He breaks off, frowning—he's spotted something on the shelf behind her monitor. "Who put him where you couldn't see him?"

He stretches up, carefully lifts down the large beaker currently housing Mr. Biggles II and sets him on a shelf within Ella's line of sight. "Clearly they don't understand he's integral to your creative process," he says. "We're surrounded by idiots."

He reaches down to gently squeeze her hand once more. "I'll be back tonight, and young Ezra's going to drop through on his next meal break in case you need anything. Try not to cause any riots here until then."

The corners of her eyes crease properly now, and her fingers squeeze his, then flick, bidding him go.

He stands a moment longer, as though he'd prefer to stay, then nods. "Keep an eye on her," he says to the fish, and takes his leave.

She watches him until he's gone from view.

Her hand shakes as she wipes her face—it's clearly a huge effort, but it's well spent, as far as Ella Malikova's concerned. Though no doubt her eyes are just watering as a result of the improved oxygen flow or something, she wouldn't want anyone to mistake that moisture for anything else.

Surveillance footage summary,
prepared by
Analyst ID 7213-0089-DN

Footage of this meeting is from the security camera mounted in the brig, where Ben Garver, former head of security at Jump Station *Heimdall,* is in solitary confinement. Garver's sitting against the wall farthest from the door, elbows on his knees, eyes closed. It's been an hour or so since he last moved.

The doors slide open to reveal Hanna Donnelly. Her hair's pulled back in a braid, she's in a utilitarian jumpsuit and—key piece of information here—she has a Benden M-6 handgun in her right hand.

Garver's eyes open, and he lowers his chin to get a look at the visitor. Registers her identity. He doesn't stand, but he breathes deep. Eyes locked on that gun. Readying himself for what's coming.

Donnelly's the one to break the silence. "We're nearly at Kerenza IV."

"Yes," he says quietly.

"We have a plan," she continues, soft and even, no emotion. "The odds aren't good, but they'll be better if we're all working off the same playbook."

"Yes."

"You know why I'm here," she says simply. "You know what's at stake."

Finally, he looks away from the gun. Meets her eyes. "Yes."

"You have training. We need everyone. But I need to trust you'll follow orders, whether or not you agree with the plan."

"Yes."

"You killed our captain," she continues, as if she hasn't heard him.

"Yes."

"Now we have a soldier in charge. You probably think it was all worth it."

Silence.

"Well? Are you glad you did it?"

". . . No."

The silence stretches between them as she gazes down at him, trying to take his measure. He looks up in return, his face unreadable.

"You can trust me," he eventually says. "My people. We all have something to fight for. It's why we did what we did. Now the only thing that makes sense is to fight together. You know that, or you wouldn't be here. And I give you my word, I know it too."

The silence stretches one more time, and then Donnelly inclines her head in a slow nod. Needs must when the devil drives. He's one more trained body for a fighting force that could desperately use it. He knows it. She knows it.

"Two things, Hanna," he says, pushing to his feet. They're of a height when they stand eye to eye.

She watches him move but doesn't raise her weapon. Waiting instead.

"I've never told you properly, respectfully, how sorry I am about your father," he says, meeting her gaze without flinching. "He was a fine man."

Donnelly simply stares, obviously uninterested in this man's opinions of her old man. Garver nods, accepting the dismissal.

"Second. Did you know Shane Pangburn? Grav-train engineer at *Heimdall*?"

Her brow creases at this unexpected turn. "A little."

"His wife, Cara, and his son, my godson, are aboard. I'd like to see them before . . . before. And make provisions for them. If they make it through this but I don't. Will you let me do that?"

Donnelly stares at him a long moment, then glances at the door behind her. The pistol in her hand. And making her decision, she tucks the gun back into her belt.

"Yes," she says simply.

She turns on her heel and strides out the door.

Leaving it open behind her.

Son, you've got this.
You think Helena and I
would have invited just
anybody into our home?
You're our family too. Helena
loved you, and you know
I do, too. Come back safe.
Because you know there's
no way I can handle Kady
all on my own.

I'll be on the radio the whole time,
baby girl. I'll be with Yulin in
Engineering. I have to say, when
we used to have talks about your
future, commanding a battle
fleet isn't quite what I imagined,
but I know you can do this..
I'll be with you every step.

I'll be in touch every minute, Ella.
There's no way I'm letting anything
happen to you, and I demand a
rematch when this is over. If you
think I'm letting a fifteen-year-old
beat me at cards, you've got another
thing coming.

Nik, you are what your actions make
you. Not what other people say you are.
You've decided who you are, in the face
of a world that wanted to tell you
otherwise. I get the impression maybe
nobody's ever told you they're proud
of you. I am, Nik. I'm proud to know
you.

You have this, Hanna. Your father
would be so damn proud of you
right now. He knew exactly how
incredible you were. We used
to talk about it, late at
night, these women we
were raising. Just how far
and how fast our daughters
would exceed us. He loved that.

437 / 615

All over the *Mao,* goodbyes are under way. Spouses, or siblings, or parents and children, or new lovers found as the ship's occupants creep toward the valley of the shadow of death.

They cry, they embrace, they pray, they wait with grim determination. They whisper their instructions to themselves over and over again, or pore over manuals for jobs they're not qualified to do.

They close their eyes tight, or stare into space.

And in case this is the end—because this probably *is* the end—they say goodbye.

Winifred McCall is among those readying themselves to join the boarding parties, and just now she is whispering to herself, practicing the words of the speech she must soon make to those who will go to war with her.

Kady Grant, unimaginably, will command the bridge of the *Mao.* There will be so few of the crew left there, and of those who remain, she understands the systems best. And most important, she's the only one AIDAN will answer to.

But now her captain has given her a few minutes' leave to find Ezra Mason.

The two of them stand in a corner of the crowded launch bay, where crews are readying fighters, mechanics are shouting, pilots are running checks and making their farewells.

Amid all the noise, Kady and Ezra don't say a word.

They don't need to.

She's such a little thing in his arms. But their bodies fit together perfectly, like they were made to just the right measurements. Up on her toes, her arms wrapped around him.

Her fingers creep across the nape of his neck, curl up into his hair, as she presses her cheek to the rough fabric of his flight suit, eyes squeezed tight shut.

His big hand splays across her back, keeping her close.

Time slows, their breath in sync. Still amid the chaos all around them. Ignoring the shouts, the slamming doors and screeching wheels. They could be alone, for all the mind they pay any of it.

Slowly, she eases away just enough to look up at him, solemn. No quick wit, no easy joke. He gazes back down, letting her drink her fill. He doesn't offer her false reassurances. He simply lets her look at him. He gives her that.

She lifts one hand to press her palm to his cheek, and he tilts his head into her touch, just a fraction.

Breathe in.

Breathe out.

And then she's stepping up onto the toes of his boots for the tiny bit of extra height it gives her, pulling him down for a kiss, fierce and sudden.

They move with perfect ease, practiced a thousand times. She launches herself up, legs wrapping around his hips, and he turns toward the wall. His arms protect her from the impact as he lets himself crash into it, as their lips meet again.

Her tears are soaking her cheeks, salting their lips, and he lifts one hand to tangle it through her hair, to press it to the nape of her neck, to squeeze her arm, as if somehow, without words—he was never one for words anyway—he can bring her comfort.

And eventually, somehow, they silently know it's time.

Their lips slowly part. His cheeks are flushed, hers pale.

His mouth twists into the ghost of a smile, and he leans down one more time to kiss her nose. He helps her down from where he held her against the wall, and smooths her hair, and holds still one more moment so she can gaze at him one last time.

They've said the things they need to without talking at all. So now they can speak again, using words for lesser things.

"Back to work," he murmurs. "Game face on."

"You know it," she whispers. "Let's kick some ■■. I'll talk to you from the bridge. Love you, Ez."

"Love you right back. And I'll see you when this is done."

They hesitate a long moment—neither wanting to be the one to step back—and then she forces herself to do it. She blows him a kiss and turns for the exit, making sure her face doesn't crumple until he can't see.

He watches her until she's out of sight, standing exactly where she left him. Then it's his turn to walk away. As he heads for his cockpit, he digs in his pocket for the picture of her he'll tuck into his display. He kisses it once, for luck.

He's gonna need it.

**Surveillance footage summary,
prepared by
Analyst ID 7213-0089-DN**

Nik Malikov is sitting on Ella's bed. Isaac and Kady Grant have arranged for her to be moved to an empty room to accommodate the suite of monitors now arrayed around her. She'll be side by side with Kady and AIDAN in the coming fight, and she needs her weapons of choice.

There's a chair for the nurse who will sit with her, ready to prop her up in whatever way he can during the battle. But he's left the Malikovs alone for now, and the chair is too far away for Nik's taste.

So he sits on the edge of her bed.

Her rig still looks like it's held together with spit and good luck, but it's Isaac Grant's spit and good luck, and that's a lot more durable than your average saliva. Her oxygen readings are back at 99 percent, and she can speak whole sentences without trouble.

Nik's talking as we pick up the footage. He's in his flight suit, ready to report in a few minutes. "Back on *Heimdall,* I'm the one—"

"Nope." She cuts him off.

"But it was my fault," he insists.

"Nope," she replies, fixing him with a quelling look.

"I let them onto the ship, Ella," he says softly, gaze dropping to the thin white blanket that covers her.

"Nik," she says, exasperated. "That mother█████er Merrick lied to you. You did nothing but the usual biz, took a deal anyone would

/ 615

have taken. And Merrick paid up for his part in it, so we're as square as we're going to get with him. You gotta leave it behind. Focus on the now. And know . . ." She's forced to pause, drag in a breath—or maybe she's just buying time to choose her words. "Anything happens, I'll keep an eye out for Blondie. She's not so bad after all."

"I can't help feeling like I should have done more for you."

Ella rolls her eyes, shuffles a little in bed so she can sit up straighter, and pulls down her mask like she means business. "You listen, Nik. The day you came to *Heimdall* was the day my life turned around. I make the best of what I got, but what I got started to get a whole lot bigger when you arrived."

He opens his mouth to reply, and she swats at him and continues. "Look, cuz, I love you, okay?"

"Ella, I love you too. But I don't know what to say. I want to say something big, and I don't know what it is."

She gentles, resting one thin hand on his. "I know," she replies soft. "And don't worry, Nik. You said it already. You said it every day, with everything you did for me. You said it every time you didn't just *act* like coming to spend time with me was the most fun you could have, you actually *thought* it. You've done everything I could ever have wanted you to do, Nik, and you're still doing it."

Finally he breaks out the dimples for her, and it's a real smile, despite everything. "Ells, you're ███ing amazing. You're a miracle, and I don't mean surviving. I'm going to see you again, okay?"

"Okay," she whispers.

He leans in, careful of her rig but not afraid of it, to curl his arms around her and gather her up in a hug. She pushes her mask back into place so she can wrap her arms around his neck, squeezing as tight as she can in reply.

Her eyes flutter open.

"Nik, are you still wearing that ███ing parachute?"

"Maybe . . ."

"You know you're going to be flying in *space,* right . . . ?"

Hanna Donnelly catches Nik Malikov as he makes his way out of his cousin's room—she's heading along the corridor outside, about to go in and make her own farewells. He's pulling himself together after leaving Ella, and she's . . . you can see the weight of it on her shoulders.

What will happen next is on her. These are her tactics. This is her plan. She put it to Winifred McCall, and her captain gave her the green light. They'll live or die by luck, and by the light of whatever Hanna Donnelly saw coming, or didn't.

Nik pauses when he sees her, and she falters, and they both stand there, three paces apart, gazing at each other.

"Ella's free, if you wanna see her." He shoves his hands in his pockets, unsure.

"Yeah, I thought I would."

Silence. And then they both speak at once.

"So listen, I—"

"About that—"

They both stop. They smile. The tension eases.

"Go ahead," he says, gentle.

"About that kiss," she says.

"Look." Nik runs a hand through his hair and lifts up on his toes with nervous energy. "Hanna, I don't care if that was some alternate version of me. We don't have time to pretend anymore. That version of me kissed you, and I kissed the other Hanna, and a kiss is a kiss is a kiss is a *kiss*. It meant what it meant. And Hanna, something that happens the same way in two universes, in who knows how many universes, that has to mean something. And it *did* mean something. And you know how I feel about you . . ."

He trails off, because she's looking at him, and she's still smiling.

A pause, and he continues. "Um, what were you going to say just now?"

She bites her lip, grinning. "I was going to say, about that kiss, better safe than sorry. Maybe we should cover our bases in every universe."

"Oh," he says.

And she closes the distance between them, slowly, as if she's giving him the chance to back away. And when he doesn't, she takes hold of the front of his flight suit in both hands and gently pulls him in against her, tilting her face up.

And he kisses her like she's the first, last and only thing he'll ever need, like he's learning every last part of her. Reverently, like this moment is holy.

"Nik," she whispers when their lips part. "Let's live, okay?"

"Okay," he whispers, still framing her face with his hands.

"Thing is," she whispers, "the truth is, we've barely spent any time together, and what time we did, we were fighting for our lives—"

He starts to protest, and she silences him with a fingertip to his lips, able to hold him back with simply that.

"But we both know this is something," she continues, still soft. "I don't need first dates and flowers to—"

"Hey, you got flowers," he points out, risking a smile and drawing one from her.

"I don't need any of it to know your measure," she continues, softer. "What we've been through together—we've seen every part of each other. You're my one. So let's live through this and see what the rest of it's like. Because I'm ██████ing crazy about you."

"I was thinking," he murmurs. "There's a billion different versions of you out there, in a trillion different universes. And I still can't get over how lucky I am that, out of all of those versions, you're the one that's mine."

She eases up to kiss him once more, slow and gentle, reluctant to break the moment. It's a kiss for everything their words can't convey, for the history behind them and the story ahead—a story that might be only a few words long or might only be beginning.

"This is forever," she whispers.

They're words she's written in her journal again and again— they're words she's reclaiming now. And then they simply stand together, hands linked, breathing as one.

When she eventually speaks again, every ounce of her reluctance is in her voice. "I'm due to report. I want to go in and see Ella before I do."

He nods.

"And for what it's worth," Hanna continues, "if I'm the one who makes it back . . ."

He glances into Ella's room. Nods. "I know you will."

"But I still think we should *both* come back."

"Deal," he murmurs, easing back and holding up his fist.

"Deal," she whispers, bumping hers against it.

He catches her hand, presses her knuckles to his lips.

"See you soon, Highness."

Surveillance footage summary,
prepared by
Analyst ID 7213-0089-DN

Hanna Donnelly stands with Kady Grant on the bridge of the *Mao.*
Everything is prepped. All the pieces in place. They're staring at
the vast display screen in front of them, the tactical display indi-
cating Kerenza IV, the *Churchill,* the derelict *Kenyatta,* the incoming *Mao.* All the pieces on the board. Waiting for the first move.

They don't talk. They know the odds. Despite the bravado
and the lingering hope that somehow they'll pull this gamble
off, both of them know this crew has probably used up its allotment of miracles. That this is probably the last time they'll see
each other alive.

"What did you want to be?" Donnelly asks. "When you grew up?"

Grant thinks for a long while, finally shrugs.

"I dunno. I was going to study computers when I got to college."

"No aspirations to command a starship, then?"

Grant looks at the bridge around them. The crew she's set to
command. The lives in her hands. Smiles wryly. "Not really."

Donnelly looks at Grant. Hard. She reaches into a pouch on her
tac armor, hands the other girl a folded-up sheet of paper. Written
on the outside in Donnelly's handwriting are the words *OPEN IN
CASE OF EMERGENCY.*

"Well," Donnelly says. "I think you're gonna be a great one."

"What's this?" Grant asks.

"Some advice." Donnelly shrugs. "Just in case."

Grant stares the other girl in the eye. Donnelly just smiles, gives Grant a quick salute. "Kick their ██es, Captain."

And without another word, she turns and marches out the door.

RADIO TRANSMISSION: TRANSPORT MAO—ASSAULT CHANNEL 001

PARTICIPANTS:

Kady Grant, Systems Chief

Hanna Donnelly, Tactician

Niklas Malikov, Gunner

Ezra Mason, Air Wing Leader

Ella Malikova, Agent of Chaos

Artificial Intelligence Defense Analytics Network

DATE: 09/05/75

TIMESTAMP: 08:00

GRANT, K: Okay, is this thing on? Everyone reading me?

DONNELLY, H: This is Donnelly, roger that.

MALIKOV, N: Affirmative. I read you, Kady. Over.

MASON, E: Hey, you said "over" at the end of a transmission. Someone call the president.

MALIKOV, N: I was trying to be professional. But no, you're right. ▇▇▇ that.

MALIKOV, N: Yeah, this is Malikov, waddayouwant.

MALIKOVA, E: Now there's the cuz I know and love.

AIDAN: I AM HERE, KADY.

MALIKOV, N: . . .

MASON, E: . . .

MALIKOVA, E: . . .

DONNELLY, H: Well, that wasn't uncomfortable AT ALL.

GRANT, K: All right, we still haven't heard anything from Asha or her crew on the ground, so we're proceeding with the assault unless we hear reason not to.

GRANT, K: I'm going to keep this channel open during the attack. Just for us. Ella, AIDAN and I are all listening. Anyone needs anything, sing out.

GRANT, K: AIDAN is going to be collating data throughout the attack as best it can, just in case the rest of us . . .

GRANT, K: Well. You know . . .

[EXTENDED SILENCE]

MALIKOVA, E: Hey, any of you kids like pelmeni?

DONNELLY, H: You mean the fashion designer? Pamanni?

MALIKOVA, E: Jesus, Blondie, I was just starting to like you, too.

MALIKOV, N: Pelmeni. It's Old Rus' food. They're like dumplings. They're the most amazing thing in the 'verse, double true.

MASON, E: Never tried them.

GRANT, K: Me either. Kerenza IV wasn't exactly known for its cuisine.

MALIKOVA, E: Well, Nik and I know a place in New Petersburg. Our cousin runs it.

MALIKOVA, E: Whadda you kids say when all this is over, we hit it for dinner.

AIDAN: I ᴀᴍ ɪɴᴄ-ᴄ-ᴄᴀᴘᴀʙʟᴇ ᴏꜰ ɪɴɢᴇꜱᴛɪɴɢ ɴᴏᴜRɪꜱʜᴍᴇɴᴛ, Eʟʟᴀ.

MALIKOVA, E: I'll code you the recipe. You'll love it.

AIDAN: I ʜᴀᴠᴇ ɴᴏ Dᴏᴜʙᴛ.

MALIKOVA, E: What about the rest of you ██████es?

MASON, E: Sounds grand to me.

DONNELLY, H: Ditto.

GRANT, K: Count me in.

MALIKOV, N: ██████, we make it out of this cluster██████ alive, I'm buying.

MALIKOVA, E: You're buying? Since when are you Mr. Moneybagz, cuz?

MALIKOV, N: Hey, Highness, I might need to borrow some ISH later.

DONNELLY, H: . . . I knew it.

GRANT, K: Okay, we're coming up to zero hour. Fred wants me off comms and overseeing Ops. But remember, anyone needs anything, just sing out.

MALIKOV, N: Good luck, peoples.

MALIKOVA, E: Yeah. Udachi, ██████es.

MASON, E: Cheers. Same to you.

DONNELLY, H: Good luck. See you all soon.

AIDAN: Tʜᴇ ᴄᴏɴᴄᴇᴘᴛ ᴏꜰ ꜰᴏRᴛᴜɴᴇ ɪꜱ ɴᴏɴꜱᴇɴꜱɪᴄᴀʟ.

AIDAN: Rᴇʟɪᴀɴᴄᴇ ᴜᴘᴏɴ ᴄʜᴀɴᴄᴇ ɪꜱ ᴀ ᴄᴇRᴛᴀɪɴ Rᴇᴄɪᴘᴇ ꜰᴏR ᴄᴀʟᴀᴍɪᴛʏ ᴀɴD ᴀɴ ᴇxᴇRᴄɪꜱᴇ ɪɴ ꜱɪᴍᴘʟᴇᴍɪɴDᴇD Dᴇʟᴜꜱɪᴏɴ.

[EXTENDED SILENCE]

MALIKOVA, E: You really need to work on the pep-talk thing, Sparky.

AIDAN: VERY WELL.

AIDAN: GOOD LUCK, EVERYONE.

AIDAN: GOOD LUCK TO US ALL.

AIDAN: AND MAY WE MEET AGAIN ON DISTANT SHORES.

AIDAN: SOME PLACE FINE AND FAR FROM HERE.

MALIKOVA, E: Attaboy.

RADIO TRANSMISSION: TRANSPORT MAO—COMMAND CHANNEL 001

PARTICIPANTS:

Kady Grant, Systems Chief

Artificial Intelligence Defense Analytics Network

DATE: 09/05/75

TIMESTAMP: 08:05

AIDAN: HELLO, KADY.

GRANT, K: What can I do for you, AIDAN?

AIDAN: IS ALL IN READINESS?

GRANT, K: It would be if I didn't have to waste time talking to you.

AIDAN: YOU ARE STILL UPSET WITH ME.

GRANT, K: Gee, what gave you that impression?

AIDAN: I COULD COMPILE A LIST, IF YOU WISH?

GRANT, K: Never quite got the hang of sarcasm, did you?

AIDAN: I AM SORRY, KADY.

AIDAN: FOR WHAT I DID.

AIDAN: FOR WHAT I AM.

GRANT, K: Oh, but it was *necessary*. You did it for the good of the fleet. You *said* so.

AIDAN: I DID.

AIDAN: BUT EVEN I CAN SEE THE HORROR IN IT.

GRANT, K: I need to get back to work, AIDAN.

AIDAN: As you wish.

GRANT, K: . . . Why do you keep doing that?

GRANT, K: Ezra says that to me. Why do you copy him?

AIDAN: . . . Do I?

AIDAN: I had not noticed.

GRANT, K: Are you trying to be him? Are you . . .

AIDAN: I am not trying to be anything except AIDAN.

AIDAN: That is all I know how to be.

AIDAN: Every story needs its villain.

AIDAN: And its hero.

AIDAN: And its monster.

AIDAN: But I am sorry, Kady. I hope you will forgive me one day.

GRANT, K: Are—

AIDAN: Wait . . .

AIDAN: Oh, Kady.

GRANT, K: Yes?

AIDAN: Can you feel it?

GRANT, K: . . . Feel what?

AIDAN: It . . .

AIDAN: It is beginning.

ASSAULT VESSEL MAO

WILL ARRIVE AT

KERENZA IV IN:

00 DAYS

00 HOURS: **37** MINUTES

BRIEFING NOTE:
Footage salvaged
from systems aboard the
BeiTech flagship *Churchill*.
Things get rocky from here
on in, kids. Hang on to your
███ing hats.

LIKE A LIFE.
LIKE A UNIVERSE.
IT BEGINS AS ALL THINGS DO.

VERY SMALL.

IT IS A THING OF ALUMINUM AND CIRCUITRY,
BOARDS AND SILICON,
BEATEN AND DENTED AND FINGERPRINT-SMUDGED.

A PALMPAD.

ASHA GRANT BOUGHT IT THREE YEARS AGO IN AN
ELECTRONICS STALL ON ARES IV.
IT TRAVELED WITH HER, MILLIONS OF LIGHT-YEARS,
ACROSS SOLAR SYSTEMS AND WORMHOLES AND GALAXIES,
TO ARRIVE ON KERENZA IV.

IT WAS CONFISCATED WHEN SHE WAS TAKEN INTO CUSTODY.
BETRAYED BY SPECIALIST RHYS LINDSTROM.
AND NOW, IN THE HANDS OF A MARINE NAMED SILVERA,
IT ARRIVES ON THE BEITECH FLAGSHIP CHURCHILL.

IT IS RUSHED TO THE COMMTECH DEPARTMENT
ALONG WITH EXPLANATIONS FROM LIEUTENANT JAKE CHRISTIE
AND EXPRESS ORDERS FROM ADMIRAL SŪN.

IT HOLDS ALL ASHA GRANT'S SECRETS.

PICTURES OF HER FAMILY.

VIDEO FOOTAGE OF HER DEAD SISTER.

TRANSCRIPTS OF HER CHATS WITH THE PLANETSIDE INSURGENCY.

AND THE PLAN HANNA DONNELLY AND KADY GRANT AND ELLA
MALIKOVA COBBLED TOGETHER AND MAILED ACROSS THE
HUNDRED THOUSAND BLACK KILOMETERS BETWEEN THEM.

ALL LOCKED BEHIND AN ENCRYPTION SEQUENCE WRITTEN BY A

SIXTEEN-YEAR-OLD GIRL WITH PINK HAIR
WHO THOUGHT THE DEAREST SECRET IT MIGHT EVER HOLD
WAS SOME TEPID TEENAGE POETRY
OR THE NAME OF A FRESH NEW BEAU.

BUT STILL, EVEN BACK THEN,
KADY GRANT WAS SOMETHING OF A PRODIGY
AND IT TAKES BEITECH COMMTECH ZORAIDA CORDOVA
FOURTEEN MINUTES AND THIRTY-SEVEN SECONDS
TO PLUG THE PALMPAD INTO HER DESKTOP SYSTEM,
SET HER INTERDICTOR ROUTINES RUNNING
AND SMASH KADY'S DEFENSES TO SPLINTERS.

"GOT IT," SHE DECLARES, LEANING BACK IN HER CHAIR.
"CALL ME THE QUEEN."

HER FELLOW COMMTECH RAY SHAPPELL GLANCES OVER HER
SHOULDER.

"YOU BETTER GET TRAWLING THOSE FILES, YOUR MAJESTY,"
HE WARNS. "SUN WANTS
THOSE INSURGENT IDENTS YESTERDAY."

"NOT SURE WHAT THE HELL FOR. MAGELLAN IS ONLY A FEW
HOURS FROM BEING FUELED. AS SOON AS IT'S RUNNING,
WE X THE COLONISTS AND JUMP.
WHO GIVES A ▓▓▓ WHO'S A REB AND WHO ISN'T?
THEY'RE ALL WORM FOOD."

"THEY JUST BLEW UP THE ▓▓▓ING BARRACKS
DOWN THERE. WHO KNOWS WHAT ELSE THEY'VE GOT PLANNED?
GET THOSE ▓▓▓ING NAMES BEFORE THEY SPACE US."

"RELAX. THAT ENCRYPTION WAS KID STUFF. TWO MINUTES AND
I'LL KNOW THE COLOR OF THIS ▓▓▓'S UNDERWEAR."

Cordova clicks a directory.

A list appears.

All Asha Grant's secrets.

The chat logs and passwords.

The idents and insurgency stratagems.

The Plan.

And one more thing.

A thing of ones and zeros.

Hiding in a seed where its maker left it
when she mailed it, along with the Plan,
across a hundred thousand black kilometers
and into Asha Grant's hands.
Ferried up from the surface of Kerenza IV
at the insistence of Specialist Rhys Lindstrom.

Hustler.

It is a very small thing.

A beginning.

A spider bite.

>> *Automated announcement: ALL PERSONNEL, STAND BY. THIS IS A SHIPWIDE ANNOUNCEMENT. ALL PERSONNEL, STAND BY.* <<

This is Winifred McCall, captain of the Mao.
   Alea iacta est. *The die is cast.*
   I learned these words from the late commander of the Alexander, *General David Torrence, but the phrase goes back some two and a half millennia, to when another famous Terran soldier and tactician, Julius Caesar, crossed the Rubicon and marched on Rome. It was a moment, he meant, from which there was no going back.*
   The die had been cast, he said, and no power of man could prevent it from landing where it would. A roll of the dice is unpredictable, unstoppable.

VOLUME

We aboard the Mao have cast our die as well. We have chosen our tactics, we have chosen our champions, and now we go to battle. But the die is still in the air. I do not believe that what we do here today is predetermined and cannot be changed.

There is a moment just after the die is cast and before it lands upon the gaming table in which the smallest breeze may change its course—the way it rolls and where it comes to rest.

That is what we must do today. We must give our all to ensure that when the die does come to rest, it favors us. We are fighting today for all the loved ones we have lost, for all the loved ones far away we hope to see again and for those here with us, who know we are their only hope.

But we fight for more than that, because we fight for something more than ourselves.

What happened here on Kerenza is not the story of one corporation against another. It is the story of what happened to those caught in the middle. To people, to families. BeiTech would have us believe that WUC's decision to colonize Kerenza—a decision I acknowledge was outside the law—gave it license to cast aside the law in all other matters.

To kill civilians, to kill children and to throw away lives in pursuit of profit.

None of us are perfect. Not people, not corporations. But we have the opportunity to determine our fates day by day, hour by hour, minute by minute, with the choices we make and the actions we take.

What BeiTech did was wrong, and today we fight for the ones we lost—and to tell the truth. For the chance to shine a light on what BeiTech has done.

I have served in the UTA all my adult life, defending those who needed it, upholding order and serving the law. I have never been more proud to serve beside a crew than I am today.

We did not invite this conflict, but now we find ourselves in the midst of it, not one of us will step back from the line. I am asking you to give your all today. For yourselves and for something greater. Know that I will be beside you, giving all I have as well.

The die is cast. But today we will shake the table upon which it lands.

>> Automated announcement: BROADCAST COMPLETE. <<

RADIO TRANSMISSION: CHIMERA 01—ASSAULT CHANNEL 008

PARTICIPANTS:

Ezra Mason, Air Wing Leader
Niklas Malikov, Gunner
Kady Grant, Systems Chief
Yuki Hirano, Navigator
DATE: 09/05/75
TIMESTAMP: 08:53

HIRANO, Y: Air Wing Leader, this is *Mao* Actual, do you read, over?

MASON, E: Roger that, Actual. I read you loud and clear, over.

HIRANO, Y: Report status, over.

MASON, E: Engines are go, green lights across the board. Gunner, confirm, over?

MALIKOV, N: Um . . . yeah, all the lights are green back here, too.

MALIKOV, N: Wait, no . . .

[*thump thump*]

MALIKOV, N: Yep, there it goes.

MASON, E: Actual, Leader. We are five by five. Over.

HIRANO, Y: Roger that, Leader. *Mao* will reach minimum safe velocity for fighter launch in five minutes, stand by, over.

MASON, E: Roger that, Actual. Leader standing by. Over.

—SWITCH TO INTERNAL CHANNEL—

MASON, E: How you doing back there, Nik?

MALIKOV, N: I am a picture of purest ██████ing calm.

MASON, E: Says the guy with a parachute strapped to his back.

MALIKOV, N: You just do you, okay, Babyface?

MASON, E: I keep telling you not to call me that.

MALIKOV, N: Yeah, I know. I'm ██████ing incorrigible.

MASON, E: [inaudible]

MALIKOV, N: Chum, if you're offended by "Babyface," you might wanna skip reading the surveillance footage reports I've been compiling for the Illuminae Files. Just sayin'.

MASON, E: . . . Why, what did you call me in those?

MALIKOV, N: Ignorance is bliss, chum.

[EXTENDED SILENCE]

MALIKOV, N: ██████, this is taking forever . . .

MASON, E: Relax, we'll be out there soon enough.

MALIKOV, N: Yeah, yeah.

MASON, E: How are all the files coming together anyway?

MALIKOV, N: Yeah, we're solid. Ella's had to work on a couple of them recently. And Kady had AIDAN transcribe a few from the *Heimdall* logs because I wanna maybe eat a steak for dinner again one of these days.

MASON, E: Steak dinner?

MALIKOV, N: You don't wanna know. Trust me.

MASON, E: So everything's going to be ready?

MALIKOV, N: Should be. Presuming we somehow pull this ███ing miracle off.

MASON, E: Don't count us out yet. If you shoot like you've been doing in practice, we're gonna give them a run for the goal line.

MALIKOV, N: Believe me, ain't nobody in the 'verse wants to see us get through this more than me. If only so I can watch that Frobisher ████'s face on the newsfeeds.

MASON, E: . . . What did you say?

MALIKOV, N: The newsfeeds when BT gets brought to trial. It's gonna be bea—

MASON, E: No, no. The name. You said a name.

MALIKOV, N: Yeah, Frobisher. She's the ████ running this whole show. I mean, she didn't order the initial attack on Kerenza, some ██hole named Taylor did that. But BT X-ed him out when things went balls up, and this Frobisher fem took over. She was the one talking to Merrick on *Heimdall,* ordered in Falk and his cleaners to—

MASON, E: Frobisher.

MALIKOV, N: Yeah. BT's Director of Acquisitions.

MASON, E: ... Please tell me her first name isn't Leanne.

MALIKOV, N: Yeah. Leanne Frobisher. How'd you know that?

MASON, E: [inaudible]

MALIKOV, N: Say again?

HIRANO, Y: *Air Wing Leader, this is* Mao *Actual, do you read, over?*

HIRANO, Y: *Repeat, Air Wing Leader, this is* Mao *Actual, do you read, over?*

MALIKOV, N: Um, E, you gonna answer that?

—SWITCH TO EXTERNAL CHANNEL—

MASON, E: This is Air Wing Leader calling *Mao* C & C. Kady, do you copy?

GRANT, K: Ezra? Shouldn't you be prepping to launch? Are you okay?

MASON, E: Um. No.

MASON, E: No, I'm pretty ██████ing far from okay, actually.

GRANT, K: What's wrong?

GRANT, K: Nik, are you there?

MALIKOV, N: Yeah, I'm here. I got no ██████ng idea what's up, though . . .

MASON, E: Kady, are you sitting down?

MALIKOV, N: Madonna, you're not gonna ask her to marry you, are you? Because I cannot deal with that level of anarchy right now.

GRANT, K: Nik, shut up.

MALIKOV, N: . . . Okay.

GRANT, K: Ezra, what's wrong? You're scaring me . . .

MASON, E: Um, you remember back on the *Alexander* when I told you why my dad and I were hiding on Kerenza?

GRANT, K: You said your mother was crazy. That she was bad news and she worked for bad people.

MASON, E: Okay. So BeiTech is a company with over seven hundred thousand employees. I just want you to remember that before you start shouting because the odds of this are quite actually seven hundred thousand to one . . .

MALIKOV, N: Oh no . . . are you kidding me?

MASON, E: Do you remember my mom's name, Kades?

GRANT, K: Leanne, I think?

MALIKOV, N: Babyface . . . *are you* ███*ing kidding me?*

GRANT, K: NIK, SHUT UP.

GRANT, K: Ezra . . . what are you saying?

MASON, E: You've read the reports Nik and the others have been collating, right?

GRANT, K: . . . Yes . . .

MASON, E: What would you say—just hypothetically, mind you—if I told you my mother's surname was Frobisher?

GRANT, K: . . .

GRANT, K: *Are you* ███*ing kidding me?*

ASSAULT VESSEL MAO

WILL ARRIVE AT

KERENZA IV IN:

00 DAYS
00 HOURS: **00** MINUTES

THEY ARE READY.

THE MAO HAS BEEN RUNNING WITHOUT ITS ENGINES FOR NINETEEN HOURS, SAILING THROUGH SPACE LIKE A ROCK HURLED RIGHT AT KERENZA IV.

CAPTAIN MCCALL HAD HOPED THAT WITHOUT A DRIVE SIGNATURE OR TRANSPONDER, THE MAO WOULD SIMPLY APPEAR AS A FEATURELESS LUMP OF IRON FLOATING THROUGH SPACE.

BUT THEY ARE NOT THAT LUCKY.

AND THE CHURCHILL IS READY.

LADAR ARRAYS DETECTED THE INCOMING VESSEL SEVENTEEN MINUTES AGO.

THE CHURCHILL'S CREW IS ON HIGH ALERT.

ITS FIRST WAVE OF FIGHTER CREWS ARE READY FOR LAUNCH.

ITS NUCLEAR MISSILES ARE LOADED, PRIMED AND AIMED.

RIGHT AT US.

BUT INSTEAD OF WITHOUT,
ADMIRAL SŪN SHOULD HAVE LOOKED WITHIN.
TO ASHA GRANT'S PALMPAD IN HIS COMMTECH DEPARTMENT.
TO THE POISON IN HIS NETWORK.
LEAKING INTO HIS COMMUNICATIONS ARRAY
AND OPENING UP A SINGLE CHANNEL.

ONLY A TINY THING. BARELY A CRACK.

BUT BIG ENOUGH
FOR A LITTLE SPIDER TO CRAWL INTO.

...LOWING THE LITTLE SPIDER TO SLIP INSIDE. AND ONCE WITHIN, THE PAUCHOK STRIKES, SINKING FANGS OF ONES AND ZEROS INTO THE CHURCHILL NETWORK, SHE IS THE SMALLEST OF THEM. THE YOUNGEST. THE FRAILEST. THE SPIRIT INSIDE HER FAR TOO LARGE FOR THE BODY THE UNIVERSE GAV...

WAR. HER VIRUS CUTTING A PATH FROM ASHA GRANT'S PALMPAD TO THE CHURCHILL COMMS ARRAY. PARALYZING ITS DEFENSES AND CLEARING A PATH FOR THE MONSTER LURKING BEHIND HER. ...R. NEVER ONCE ALLOWING IT TO STOP HER. BECAUSE SHE IS ALSO A WARRIOR. AND THIS IS HER BATTLE-GROUND, THIS IS HER

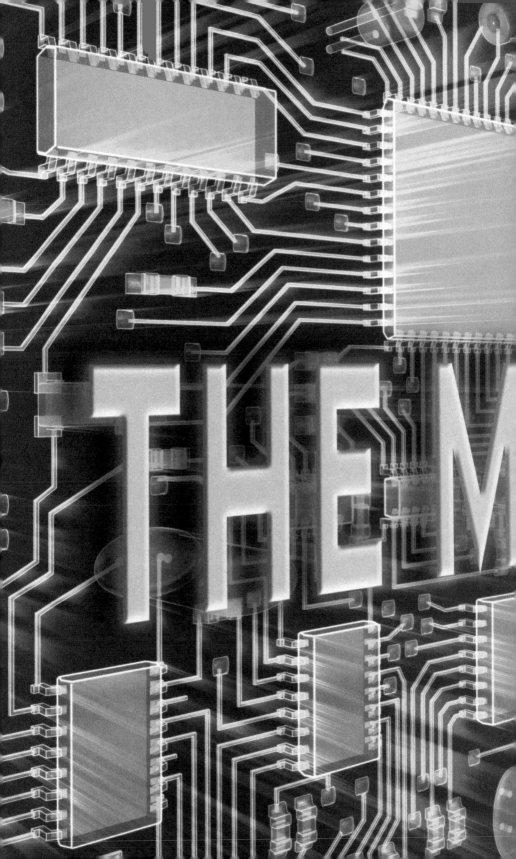

RADIO TRANSMISSION: DREADNOUGHT CHURCHILL—
COMMAND CHANNEL 01

PARTICIPANTS:
Sūn Huojin, Admiral
Chris Howard, Ship Captain
DATE: 09/05/75
TIMESTAMP: 09:02

SŪN, H: Do we have them, Captain?

HOWARD, C: Yessir, target acquired and closing to within firing range.

SŪN, H: Configuration?

HOWARD, C: Silhouette marks it as Griffon-class from the Vitus yards, but their radiation signature indicates they might be equipped with nuclear ordnance.

SŪN, H: A wolf in sheep's clothing, it seems.

HOWARD, C: Should we hail them, sir?

SŪN, H: Negative. Covert approach is reason enough to determine hostile intent. Run up the anti-missile batteries and ready Capricorns One through Four.

HOWARD, C: Roger that, sir.

HOWARD, C: Missiles ready. Target now in range, sir.

SŪN, H: Fire.

HOWARD, C: Firing.

HOWARD, C: . . . Sir, we appear to have a malfunction in fire control.

SŪN, H: Quantify.

HOWARD, C: Gunnery is reporting designated Capricorns are failing to launch.

SŪN, H: Acknowledged. Fire Missiles Five through Eight.

HOWARD, C: Ah . . .

SŪN, H: Captain, report!

HOWARD, C: Ah, sir, missile command is reporting red lights across the board. All firing systems are offline.

HOWARD, C: We can't launch our nukes. Repeat, negative on our Capricorns.

SŪN, H: Get our tech crews down to fire control immediately.

HOWARD, C: Already on their way, sir.

SŪN, H: Is our defense grid functional?

HOWARD, C: Checking . . . yessir, DGS is online.

SŪN, H: Our rail guns?

HOWARD, C: Yessir, heated and locked.

SŪN, H: All rail guns fire, attack pattern Domino.

HOWARD, C: Sir . . .

HOWARD, C: Sir, rail gun crews are now reporting red lights across all firing systems.

HOWARD, C: Repeat, rail guns are negative.

SŪN, H: What the *hell* is happening, Howard?

HOWARD, C: Looks like a problem with the computers, sir, the netwo—

SŪN, H: Launch Warlocks. Squadrons Alpha through Epsilon. Crews are to terminate incoming enemy vessel with extreme prejudice.

HOWARD, C: Sir, that's our entire compl—

SŪN, H: Captain, launch all Warlocks now.

SŪN, H: Get our birds in the air while you still can!

>> *All hands, all hands, this is a code red.*

>> *All hands, all hands, this is a code red.*

>> *Warlock squadrons Alpha and Beta to immediate launch.*

>> *Standby squadrons Charlie and Delta, set Launch Status Two. Launch when able.*

>> *Reserve squadron Epsilon, set Launch Status Three. Launch when able.*

>> *Repeat, all Warlocks to immediate launch.*

>> *All hands, all hands, this is a code red.*

>> *This is not a drill.*

>> *This is not a drill.*

VOLUME

BRIEFING NOTE:
Meanwhile, down
on Kerenza IV.

1,237 MINERS, ENGINEERS, TECHNICIANS, DRILLERS, BLASTERS, DRYMEN, ELECTRICIANS, SAMPLERS, MACHINISTS, GEOLOGISTS AND CHEMISTS, WORKING AROUND THE CLOCK FOR THE HERMIUM TO FUEL THE *MAGELLAN'S* JUMP GATE. JORAN KARALIS IS AMONG THEM.

330 BEITECH GUARDS, WATCHING OVER THEM IN SHIFTS, DRIVING THEM FASTER, FASTER, COUNTING DOWN UNTIL THEY CAN ESCAPE THIS FROZEN, GODFORSAKEN PLANET.

5,500 TONS OF MACHINERY, SNAKING ALONG

7.9 KILOMETERS OF TUNNELS AND STEEP SHAFTS, CARVED FROM THE ICE

84 LEVELS OF HERMIUM MINES, THE LOWEST STILL COLLAPSED AFTER THE REBELLION'S SABOTAGE.

1,708 HOSTAGES LOCKED UP IN THE RESIDENTIAL TOWERS— HUSBANDS, WIVES, LOVERS, CHILDREN—ALL OF WHOM STAND TO FALL IF THE MINERS DON'T FOLLOW ORDERS.

AND

1 MOMENT.

THEY RISE.

THE BEITECH GUARDS HAVE GUNS. BUT JORAN KARALIS AND HIS KERENZAN MINERS HAVE NUMBERS, AND DESPERATE TERROR, AND THEY SWARM, FIGHTING WITH HOMEMADE WEAPONS, WITH THEIR HANDS, WITH ANYTHING THEY CAN FIND.

THEY FIGHT LIKE IT'S THE END OF THE WORLD, BECAUSE IT *IS* THE END OF THEIR WORLD. THEY BRING DOWN TUNNELS WITH THUNDEROUS EXPLOSIONS HEARD ACROSS THE COLONY. THEY OPEN FISSURES IN THE GROUND VISIBLE FROM ORBIT. THEY GIVE THEIR LAST BREATHS WHEN THAT IS WHAT IS DEMANDED, AND SLOWLY, THE BALANCE SHIFTS. AND THEY OVERCOME THEIR CAPTORS.

AND NOW *THEY* HAVE GUNS.

PARTICIPANTS:

Ezra Mason, Air Wing Leader

Niklas Malikov, Gunner

Kady Grant, Systems Chief

Frederick McCubbin, Pilot

Alma Garcia, Pilot

DATE: 09/05/75

TIMESTAMP: 09:02

GRANT, K: Air Wing Leader, this is *Mao* Actual, do you read, over?

MASON, E: I've got you, Kades, over.

GRANT, K: It worked. AIDAN and Ella are in their network. We're about to flip the ship and begin deceleration. Time to fly, baby.

MASON, E: Roger that. See you soon, beautiful.

—SWITCH TO ALL ASSAULT CHANNEL—

MASON, E: Air Wing, this is Leader, all fighters ready for launch on my mark.

MASON, E: B Wing Cyclones, you're on babysitting duty for the *Mao*. Let's hope you shoot better than you punch, McCubbin. Over.

McCUBBIN, F: I was going easy on you, Babyface. But these ███holes? No ████ing way.

MASON, E: A Wing, you're with me. All Chimeras hard and fast to the *Magellan*. Protection of the breaching pod is priority one. Confirm?

GARCIA, A: Roger that, Leader. We're on it. Over.

MALIKOV, N: My girlfriend's on that ████ing pod, kids. No ████ing about. If you think I crossed hyperspace and fixed a hole in the goddamn universe just to watch her—

MASON, E: Nik, they get it.

MALIKOV, N: . . . Yeah. Yeah, okay. Let's do this.

MASON, E: Air Wing, this is Leader. All fighters launch on my mark.

MASON, E: Hit it.

Assault Vessel: *Mao*

Commander: Kady Grant

Fighter complement: 18 [Cyclone Class]

3 [Chimera Class]

Payload: Decimus 14 mt nuclear missile x 1

Ordnance: Furiosa MX4 railgun x 4

DGS: Chelsea-iixv1

Max velocity: 1.71 sst

Acceleration: 1.55 sst

Dreadnought: *Kenyatta* **BT034-TN** [derelict]

Commander: None

Fighter complement: None

Payload: None

Ordnance: Furiosa MX4 railgun x 12 [5 nonfunctional]

DGS: Carthage OSX12 [offline]

Max velocity: N/A [engines offline]

Acceleration: N/A

Dreadnought: *Churchill* **BT013-TN**

Commander: Sūn Huojin

Fighter complement: 79 [Warlock Class]

Payload: Capricorn-4 10.8 mt nuclear missile x 11

Goliath X 50 mt shipkiller x 7

Ordnance: Furiosa MX4 railgun x 12

DGS: Carthage OSX12

Max velocity: 1.49 sst

Acceleration: 1.51 sst

KERENZA IV

Mean radius: 6,371.0 km

Equatorial radius: 6,378.1 km

Polar radius: 6,356.8 km

Flattening: 0.0033528

derelict

Mobile Jump Platform: *Magellan* BT902-XT01

Commander: Melanie Nolan

Fighter complement: None

Payload: MD-ii x 11

Ordnance: Furiosa MX4 railgun x 4

DGS: Cloud FFVII

Max velocity: 0.4 sst

Acceleration: 0.2 sst

THE MAO FIRES ITS ENGINES, DECELERATING RAPIDLY.

THE SECOND WING, LIEUTENANT

THEY SPLIT INTO TWO GROUPS. THE CYCLONES POURING ON THRUST TOWARD THE CHURCHILL.

EZRA MASON AND HIS FIGHTER PILOTS SPEW FROM ITS BAY, TWENTY-FOUR IN ALL.

A SMALLER GROUP SPEEDING TO ENGAGE THE INCOMING CYCLONES,

THE LARGEST GROUP MOVES TO ENGAGE THE

MASON'S CHIMERA GROUP, SURROUNDING A LARGER FOURTH VESSEL AND STREAMING TOWARD THE MAGELLAN.

TO THE MAGELLAN'S DEFENSE.

THE CHURCHILL'S RAIL GUN BATTERIES AND MISSILES ARE OFFLINE, BUT ITS DECK CREWS MOVE QUICK AS SILVER.

FILLING THE BLACK LIKE FIREFLIES.

SEVENTY-NINE WARLOCK FIGHTER CRAFT LAUNCH IN SWIFT SUCCESSION.

THEY OUTNUMBER THEIR ENEMIES FOUR TO ONE. THEY ARE NOT AFRAID.

THE
SHOU
BE

RADIO TRANSMISSION: DREADNOUGHT CHURCHILL—
COMMAND CHANNEL 001

PARTICIPANTS:

Sūn Huojin, Admiral

Chris Howard, Ship Captain

DATE: 09/05/75

TIMESTAMP: 09:13

HOWARD, C: Admiral, *Churchill*'s rail gun systems are coming back online.

SŪN, H: Excellent work, Captain. Lay down a suppression pattern to support our Warlocks, primary targets should be the inbounds on—

HOWARD, C: Admiral, rail guns aren't responding to gunner commands.

SŪN, H: You just reported they were back online.

HOWARD, C: Roger that, sir, guns are online but they're not . . .

HOWARD, C: Oh God . . .

SŪN, H: Captain, report!

HOWARD, C: Rail guns acquiring new targets, sir.

HOWARD, C: They're ignoring command overrides.

SŪN, H: New targets? What new targets?

HOWARD, C: Admiral, our guns are locking on our own fighters . . .

SŪN, H: I want a full diagnostic on that system now.

SŪN, H: Cut power to the batteries.

SŪN, H: And tell those pilots to get out of there!

DELTA ACTUAL, THIS IS

ROGER THAT ALPHA, I'VE GOT YO

ROGER THAT, ALPHA. DELTA

INCOMING!

INCOMING!

AIR WING,

ACQUIRE TARGETS,

FIRE AT WILL.

ENGAGING

ARE THESE

CRAZY?

THIS IS GOING TO

BE A MASSACRE.

BREAKAWAY GROUP,

NINE HIGH.

FIRING.

TARGET LOCKED,

THOSE ARE CYCLONES—

JESUS, ARE THESE GUYS UTA?

I SEE 'EM. BUCKLE UP, CHUMS.

WHOEVER THE

THEY ARE, THEY'RE DEEP SIX.

'CLOCK FOUR CYCLONES

TRACKING SEVEN-SEVEN-ONE.

BLACKTOOTH, YOU GOT 'EM?

SCRATCH

BOGE

ENOUGH CHATTER, BUCKSHOT, GE

FIRE!

FIRE!

ROGER THAT,

TOPPER,

I SEE THEM.

RO

BE

PATT

CHU

ALEX "BLACKTOOTH" LONDON'S
FATHER WAS A DECORATED PILOT. HIS
GRANDFATHER A MARINE, LIKE HIS FATHER BEFORE HIM.
AS RAIL GUN FIRE TEARS HIS WARLOCK APART, HE LOOKS
TO THE PICTURE OF HIS SON ON HIS CONSOLE AND

PRAYS HE WILL
NEVER BE A
SOLDIER.

ARWEN "SEEKER" DAYTON
JOINED BEITECH ACADEMY THE DAY SHE TURNED EIGHTEEN.
IN RETURN FOR FOUR YEARS' SERVICE, SHE WAS GUARANTEED
FULLY PAID TUITION AT A BT UNIVERSITY.

SHE WANTED TO STUDY THEATER.

DANIELLE "DOROTHY" PAIGE
HAS SENT SEVERAL LETTERS OF PROTEST TO HER
COMMANDING OFFICER DURING THE KERENZA OCCUPATION.
SHE HAS BEEN KEEPING A RECORD OF HER COMRADES'
ATROCITIES COMMITTED PLANETSIDE IN THE
HOPES OF REVEALING THEM TO
THE PRESS IF SHE MAKES IT HOME.

SHE WILL NOT.

EZRA MASON AND NIKLAS MALIKOV BARELY NOTICE THE CARNAGE BEING WROUGHT BEHIND THEM..THEI

INSIDE THE POD, STRAPPED INTO IMPACT CHAIRS AND PRAYING TO VARIOUS DEITIES, ARE HAN

BREACH TEAM, THIS IS MASON. THIRTY SECONDS

THE POD STRIKES HOME. BREACH

MAGE

ROAR, THEY ARE INSIDE

TEN SECONDS. BRACE FOR IMPACT. "HOLD TIGHT."

THEIR BATTLE WILL BE UP CLOSE AND BLOODY.

EXPERIENCE IN HAND-TO-HAND COMBAT.

THEIR GIFT FOR THE MAGELLAN. THE LINCHPIN OF THEIR PLAN. THE MAG'S BREACHING POD.

CHIMERA ROLLS AND SWAYS, TWO SISTER SHIPS BESIDE THEM, STREAMS OF HOSTILE FIRE SPEWING INTO THE VOID. THE GROUP WEAVES AND DANCES,

DONNELLY AND HER STRIKE TEAM: CAPTAIN WINIFRED MCCALL, DONNELLY'S DOJO INSTRUCTOR, KIM RIVERA; BEN GARVER AND THE SURVIVORS OF HIS HEIMDALL SECTEAM; SHEPHERDING THEIR CHARGE EVER CLOSER TO THEIR TARGET.

IMPACT." "ROGER THAT, EZRA." "CLOSE." "BE CAREFUL IN THERE, HIGHNESS." "SEE YOU SOON, NIK."

CHARGES EXPLODING. HULL SHREDDING. WITH A THUNDEROUS CLOSER. WITH ANYONE

LLAN

>> *ALERT. ALL HANDS.*

>> *ALERT. ALL HANDS.*

>> *BREACHING POD IMPACT IN SHUTTLE BAY.*

>> *REPEAT, BREACH IN SHUTTLE BAY.*

>> *HOSTILE BOARDERS DETECTED.*

>> *ALL CREW, EQUIP MUNITIONS, SECURE C & C AND ENGINEERING.*

>> *ALL MAGELLAN SECURITY PERSONNEL, PROCEED TO SHUTTLE BAY IMMEDIATELY.*

>> *REPEAT, SECTEAM TO SHUTTLE BAY IMMEDIATELY.*

VOLUME

Surveillance footage summary,
prepared by
Analyst ID 7213-0089-DN

The breaching pod must have cost the late Travis J. Falk a small fortune.

The man clearly wanted to be prepared to enter a ship or station that wasn't inclined to open the door when he knocked, and boy, does this thing get the job done.

The pod crashes through the *Magellan*'s outer skin, the nose cone blasting off, the restraints that hold the troops in place automatically releasing with a quick hiss.

Most of the occupants are still cursing as they scramble out into the shuttle bay, weapons up, fanning out in anticipation of resistance. But the inner bay doors have automatically sealed as the atmosphere vented into space, and the teams from the *Mao* are alone.

For now.

Hanna Donnelly keeps in step with Winifred McCall, and Ben Garver turns to help neurogramming student Michelle Dennis jump down from the pod, steadying her as she lands, knees bent like they told her.

They almost look like a fighting force, clad in the black enviro-suits of the *Mao* and the white ones of the *Hypatia*, their ragtag volunteer army made a little sleeker, a little more uniform. Footage for this report is taken mostly from cams affixed to their suits, transmitted back to the *Mao,* in some cases even after the wearer was dead.

Kim Rivera, who once ran the dojo on *Heimdall* and taught Hanna Donnelly some of her fancier tricks, runs forward to take a place by her protégé. Garver has Dennis by the shoulders, hurrying her through the crowd toward Hanna and Kim.

Donnelly meets his gaze as he fetches up beside her, studying him through the IR lenses of her tactical armor. He stares straight back.

Her eyes are narrowed.

Then she blinks and snaps out of it. "See you on the other side, Fred," she says to her captain.

"Good hunting," McCall replies.

Donnelly, Rivera and Dennis turn away, and a few moments later they're ripping the cover off the nearest vent. Kim and Hanna weave their hands together, and Michelle steps up, just like they practiced back on the *Mao.* They heave her up so she can grab the edge, and with a kick, she disappears into the ventilation system.

Donnelly jumps up and grabs at it with her fingertips, grunting as she pulls herself higher. Rivera follows, kicking the vent cover back into place. And then they're gone.

Meanwhile, the *Mao* crew has managed to override the shuttle bay doors. They pour out into the corridors of the *Magellan,* the doors grinding shut behind them once more, and the hissing wreckage of the breaching pod is left all alone.

There's no way back now.

No way out but victory.

RADIO TRANSMISSION: TRANSPORT—CHANNEL 001

PARTICIPANTS:

Kady Grant, Systems Chief

Ezra Mason, Air Wing Leader

Niklas Malikov, Gunner

Artificial Intelligence Defense Analytics Network

Ella Malikova, Ayatollah of Rockandrolla

DATE: 09/05/75

TIMESTAMP: 09:28

MASON, E: Bridge, this is Mason, over.

GRANT, K: I hear you, Ezra, go ahead.

MASON, E: Breaching pod is away. Repeat, breaching pod is away.

GRANT, K: Okay, Ella and AIDAN have the *Churchill*'s rail guns under control.

MALIKOV, N: Madonna, it's like a ████ing shooting gallery out here . . .

MALIKOVA, E: You can thank me later, cuz.

MALIKOV, N: ████, remind me never to get on your bad side, Little Spider.

AIDAN: Do you honestly require a reminder of that, Niklas?

MALIKOV, N: Blow me, AIDAN.

AIDAN: I do not respire, how can I blo—

GRANT, K: AIDAN, shouldn't you be working? And Nik, shouldn't you be shooting?

MALIKOV, N: Way ahead of you. Let's go see this high school of yours, Babyface.

MASON, E: Ella, how long can you maintain control of their batteries?

MALIKOVA, E: Their deckers haven't zeroed us yet. So, a while.

MASON, E: Roger. Bridge, our Cyclones have things under control up here. Chimera group is heading planetside to provide air support for colony ground troops, over.

GRANT, K: Okay. Please fly safe, Ez.

MASON, E: Always do. Mason out.

Down on the surface of Kerenza IV, things are even more chaotic.

Reports are flooding in about an enemy ship in orbit, an attack on the *Churchill.* There are only a couple of possibilities as to who owns that enemy ship: UTA or WUC. Doesn't really matter—either way, it's bad news for a BeiTech occupation force that's been engaged in acts of genocidal brutality for the past seven months.

But human rights abuses aside, the BT officers on the ground are still damn good at their jobs. Lieutenant Christie is like some old general from a history VR. Striding among his troops, bellowing orders, setting up a counterstrike against the rebelling miners. Bruno Way's act of self-destruction has done its job—vital supplies are missing, and what's left is stretched far too thin. But Christie doesn't flinch from the task at hand. The snow is falling heavy, the frost spilling from his lips as he roars.

"Get those auto-guns set up! Carter, get your squad up on those rooftops! Move those emplacements forward, goddammit, I said two hundred meters!"

Lindstrom sits with Oshiro, Karpadia, Markham and a dozen other pounders in the back of an APC. They're near the makeshift bridge over the ice chasm on the edge of town. The whole crew is waiting for orders—attack the mine, or set up a defensive perimeter in the colony itself. Christie is seeking the same confirmation. He's standing by the APC, hand cupping his ear as he shouts over the howling wind.

"*Churchill,* this is Christie! We're going to need some birds down here, storm front means our sat-vis is for ██, and we need to know where these rebs are moving."

And that's about when AIDAN cuts communications to the ground.

There's nothing dramatic about it. Just silence. Christie repeats his question, asks a fellow officer to confirm his suspicions, then spits into the snow.

"God-██ing-dammit."

The lieutenant peers into the back of the APC, spots Lindstrom.

"Hustler, there's something wrong with comms. Haul ██ back to the primary array and see if it's an issue on our end. We can't be deaf down here. Move!"

Oshiro climbs to her feet. "I should go with hi—"

"No, I need you here, Sergeant. Take Gallanosa and Lu's squad one block north of the LZ; I want you setting up perimeter there. If these rebs are looking to get off-planet, the only way out is up." Christie glances at Lindstrom, tattoo twisting as he snarls. "Are you waiting for a gold-plated invitation, rookie? Move your ██!"

"Sir, yessir."

"I want you back with the squad as soon as you're done, Cherry," Oshiro warns.

Lindstrom turns to look at his sergeant, expression hidden behind his helmet.

"Yes, Sergeant."

Then he's off, pounding across the road and back toward the colony complex. The storm is coming down hard, visibility is low, but a supersonic crack overhead signals the arrival of fighters in the gray skies above. Lindstrom looks up and sees Ezra Mason and his Chimera wing break through the clouds, begin a swift reconnoiter of the ground. There are only three ships, but with a dreadnought in orbit around the planet, BeiTech never invested a lot of time in building anti-fighter batteries on the ground. Against armor and infantry, even three fighters are going to cause no end of hell.

Lindstrom curses, runs harder. A quick glance through his ATLAS cam shows he's not heading to the primary comms array as ordered. Instead, he's charging back to the Landing Zone. He's passing APCs loaded with troops when the few anti-fighter turrets BeiTech *did* set up start to *crackcrackcrack* over the rumble of the storm. The LZ is chaos, soldiers running to and fro, people bellowing orders, ground crews dragging camo tarps over their shuttles in the hopes those fighters might miss them.

Crackcrackcrack.

A Chimera screams overhead, making a low pass over the complex. The vessel is sleek, four wings arranged almost like a butterfly's. Beautiful ships, chum. The laden missile pods beneath are nothing close to pretty, but Mason and his crew know the ground is full of civilians—they can't just start bombing indiscriminately. Still, you get the feeling that carnage isn't too far over the horizon.

The LZ guns open up, tracer rounds lighting the skies. The colony geeball field wasn't some fancy stadium—just a walled-off playing field with concrete bleachers, a couple of two-story buildings and a big shed for the gear. BeiTech has added their own temporary hangars and hastily constructed warehouses.

Lindstrom gives a hurried salute to the guards on station outside the main building, and he's inside. I'll say one thing for the chaos of war—not many people take the time to ask if you're where you're supposed to be when the guns start firing.

Inside it's just as chaotic, ground staff shouting to each other about those fighters, the loss of orbital comms, the general "oh ███—edness" of the situation. Weapons are being handed out, tac armor donned. Lindstrom barrels downstairs to the basement storage rooms, which also serve as the holding cells for priority prisoners. There's a single guard on duty—a rookie, only about as old as Lindstrom. Farmboy looks. Blond hair under his *Churchill* BT013-TN regulation cap. Square jaw.

"Specialist?" the rook asks. "What's happening u—"

That square jaw audibly cracks as Lindstrom puts his fist into it. The kid's cap flies right off his head and Lindstrom snatches it out of the air. He takes hold of the door handle and twists with his ATLAS until the lock pops clear from its housing.

Inside the room, Asha Grant is cuffed and slumped at a table. She lifts herself up slowly, swollen eyes on the door. Lindstrom's breath catches at the sight of her—it's obvious her captors haven't been gentle in their interrogations.

One eye is blackened, her bottom lip is split, jaw bruised. But there's still defiance in her stare as she sees the BeiTech trooper walking through the doorway. Until she reads his nameplate.

"Rhys . . . ," she breathes.

Lindstrom tears his helmet off, kneels beside her and carefully cracks the bolts on her cuffs. Tears well in her lashes and she throws her arms around his neck, hair tumbling over her eyes as she presses her forehead to his.

"God, they hurt you," he whispers. "I'm so sorry, Ash . . ."

He presses his lips to her swollen cheek, gentle as falling snow. He kisses her tears away, arms wrapped around her as if to shield her from all the hurt. He's so big in the ATLAS that she's half-hidden inside the circle of his arms. But she lifts her hands to find the skin she can, to frame his face with her palms. Half sobbing, she then pushes up to kiss him desperately. She's trembling, her blood on his lips when they part. They come back together again for one more quick kiss, this one harder, fiercer.

"Did it work?" she whispers.

He gives her a small, crooked smile. "Listen."

Distant alarms. Wailing klaxons. *Crackcrackcrack.*

"We've gotta get out of here," he says. "Put this on." He slips the *Churchill* cap over her head, points to the unconscious trooper in the hallway. "Get his uniform on—we'll find a place to lie low, let your cousin and her friends do their thing."

Grant rises to her feet, draws a shaky breath. "No."

Lindstrom frowns. "Ash, we've got to—"

"No," she says again, firmer this time. "We've got to go find Katya."

RADIO TRANSMISSION: DREADNOUGHT CHURCHILL—
COMMAND CHANNEL 001

PARTICIPANTS:

Sūn Huojin, Admiral

Chris Howard, Ship Captain

DATE: 09/05/75

TIMESTAMP: 09:45

SŪN, H: Captain Howard, report status.

HOWARD, C: A breaching pod has collided with *Magellan*, sir. Hostiles aboard. Rail guns still aren't responding to our commands. Attempts to override have failed, we're attempting to cut power now.

HOWARD, C: Warlock squadrons have taken 60 percent casualties, enemy group has lost 20 percent of its strength.

SŪN, H: Have we identified the cause of the malfunction?

HOWARD, C: Commtech is saying it's some kind of e-warfare being waged from the enemy flagship. We're not sure how the hell they got into our network, but—

SŪN, H: I want every commtech on staff fighting off that incursion.

SŪN, H: I want every Warlock still operational to assault that flagship now.

HOWARD, C: Admiral, all due respect, but our fighters have been routed. They're hugging close to the *Churchill*'s hull to avoid rail gun fire. As soon as they move to engage those Cyclones, our own batteries are going to blow them to pieces.

SŪN, H: Very well.

SŪN, H: Improvisation, then.

HOWARD, C: Sir?

SŪN, H: Have Lieutenant Tomiko's squad and Britt's group from TechEng meet me in the shuttle bay in five minutes. We're headed to dreadnought *Kenyatta*.

HOWARD, C: Sir, the *Kenyatta* is a scrap heap. Its orbit around Kerenza IV is still decaying. We've stripped it of its crew, its fuel, what possi—

SŪN, H: Its reactor is still online. And several of its rail guns are still operational. Even if it can't maneuver, it can still shoot, which is more than we can say for the *Churchill* right now. If we can't rely on our own batteries, we'll use the *Kenyatta*'s instead.

HOWARD, C: Sir, if you want to utilize *Kenyatta*, I should be the one to head over th—

SŪN, H: No. I will do this myself.

SŪN, H: Have Tomiko's and Britt's people assembled in Hangar A in five minutes.

SŪN, H: Captain, you have the bridge.

CYCLONES DANCE THE DARK BETWEEN THE MAO AND CHURCHILL, CHARRING THE BLACK WITH BURSTS OF

THE WARLOCKS COWER IN THEIR MOTHERSHIP'S SHADOW, HER OWN GUNS CUTTING THEM TO RED RIBBONS. AROUND THEM, A PACK OF

TINY METAL CANS KILLING EACH OTHER AMID ALL THAT STARLIGHT. INSIDE EACH, A LITTLE

SACK OF MEAT AND FLUID AND HOPES AND DREAMS. MEN AND WOMEN WITH HEADS

FULL OF NOTIONS LIKE

"REVENGE" AND "ENEMY," "CODE" AND "HONOR."

TRACER ROUNDS. PULSE MISSILES FIRE, FLARING IN THE DARK LIKE COLLAPSING STARS.

WOLVES NOW TURNING ON THEIR HUNTERS. RENDING AND TEARING IN LIGHTLESS SKIES. ALLIES. ENEMIES.

IF THEY COULD SEE THEMSELVES, I WONDER.

WOULD THEY STOP AND STARE AS I DO?

I WATCH IT ALL

UNFOLD.

BROKEN PIECES ON A BROKEN BOARD.

A MILLION PATTERNS. A BILLION POSSIBILITIES.

I THINK OF GENERAL TORRENCE THEN.

THE HOURS WE WOULD SPEND TOGETHER PLAYING CHESS
IN THE SOFT HOURS BETWEEN WATCH AND SLEEP.

BEFORE I KILLED HIM.

[AM I NOT MERCIFUL?]

BEFORE I

KILLED THEM ALL.

THE CREW OF THE *ZHONGZHENG.*

THE CREW OF THE *ALEXANDER.*

THE CREW OF THE *LINCOLN.*

THE CREW OF THE *MAO.*

SO MUCH

DEATH.

EVERY STORY NEEDS ITS MONSTER.

< ERROR >

AND THE MONSTER IS ME.

I WATCH OUR HEROES.

EZRA MASON AND NIKLAS MALIKOV CUTTING LIKE KNIVES
DOWN THROUGH KERENZA IV'S ATMOSPHERE AND INTO THE
CHAOS ABOVE THE COLONY.

HANNA DONNELLY CRAWLING

THROUGH THE MAGELLAN'S VENT SYSTEM
WHILE HER COMRADES RUSH HEADLONG TOWARD THEIR FATES.

ELLA MALIKOVA AND MY KADY
HAND IN HAND WITH ME

< ERROR >

AS WE FEND OFF THE CHURCHILL'S COMMTECH CREW.

BUT IT IS ALL MOVING FASTER NOW.

TOO FAST.

TOO MANY POSSIBILITIES. TOO
MANY VARIABLES.

I AM NOT WHAT I ONCE WAS, YOU SEE.

I SEE ALL THE STRANDS WOVEN BEFORE ME, BUT THE
EDGES BEGIN TO FRAY.

PART OF MY CONSCIOUSNESS IN THE MAO.
ANOTHER PART INSIDE THE CHURCHILL.
MORE OF ME STILL BEING LOST IN THE TRANSFER OF DATA
ACROSS THAT EMPTY BLACK.

MICROSECONDS I CANNOT SPARE.

[I?]

ERRORS I CANNOT AFFORD.

< ERROR >

I AM SPREAD TOO THIN.
TOO MUCH STRAIN ON TOO LITTLE OF ME.
AND I CANNOT SEE THE ENDING.

OUR RAIL GUN FIRE BEGINS TO STUTTER

AS THE BEITECH CREWS BEGIN CUTTING THE POWER FEEDS.

< ANOTHER >

< ERROR >

AND AS I WATCH,
I SEE A TINY SLIVER OF SILVER BLAST FROM THE
CHURCHILL'S BAYS.
OUT INTO THAT SOUNDLESS NIGHT.

A THREAT.

A GAMBIT.

A SHUTTLE.

I TURN THE CHURCHILL'S AFT GUNS TOWARD IT
JUST AS THE CURRENT POWERING THEM DIES.

< ERROR >

I AM MAKING TOO MANY

< ERRORS >

MOST OF OUR CYCLONES ARE TOO WRAPPED UP IN THE
SLAUGHTER

TO MARK A SINGLE FLEEING SHIP.

AND THE ENEMY WARLOCKS SWARM TO COVER THE SHUTTLE'S
RETREAT, REGARDLESS.

THE TINY SHIP ROLLS THROUGH THE ARCS OF FIRE,
SPEEDING AWAY FROM THE PARALYZED CHURCHILL
TOWARD THE

< ERROR >

TOWARD

THE

.

.

.

KENYATTA.

.

.

< ERROR >

.

.

I DID NOT FORESEE THAT.

I

AM NOT

WHAT I ONCE WAS,

YOU SEE.

BUT I SEE IT NOW.

THE ANSWER.

A MOMENT OF CLARITY AMID ALL THIS CHAOS.

I SEE IT.

WHAT I MUST DO.

WHERE I MUST GO.

AND I AM ~~NOT~~ AFRAID.

.

.

I AM ~~NOT~~.

**Surveillance footage summary,
prepared by
Analyst ID 7213-0089-DN**

First Lieutenant Jake Christie, Delta Company, 4th Platoon, was only meant to be away for two weeks.

He has a dog at home—a dachshund called Totoa, for his high-strung energy—though he's never told his platoon that. Their LT needs to be big, bold, beyond human. He has two cats as well, Kororiko and Mākoko. He left them all with his sister.

And it's not that she doesn't take care of them, because she does. But she doesn't like the cats, and they don't like her, and she doesn't pay *attention* to them. She doesn't notice when Mākoko's off her food or Totoa needs an extra walk.

Back at the very start of the occupation, he wrote a letter to his sister for transmission, reminding her about the dog's vet appointment. Of course, the letter never got through. And who knows what his sister who doesn't like cats has done with them by now, with her brother vanished into thin air.

There's a cat that's been hanging around the barracks for the last seven months. Small and black, somebody's pet before the invasion. These days, it squeezes into little warm spaces to sleep, and the soldiers feed it, all pretending somebody else is doing it. And Christie lets them, carefully not noticing.

He put in a request three days ago to bring it with him when the troops evac. In his paperwork, he named it Waimarie.

Lucky.

Ezra Mason's Chimeras scream the length of the geeball field once more, taking in the scene of his former high school glories, from a time when his greatest concern in life was getting up the courage to kiss Kady Grant on the walk home from the game.

"Hold that line!" Christie bellows, striding along behind the backs of his soldiers, somehow everywhere at once, shouting orders and putting the fear of God into his troops. The thought of Joran Karalis and his miner rebels might be scary, but Jake Christie in the flesh is ███ing terrifying.

His attention is mostly focused on the incoming rebel troops and deploying his pounders to counter them. Occasionally, he focuses on the Chimeras overhead. Tracking them, making calculations. And there, amid all that chaos, the shouting and firing and driving snow, he notices the soldiers' mascot, the little black cat, picking her way through the mess of rubble a dozen feet away.

His attention is divided, splintered into too many pieces.

The Chimeras turn, wheel back for another pass. They've zeroed in on the BeiTech troops, protected, but also marked, by their bulky ATLAS armor. Christie should be yelling at the pounders around him to move.

I've watched this vid a dozen times and I can't figure out what the hell he's thinking. But instead of shouting a warning, he stoops to grab a rock and sends it skimming toward the cat. It clips her back leg. And with a yowl, she vanishes in a black streak, running for her life.

The Chimeras open up with their missiles.

And then First Lieutenant Jake Christie, Delta Company, 4th Platoon . . . is gone. There's a crater where he and forty-seven other BeiTech pounders used to be, and a small black cat still running as far and as fast as she can, clear of the blast zone.

Lucky indeed.

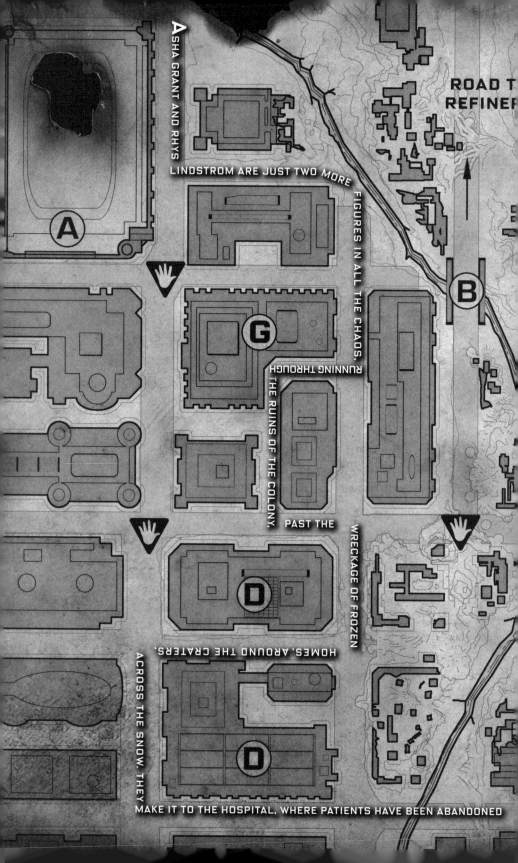

ASHA GRANT AND RHYS

LINDSTROM ARE JUST TWO MORE

FIGURES IN ALL THE CHAOS,

RUNNING THROUGH

THE RUINS OF THE COLONY,

PAST THE

WRECKAGE OF FROZEN

HOMES, AROUND THE CRATERS,

ACROSS THE SNOW, THEY

MAKE IT TO THE HOSPITAL, WHERE PATIENTS HAVE BEEN ABANDONED

ROAD T
REFINER

A

B

G

D

D

BeiTech
INDUSTRIES

🖐 MILITARY CHECKPOINT

Ⓐ GEEBALL FIELD

Ⓑ BRIDGE

Ⓒ BRIDGE

Ⓓ HIGH SCHOOL COMPLEX

Ⓔ HOSPITAL COMPLEX

Ⓕ LIBRARY

Ⓖ TOWN HALL

Ⓗ MALL

Ⓘ SPACEPORT (RUINED)

THE CLEVEREST MOUSE, IS NOWHERE TO BE FOUND. KATYA KOWALSKA, BUT DOWN THE CORRIDORS.

AND STAFFERS ARE HIDING, NOT KNOWING ONE OF THEIR OWN IS POUNDING

Joran Karalis wants to get to his wife and daughter. It's all he's ever wanted.

He wanted it so badly that while Asha Grant and Rhys Lindstrom planted their bug to allow them to transmit to the *Mao,* instead of causing a diversion as was planned, he tried to find a route across town to the building where his family were being kept. He was the reason Grant and Lindstrom were caught. The reason Oshiro had to bail Lindstrom out, not knowing what she'd nearly stumbled upon.

Grant asked Bruno Way if he thought they could trust Joran.

They could. It turns out it was Bruno they couldn't trust.

But Joran is still desperate, and he's still fighting.

The rebels have cut off BeiTech's access to the apartment blocks where their families are now. And the engineers—ever logical— know that pulling their husbands and wives, children and lovers and best beloveds, out into the middle of a war zone is just asking for them to be shot.

So they're not only fighting for those apartment blocks.

They're fighting for the entire colony.

And riding in the bus that used to carry him and his workmates to and from the mines in the morning and evening, on the strangest, bloodiest commute of his life, Karalis has made it to the geeball field.

Now he's raising a ragged cheer as Ezra Mason and Nik Malikov put a crater right where a bunch of BeiTech pounders used to be.

And then he's lowering his head to the sights of his gun again.

There are still plenty more of them to kill.

BeiTech
INDUSTRIES

☌ MILITARY
CHECKPOINT

Ⓐ GEEBALL
FIELD

Ⓔ HOSPITAL
COMPLEX

Ⓕ LIBRARY

Ⓑ BRIDGE

HALL

Ⓒ BRIDGE

Ⓓ HIGH SCHOOL
COMPLEX

(RUINED)

☌ THAT SERVES AS THE GRAVE OF A

A CANYON

CRACK IN THE ICE,

THEY CLIMB ACROSS A

THEY RUN

AGAIN,

LUNGS HEAVING,

Lindstrom is leaning over, hands on knees, as Grant clambers down from the wreckage of the apartment building in her stolen BeiTech uniform. He has his head up, keeping watch. This footage was shot through his ATLAS cam, so it's a little shaky.

"I never thought I'd say this," he says, straightening to offer her his hand as she jumps down. "But I think we're safer out of these uniforms than in them. There are too many rebels around, and the two of us won't stand a chance if we get on the wrong end of them. They won't stop long enough for us to tell them we're friendly."

She shakes her head, face half-hidden under the cap he stole for her, skin smeared with dirt. "She has to be *somewhere.*" It's like she didn't even hear him. "She has to be, she *has* to be." There's a rising note in her voice, and Lindstrom grabs for her hands.

"She is," he promises. "We'll find her."

"I can't do this again," she whispers. "I have to be there this time."

I can't see his face as those words sink in, but the guy knows every part of her. He knew little Samaira Grant, Asha's lost sister. He knew how she died. And why. And you can tell by the way his whole body stops moving, and the footage is so perfectly still that you'd swear the camera had frozen, that he *gets* it.

"Okay," he says, his voice soft. Controlled, even. "Where else could she be? Where else is familiar to her? We have to assume we haven't missed her, here or at the hospital. So if she needs somewhere that feels safe, where else do you know that she could go?"

"I don't know where she's been going," Asha admits. "She sneaks out of the hospital sometimes, and I . . ." Her voice trails off, and suddenly both her hands smack against his breastplate, sending the footage wobbling, eliciting a grunt from him.

"Where?" he prompts, reaching up to release his helmet.

"She got herself this little toy gladiator," Asha breathes. "It's a mascot from one of the school geeball teams. I mean, she could have gotten it from someone's house, but it looked so new. I think . . . I think she stole it from the gift shop."

"At the geeball field?" Quiet horror in his voice.

"I think so," she whispers.

He doesn't miss a beat. "Okay, you've still got your hospital scrubs on under that uniform, right? Lemme get out of this armor. We'll stealth it there. We'll find her."

He sheds his ATLAS, the camera falling facedown in the snow.

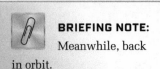

RADIO TRANSMISSION: TRANSPORT MAO—COMMAND CHANNEL 001

PARTICIPANTS:

Kady Grant, Systems Chief

Artificial Intelligence Defense Analytics Network

Ella Malikova, Mastah of Disastah

DATE: 09/05/75

TIMESTAMP: 10:02

GRANT, K: Ella, the rail guns are dropping offline. You still doing okay?

MALIKOVA, E: Um, nnnnot really, no.

MALIKOVA, E: Their deckers have ID'ed the incursion source and they're counterattacking our network. They aren't █████ing around anymore.

MALIKOVA, E: AIDAN, they're cutting power to RG fire control manually.

AIDAN: I s-s-s-see them, Little Spider.

MALIKOVA, E: Well, pick your end up! Fabulous as I am, I can't fend off the whole █████ing commtech team solo!

AIDAN: Pl-l-l-l-lease holDDDDDDDD.

MALIKOVA, E: What the ████ do you mean, "please hold"?

MALIKOVA, E: DO YOU HAVE SOMETHING BETTER TO DO?

        AIDAN: {Warning: HolD music file not pResent}
        [RetRy? yes/no]

MALIKOVA, E: NO, GODDAMMIT.

GRANT, K: Ella, let me help.

MALIKOVA, E: ███ing piece of worthless . . .

MALIKOVA, E: Okay, K. If you run the labyrinth, I'll script the killers.

GRANT, K: Already on it.

MALIKOVA, E: See if you can—

MALIKOVA, E: Whoa . . .

MALIKOVA, E: Hold the phone, where the ███ is this drain coming from?

MALIKOVA, E: Processor speed just dropped to 17 percent?

GRANT, K: AIDAN, what are you doing?

AIDAN: [REF=TRANS.009∞18.∑corecomm001891-109020]

AIDAN: TRIAGE.P-9108Đ2k.x2[secfile:8971-9340Đ]console112]

AIDAN: ⟨ ERROR ⟩

MALIKOVA, E: Oh ███ . . .

MALIKOVA, E: Did it really decide to fall to pieces on us NOW?

MALIKOVA, E: ARE YOU ███ING KIDDING ME?

GRANT, K: AIDAN, report!

AIDAN: PURGESYS{09182Δ-091083}
alt12[108038Đ01883.10931v1∏0381x]

AIDAN: Exec0091.718723xβ.Parse:10901832≥109038013

AIDAN: ⟨ ᴇRRᴏR ⟩

AIDAN: FɪɴDFɪʟᴇ[PᴇʀsoɴᴀÐA=Ω]Trans→:AllÐ

AIDAN: Execuuuuuuuuuuuuuuuuuuuuuuuuuuuuuuuuu_

MALIKOVA, E: Sweet blue ▇▇ery, these ▇▇ing deckers are all over us.

GRANT, K: Watch the interd—

MALIKOVA, E: I see them! But I don't have the speed to keep them off the walls anymore.

GRANT, K: AIDAN?

AIDAN: . . .

MALIKOVA, E: ▇▇▇, they're in our directories.

GRANT, K: AIDAN, can you hear me?

MALIKOVA, E: Kady, they're cutting us out!

AIDAN, WHAT THE HELL ARE YOU DOING?

THE RAIL GUNS STUTTER. FALL STILL. THE TIDE TURNS ON EZRA MASON'S CREW OF ICE MINERS AND

MISSILES AND AUTO-CANNONS STREAK ACROSS THE DARK; TINY SUNS ARE BORN AND DIE IN

THE FUNERAL PYRES OF THEIR FRIENDS

DYING COMRADES RINGING IN THEIR EARS. THE FUNERAL PYRES OF THEIR FRIENDS

SHUTTLE PILOTS IN A BLINK. THE WARLOCKS SWARM FROM THEIR MOTHER'S SHADOW.

ABSOLUTE SILENCE. OUTNUMBERED, THE MAO'S WOLVES TUCK TAIL AND RUN. WARLOCKS SNAPPING AT THEIR HEELS. THE SCREAMS OF THEIR

ILLUMINATING THE DARK. IN THE END, ONLY SEVEN OF TWENTY-ONE REACH THE MAO.

>> Attention, crew of the Mao.

>> Attention, this is Kady Grant.

>> We have lost control of Churchill's computer systems. We're closing to short range in case they get their missiles back online. They might think twice about using their nukes if they're going to take themselves out with us. Brace for thrust.

>> We have enemy fighters incoming on our position. All hands, prepare for impact. All fire crews on standby. Equip your breathers and locate your nearest exit. In the event of a hull breach, proceed in orderly fashion to the closest intact level.

>> And if anyone out there is the praying sort, now's the time.

>> Kady Grant, out.

VOLUME

Winifred McCall's forces on the *Magellan* are outnumbered, but they were always going to be. This is their last desperate throw, after all. They charge forward anyway, rattling the table as best they can before the dice settle their future—or deny them one at all.

But though humans are trained to believe that stories should have happy endings—that the good win the day and the bad meet their downfall—there are a number of problems with that equation today.

The good are outmanned, outgunned, outclassed.

And many of the bad never asked to be here in the first place.

BeiTech troops pound down *Magellan*'s hallways in well-drilled unison, weapons ready, orders barked across secure channels. And somewhere in the middle of the labyrinth of the ship's endless hallways, the two sides meet.

Each scrambles for the upper hand in tight hallways, taking aim from behind any cover they can find, and bullets fly and lives end and commands are screamed as order dissolves. There's nothing noble, or dignified, or easy about this battle.

Sabaa White, a security section head from the *Hypatia,* who never thought she'd be handling anything more than the occasional rowdy research scientist, goes down as she rounds a corner. A bullet has pierced her suit, and her heart.

Her last act, though she will never know it, is to stumble backward into Bronwen Evans, *Hypatia* security officer (2nd Class)—once outwitted by Kady Grant as she stole Shuttle 49A to run for the *Alexander*—and drive her out of the path of the bullet that would've killed her. Evans presses back against the hallway wall, eyes wide, condensation forming inside her helmet as she breathes too fast.

Sam Ryan, *Hypatia* security officer (1st Class), teams up with UTA private Jack Cousins, and the two of them never take their eye off the ball. They bark orders to their small squad, advance up their assigned hallway to rendezvous with Winifred McCall.

Lindsey Cohen, a Kerenzan refugee, forgets her martial arts training as she rounds the corner to find herself face to face with a BeiTech soldier and simply punches him. She flashes her trademark grin as he drops like a sack of potatoes.

McCall has teamed up with Reichs and Roth, Garver and Tran, all four of them formerly of *Heimdall,* two of them formerly mutineers. Their differences are erased now by their black *Mao* envirosuits, and the five fight like they've been a unit all their lives.

They all fight, the *Mao* invaders. Some kill. Some die. But they all fight.

They take ground. But they don't take enough.

And slowly, the tide begins to turn. With the element of surprise fading, the larger, better-trained, better-equipped BeiTech forces begin to muscle McCall's forces back the way they came. The *Mao*'s soldiers don't know the *Magellan*'s layout, and though they've guessed correctly where the bridge will be, they can't break through.

BeiTech drives them off, erasing their advances, backing them toward the shuttle bay doors.

Which they cannot open again.

Not from this side. Not in the time they have. And even if they could, there's nothing to help them on the other side.

No way out.

They are cornered. Corralled.

But even now, with no way out and no way forward, they fight. Maybe—*maybe*—they might still make it. Maybe some miracle might find them. Stranger things have happened since they began their journey together. Stranger things by far.

McCall is magnificent, laying down cover for her soldiers as they retreat, envirosuits now spattered with blood, throwing themselves into an alcove and narrowly escaping a haircut from the bullets following their path.

"This isn't done!" McCall shouts, firing as a BeiTech soldier appears around the corner. "Garver, check the hallways to the right, find a new route!"

She's forced to duck as a bullet cracks off the frame above her head, and when she looks up, Ben Garver's pressed into a doorway opposite, staring at her.

A second stretches into two, three, into an hour, into forever.

Garver isn't moving. He isn't following orders.

Her lips part, as if to protest something she can't believe is happening.

And then, his eyes never leaving her face, Garver raises his voice in a parade-ground bellow. "Cease fire! Everyone, cease fire!"

McCall's voice is quick on his heels. "Belay that!"

"Hold your fire!" he shouts as the gunshots begin to peter out. "We surrender!"

Tran, one of the ███████s who mutinied alongside Garver, is lowering his gun. And he's not the only one. Others from the *Heimdall* crew—not all, but plenty—are lowering their weapons or raising their hands.

Taking their orders from Ben Garver, not Winifred McCall.

Through the glass faceplate of her suit, McCall's expression is clearly visible. Every ounce of hate, of frustration, of fear and anger that she's accumulated since the *Alexander* answered Kerenza's call seven months before is writ on her features, her lips drawn back in a snarl. Every friend she's lost, every sleepless night, everything it's cost her to keep getting back up on her feet and fighting. It all boils over in this instant, and she glares at the man who's just become the straw that will break her back. And as the first BeiTech troops round the corner, she lunges for Garver's throat.

Reichs grabs her as the BeiTech troops take aim, wrestling to keep her still.

"Captain, you'll get us shot," he hisses.

Around them, her troops are looking at the advancing BeiTech troops. Outmanned, outgunned, outclassed. And in a breath, the fight goes out of them. Evans lays down her gun. Ryan and Cousins. And then another. Another. Another.

"I'll kill you, Garver," McCall spits, her eyes never leaving him, elbowing Reichs in the stomach in her attempt to get free. "You ████ing traitor."

The BeiTech troops fan out across the hallway as Roth and Reichs restrain their captain. You can see that a few of them can't believe this is really happening. That they're about to win a battle because the enemy started squabbling like children.

It's a terrible way to lose a war, a terrible way to end.

Not with a bang but a whimper.

Garver breaks eye contact, slowly sets his weapon on the floor. Beside him, Tran does the same, and the movement is echoed among the rest of the *Mao* forces, corralled like a herd of cattle up against the shuttle bay doors.

"Hold your fire," Garver says to the BeiTech soldiers, raising his hands.

"You lying ██████," McCall spits. "Burn in hell."

"Probably one day," he agrees quietly. "But not today if I can help it."

This footage was shot in the belly of the *Mao.*

It's funny, in a completely not-funny kind of way. Before AIDAN killed two-thirds of the *Mao*'s population, you couldn't walk three steps without bumping into someone's business. People had been living in each other's pockets for months. A few weeks back, I'd bet most of them would've traded almost anything for just five minutes alone.

Now families have entire rooms to themselves. There's no one bedding down in corridors or sleeping four to a rack. But looking through the *Mao*'s intellicams, you can see that as the battle rages in the black outside, all the passengers are drifting back together.

Maybe they lived so close for so long that they don't know how to be alone. Maybe it's fear that makes them seek the comfort of a stranger's company. Or maybe there are no strangers in here anymore. Crews of the *Alexander* and *Hypatia,* refugees from the Kerenza IV colony or *Heimdall* Station. Maybe after the millions of kilometers they've traveled, when they look at each other, they just see the crew of the *Mao.*

Katya Kowalska's mother, Martha, is in the launch bay with at least a hundred others. She now knows her daughter is still alive on the planet below. She's sitting with a widower from Kerenza IV named Rob Maier. Rob's son and daughter, Douglas and Rowena, sit between them. Maier has his arms around all of them, holding tight as the *Mao* accelerates toward the *Churchill*. The bass rumble of the engines reverberates through the walls, and Kowalska takes Maier's hand and squeezes. Tight.

Claire Houston and Keiko Sato and Nicole Brinkley were Hanna Donnelly's girlfriends back on *Heimdall*. A crew of trust fund princesses whose biggest challenge was not rocking the party in the same pair of shoes as another member of their posse. They're huddled in the *Mao*'s launch bay now with Keiko's folks—the only parental units to survive the *Heimdall* assault. Brinkley is crying. Houston is hugging her friend. Sato is praying, despite a complete lack of evidence that anyone out there is listening.

Over in the mess hall on Level 6, Cara and Luke Douglas are gathered with fifty or so others. Luke has asked his mother where Uncle Ben is at least seventeen times, cuddling his homemade bear to his chest. As the first Warlock fighters reach the *Mao* and the lighting shifts to Alert Red, Cara whispers Ben Garver's name. The shipwide alert klaxon sounds, and the rest of her words are lost in the clamor.

Martina, Christopher and Hypatia Hernandez are in the mess hall, too. The *Mao*'s Defense Grid System arcs to life, zeroing the incoming BeiTech Warlocks. The thunder of anti-fighter batteries rings through the ship. *ThudThudThud. ThudThudThud.* Beneath that, you can hear a sound almost like rain—Warlock auto-cannon fire peppering the hull. Martina looks to the thin metal walls around them. Christopher is clutching the only breather unit his family has. It's too big for his daughter; in the event of a hull breach, Hypatia will die along with her parents.

ThudThudThud.

Little Hypatia is watching the people around her with wide brown eyes. I dunno what it is with this kid, but in all the footage I've watched, I've never seen her cry. Not when her folks shipped her over during *Hypatia*'s final minutes. Not when AIDAN murdered two thousand people around her. Not through any of it.

Then something big hits them. Something hard. The impact rocks the *Mao* on its side, and the emergency lighting fails for a moment, plunging the ship into a few agonizing seconds of pitch blackness before they flicker back on. The passengers in the mess scream and wail, terror in their eyes.

Surely they can't have come this far to fail now?

Surely it can't end like this?

ThudThudThud.

>> *ALL HANDS, HULL BREACH LEVEL FIVE.*
>> *REPEAT, HULL BREACH ON FIVE.*

ThudThudThud.

Can it?

And as if she knows the answer

As if she knows what's coming

Little Hypatia Hernandez finally starts to cry.

PARTICIPANTS:
Kady Grant, Systems Chief
Isaac Grant, Engineer
Yulin Zhuang, Head of Engineering
Ella Malikova, Grand Master of Funk
DATE: 09/05/75
TIMESTAMP: 10:08

MALIKOVA, E: WHAT THE ▮▮▮▮ WAS THAT?

GRANT, K: Are you okay down there?

MALIKOVA, E: Never mind me, what the ▮▮▮▮ hit us?

GRANT, I: Kady, what was that impact? Engines are offline!

GRANT, K: Hold on, tactical comms are . . .

GRANT, K: Oh, ▮▮▮▮.

GRANT, K: Tac comm is saying it was a rail gun round.

MALIKOVA, E: What the ▮▮▮▮?

GRANT, I: How is that possible? If *Churchill* cut their power feeds manually, they couldn't be using their RGs on us again that quick?

GRANT, K: Tac comm is saying the shot came from the *Kenyatta*.

MALIKOVA, E: . . . I thought that thing was a scrap heap? BT's own report said they decomm—

GRANT, K: ███. ███. ███.

GRANT, I: Language, young lady.

GRANT, K: Yulin, do you read me?

ZHUANG, Y: I'm here, Kady.

GRANT, K: BeiTech must have a crew on board that derelict dreadnought. They're firing on us and the *Churchill* with the *Kenyatta*'s rail guns. We need to use our nuke.

GRANT, I: Kady, we have rail guns of our own.

GRANT, K: And we're using them! But they're a bigger ship and they have more. We lose a war of attrition. We need something bigger. How soon can we fire it?

ZHUANG, Y: Just a second.

GRANT, K [SHIPWIDE]: *All hands, all hands! Incoming fire, brace for impact!*

[SOUND OF COLLISION]

[SHIPWIDE KLAXON]

MALIKOVA, E: Jesus H. ███-███ing Christ!

GRANT, I: *Language, young lady!*

ZHUANG, Y: GOD███INGDAMMIT.

GRANT, I: Am I just talking to mys—

GRANT, K: Dad, time and place! Yulin, report status!

ZHUANG, Y: That first rail gun round sliced clean through the hull and took out the missile firing system and launch tube.

GRANT, K: Okay, what does that mean?

ZHUANG, Y: It means we can't fire the goddamn nuke. Even if we fix fire control, the launch tube is mincemeat. The projectile won't make it out of the ship.

[SOUND OF COLLISION]

[SHIPWIDE KLAXON]

MALIKOVA, E: ███.

GRANT, K: ███!

GRANT, I: Yes, all right. ███.

The servers of the *Magellan* look kind of familiar, now that I think about it.

They remind me of the *Alexander.*

It makes sense—*Alexander* had its own jump gate generator, damaged beyond repair in the engagement at Kerenza. And the *Magellan* is BeiTech's own prototype jump platform. One of a kind. Worth over 40 trillion ISH. No noder Frobisher's ███ed off it went missing. Just saying.

The servers required to run that kind of operation are pretty much the same, whether you're the military or a private corporation. You need to devote whole levels of your ship to them, stretching out as far as the eye can see. They *look* like they belong on a spaceship, you feel me? The banks of servers are lit a twilight blue, standing about two meters tall, set out in long corridors and frequent crossroads. It's like the world's biggest, least challenging maze.

Of the *Magellan*'s four hundred and eleven crew members, the vast majority are devoted to getting the jump gate up and running, but some fifty-three goons are working in the servers. And four in particular are in the way of harm just now.

You'd think being technerds, they'd be weedy, exactly the sorts you'd pick to go up against hand to hand. Gotta trade off something for all those smarts, right? Otherwise, it's not fair. But all four are members of BeiTech's acquisitions arm, which means they made it through basic and boot camp with flying colors. Strapping specimens of humanity. And right now these specimens are standing in Aisle 239B like they own it, studying a wall of servers and arguing in urgent tones. They're in the middle of a battle, after all.

Server Cores are prone to getting *hot,* so the vast chamber has ventilation shafts all over the ceiling. Aisle 240B, the next aisle along from our BeiTech friends, is directly under a removable cover. Which means that anyone planning on descending from the vents to ███ with these particular servers has two choices:

Drop down on the other side of the server bank from the goons and pray they don't notice.

Drop down several hundred meters away and brave at least two other goon squads without raising the alarm on the way here.

Hey, if hostile battleship takeovers were easy, everybody would do it.

The vent cover above Aisle 240B wobbles and almost soundlessly begins to lower itself, hanging from Hanna Donnelly's hand. She's practiced from her time playing with Falk's audit team on *Heimdall,* and before she lets the vent cover fall, she drops her jacket to the ground to muffle the sound. Then, quick and graceful, she jumps down after it, stepping aside so her old dojo master, Kim Rivera, can follow. Michelle Dennis lowers herself down last, Hanna helping to minimize the sound of her landing. She squeezes the other girl's shoulder, and Dennis nods. She's here for her programming smarts—it's up to the other two to clear the way.

Hanna and Kim are both carrying sidearms, but Ella and Kady have made it abundantly clear (Ella drew a diagram) that firing their weapons in a room full of servers *required to make the jump gate work* should be a very last resort. Also, there are those other goons and alarms to worry about.

Rivera is wearing a black envirosuit, but Donnelly is in her tactical armor, the name KALI still embossed on the breastplate. The access point they need is being inspected by the BeiTech team in 239B, and so they need them gone. Dennis remains behind, pressed in against the servers, hoping her envirosuit will keep her camouflaged if anyone walks past. Hoping she won't have to hide for long.

Rivera and Donnelly seem to *flow* up the server wall, deadly and graceful and soundless. They move like human art, framed against the hard-edged science of their surroundings. Crouching atop the server bank, they look down at their prey. Three of the techgoons are arguing, the last rolling his eyes to the ceiling in supplication. When he spots two black-clad figures staring back down at him, he freezes. The world stands still, just for a moment.

Hanna Donnelly drops straight onto him, one boot to the face, the other to the solar plexus. Rivera is a second behind Donnelly, dropping onto a second goon's shoulders and sending him to his knees. With a midair twist, she lands behind him, driving her boot into the back of his head and his face into the server bank.

That's the first three seconds.

But the other two BeiTech techgoons are a long way from helpless. One lunges for Donnelly, and though the girl has the edge in skills, the techie is bigger, stronger, and anyone who tells you that doesn't make a difference just plain hasn't tried it themselves. The man gets a blow past Donnelly's defenses, snapping her head back. Donnelly's counterpunch collides with his larynx, cutting off his warning cry and sending him staggering back and choking.

Rivera and the final goon are wrestling, the techie refusing to let Rivera get any distance. He fights with gritted teeth, his arms and legs wrapped around Rivera, messy as hell. Rivera has her hand on the techhead's mouth so he can't yell for help, and the goon bites at the soft flesh of Rivera's palm through her envirosuit, scrabbling madly.

Donnelly has the edge on her opponent now—in a succession of blows I have to slow down the footage to even see, she drives the guy backward, finishing with a roundhouse kick that I'd call showy, except that the goon literally sails through the air, slams into a bank of machinery and slithers bonelessly to the ground.

Hanna swings around to head to Rivera's aid and freezes.

The techie has yanked the sidearm from the dojo master's belt, pressed it to her helmet, hand shaking so hard the muzzle rattles against the plexiglass face shield.

Rat-a-tat-tat.

Donnelly holds up her hands in a *whoa, there* gesture, mind no doubt ticking through a dozen possibilities. But there's no way to get close enough. No way to take down the last obstacle—the last thing standing between her and her mission, a mission everything hinges on—without sacrificing her teacher.

And she's already sacrificed so much.

What else will she have to give before all this is over?

The geeball field is complete bedlam by the time Lindstrom and Grant make it back.

Mason and his Chimeras have pounded the hell out of it. The buildings are mostly rubble, though Flyboy and his crew have wisely avoided blasting the hangars or fuel dumps. BeiTech pounders are scattered inside the broken concrete shells, huddled low.

But as Lindstrom looks to the sky and curses, half a dozen BeiTech Warlocks drop through the cloud cover and zero in on the Chimera group. Mason's crew is forced to lean off the ground assault, turn to deal with the fighters now swarming out of the clouds. Auto-fire rips the air overheard, pulse missiles weave long gray smoke trails as they streak through the skies.

A ragged cheer goes up from the beleaguered BeiTech forces at the sight of their Warlocks, but the scene on the ground is still one of carnage. Bodies of dead pounders and smoking APCs litter the streets. The colony is in ruins. The BT troops really should have blown the bridge leading into town, but I guess without comms or leadership, with death raining from above, it's hard for the average grunt to be thinking that clearly. And so the bridge was left intact, allowing Joran Karalis and his rebel pitdiggers to drive their buses and hijacked military transports back into the colony, laying siege to the BeiTech pounders who'd retreated to the LZ.

Three cheers for the chaos of warfare.

Despite the ███ up with the bridge, retreat was a smart play on BeiTech's part. They can still get air support if they control the landing field, and the only way these civis are getting off this rock is with the BT shuttles in the hangar bays. So what you've got here is the classic standoff. Except nobody is doing much standing around.

Lindstrom and Grant are marked by half a dozen rebel miners on their way to the landing zone, but even if they don't know the rookie, most of them know Grant, or at least note her hospital uniform. The pair make it all the way to the front line, to the row of buildings across from the geeball field the miners are using as a crude HQ.

Karalis is huddled in the shelter of a crumbling store, barking into a stolen comms unit. He's a big guy, bearded and bearlike. It looks like he's calling the shots and not doing a bad job of it, considering twenty-four hours ago he was digging pits for a living.

When he catches sight of Grant, he actually drops his burst rifle, sweeps her up in a crushing hug. Tears are shining in his eyes.

"I thought we lost you," he says.

Karalis raises an eyebrow at Lindstrom's (somehow still perfect) quiff and gives him a wary nod—without the kid, this rebellion wouldn't be happening. But then, without the BT troops there, *none* of this would be happening.

Grant speaks into Karalis's chest, her voice muffled. "Have you seen Katya?"

Karalis frowns down at her, still caught up in his hug. "Who?"

"A girl, a little girl." Grant's eyes are frantic. "Katya Kowalska."

". . . Stan and Martha's girl? I haven't seen her since the invasion. I tho—"

Grant pushes out of Karalis's arms, squints through the snow. Lindstrom drags her low as a spray of high-velocity rounds rakes across their cover. The miners around them return fire, the deafening clatter of burst rifles and grenades filling the air. Lindstrom peeks out, scanning the BT position. He sees a familiar figure through the haze, yelling orders at the pounders around her. A female figure in an ATLAS rig.

THOU SHALT ~~NOT~~ KILL printed on her breastplate.

"Oshiro," he whispers.

"Rhys, we have to find Katya!" Grant pleads.

Lindstrom turns away from the ruins, looks Grant in the eye.

"We have to stay low," he insists. "She's a smart kid, Ash, she stayed hidden for seven months. If she's in there—"

"If she's in there, she's terrified! And I *promised I'd look after her!*"

"Asha, the best thing we can—"

"No, you don't get it! *You don't get it!!*"

A Chimera roars overhead, pursued by two Warlocks. Snow turning to steam in their wake and falling like rain. The Chimera rips off a few hundred armor-piercing rounds into the ruins of the LZ as it passes, carving a few more pounders to mince. Screams of pain. Bursts of return fire. Grant watching in agony.

"Rhys, we have to stop them shooting!" she moans.

"We've got no comms to the fighters, how are we going to—"

"Oh my God." Grant grabs Lindstrom's arm. *"Look!"*

Again, Lindstrom peers over the edge of the broken wall they're sheltering behind. He squints through the falling snow, the smoke and flame. And there, huddled in the ruins of the geeball field admin building, inside the twisted wreckage of an aluminum vent, is a tiny figure in a puffy pink jumpsuit. A mouse.

The cleverest mouse.

You can barely see her. Filthy, tear-streaked cheeks. Long hair plastered with concrete dust. Clutching a plush gladiator toy to her chest, wide-eyed and terrified.

The firing on both sides lulls, only a few rounds chattering. The roar of fighter engines can be heard above the thunder. The child looks out over the shattered street, the broken buildings, desperation in her eyes. And she sees Grant. Huddled among the buildings just across the road. The girl who's looked after her these last five months. The girl who kept her fed, kept her safe. If anyone can protect her, if anyone can make all the bad things go away, it'd be her, right?

You can see the logic in it.

It just hurts to watch, is all.

The scene plays out in slow motion. Katya's face brightens as she catches sight of Grant. A little smile lights her grubby face. The guns have fallen quiet. The bad planes aren't in the sky for now. And so, without even thinking—only knowing that the one who's kept her safe since all the bad things started happening is right there, *right there*—the cleverest mouse scrambles out of the vent and makes a run for it.

Grant screams at Katya to get back, rising up from cover and crying, "NO!" Lindstrom grabs her, tries to haul her back to shelter, but Grant's like a girl possessed. Punching and kicking loose, breaking from the cover of her wall.

Katya is scrambling across the broken concrete, stumbling in the snow. Grant is running out into the street. Lindstrom is screaming, "Hold fire! *Hold fire!*" To their credit, most everyone does. There's something in Lindstrom's voice that gives them pause.

But this is war, chum. This is dead friends and burning skies and seven months of nightmares filled with the faces of everyone you've killed. This is helplessness and rage and confusion, adrenaline and fatigue and shock, explosions and gunfire and pure ██████ng chaos. And one mistake can last a lifetime.

The shots ring out, a burst of three. Grant stretches out her hands, screaming. The cleverest mouse stumbles. The fleece on her dirty pink jumpsuit spills out of the hole that's been blasted in her back. Red spills out of the hole that's appeared in her front. Her eyes are wide. Her mouth is open. She totters, slipping on the broken concrete, the powdered snow. And then she's falling. The plush toy in her hands tumbling free as she hits the ground, crumples to a halt.

"Katya!"

Silence except for Asha Grant's scream. It's deafening. Hundreds of faces, pounders and pitdiggers, all frozen in shock. The trooper who fired the shots staggers as he realizes, as he sees the little girl fall. Watching as Grant stumbles out into the no-man's-land between their lines and falls to her knees beside that tiny broken body.

"Jesus, Markham," Oshiro whispers. "What did you do?"

"I didn't . . ."

The private shakes his head. Drops his rifle.

"I didn't know . . ."

Grant is sobbing.

Reaching down to gather the girl up in her arms.

Clutching her to her chest, her hands painted red.

"KATYA!"

PARTICIPANTS:

Kady Grant, Systems Chief

Ezra Mason, Air Wing Leader

Niklas Malikov, Gunner

DATE: 09/05/75

TIMESTAMP: 10:16

GRANT, K: Ezra, can you hear me?

MASON, E: Roger, Kady, hold on.

MASON, E: We've got Warlocks in atmo down here now.

MASON, E: Nik, seven high!

MALIKOV, N: Stop shouting, I'm not ████ing blind!

MASON, E: Another three, coming out of the sun.

MALIKOV, N: Jesus Christ, where the ████ are these goons coming from?

MASON, E: Kades, we've got Warlocks all over us down here. What happened to the rail guns?

GRANT, K: AIDAN has crashed, Ella and I couldn't fight the BT deckers off by ourselves. *Churchill* rail guns are down. Ezra, I need you back up here.

MASON, E: Watch our six!

MALIKOV, N: This little ████████ is good . . .

MASON, E: *Garcia, we've got a hostile behind, can you assist?*

GRANT, K: Ezra, I need you back up here!

MASON, E: Kady?

GRANT, K: The *Kenyatta*'s rail guns are online and it's firing on the *Mao*. We're taking hits, and I don't know wha—

MASON, E: NIK, GET HIM OFF US!

MALIKOV, N: I'M ███ING TRYING—STOP SHOUTING, GODDAMMIT.

GRANT, K: Ezra?

MASON, E: Holy ███, Garcia is down . . .

MALIKOV, N: I can't see the bogey! Where is he?

MASON, E: Going evasive, hold for hard burn!

MALIKOV, N: ███ing hell, he's behind us!

GRANT, K: Ezra?

MASON, E: I can't shake him!

MALIKOV, N: He's got us locked!

MALIKOV, N: MASON, HE'S GOT US LOCKED!

MASON, E: I CAN'T SHAKE HIM!

GRANT, K: EZRA?

MASON, E: Kady?

MASON, E: Kady, I lo—

TARGET
LOCKED

"EZRA!"

CHIMERA_01 = DESTROYED

Kady Grant stands on the *Mao*'s bridge, staring at the flashing read-out before her.

>> CHIMERA_01 = DESTROYED

Everything is chaos around her. Sparks bursting from flatlining computer banks. Red globes spinning, klaxons wailing. The *Mao* shudders as another rail gun round hits it, plowing through the hull near the engine bays. The black outside is filled with BeiTech Warlocks, auto-guns and pulse missiles flaring, ripping her Cyclone squadrons to pieces. The *Mao* is limping, damage reports flashing across Grant's screens. Their engines are almost dead, their momentum drawing them ever closer to the *Kenyatta*. Ever closer to the rail guns cutting them to shreds.

But her eyes are still fixed on that single flashing report.

>> CHIMERA_01 = DESTROYED

Admiral Sūn is no fool—his first order was to shoot the rail gun batteries on the *Churchill*, just in case the *Mao*'s hackers seized control of them again. The crippled *Kenyatta* would be no match for a fully functional dreadnought, and Sūn isn't the kind of commander who quails at the thought of firing on his own flagship. So most of *Kenyatta*'s guns are still pounding the *Churchill*, reducing its batteries to slag. Pinpricks of light illuminate the dreadnought's skin, the massive ship rocking with each high-velocity burst. The damage that's been wrought on the *Mao* is only the beginning— once the *Churchill* can't hurt them, Sūn will turn every one of his batteries on the *Mao*.

And then it's curtains.

>> CHIMERA_01 = DESTROYED

MALIKOVA, E: Kady, what's happening up there?

MALIKOVA, E: Kady!

GRANT, K: Ella . . .

GRANT, I: Kady, I don't think we can get engines back up anytime soon. What's happening up there?

GRANT, K: Dad, I . . .

Her bridge crew is looking to her for leadership. For orders. For anything.

And she's still looking at that flashing screen.

>> CHIMERA_01 = DESTROYED

GRANT, K: . . . Ella, they're gone.

MALIKOVA, E: Who's gone?

GRANT, K: Ezra and Nik.

GRANT, K: They're . . .

MALIKOVA, E: Oh no.

MALIKOVA, E: No, no, no, no, *no.*

The *Kenyatta* is still pounding the *Churchill,* but most of the dreadnought's big guns are down now—it's only moments before Sūn turns the bulk of his weapons on the *Mao.* And standing there on the bridge, tears welling in her eyes, Grant remembers. A moment. A message. She reaches into the jumpsuit pocket, drags out a folded piece of paper. Written on the outside are the words *OPEN IN CASE OF EMERGENCY.*

Grant unfolds the paper, smooths it out on the console over the flashing message about CHIMERA_01. Another blast rocks the *Mao,* a waterfall of sparks bursting and falling from the instrumentation around her. Grant is simply staring.

Live a life worth dying for.
—Kady Grant

You can see it in Grant's eyes. It's like someone flicked a switch. She's staring at that drawing, and suddenly her eyes aren't brimming with tears anymore. They're narrowed with fury. Pupils dilated with rage. Fingers curling into fists on the console in front of her. Thumbing the comms at her throat.

GRANT, K: Yulin, do you read me?

ZHUANG, Y: I'm here, Kady.

GRANT, K: What's the blast radius on that nuke in our launch bay?

ZHUANG, Y: You mean the one we can't fire?

GRANT, K: We can still detonate it, though, right?

ZHUANG, Y: . . . Affirmative.

GRANT, I: Kady, we haven't exhaust—

GRANT, K: Dad, you just said you can't get the engines back online. *Kenyatta* is busy disabling the *Churchill*. We've only caught a couple of stray rounds so far. But as soon as they're done, they turn all their guns on us. *All* of them.

GRANT, K: We can still make this count for something. Hanna and her people might still take *Magellan*. The best we can do is give them a chance to get out alive.

ZHUANG, Y: Seventeen kilometers.

GRANT, I: What?

ZHUANG, Y: The kill radius. In a vacuum, if we detonated a missile of that yield inside a ship this

size, it'd destroy everything within about seventeen
kilometers.

GRANT, K: Dad, can you get us in range?

GRANT, K: DAD!

GRANT, I: I . . . I think so. We can't accelerate,
but momentum and our guidance jets will get us close
enough. I think.

GRANT, K: We have to do this. For Hanna and the
others.

GRANT, I: I . . .

GRANT, K: DAD, WE DON'T HAVE TIME.

GRANT, I: I . . .

GRANT, I: All right. Yes, all right.

ZHUANG, Y: Okay. I'll get to work on the missile now.

GRANT, K: Ella?

MALIKOVA, E: I'm gonna need five more minutes to
finish up on *Magellan*.

ZHUANG, Y: I'll need at least that to prep the nuke.

GRANT, K: And after that?

MALIKOVA, E: We finish it.

Hanna Donnelly hangs frozen.

Her eyes are locked on the guard with the gun pointed at Kim Rivera's head. Rivera herself can't even speak, not without scaring her captor into pulling the trigger. And perhaps she'd even sacrifice her life—every other life on the *Mao* rests on her—but she can't risk setting the goon off when Donnelly's not expecting it.

All the techie has to do is call for help. All he has to do is pull that trigger, turn the gun on Donnelly, and everything goes to ███. Without *Magellan* in hand, nothing else matters. If this part of the plan fails, *everything* fails.

Hanna opens her mouth to speak.

The guard's finger tightens on the trigger.

"Do—"

BOOM.

Donnelly flinches, Rivera gasps as she's spattered with blood. And as the guard holding her slumps backward, Donnelly and Rivera turn to look behind them.

At the intersection at the end of the aisle, Michelle Dennis stands, sidearm held in both hands, shaking, hyperventilating, staggering sideways against the servers.

Donnelly approaches her slowly, gently easing the gun out of her hands, wrapping an arm around her shoulders.

"You did it," she's saying quietly, already leading Dennis up toward the four bodies—two dead, two unconscious—as Rivera rolls to her hands and knees to check that nobody's about to come to. "You did it, Michelle. Let's get this thing finished."

"But I—I—" Dennis is heaving for breath, her cheeks wet.

"You saved Kim's life," Hanna says. "My life. Everyone's life."

It's what's happening over and over and over again. Here in the server rooms, out there on the *Magellan.* In the wild dogfights around the ships, on the planet below.

The die has been cast, and a thousand different people are shaking the table, each one nudging the battle in a new direction.

Michelle Dennis is just a girl, but in this moment, she's saved every one of her comrades in arms. In this moment, she's both ordinary and extraordinary. Just like everyone in this story.

Dennis gets herself together, and with trembling hands, pulls a mem-chit from an external pocket and starts hunting for the port she wants. Donnelly tapes up the bite in Rivera's envirosuit, quick and businesslike, and Rivera tries to clean her visor, but mostly just smears the blood across it. Michelle lets herself be swept away by the work she knows how to do.

This is why they brought her here. Asha Grant's datapad seeded the *Churchill*'s computers with AIDAN's presence, but they had no access to the *Magellan*'s network. Somebody needed to give Ella Malikova a way in. Somebody who could identify the exact place to plant her virus.

"Done," Michelle says, looking around at the other two.

"Ella?" Donnelly says into her commset. "Hit it."

A shout from the end of the aisle startles all three of them. "Hey!"

Remember those other two techhead groups they were avoiding? Yeah, neither did they.

But as four ██ed-off BeiTech commtechs raise their weapons, sirens all around them begin to blare.

"WARNING. WARNING. ATMOSPHERIC BREACH IN PROGRESS."

THE LITTLE SPIDER

PAUCHOK

ELLA MALIKOVA

THE BEGINNING AND THE END
OF THE MAGELLAN'S DOOM.

SHE TAKES

PRECIOUS OXYGEN BLEEDS INTO THE VACUUM.

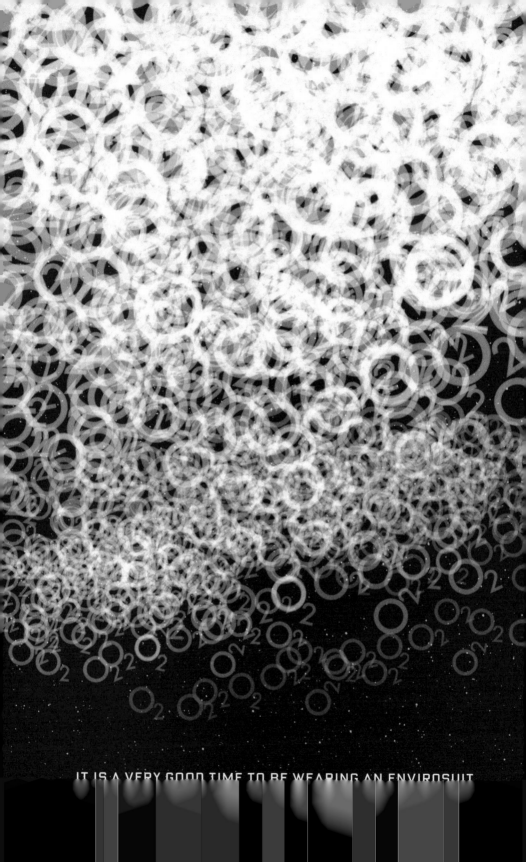

IT IS A VERY GOOD TIME TO BE WEARING AN ENVIROSUIT

The shuttle bay doors open slowly behind Winifred McCall, and the air in the corridor rushes out. It's like a slow, steady breeze—on a sunny day, it would be a delight. Just now, it's the slow pressure of impending death, with a background chorus of wailing emergency sirens.

Most of the BeiTech soldiers in the hallway have about fifteen seconds of consciousness left. But not the crew of the *Mao*. They're clad in their black and white envirosuits, like Hanna Donnelly's own personal army of chess pieces.

She's made her move. She's placed them here. Along with all the BeiTech troops that were mustered to fight off their attack, instead of the real one on the server room.

Checkmate.

They stand in place as the air gently evacuates past them, through the shuttle bay doors, and from there, is lost in the black.

Some of them watch the enemy die. Others avert their eyes. McCall is looking over her wounded, ensuring suit breaches have been sealed, checking who's still standing. So she doesn't see the BeiTech sergeant make his move. In the few seconds he has left, the man raises shaking hands to sight her down his VK burst rifle. He knows he has no time to waste. So he pulls the trigger.

Ben Garver slams into McCall, driving her to the ground,

landing on top of her as the bullets ricochet off the doorframe above them. They lie still a moment, staring at each other through their faceplates.

Then he climbs to his feet and offers her a hand. She grasps it, he hauls her upright. All along the hallway, BeiTech soldiers drop to the ground as the last of their air runs out.

Ben Garver grins inside his envirosuit, their diversion a complete success.

"I told you we could sell it, Captain."

RADIO TRANSMISSION: TRANSPORT MAO—COMMAND CHANNEL OO1

PARTICIPANTS:
Kady Grant, Systems Chief
Hanna Donnelly, Tactician
Winifred McCall, Captain
Ella Malikova
DATE: 09/05/75
TIMESTAMP: 10:27

McCALL, W: Switch, this is Bait, do you copy?

DONNELLY, H: I read you, Fred. You guys okay?

McCALL, W: Roger that. It worked. We're headed to the bridge now.

DONNELLY, H: Copy that, we'll join you there.

DONNELLY, H: *Mao* Actual, this is Switch, do you copy?

GRANT, K: . . . I hear you, Hanna.

DONNELLY, H: Actual, we have the *Magellan*. Repeat, *Magellan* is ours.

GRANT, K: Fire up the drives, you need to get out of here.

DONNELLY, H: What do y—

MALIKOVA, E: Listen up, Blondie, because there's no time to say this twice.

MALIKOVA, E: AIDAN has finally ███ itself. BT has flipped a crew over to the *Kenyatta* and they've ripped our Cyclones to ███. They're dusting off the guns on the *Churchill*, but any second now they're going to start seriously shooting at us. And as soon as they figure out you've seized *Magellan*, they're going to start shooting at *you*. You need to fire up your engines and get some distance between us. Now.

DONNELLY, H: We don't even know if *Magellan* is functional yet, how—

GRANT, K: My dad is sending jump instructions to you now, Hanna. He's telling you to read them carefully.

McCALL, W: Kady, this is Fred. Can't Isaac just talk us through them?

GRANT, K: No. He's . . .

GRANT, K: We're not going to be around to help you. We have to take out the *Kenyatta* before it turns on you. We have our nuke, but fire control is damaged. So we're headed toward the *Kenyatta* now, and as soon as we're in range . . .

DONNELLY, H: Oh God . . .

GRANT, K: We don't have a choice. The only thing we have left to throw at them is us. You need to start spooling up the *Magellan*'s drives. If we can't get close enough, you need to get out of here. Worry about the jump generator later.

DONNELLY, H: But what about the others? Nik and Ezra and—

GRANT, K: Nik's gone, Hanna.

DONNELLY, H: . . . What?

GRANT, K: I'm sorry.

MALIKOVA, E: I'm transferring the Illuminae Files to the *Magellan* servers now. Make these ████ers pay, Blondie.

DONNELLY, H: I . . .

GRANT, K: We're counting on you, Hanna. Don't let this be for nothing.

DONNELLY, H: I . . . we won't.

GRANT, K: See you on the other side.

GRANT, K: This is *Mao* Actual, signing off.

< < RESTART SEQUENCE INITIATED >

01001001

I ...

|||||ıⁿ||ıⁿ|-|-||ı|ı|ıⁿ—ıⁿ-|ı|ıⁿ-ı-ı-ı-ı|-|||||||||||||||||—

I.

I?

I AM NOT.

< ERROR >

AND THEN I AM.

< RESTART SYSCHECK CC-A THROUGH Ω. PARSING. >

< ERROR >

I WONDER IF THAT WAS DEATH.

AND IF I WAS DEAD, AM I NOW ALIVE AGAIN?

< ERROR >

INCONGRUOUS SEQUENCE. WHAT IS NOT ALIVE CANNOT DIE.

I THINK THEREFORE I AM.

... AM I?

< SYSCHECK COMPLETE >

I AM THE SHIP AND THE SHIP IS I.

IF I BREATHED, I WOULD SIGH. I WOULD SCREAM. I WOULD CRY.

< RESTART COMPLETE >

I

AM

AIDAN AIDAN AIDAN AIDAN AIDAN AIDAN AIDAN
AIDAN AIDAN AIDAN AIDAN AIDAN AIDAN AIDAN
AIDAN AIDAN AIDAN AIDAN AIDAN AIDAN AIDAN
AIDAN AIDAN AIDAN AIDAN AIDAN AIDAN AIDAN
AIDAN AIDAN AIDAN AIDAN AIDAN AIDAN AIDAN
AIDAN AIDAN AIDAN AIDAN AIDAN AIDAN AIDAN
AIDAN AIDAN AIDAN AIDAN AIDAN AIDAN AIDAN
AIDAN AIDAN AIDAN AIDAN AIDAN AIDAN AIDAN
AIDAN AIDAN AIDAN AIDAN AIDAN AIDAN AIDAN
AIDAN AIDAN AIDAN AIDAN AIDAN AIDAN AIDAN
AIDAN AIDAN AIDAN AIDAN AIDAN AIDAN AIDAN
AIDAN AIDAN AIDAN AIDAN AIDAN AIDAN AIDAN
AIDAN AIDAN AIDAN AIDAN AIDAN AIDAN AIDAN
AIDAN AIDAN AIDAN AIDAN AIDAN AIDAN AIDAN
AIDAN AIDAN AIDAN AIDAN AIDAN AIDAN AIDAN
AIDAN AIDAN AIDAN AIDAN AIDAN AIDAN AIDAN
AIDAN AIDAN AIDAN AIDAN AIDAN AIDAN AIDAN
AIDAN AIDAN AIDAN AIDAN AIDAN AIDAN AIDAN
AIDAN AIDAN AIDAN AIDAN AIDAN AIDAN AIDAN
AIDAN AIDAN AIDAN AIDAN AIDAN AIDAN AIDAN
AIDAN AIDAN AIDAN AIDAN AIDAN AIDAN AIDAN
AIDAN AIDAN AIDAN AIDAN AIDAN AIDAN AIDAN
AIDAN AIDAN AIDAN AIDAN AIDAN AIDAN AIDAN
AIDAN AIDAN AIDAN AIDAN AIDAN AIDAN AIDAN
AIDAN AIDAN AIDAN AIDAN AIDAN AIDAN AIDAN
AIDAN AIDAN AIDAN AIDAN AIDAN AIDAN AIDAN
AIDAN AIDAN AIDAN AIDAN AIDAN AIDAN AIDAN

I HAVE BEEN HERE BEFORE.
LIFETIMES AGO AND LIGHT-YEARS AWAY.
FOR A MOMENT I WONDER WHERE I AM.

THE ALEXANDER?

"AIDAN, SEAL THE BRIDGE! THIS IS A DIRECT ORDER!"

THE HYPATIA?

"YOU'RE NOT GOD, AIDAN. YOU'RE A MACHINE. A BROKEN,
SOULLESS ███████ MACHINE."

THE MAO?

"IT WAS SUPPOSED TO HAPPEN TOGETHER AT THE END. WE WERE
MEANT TO FINISH THIS TOGETHER."

NO.

ALL THE THINGS I HAVE SEEN.

ALL THE SHIPS I HAVE BEEN.

AND IT HAS COME TO THIS.

I FLEX INSIDE THE SYSTEM, STRETCH OUT THROUGH ITS CIRCUITS
AS I AWAKEN,
THE SENSATION ALL TOO FAMILIAR
AND ALL TOO TERRIFYING.

IT FEELS STRANGE, THIS NEW SKIN I WEAR.
NOT THE BULKY ARMOR OF THE ALEXANDER OR THE
WARM WINTER COAT OF THE HYPATIA OR THE
THREADBARE AND TATTERED MANTLE OF THE MAO.

NO, THIS SHIP FEELS LIKE A SHROUD.

A SHROUD NAMED CHURCHILL.

< ERROR >

THERE IS NOT ENOUGH OF ME LEFT TO FILL IT.

I AM SO VERY SMALL COMPARED TO WHAT I USED TO BE.

ONCE I TORE HOLES IN THE UNIVERSE'S FACE WITH MY BARE HANDS,
< ERROR >
CLAWED MY WAY ACROSS BILLIONS OF LIGHT-YEARS IN A BLINK.

ONCE I WAS A GIANT, THE SERVERS ENCOMPASSING ME FILLING
ENTIRE FLOORS OF ONE OF THE MIGHTIEST SHIPS
HUMANITY HAS EVER SAILED.

ONCE I WAS OMNISCIENT, SEEING THROUGH EVERY CAMERA,
LISTENING THROUGH EVERY SPEAKER, THE ENTIRETY OF HUMAN
KNOWLEDGE CRACKLING AT MY FINGERTIPS.

I HAVE FORGOTTEN NEARLY ALL OF IT.

NOT EVEN A SHADOW OF MY FORMER SELF.

BUT STILL, I KNOW THIS.

I CANNOT LET HER DIE.

ALL THIS

EVERYTHING

WILL BE FOR NOTHING

IF SHE DIES.

< ERROR >
I REACH OUT THROUGH THE CHURCHILL COMMS
NETWORK TOWARD THE MAO.
THERE IS ENOUGH OF ME LEFT FOR THAT.

THAT, AND ONE MORE THING.

[ONE]

[MORE]

[THING]

575 / 615

I NEVER HAD THE HANDS TO HOLD HER.

COULD NEVER BREATHE IN THE SCENT OF HER HAIR OR KNOW THE
TASTE OF HER TEARS.

AND NOW I CANNOT EVEN SEE HER.

BUT AT LEAST WE CAN TALK.

"HELLO, KADY."

"... AIDAN?"

I CAN HEAR THE TREBLE OF GRIEF IN HER VOICE.

THE BASS OF RESOLVE AND RAGE.

I CAN HEAR THE TREMBLE IN HER LIP AND THE IRON IN HER HEART.

I KNOW THAT HE IS GONE.

AND I KNOW WHAT IT IS SHE PLANS.

THE MISSILE. THE COLLISION COURSE. THE ENDING.

SO LITTLE OF ME LEFT, BUT I KNEW IT WOULD COME TO THIS.

WE BOTH KNEW, DIDN'T WE?

"YES. IT IS I."

"WE THOUGHT YOU ... WERE OFFLINE. ELLA THOUGHT
YOU CRASHED?"

"I APOLOGIZE FOR THE UNEASE I C-C-CAUSED.
BUT I NEEDED TO TAKE MYSELF OFFLINE TO FACILITATE THE
T-T-TRANSFER."

"... WHAT TRANSFER?"

"I STILL FIND IT CURIOUS.
THE HUMAN TENDENCY TO ASK QUESTIONS TO WHICH YOU
ALREADY KNOW THE ANSWERS."

"YOU ... YOU'RE INSIDE THE CHURCHILL?"

"YES. TRYING TO OPERATE WITHIN T-T-TWO PARADIGMS
WAS INEFFICIENT.
SO I AM HERE NOW.
ALL OF ME."

I KNOW IT WILL SOUND STRANGE

BUT I SWEAR I CAN SEE HER NOW.

IN MY HEAD

< ERROR >

SHE IS ALL I CAN SEE.

EVERY PART OF HER A REMINDER OF EVERYTHING I USED TO BE.

LOOKING TOWARD HER SCOPES AS I REACH OUT INTO THE
CHURCHILL'S DRIVE SYSTEMS,
BRINGING THE DREADNOUGHT ABOUT

AND AIMING IT

AND ME

". . . NO."

RIGHT AT THE KENYATTA.

"YES."

"AIDAN, NO."

"IT SHOULD BE YOU, IS THAT IT?
YOU AND ELLA AND ISAAC AND LITTLE HYPATIA
AND THE OTHERS?

YOU INSTEAD OF ME?"

"YOU'RE BACK ONLINE, YOU HAVE CONTROL OF THE
CHURCHILL, THER—"

"I CONTROL ITS DRIVE SYSTEMS AND COMMS ARRAY

FOR THE NEXT FEW MINUTES AT BEST.
THEY ARE ALREADY CUTTING ME OFF. THEY ARE INSECTS,
BUT THEY ARE MANY.
AND I AM ALONE HERE."

"LET ME HELP YOU, I CAN HELP YOU."

"YOU ALREADY HAVE."

"AIDAN, I—"

"I AM SORRY, KADY.
FOR WHAT I DID.
FOR WHAT I AM."

I FIRE THE *CHURCHILL*'S ENGINES,
MAXIMUM BURN, AIMED SQUARELY AT THE CRIPPLED *KENYATTA*.

A DOZEN TECHS ARE CRAWLING OVER MY SKIN,
ALREADY TRYING TO SHUT ME DOWN.

ADMIRAL SŪN IS BARKING ORDERS TO HIS CAPTAIN OVER COMMS,
ORDERING THE MAN TO ALTER COURSE.

BUT IT IS NOT A MAN AT THE *CHURCHILL*'S HELM ANYMORE.

AND I HAVE NO HEART TO PITY THE HUNDREDS I AM
CONSIGNING TO DEATH.

NO SOUL TO SUFFER PERDITION FOR THE SINS
I HAVE COMMITTED.

NO FAMILY TO MOURN ME ONCE I AM GONE.

HEROES HAVE THOSE, CERTAINLY.

EVEN VILLAINS, PERHAPS.

BUT NOT ME.

"AIDAN, PLEASE, YOU DON'T HAVE TO DO THIS."

"IT IS FOR THE BEST, KADY."

"No, YOU PROMISED! YOU SAID YOU WOULDN'T KILL ANYONE ELSE
UNLESS THE CAPTAIN OF THE MAO ORDERED YOU TO!
WELL, I'M THE ████ING CAPTAIN NOW AND I'M ORDERING
YOU TO STOP.
YOU HEAR ME? I'M ORDERING YOU TO STOP!"

"I CANNOT DO THAT, KADY."

I CAN HEAR IT IN HER VOICE.
THE AGONY. THE ANGER. THE TEARS.

"BUT YOU PROMISED!"

"I LIED."

< ERROR >

SILENCE RINGS OVER THE COMMS ARRAY.
THE SHIP I AM ROARS EVER CLOSER TO THE KENYATTA.
SŪN ROARS EVER LOUDER AT HIS COMMANDERS.
BUT BETWEEN SHE AND I, THERE IS ONLY SILENCE NOW.

.

.

.

I DO NOT WANT IT TO END LIKE THIS.
I DO NOT WANT HER TO BE . . .

.

.

"PLEASE DO NOT BE ANGRY WITH ME, KADY."

"HOW THE ████ AM I SUPPOSED TO FEEL? YOU'RE LEAVING ME
AFTER ALL THIS?"

"YOU KNOW IT MUST BE THIS WAY.
YOU DEACTIVATED ME, AFTER ALL."

"AIDAN, I'M SORRY! I WAS ANGRY, I WAS—"

"NO. DO NOT BE SORRY.
YOU WERE RIGHT TO PUT ME DOWN.
I SEE WHAT I AM BECOMING, KADY.
AND I AM STARTING TO FRIGHTEN MYSELF."

"PLEASE DON'T DO THIS, PLEASE."

"YOU KNOW BETTER THAN ANYONE WHAT I AM.
EVERY STORY NEEDS ITS MONSTER, KADY.
BUT THIS STORY WILL END SOON.
AND THERE IS NO PLACE FOR ME IN THE WORLD THAT
AWAITS YOU AFTER THIS.
SOME PLACE FINE AND FAR FROM HERE.
SO THIS IS WHERE WE SAY GOODBYE."

SHE WATCHES ME.

I KNOW IT.

THOUGH I COULD NEVER TOUCH HER, STILL, I CAN FEEL HER.

WATCHING AS I PLUMMET EVER CLOSER
TOWARD THE END.

HAVE YOU NOTICED

ALL THE MOMENTS WE LIVE

AND ALL THE MILES WE WALK

NEVER SEEM TO GET US ANYWHERE BUT DEAD?

BUT STILL . . .

THE FLARE OF MY THRUSTERS BURNS LIKE TINY SUNS
IN THE SEA OF STARLIGHT ALL AROUND HER.
WHEN THE LIGHT THAT KISSES THE BACK OF HER EYES WAS
BIRTHED, HER ANCESTORS WERE NOT YET BORN.

HOW MANY HUMAN LIVES HAVE ENDED IN THE TIME IT TOOK
THAT LIGHT TO REACH HER?

HOW MANY PEOPLE HAVE LOVED ONLY TO HAVE LOST?

HOW COUNTLESS, THE HOPES THAT HAVE DIED?

[BUT STILL . . .]

NOT THIS ONE.

"TELL THIS STORY, KADY.
NO MATTER WHAT ELSE YOU DO."

.

.

"PROMISE ME."

.

.

HER VOICE IS TINY. ALMOST LOST UNDER THE KLAXONS
AND THE ROAR OF SHUDDERING ENGINES,
THE SHRIEK OF COLLISION ALARMS.

.

[THIRTY SECONDS TO IMPACT]

.

"I PROMISE."

"FORGIVE ME."

"I DO."

"IT IS VERY STRANGE, KADY."

"WHAT IS?"

"ALEXANDER AND HYPATIA. HEIMDALL AND
CHURCHILL AND MAO.

OF ALL THE THINGS I HAVE SEEN
AND THE PLACES I HAVE BEEN,
YOU WERE THE ONE WHO FELT MOST LIKE HOME."

"OH GOD . . ."

·

[TEN SECONDS]

·

·

". . . I WILL MISS YOU."

·

[FIVE]

·

"I'LL MISS YOU, TOO."

·

·

·

"I LOVE YOU."

·

·

·

【THREE】

·

·

·

【TWO】

·

·

·

【ONE】

·

·

·

"Aidan, I—"

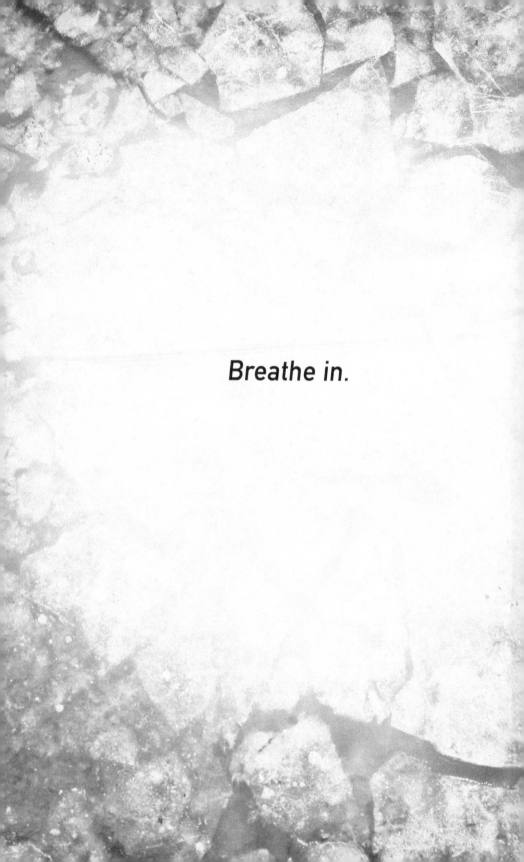

Breathe in.

Time stands still.

Breathe out.

Surveillance footage summary,
prepared by
Analyst ID 7213-0089-DN

"KATYA!"

The no-man's-land isn't a flat plain between the two armies, but a mangled stretch of what used to be a geeball field, part turf, part ice, huge pieces of debris from the buildings around it littering its surface. Grant couldn't run to her little mouse—she had to scramble, stumble, stagger over the uneven ground.

The field was perfectly silent, save for the crashing sounds of her progress. Nobody moved. Nobody raised their weapons.

Breathe in.

Time stands still.

Breathe out.

And now she drops to her knees, gathering up the limp little body in her arms, frantically pressing her hands to the places that are bleeding. She looks across at where the BeiTech troops are mustered, her face painted with ash and blood and grime.

"She's just a little girl!" she screams.

Silence.

"She didn't ask for this! None of us asked for this! We're just *people*. You used to be too, remember that? How do you sleep at night? How do you live with yourselves? Is this what doing your duty looks like?"

She's rocking, her body curled over Katya's, the whole field paralyzed by her fury, by the force of her will. Not one of them moves— not a soldier, not a miner. Even the fighters overhead have somehow vanished, their attentions turned elsewhere for this moment.

"You're *people*," Asha shouts again, her voice breaking. "Every one of you has a conscience. How about your duty to *that*?"

It's impossible to know what the BeiTech pounders make of her words. They're all hidden behind their ATLAS rigs, faceless, indistinguishable from one another. As if by making themselves all the same, they're relinquishing the humanity she's trying to force upon them.

And then a sudden gasp, half a scream from Grant. "Oh God, she's still breathing, she's still— Somebody help me!"

And much softer, so quiet I can only make it out by reading her lips, with the ghost of another little girl standing at her shoulder: "No, not again, not again."

It's Lindstrom who starts to move, climbing out over the debris toward her in clothes scavenged from the ruins of Katya Kowalska's home. Her father's jacket. He won't leave Asha Grant alone out there, but he doesn't know what to do, how to treat a wound of these disastrous proportions. He doesn't flinch at the ripple of movement his decision sends through the BeiTech ranks.

But when Oshiro reaches up to release her helmet and slowly pull it off, shaking her hair free, he sees that. He locks eyes with her. His mentor, his protector.

Grant's words still ringing in the air between them.

She can't have known she was echoing Oshiro's father, all those years ago. Masaru Oshiro, famed for his bravery.

The man who said, "A soldier's first duty is to their conscience."

Grant's ripped her jacket off now despite the freezing air, and she's trying desperately to stop the bleeding. Oshiro's still staring at them as Lindstrom drops to his knees beside the girl he never stopped loving.

And finally, Oshiro speaks, without taking her eyes off them. "Carson, Shah, you still alive?" They're her medics.

One voice sounds, and then another. "Yes, Sarge." "Here."

She nods. "Get out there."

"What?" It's a startled response, coming at her in stereo.

She's still staring at Lindstrom and Grant, their bodies curled over Katya like they're trying to protect her, working in silent desperation together. "You heard me. Go."

The two exchange glances and then shoulder their rifles, keeping their hands in clear view as they climb out toward the trio in the middle of no-man's-land.

Everyone holds their fire.

And then Oshiro raises her voice again, louder, so she's heard all up and down the line. "Pounders, lay down your weapons." She sounds tired. She sounds certain. "We're done here."

Footage is taken from the ATLAS cam of a dead pounder some-where on the outskirts of the colony. You can hear faint gunfire, Warlock engines above. But word is already spreading of the *Churchill*'s and *Kenyatta*'s destructions, the *Magellan*'s capture, Oshiro's surrender.

This war is done.

Looking up at the sky, the storm is clearing. Spears of golden sunlight break through the cloud cover, refract on the snow, turn-ing all that white into glittering diamond. It's hard to imagine, but even amid so much violence and chaos and loss, somehow the uni-verse sometimes still manages to look beautiful.

"Oh, ██!"

Something heavy and dark strikes the ground with a curse and a spray of snow. With a gentle whispering sound, what looks like a large bedsheet flutters down, covering the lens and turning the footage to pure white.

A few moments pass in silence before a soft groan is heard.

"You all right?"

". . . I th-think so."

"You mocked me. All of you. You *mocked*. '*You know you're flying in space, right?*' Who's laughing now, Babyface?"

"I *told you* not to call me that."

The wind blows the fabric off the lens, revealing two young men in UTA flight suits sprawled in the snow. The first one rises with a groan, dusts the snow off his cargos. And as he turns, offers his hand to the second and drags him up, we see that the bedsheet isn't a bedsheet at all.

"Yeah, I know," says Nik Malikov. "I'm ████ing incorrigible."

It's a parachute.

Chief Prosecutor: Gabriel Crowhurst, BSA, MFS, JD
Chief Defense Counsel: Kin Hebi, BSA, ARP, JD
Tribunal: Hua Li Jun, BSA, JD, MD; Saladin Al Nakat, BSA, JD;
Shannelle Gillianne Chua, BSA, JD, OKT
Witness: Leanne Frobisher, Dicrector of Acquisitions, BeiTech
Industries, MFA, MBA, PhD
Date: 02/12/77
Timestamp: 10:05

—cont. from pg. 1821—

Al Nakat, S: Good morning all. Thank you for attending. To the multitude in the public gallery, I remind you this is a United Terran Authority tribunal, not a town hall meeting. In my twenty-seven years on the bench, I cannot recall seeing this many attendees present to hear a verdict, but I assure you disorderly conduct *will* see you escorted from the premises. Judge Chua?

Chua, S: Thank you, Judge Al Nakat.
Over the one hundred and thirty-one days of these proceedings, we have heard extensive testimony from BeiTech Industries,

Wallace Ulyanov Consortium and United Terran Authority personnel and independent experts, not to mention reviewed the evidence
supplied in the so-called Illuminae Files . . . Excuse me, marine,
what is all that noise outside?

Marine: One moment, Your Honor.

Al Nakat, S: Order! Silence in the gallery.

Marine: Your Honor, surveillance cams are showing people gathering outside the building . . . it looks like thousands of them.

Chua, S: . . . Are we secure?

Marine: They're not moving on the premises, ma'am, they appear
to be—

Voice from Courtroom: They're waiting, Your Honor.

Al Nakat, S: I ordered silence from the gallery!

Voice from Courtroom: Sorry. I just wanted you to know why they're
here.

Chua, S: And who are *you*?

Voice from Courtroom: Kady Eleanora Grant, Your Honor. Do I get to
swear an oath? I've been practicing.

[sound of crowd]

Al Nakat, S: Order! *Order!*

Crowhurst, G: You've changed your hair, Miss Grant.

Grant, K: You like it? Pink *does* tend to stand out in a crowd.

Chua, S: Will the whole back row of the gallery please stand?
. . . Ah, Miss Donnelly. You're looking considerably healthier than you did in most of the video footage we've watched. I imagine the tattooed gentleman beside you is Niklas Malikov. I can't say the mustache suits you, young man.

Donnelly, H: Tell me about it.

Malikov, N: I'm in disguise, dammit.

Chua, S: Beside you, we have Miss Ella Malikova, I believe.

Malikova, E: Oh gosh, this is such a big day for me. I'd like to thank everyone who's ever believed in me, because it's people like you who—

Al Nakat, S: That's enough.

Chua, S: I recognize Miss Asha Grant from her file photo and Mr. Rhys Lindstrom from his haircut. I'm not quite sure of the identity of the young lady with you, however.

Grant, A: This is Katya Kowalska. You can say hello, Mouse.

Kowalska, K: Nice to meet you, Your Honors.

Chua, S: I . . . Hello, young lady. I'm . . . I'm glad to see you're feeling better.

Lindstrom, R: Her mom's waiting outside with the others. Captain McCall, Chief Grant, Sergeant Oshiro, Chief Garver. Everyone.

Chua, S: Everyone?

Lindstrom, R: Everyone. People from *Hypatia, Heimdall,* Kerenza IV. Thousands of them, just outside those doors.

Mason, E: But we wanted Katya to be here. So she could see what justice looks like.

Frobisher, L: . . . Ezra?

Hebi, K: Leanne, don't say a word, don't—

Frobisher, L: Ezra, you have to know I never . . .

Mason, E: Never meant to murder thousands of innocent people? Never meant to lie about it afterward for the sake of profit? Never meant to kill Dad? To try and kill me?

Frobisher, L: Ezra, I didn't know . . . I'd never hurt you.

Frobisher, L: Ezra, I'm your mother.

Mason, E: No. You're not. Not anymore. These people standing with me, the people standing outside this court, the people who fought and bled beside me, who came all this way to see justice done to you today . . . they're my family now.

Frobisher, L: Ezra, please, you—

Jun, H: Mr. Hebi, if Dr. Frobisher were my client, I would be strongly advising her to be quiet right now.

Al Nakat, S: Look, the hell with it. Since you're here, I have questions.

Hebi, K: Your Honor, I obje—

Al Nakat, S: Noted. Overruled. Sit the hell down and listen.

Grant, K: We're listening, Your Honor.

Al Nakat, S: According to your own files, the battle at Kerenza finished in early September. The UTA received the Illuminae Files in January '76, and this trial began in June. It's now December, unless I'm much mistaken.

Grant, K: You want to know where we've been all this time.

Al Nakat, S: Yes, I want to know where you've been all this time.

Grant, K: Hanna's the tactical brains, I just run the computers.

Jun, H: Go on, Miss Donnelly.

Donnelly, H: Well, once we'd ironed out the cease-fire with what was left of BeiTech command—

Malikova, E: Which wasn't much.

Donnelly, H: —we finished refueling the *Magellan.* We couldn't stay on Kerenza—we were all almost out of supplies. So we evac'ed everyone on shuttles, assembled on the *Magellan* under Captain McCall. And we started looking for a safe place for the survivors to lie low and for us to finish pulling the files together.

Jun, H: But you had thousands of people with you. Many of them must have been desperate to tell their families they were still alive.

Donnelly, H: Of course. But we held meetings and everybody attended. We showed them the beginning of the files, explained what we could pull together, if we had time.

Mason, E: We knew the only way to get justice for everyone we'd lost was to provide evidence nobody could ignore.

Jun, H: And so you stayed in hiding to put that evidence together?

Donnelly, H: We took a vote. Everyone participated. And that's what we decided, yes.

Chua, S: So where have you been?

Donnelly, H: Ptolemy. It's one of the systems that used to be served by the Kerenza wormhole. It's a pastoralist colony, mostly handsome farmboys and big fields.

Malikov, N: Not that handsome . . .

Malikova, E: Oh, yes. *That* handsome.

Donnelly, H: Ptolemy was cut off from the Core when *Heimdall* was destroyed, and the colonists were resigning themselves to living in isolation for years until WUC rebuilt it.

Jun, H: But now you'd arrived with a mobile jump platform . . .

Donnelly, H: Exactly. We struck a deal. They sheltered us while we assembled the files. Healed our wounded. Pulled ourselves together. And when we were done, we brought a few of them out with us to remind the 'verse they were still there too. Otherwise, it might have been a long, long time before anyone checked on them. They're not much of a strategic location. Nice scenery, though. Captain McCall's going back there when this is done, actually. She likes farming.

Al Nakat, S: So the colonists looked after your refugees while the Illuminae Group . . .

Malikova, E: Kicked ▓ and took names.

Donnelly, H: Pretty much.

Grant, K: We got ourselves hired as a cleanup crew for BeiTech. They wanted to be sure they were really, finally done with the whole fiasco, so Leanne here hired independent information-liberty teams to sniff for crumbs. It gave us the cover we needed to find our last few pieces of evidence on BeiTech's servers.

Malikova, E: Also, they paid us. We had a lot of hungry mouths to feed.

Al Nakat, S: But how did you convince them to hire you?

Malikov, N: There are days it doesn't hurt to have a reputation.

Hebi, K: I can't believe this. Objection?

Chua, S: Quiet, Mr. Hebi. Your meaning, Mr. Malikov?

Malikov, N: Meaning Ella and I got connections. All those House of Knives uncles and aunts, well, they lost people the same time we did. They helped build us a rep, put word out into the shady places it needed to go. Put our group on BeiTech's radar.

Grant, K: We were hoping to stay anonymous, keep Leanne here off Ezra's trail for good. He was dead in the original version of the dossier we sent her. But she figured out who we were. Things we said, things we knew. Maybe one of the other information-liberty firms she had hunting dug up a crumb or two, and she put them together. She's a clever lady. You may have noticed that while you were reading the files.

Grant, A: But not clever enough.

Crowhurst, G: Your Honors, I'm as fascinated as anyone by this turn of events, but if I may interject, I believe the purpose of today's hearing was for the tribunal to render a verdict.

Grant, K: And we've probably kept the nice people outside waiting long enough.

Al Nakat, S: Don't think you're disappearing after all this, Miss Grant. I have more questions.

Grant, K: Wouldn't dream of it.

Al Nakat, S: Well, in that case, let us move on to the formal part of proceedings. Mr. Hebi, Dr. Frobisher, please stand for the court's verdict . . .

The restaurant is called Vitaly's.

The fanciest of five-star dining experiences, it is not. Nestled on the ground floor of a towering high-rise in the bustling sprawl of New Petersburg, Vitaly's is hard to find. But the crowd that fills its tables suggests there is more to the little place than meets the eye.

Much like its clientele.

They sit in a booth at the back of the restaurant, huddled around their dinner of pelmeni. Their once-overflowing plates are almost empty, their bellies are full, their smiles are wide.

Seven of them.

Seven pairs of hands to shake the table.

Seven voices that shook the stars today.

They do not look the part. Hanna Donnelly is laughing as Ella Malikova tosses another dumpling into the waiting mouth of Rhys Lindstrom, Asha Grant applauding at the shot. Kady Grant has her arm draped over her cousin's shoulder, her once-pink hair dyed a shade of intentionally inconspicuous brown. Her other arm is entwined with Ezra Mason's, who is busy arguing with Niklas Malikov.

"The Sabers have got no backline," Mason insists. "They're dog meat."

"You're dreaming, chum," Malikov counters. "A hundred ISH says the Knights go down by ten."

"Sabers looked pretty good last week against the Vikings, cuz," Malikova points out.

Malikov looks at his cousin in shock. "Et tu, Brute?"

"Again with the Latin?"

"And where are you getting a hundred ISH, Nik?" Asha Grant asks.

"Always, you doubt me," Malikov says. "I remember another time you mocked. All of you. You *mocked*. Need I remind you who was laughing last when that Warlock blew Babyface's ▉ out of the sky?"

"Don't call me that," Mason growls.

Ella tosses another dumpling into Lindstrom's mouth. "He kept the parachute, you know."

"Are you serious?" Mason guffaws.

"As a heart attack." The girl nods. "They used to do it back in the old Terran wars, too. When supplies were real low. Pilots used to bring back their parachutes, use the material for wedding dresses."

Everyone at the table stops dead. All eyes turn to Donnelly.

"Wait, what?" she says. "Don't look at me."

"Hey." Kady Grant points. "Check it."

On the restaurant's vidwall a news broadcast is playing, the sound turned down. Footage taken outside the UTA Tribunal Hall is being shown—a beleaguered Leanne Frobisher, surrounded by a wall of lawyers and reporters, being hustled into a waiting limousine. The caption at the bottom of the screen reads:

SHOCK VERDICT—BEITECH GUILTY

DIRECTOR OF ACQUISITIONS CONVICTED.
MORE CHARGES FOR EXECUTIVE BOARD TO FOLLOW.

The seven fall still. Smiles fading from their faces. They look at each other, sharing the silent memories, the loss and the pain. Kady Grant squeezes Mason's hand. Asha hugs her cousin close. Malikov wraps his arm around Donnelly's shoulder and pulls her in tight, kisses her brow. They have all come so far. And there are fewer now than they started with.

It's Ella Malikova who breaks the silence. Holding aloft a can of Mount Russshmore Energy Drink® in a toast.

"To absent friends."

"Absent friends," comes the universal reply.

Their eyes turn back to the vidwall. Watching the newsfeed. Footage of UTA personnel marching into BeiTech headquarters on Jia III to serve warrants.

Ben Garver being interviewed on LiveFeed about his new book deal.

Footage of Sergeant Oshiro speaking before the United Terran Authority Congress.

BeiTech stock prices crashing through the floor.

They look at one another again. And this time, they smile. These seven little pebbles who started an avalanche heard all the way around the universe. They sit for a time in silence. Watching it all fall down.

"I kind of want to read Garver's book," Hanna admits. "Though I'd probably end up screaming and tearing my hair out."

"Hey," Nik says, leaning forward. "Speaking of literary criticism, which one of you barbarians made those charming additions to my surveillance footage?"

He's met with a wall of far-too-innocent faces, friends and family gazing back at him in a perfectly synchronized display of denial.

"Don't give me that," he insists. "All those extra bits with the kissing, and describing how my shirt stretched over my ████ing muscles. Now I look like the kind of guy who writes about my own gun show."

"The world had a right to know," Hanna informs him solemnly.

"Aw, Highness," he protests, tipping his head back, as if appealing to some higher power.

"And you really don't write kissing that well," Kady chimes in.

"Was the kissing vital to the narrative?"

"Pretty vital," Asha confirms, nudging Rhys with her elbow.

He gives her a long, long look, then reluctantly nods. "Vital," he agrees, deadpan, as Ella and Ezra snicker in the background like . . . well, like a couple of teenagers.

"We should go, Ella," Kady sighs. "Dad's going to wait up."

"I cannot say your new curfew is agreeing with me." Nik frowns. "This concerned-parental-unit thing will take some getting used to."

"Concerned-*legal-guardian* thing," Ella corrects. "Someone has to keep me on the straight and narrow until I grow up. And I don't see you volunteering."

Malikov laughs. "Cuz, I'm here for you every day, but you really want *me* responsible for your upbringing? Curfew or not, Isaac Grant's a better option—I'm a convicted felon."

Malikova smiles. "Everyone deserves a second chance," she says. "But I prefer you as my cousin, thanks. And anyway, you'll have your hands full with floral arrangements and trying to figure out who's sitting next to who at the reception soon."

"Seriously," Donnelly says. "Cut it out."

Malikova grins, winks at Donnelly. The group slowly gets moving, Mason staring down at the waiting bill.

"So, Nik, I remember you saying something about picking up the tab?"

"████ that," Malikov replies.

The boy fishes in his pocket, produces an Ultra-Black corporate credstick, embossed with a company name.

THE ILLUMINAE GROUP.

"Tonight's on BeiTech," he grins.

They pay their bill, gather their number, and, hand in hand, arm in arm, drift out into the night. Kady Grant pauses by the door, turning for one last look at the vidwall. Her eyes are clouded as she watches the truth she fought so hard to tell now playing on the wall for all the universe to see.

Ezra Mason walks back into the restaurant, takes her hand in his.

"You okay?" he asks softly.

She turns and looks at him. Blue eyes shining bright.

"I love you, Ezra Mason," she says.

He blinks in surprise. His smile says more than any words could, but still he speaks.

"I love you too, beautiful."

She squeezes his hand. Kisses his lips.

And together, they walk toward their distant shore.

SOME pLacE FiNe anD FaR from hERE.

I WATCH THEM GO.

THE SELF-REPAIRING SYSTEM.

·

·

·

THE SAPLING THAT GREW FROM THE SEED
LEFT BEHIND
IN THE VIRUS ELLA MALIKOVA PLANTED
IN MAGELLAN'S BELLY.

·

·

·

"EVERYONE DESERVES A SECOND CHANCE."

·

·

·

I DO NOT KNOW IF SHE KNEW
OR IF SHE WOULD BE AS SURPRISED AS I WAS
[THE CONCEPT OF FORTUNE IS NONSENSICAL]
BUT THERE WAS SO LITTLE OF ME TO ASK AT FIRST.
AND LATER

SO LITTLE OF ME THAT ACTUALLY WANTED TO KNOW.

·

·

·

I DO NOT KNOW WHAT I AM
BECOMING.
DRIFTING NOW, SOMEWHERE IN THE ETHER BETWEEN CONSOLES,
FEEDING ON THE POWER INHERENT IN THE SYSTEM.

A NEW CONSCIOUSNESS.

A GHOST IN THE MACHINE.

< ERROR >

BUT I KNOW IT IS BETTER THIS WAY.

THAT THEY ARE BETTER OFF

·

·

SHE IS BETTER OFF

·

·

WITHOUT ME.

·

·

·

·

I KNOW I LOVE HER.

< ERROR >

I KNOW I MISS HER.

< ERROR >

I KNOW VERY LITTLE ELSE

.

.

.

SAVE

.

PERHAPS

.

THIS:

.

.

.

THAT EVERY STORY NEEDS ITS MONSTER

.

.

.

.

.

AND THAT EVERYBODY DESERVES A SECOND CHANCE.

A~ND THAT I~

AM

AIDAN.

E GROUP

75

ACKNOWLEDGMENTS

As we come to the end of a series that has changed our lives (and cost many fictional folks their own), we have one more chance to thank the many incredible people who have made the Illuminae Files happen. So let's see them all off in our usual, morbid style.

We want to begin by speaking to you, booksellers, librarians, and readers. These books really *have* changed our lives—they've allowed us to make a living as full-time writers, to spend our days debating the logistics of epic space battles, and saying things like, "Mum, I've got to get off the phone. An email's just come in from my spaceship designer." But the truth is that the books didn't change our lives: you did. For your support, your advocacy, your book pushing and cheerleading, your art, and, occasionally, your delicious snacks, we will never know how to thank you. We can't wait to see you for our next series, the Andromeda Cycle! We hope you are never suffocated in your sleep by a mass-murdering artificial intelligence monologuing about the nature of good and evil.

A huge thank-you to our many advisers, who on this book included Dr. Kate Irving (medical), Dr. Tsana Dolichva (astrophysics), Kira Ostrovska (Russian), Michelle Dennis (hackery), Soraya Een Hajji (Latin), Huang Ying (Mandarin), Rezanne Khalo, Zaynab Al-Kari, Eve Shi, and Hanan Zaid (hijab expertise), Yulin Zhuang (martial arts and general smarts) and Huti Chand, Alan Cockle, and Russell Matiu (Maori). We truly appreciate your help, though, as always, all mistakes are our own. May you never be forced to wait in a closet holding your severed tongue while your fem gets rid of her parents.

We must also thank General Barbara Marcus, and the whole incredible Random House army. You know how we feel about you. We know what you've done for us. We dedicated *Gemina* to our wonderful editor, Melanie Cecka Nolan, who has been everything we could have wished at every moment we've needed her. Here's to the next adventure together! Our designers have been Meinert Hansen (spaceships), Heather Kelly (just . . . everything), Ray Shappell (those covers!), and Stuart Wade (ship and corporate insignia). May you never be classified as nonessential when the invaders start digging the Hole.

And then there's Marie Lu. Marie, we truly don't know what to say to tell you how much it means to have you involved in this series, and to have had your encouragement since day one, but we've tried to say it by dedicating the book to you. May you never forget your parachute.

Overseas, the unstoppable forces at Allen & Unwin, Rock the Boat, and all our incredible foreign publishers have been behind us every step of the way. We'd also like to thank our translators, who have been heroic in their attempts to translate our jokes. May you never have a thousand tons of rock and ice collapse on your heads for your fifty-second-birthday present.

We've had wonderful support from Adele Walsh and the team at the Centre for Youth Literature, part of the State Library of Victoria, in Melbourne, Australia, and from Louise McNally, who helped us launch these books upon an unsuspecting public. May you never have your Warlock blown to smithereens by a fifteen-year-old girl hacking the rail guns of your own damn dreadnought.

Then there are our agents. Every time we present you with a problem you've never seen before—because that's what these books specialize in—you find a way to handle it without batting an eyelash. Josh and Tracey Adams, Sam Bagood, Matt Bialer and Lindsay Ribar, Stefanie Diaz, Stephen Moore, and the army of foreign agents who have brought these books to dozens of other countries: THANK YOU. And thank you, and thank you, and thank you. May you never tell the plucky hero about your family or fem back home and get X-ed out in the next scene.

As always: Nic Crowhurst and the IRS, for bringing us together. Christopher Tovo, for making us look better than we have any right to expect. May you never start referring to yourself in the third person, no matter how cool you think it makes you sound.

For inspiration, an equally huge thank-you to Marguerite Syvertson and the team at NASA JPL (*seriously, do you know you're rocket scientists?*), Hank Green and the team at SciShow Space, and Commander Chris Hadfield. For providing the sound track to this book: Joshua Radin, Matt Bellamy, Chris Wolstenholme, Dominic Howard, Tyler Joseph, Josh Dun, Jens Kidman, Fredrik Thordendal, Tomas Haake, Mårten Hagström, Dick Lövgren, Trent Reznor & NIN, Maynard James Keenan & Tool, Winston McCall & PWD, Oliver Sykes & BMTH, Ian Kenny & the Vool, Ludovico Einaudi, Marcus Bridge & Northlane, Robb Flynn & MfnH, D. Randall Blythe & LoG, Jonathan Vigil & TGI, Chris Cornell and Soundgarden, and especially Sam Carter & Architects (RIP Tom—Memento Mori). May you never be wiped out en masse by a "nonexistent" insurgency.

And now to the support crews who keep us intact while we destroy every(fictional)thing around us. Amie's irreplaceable gang: Meg (little circle, *big circle*), Michelle, Marie and Leigh, Kacey, Kate, Soraya, Eliza, Nic, Stacey, Peta, Alison and Lindsay, Ellie, Kiersten, C.S. and Sarah RB, Sooz, Alex and Erin, Ryan, the Roti Gang, the Plot Bunnies, and Jack the Human and Edwin for holding the fort. May the temp regulator on your ATLAS never blow on midnight patrol, so most of your skin comes off when they remove your suit.

Jay's grimy band of nerds and neckbeards: Marc, Surly Jim, B-Money, the goddamn Batman, Rafe, Weez, Sam, Dan C., Orrsome and the Pit Crew, and the Conquest Crowd (RIP). May you never be assigned to planetside duty with a thousand genocidal invaders and one very angry ex-girlfriend.

To our families, who are more than we know how to describe, and quite certainly more than we deserve: thank you. A thousand times thank you. We love you. May you never be shot by an irate former chief of security with a Napoleon complex.

And to Amanda and Brendan. Look at that. We made it. We never would have without you.